mars attack

CW01457238

by Bogdan Lalić

EVERYMAN CHESS

Gloucester Publishers plc   www.everymanchess.com

First published in 2003 by Gloucester Publishers plc (formerly Everyman Publishers plc), Gloucester Mansions, 140A Shaftesbury Avenue, London WC2H 8HD

British Library Cataloguing-in-Publication Data
A catalogue record for this book is available from the British Library.

ISBN 1 85744 244 X

Distributed in North America by The Globe Pequot Press, P.O Box 480, 246 Goose Lane, Guilford, CT 06437-0480.

All other sales enquiries should be directed to Everyman Chess, Gloucester Publishers plc, Gloucester Mansions, 140A Shaftesbury Avenue, London WC2H 8HD
tel: 020 7539 7600 fax: 020 7379 4060
email: info@everymanchess.com
website: www.everymanchess.com

EVERYMAN CHESS SERIES (formerly Cadogan Chess)
Chief advisor: Garry Kasparov
Commissioning editor: Byron Jacobs

Typeset and edited by First Rank Publishing, Brighton.
Cover design by Horatio Monteverde.
Production by Navigator Guides.
Printed and bound in Great Britain by Biddles Ltd.

CONTENTS

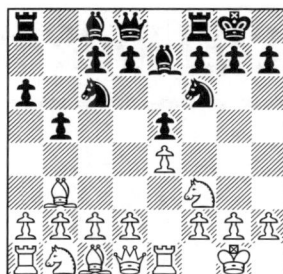

BIBLIOGRAPHY

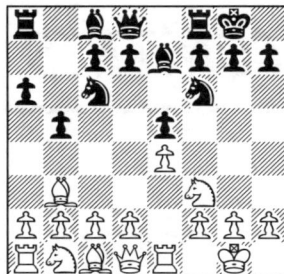

Books
Informators 1-85
NIC Yearbooks 1-63
Chess Informant Monograph C89 (Anand)
Encyclopaedia of Chess Openings: Volume C (4th Edition)

Databases
ChessBase Mega Database 2002 CD

INTRODUCTION

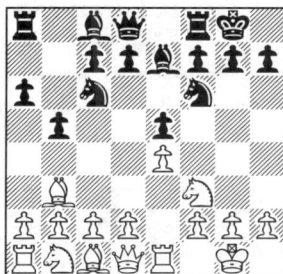

The Marshall Attack is nowadays regarded as one of the most popular and reliable of openings against 1 e4. One only has to point to the top players and specialists who play it: Adams, Ivan Sokolov, Svidler, Short, Khalifman, Kamsky (before he retired), Nunn, Blatny etc.

What has attracted all of them to the Marshall Attack? Certainly the fact that the Marshall is a counterattacking opening helps a lot. With a bold opening Black wants, from the start, to take the initiative from White.

Basically, Black in the Marshall Attack gets the type of position he wants, usually at the cost of a pawn, which does not happen in other semi-open openings such as the French, Caro Kann, Alekhine, Pirc and Scandinavian. In the Marshall Black enjoys plenty of space for his pieces and the sacrifice of a pawn is a small price to pay for it. With energetic play, Black strives for the initiative, which forces White from the start to decide whether to accept the gauntlet by taking the gambit or to chicken out.

The other argument can be that the Marshall Gambit consists of many drawish lines – note that even Anand has recently been known to prepare forced drawing variations for Black in important games. This is true and is probably the main reason why Gary Kasparov, with the white pieces, never allows the Marshall Gambit.

I have to admit that it was a big job for me to include both the Marshall Gambit and the Anti-Marshall, especially due to space limitations. Surely there are more, much more, than around 100 important games played in such a complicated opening? Therefore I had to minimise coverage in some variations due to lack of space (for instance, in the 8 a4 ♗b7 9 d3 Anti-Marshall I have concentrated mainly on the promising sideline 9...♖e8!?). In general I have tried to deal with the most important recent games, including those played in early 2003.

The book is divided into three parts:

Part 1: The Main Line Marshall
Part 2: Other Marshalls
Part 3: The Anti-Marshall

Altogether there are 105 games over ten chapters. In each chapter I have done a survey explaining the various ideas, often recommending what to do and what not to do.

In the Anti-Marshall I have included all lines where White avoids the critical position after 8 c3 d5, plus the extra option of the increasingly popular 8 c3 d5 9 d4!?.

First of all, one should be made aware of

5

how this fascinating opening unfolded. It started with the following game.

Capablanca-Marshall
New York 1918

1 e4 e5 2 ♘f3 ♘c6 3 ♗b5 a6 4 ♗a4 ♘f6 5 0-0 ♗e7 6 ♖e1 b5 7 ♗b3 0-0 8 c3 d5

9 exd5 ♘xd5 10 ♘xe5 ♘xe5 11 ♖xe5 ♘f6?! 12 ♖e1 ♗d6 13 h3 ♘g4

Capablanca must have had a deep think here.

14 ♕f3 ♕h4 15 d4 ♘xf2 16 ♖e2!

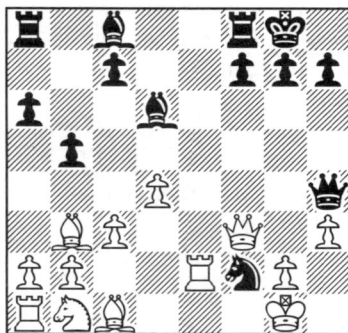

Surprised by a home-prepared new variation, Capablanca finds at the board the best way out of the complications and refutes Black's plan.

16...♗g4 17 hxg4

Not falling for 17 ♕xf2 ♗g3 followed by ...♗g4xe2 and ...♖a8-e8, after which White

could resign.

17...♗h2+ 18 ♔f1 ♗g3 19 ♖xf2 ♕h1+ 20 ♔e2 ♗xf2 21 ♗d2 ♗h4 22 ♕h3 ♖ae8+ 23 ♔d3 ♕f1+ 24 ♔c2 ♗f2 25 ♕f3 ♕g1 26 ♗d5 c5 27 dxc5 ♗xc5 28 b4 ♗d6 29 a4!

After patient defence White takes a chance and starts a counterattack.

29...a5 30 axb5 axb4 31 ♖a6 bxc3 32 ♘xc3 ♗b4 33 b6 ♗xc3 34 ♗xc3 h6 35 b7 ♖e3 36 ♗xf7+ 1-0

This defeat did not deliver a final blow to the whole opening. Black started to adopt a new system with the move 11...c6 instead of 11...♘f6?!.

A lot of thanks should go to former World Champion Boris Spassky, who was playing it successfully in his Candidate matches in the mid 1960s (he blunted Mikhail Tal's favourite move 1 e4 in their 1965 match) and soon the Marshall Gambit gained the nickname 'drawing weapon'.

However, in this book the reader will see plenty of beautiful sacrifices and nice kingside attacks by both White and Black (I tried to be objective). Sometimes I was having sleepless nights checking analysis and critical positions with *Fritz 7* and the results were amazing – once the legendary late World Champion Mikhail Tal gave a wrong assessment! This just confirms how the Marshall Gambit is rich in possibilities for both sides and it will be some time, if ever, before the refutation is found.

I would like to thank James Coleman and Dave Bland for supplying me with games that had not appeared in my database.

Also, I would like to devote this book to my late parents Dr Dragan Lalić and Dr Nellie Lalić, who supported me with my chess during their lives.

Bogdan Lalić,
Sutton,
June 2003

CHAPTER ONE

The Old Main Line: 12 d4 and 15 ♗e3

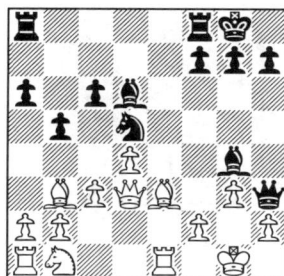

1 e4 e5 2 ♘f3 ♘c6 3 ♗b5 a6 4 ♗a4 ♘f6 5 0-0 ♗e7 6 ♖e1 b5 7 ♗b3 0-0 8 c3 d5 9 exd5 ♘xd5 10 ♘xe5 ♘xe5 11 ♖xe5 c6 12 d4 ♗d6 13 ♖e1 ♕h4 14 g3 ♕h3 15 ♗e3 ♗g4 16 ♕d3

In this chapter we deal with the old main line of the Marshall, where the real struggle begins around move 30. To complete the state of theory we have to thank a lot of correspondence players, although there are still a lot of positions that need to be tested.

The main continuation, 16...♖ae8 17 ♘d2 ♖e6, we see in Games 1-4. After 18 a4 bxa4 19 ♖xa4 f5 20 ♕f1 ♕h5 we come to the critical position (Games 1-3). After 21 f4 (Game 1) Black does best by playing 21...♖b8, thus switching play to the b-file. Excellent attacking chances are given to Black after 21 c4? f4! 22 cxd5 ♖xe3! (Game 2). Ivanchuk's cold blooded 21 ♖xa6!? should have led to a draw in Game 3 if, instead of playing for a win with 28...h5?!, Black had played the correct 28...♖xf4!. The positional continuation 18...♕h5 is seen in Svidler-Kamsky (Game 4), in which the new plan starting with 20 ♘e4 has been nicely neutralised by Kamsky's purposeful play.

In Morovic-Adams (Game 5) Black plays 17...♕h5 with the independent idea of playing ...♗g4-f5 chasing away White's queen.

However, this idea of achieving an easy draw with Black doesn't get the desired result and White is clearly better with correct play.

16...f5?! (Games 6-8) is a sideline with which Black is trying to avoid the main lines beginning with 16...♖ae8. Kindermann-Sokolov (Game 6) witnesses the paradoxical situation for the Marshall Gambit, where the swap of queens actually helps Black rather than White – this means 17 ♕f1?! is out of business. In Game 8 Black actually played 16...♔h8?!. However, the position transposed to lines with 16...f5?!

The correct continuation is 17 f4, which we see in the remaining two games of this chapter. In both games Black goes for outright attack by playing ...g7-g5. However, by playing a2-a4! quickly and keeping the vital f4-square constantly under control (i.e. not capturing on g5 too early), White's chances are clearly better.

1 e4 e5 2 ♘f3 ♘c6 3 ♗b5 a6 4 ♗a4 ♘f6 5 0-0 ♗e7 6 ♖e1 b5 7 ♗b3 0-0 8 c3 d5 9 exd5 ♘xd5 10 ♘xe5 ♘xe5 11 ♖xe5 c6 12 d4 ♗d6 13 ♖e1 ♕h4 14 g3 ♕h3 15

♗e3 ♗g4 16 ♕d3 ♖ae8 17 ♘d2 ♖e6

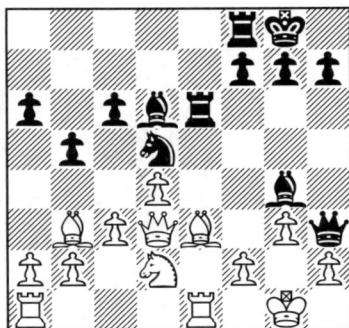

This is a multipurpose move – Black prepares to double the rooks on the e-file thus putting pressure on White. For the time being he refrains from playing ...f7-f5. However, it should be mentioned that in many lines Black can still revert to the standard ...f7-f5 plan. So basically his options are kept open.

18 a4

Before Black launches his kingside attack, White must seek counterplay on the opposite wing and the opening of the a-file will suit this aim. White's plan is rather obvious and straightforward – by playing 19 axb5 axb5 20 ♖a6! he will force Black to defend against the threats on the sixth rank.

18...f5 19 ♕f1 ♕h5 20 f4 bxa4

At first glance breaking up the pawn chain might seem anti-positional but the text has the following points:

1) If White takes on a4 with his rook, his first rank will be weakened.

2) Black will search for counterplay along the b-file.

However, for his activity Black will have to pay a price in that his a6-pawn is left at White's mercy and is doomed to fall.

21 ♖xa4 ♖b8 22 ♕f2?

Also bad is 22 ♕xa6? ♖xb3! 23 ♘xb3 ♘xe3 24 ♕c8+ ♖e8 25 ♕xc6 ♗f3! 26 ♕xd6 ♕h3! and White cannot avoid being mated, while 22 ♖xa6?! ♖xb3 23 ♘xb3 ♘xe3 is very

complicated but good for Black. These variations demonstrate that White has to watch out for the sacrifice on b3 all the time.

22...♖xb3! 23 ♘xb3 ♗d1!

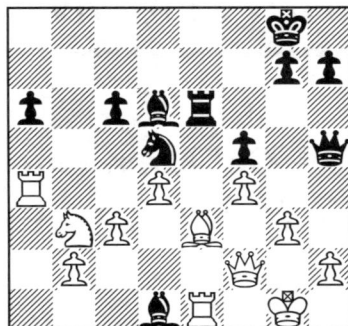

The point behind 22...♖xb3!. Despite the fact that with rook and two pawns against two minor pieces White (after his twenty-fifth move) is not doing too badly from the materialistic point of view, there are many weak points in White's camp and this leads to a near-decisive advantage for Black.

24 ♘c5

24 ♖xa6 ♗xb3 25 ♖a8+ ♔f7 26 ♖a7+ ♔g6, as in Gorkievich-Vitomskij, correspondence 1979, is also very gloomy for White.

24...♗xc5 25 ♖xa6 ♗f8 26 ♗d2 ♖g6! 27 c4 ♘f6 28 ♖a8 ♗f3 39 d5 ♘e4 30 ♗b4 ♖f6 31 ♖xe4

Desperation, but 31 ♕e3? ♕xh2+! 32 ♔xh2 ♖h6+ 33 ♔g1 ♖h1 mate is a nice finish.

31...♖xe4 32 ♕c5 ♕d1+ 33 ♔f2 ♕f3+ 34 ♔e1 ♕h1+ 35 ♔e2 ♕xh2+ 36 ♔d1 ♕h1+ 37 ♔d2 ♕g2+ 38 ♔e1

Or 38 ♔d1 ♕c2+ 39 ♔e1 ♕b1+ followed by ...♕xb2+ with an easy win for Black.

38...♕xg3+ 39 ♔e2 ♕g4+ 0-1

Game 2
J.Fernandez-Claridge
Correspondence 1998

1 e4 e5 2 ♘f3 ♘c6 3 ♗b5 a6 4 ♗a4 ♘f6

5 0-0 ♗e7 6 ♖e1 b5 7 ♗b3 0-0 8 c3 d5 9 exd5 ♘xd5 10 ♘xe5 ♘xe5 11 ♖xe5 c6 12 d4 ♗d6 13 ♖e1 ♕h4 14 g3 ♕h3 15 ♗e3 ♗g4 16 ♕d3 ♖ae8 17 ♘d2 ♖e6

An alternative is 17...f5 18 f4

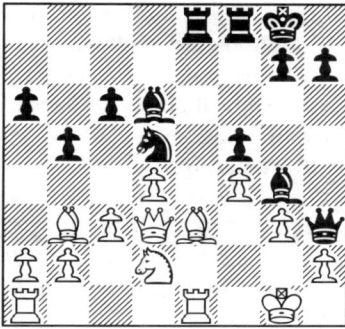

and now:

a) 18...g5?! 19 ♕f1 ♕h5 20 ♗xd5+! cxd5 21 ♕g2 ♖e4 22 fxg5 ♗h3 23 ♕f3 ♗g4 24 ♕f2, when Black's attack comes to an end, while White's material advantage should prevail.

b) 18...♔h8!? might be playable for Black: 19 ♗xd5 cxd5 20 ♕f1 ♕h5 21 ♕g2 ♖e4 22 h4! (preventing ...g7-g5) 22...h6 23 ♘xe4 fxe4 24 ♖f1 ♖f6 25 a4! ♖g6 26 axb5 axb5 and now according to Topalov 27 ♖a7 would have given some advantage to White in Anand-Topalov, Las Palmas 1993. However, Black is certainly not without counterplay due to the weak squares around White's king.

18 a4

Other moves are clearly weaker:

a) 18 ♗d1?! ♗xd1 19 ♖axd1 f5 20 ♘f3 ♖g6! 21 ♕f1 ♕h5 22 ♘e5 ♗xe5 23 dxe5 f4 24 ♗c1 ♖h6 25 ♕g2 f3 26 ♕h1 (not a very attractive square for the white queen) 26...♖e6 27 h4 and now in the game Ljubojevic-Nunn, Amsterdam 1988 Black missed the strong reply 27...♕f5!, which would have kept White's queen in prison.

b) 18 c4? ♗f4! 19 cxd5 ♖h6 20 ♕e4 ♕xh2+ 21 ♔f1 ♗xe3 22 ♖xe3 ♖f6 23 f3 ♗f5 24 ♕e5 ♕xd2 25 ♔g1 cxd5 26 ♗xd5

♕xb2 with both a positional and material advantage to Black according to Yugoslav GM Dragoljub Minic.

c) 18 ♗xd5 cxd5 19 a4 bxa4 20 c4 (worse is 20 ♖xa4? f5 21 ♕f1 f4! 22 ♗xf4 ♕xf1+ 23 ♖xf1 ♗xf4 24 gxf4 ♗h3 and Black wins at least the exchange) 20...dxc4 21 ♕xc4 h5! with a strong initiative on the kingside according to Mikhail Tal.

18...bxa4 19 ♖xa4 f5 20 ♕f1

White has to think about the safety of his monarch because the foolhardy 20 ♖xa6? f4! would have led to an irresistible attack for Black on the kingside in all variations.

20...♕h5

The old game Parma-Spassky, Yugoslavia-USSR 1965 saw 20...f4?, which led to a very bad position for Black after 21 ♕xh3 ♗xh3 22 ♖xa6! fxe3 23 ♖xe3 ♖xe3 24 fxe3 ♗e7 25 e4 ♗g5 26 exd5 ♗xd2 27 dxc6+ ♔h8 28 ♖a1 etc.

21 c4?

This position deserves a diagram.

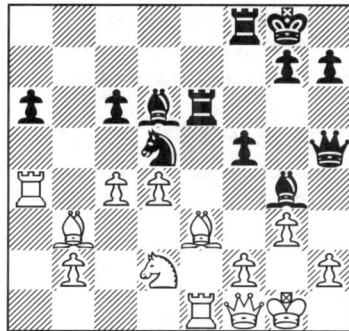

With his last move White wins material, leaving Black with no choice but to go 'all-in'. The position is difficult to evaluate because of the unequal material and it is no wonder that even the late great World Champion Mikhail Tal gave a wrong assessment. Currently this move is considered bad, yet a long time ago it was considered the best for White!

21...f4!

Obviously Black has no choice because 21...♘xe3?! 22 fxe3 c5, although possible, would have kept Black's attacking chances on the kingside to a minimum.

22 cxd5 ♖xe3!

Again the strongest move because 22...fxe3?! 23 dxe6 ♖xf2 (of course not 23...exf2+? 24 ♕xf2 ♖xf2 25 e7+! winning for White) 24 e7+ ♔h8 25 e8♕+! ♕xe8 26 ♖xe3! ♖xf1+ 27 ♘xf1 with 28 ♖xa6 to follow gives an obvious advantage for White according to the analysis of the recently deceased Russian GM Alexey Suetin.

23 fxe3 fxg3 24 dxc6+! ♔h8 25 hxg3 ♖xf1+ 26 ♖xf1

Forced because 26 ♘xf1? ♗f3! is very bad for White.

26...♕g5!

Black can draw here with 26...♕h6 27 ♘c4 ♕h3! 28 ♘xd6 ♕xg3+ and it's perpetual check, The text, as we shall see, is even stronger.

27 ♖f4

Should White defend the e-pawn by 27 ♘c4, there follows 27...♗e2! winning material so White decides to give up the exchange in order to diminish Black's attacking potential.

27...♗xf4 28 exf4 ♕e7 29 ♘f1

Forced because 29 ♖xa6?? loses outright after 29...♕e3+ 30 ♔f1 ♕e2+ picking up the rook.

29...♕e4!

This is stronger than the alternatives:

a) 29...h5 30 ♖xa6 ♕e2 31 ♖a8+ ♔h7 32 ♗g8+ ♔g6 33 ♗d5 ♗h3 34 ♖a1 ♕xb2 35 ♖d1 ♕e2 with roughly equal chances, Kaiumov-Sternberg, Beltsy 1979.

b) 29...♕e2!? 30 ♖b4 h5! is a promising continuation for Black. Now 31 ♖b8+ ♔h7 32 ♗g8+ was wrongly assessed by Tal as clearly better for White but in fact after 32...♔h6! (not 32...♔g6? 33 c7! threatening ♖b8-b6+ and it is White who is winning) 33 ♗f7 g6! 34 ♖e8 ♕f3! it was White who found himself in a critical position in Rooks-

Kotzem, correspondence 1992.

30 d5

Or 30 ♖xa6 ♕xd4+ 31 ♔g2 ♕xb2+ 32 ♔g1 h5! with excellent winning chances for Black, while after 30 ♖b4 ♕xc6 31 ♖b8+ ♗c8 32 ♗d5 ♕c7 33 ♖a8 ♕d7! 34 f5 h5 35 ♗e6 ♕xd4+ Black's attack comes first. The general conclusion is that, despite White having enough material for the queen, all the chances are with Black due to the weakened position of the white king.

30...♕d3 31 ♖b4 g5!

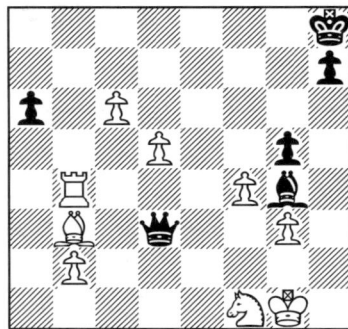

Giving the black king some air and simultaneously softening up the white kingside.

32 c7

Or 32 ♗c4 ♕d4+ 33 ♔g2 gxf4 34 gxf4 ♕xf4 35 ♔g1 h5 36 b3 h4 37 ♖a4 ♕d4+ 38 ♔g2 ♕b2+ 39 ♔g1 h3 0-1 Frost-Claridge, correspondence 1998.

32...♔g7 33 ♗c4 ♕d4+ 34 ♔g2 ♕e4+ 35 ♔f2

Alternatives are no better: 35 ♔h2 ♗f3! or 35 ♔g1 gxf4 36 gxf4 ♗h3 with an easy win for Black in both cases.

35...gxf4 36 gxf4 ♕xf4+ 37 ♔g1 a5 38 ♖a4 ♕d4+ 39 ♔g2 ♕e4+ 40 ♔f2 ♕f3+ 41 ♔e1 ♕d1+ 42 ♔f2 ♕xa4 0-1

Game 3
Ivanchuk-Short
Riga 1995

---

1 e4 e5 2 ♘f3 ♘c6 3 ♗b5 a6 4 ♗a4 ♘f6

dxc4 27 ♕xc4 ♕xc4 28 ♘xc4 but even here Black is facing an uphill struggle to draw in the arising ending, Chandler-P.Littlewood, London 1987.

All these examples show that Black still has to demonstrate a way to equality in the jungle of variations starting with 18...f5.

19 axb5 axb5 20 ♘e4

This is the idea of super-GM Viswanathan Anand. An alternative is the older continuation 20 ♘f1 which does not cause Black any problems after 20...♗f5 and now:

a) 21 ♕d2 ♗e4 22 ♗c2 f5 23 ♗d1 ♕h3 24 f3 f4! 25 fxe4 fxg3 26 ♕g2 gxh2+ 27 ♔h1 ♕xg2+ 28 ♔xg2 ♖xe4 29 ♗b3 h1♕+! 30 ♔xh1 ♖h4+ 31 ♔g2 ♖g4+ with a drawn position as in Rubinchik-Vitomskis, correspondence 1989. It is very risky for White to continue to play for a win with 32 ♔h3 because of 32...h5 33 ♗d1 ♖xf1! 34 ♖xf1 ♖g3+ 35 ♔h4 ♘e3 etc.

b) 21 ♕d1 ♗g4 22 ♕d2 ♕h3 23 ♗d1 ♗xd1 24 ♖axd1 f5 25 f4 g5! 26 ♕g2 ♕xg2+ 27 ♔xg2 ♖fe8 28 ♗d2 ♖xe1 29 ♖xe1 ♖xe1 30 ♗xe1 gxf4 with an equal ending in Karpov-Short, Tilburg 1991.

20...♗f5

Against 20...♗c7?! there is a devilish idea after 21 ♗d2 ♖fe8 22 ♗d1! ♗xd1 23 ♖exd1 when 23...♖xe4? 24 ♕xe4! ♕xd1+ 25 ♔g2!!

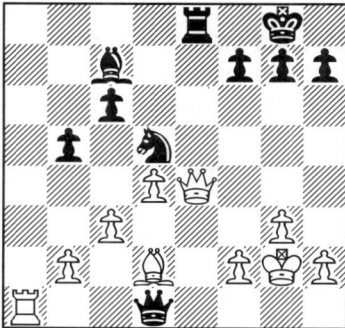

when Black is lost due to the weakness of his back rank. In the game Anand-Kamsky, Sanghi Naghar (1st matchgame) 1994 Black

played 23...f5 24 ♘g5 ♖e2 and now 25 ♕f3 would have left White with a clear advantage. **21 ♗d2 ♖xe4! 22 ♖xe4 ♘f6 23 f3 ♕g6!**

Hitting both e4- and g3-squares, which means Black will restore the material balance. **24 ♕f1 ♘xe4 25 fxe4 ♗xe4 26 ♗f4 ♗d3 27 ♕f2 ♗xf4 28 ♕xf4 h6 29 ♕f2 ♖e8 30 ♖e1 ♖xe1+ 31 ♕xe1 ♗e4 32 ♕f2 ½-½**

Game 5
Morovic-Adams
Santiago 1997

1 e4 e5 2 ♘f3 ♘c6 3 ♗b5 a6 4 ♗a4 ♘f6 5 0-0 ♗e7 6 ♖e1 b5 7 ♗b3 0-0 8 c3 d5 9 exd5 ♘xd5 10 ♘xe5 ♘xe5 11 ♖xe5 c6 12 d4 ♗d6 13 ♖e1 ♕h4 14 g3 ♕h3 15 ♗e3 ♗g4 16 ♕d3 ♖ae8 17 ♘d2 ♕h5

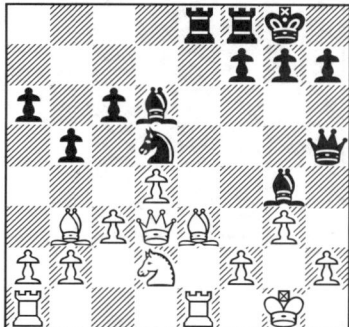

This move can lead by transposition to the

line 17...♖e6 18 a4 ♕h5. Here Black tries to sidestep this variation and to force a draw by a perpetual attack against White's queen. However, White has a way to avoid this draw.

18 a4

The strongest reply. Black quickly achieved the initiative after 18 ♘f1 ♖e6 19 ♗d1?! (better was 19 a4 transposing to 17...♖e6 18 a4 ♕h5 19 ♘f1 etc.) 19...f5 20 ♗xg4 ♕xg4 21 ♗d2 ♖g6 22 ♔g2?! (Black gets a promising attack after both 22 c4 bxc4 23 ♕xc4 ♔h8 and 22 f3 ♕h3 23 ♕e2 f4 24 ♕g2 ♕d7 25 g4 h5 26 h3 hxg4 27 hxg4 c5 but the text is clearly worse) 22...f4 23 f3 ♕h5 24 g4 ♕h4! 25 ♗e2 ♖xg4+! 26 fxg4 f3+ 27 ♔h1 (forced since after 27 ♕xf3 ♖xf3 28 ♔xf3 ♕h3+ 29 ♘g3 ♘f6 Black's attack breaks through) 27...fxe2 28 ♕xe2 ♔h8 29 ♔g1 h6 30 ♕g2 ♗f4 31 ♖e1 ♕g5 32 h3?! (better was 32 ♖d1 preventing the late intrusion of the Black queen to d3) 32...♕g6! 33 ♖d1 ♗b8 34 ♖d2 ♕b1 35 ♗f2 ♔g8 (White is in a kind of zugzwang and the pin along the first rank is decisive) 36 b3 ♗f4 37 ♖e2 ♘xc3 38 ♖e6 ♕xa2 39 ♖xc6 ♕xb3 40 ♖xa6 ♘e2+ 41 ♔h1 ♗b8 42 ♗e1 ♕d1 0-1 Ivanchuk-Adams, Terrassa 1991.

18...♗f5?!

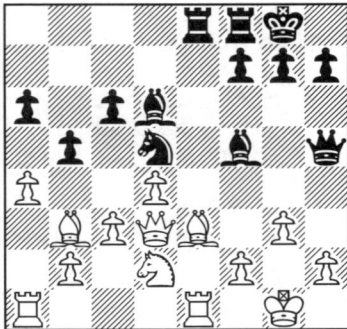

A better option was 18...♖e6. With the text Black aims to force a draw by repetition.

19 ♕f1

19 ♗d1 appears to be a blunder but is actually playable: 19...♕xd1 (worse is 19...♕g6?! 20 ♕f1 ♘xe3 21 ♖xe3 ♗f4 22 ♖xe8 ♖xe8 23 ♘f3 ♗d3 24 ♕g2 – of course not 24 ♘h4? ♗xf1 25 ♘xg6 ♖e1! etc. – 24...♗d6 25 axb5 axb5 26 ♘e5 with advantage to White) 20 ♕xf5 ♘xe3 21 ♕d3 ♕c2 22 ♖xe3 ♕xb2 23 ♖b1 ♕a2 24 axb5 axb5 25 ♘e4 ♗e7 26 ♖be1 ♖d8 with equal play in Leyva-Pupo, Holguin 1992.

19...♗h3 20 ♗d1 ♕f5 21 ♕e2 c5

Or 21...♘f4 22 ♕f3 ♘d3 23 ♕xf5 ♗xf5 24 ♗c2! with advantage for White because after 24...♘xe1? 25 ♗xf5 Black's knight on e1 is trapped.

22 ♘f3 b4

White is also much better after 22...♗f4 23 ♕d2 ♘xe3 24 fxe3 ♗h6 25 axb5 axb5 26 ♖a5!? etc.

23 ♕xa6 bxc3 24 bxc3 ♘xc3 25 ♕xd6 ♘xd1 26 ♘h4! ♖xe3

Obviously the only move because otherwise Black would be a whole piece down for nothing.

27 ♖axd1

Of course not 27 ♘xf5?? ♖xe1 mate or 27 fxe3?? ♕f2+ with mate to follow, but 27 ♖exd1?! was possible and leads to a draw after 27...♕e4! 28 dxc5 (or 28 fxe3 ♕xe3+ 29 ♔h1 ♕e4+ with perpetual check) 28...♖e8! (threatening the nasty ...♖e3-e1+ mating) and White has nothing better than 29 fxe3 ♕xe3+ 30 ♔h1 ♕e4+ with a draw.

27...♖xe1+ 28 ♖xe1 ♕c2 29 dxc5 ♕xa4 30 ♘g2! ♕b4 31 ♕e5

Deserving of attention is 31 ♖d1!? ♗g4 32 c6! etc.

31...♗d7 32 ♘f4 ♗c6 33 ♘h5 f6 34 ♕e7?!

Stronger is 34 ♕e6+ ♔h8 (forced because after 34...♔f7? 35 ♖d1 White immediately wins) 35 ♕e7 ♖g8 36 ♘f4.

34...♖f7 35 ♕d8+ ♖f8 36 ♕e7 ♖f7 37 ♕e6 ♗d7?!

Simpler was 37...♕xc5 38 ♖d1 h6! which leads to a draw. 39 ♖d8+ followed by ♕xf7 is not possible because White would get mated first by ...♕c5-c1+.

38 ♕e3 ♖f8 39 ♕e7 ♖f7 40 ♕e3 ♖f8 41 ♕c1 ♖e8 42 ♖xe8+ ♗xe8 ½-½

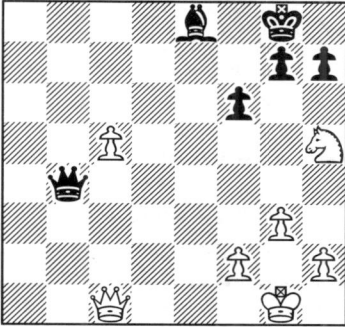

After 43 ♘f4 ♗c6 it would be very difficult, if not impossible, to convert White's extra pawn into a win due to Black's bishop being stronger than White's knight.

Game 6
Kindermann-I.Sokolov
Biel 1988

---

1 e4 e5 2 ♘f3 ♘c6 3 ♗b5 a6 4 ♗a4 ♘f6 5 0-0 ♗e7 6 ♖e1 b5 7 ♗b3 0-0 8 c3 d5 9 exd5 ♘xd5 10 ♘xe5 ♘xe5 11 ♖xe5 c6 12 d4 ♗d6 13 ♖e1 ♕h4 14 g3 ♕h3 15 ♗e3 ♗g4 16 ♕d3 f5?!

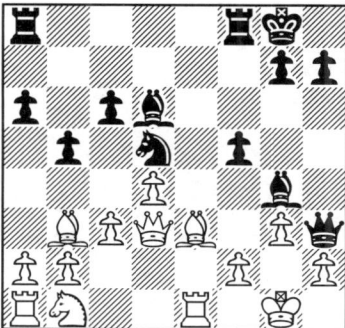

This rare move is played with the aim of avoiding the jungle of variations you need to memorise in the long old main line of the Marshall starting with 16...♖ae8 etc. Black, without hesitation, gets on with his kingside attack, thus trying to save an important tempo by not playing ...♖a8-e8.

From White's point of view he should prevent Black from playing ...f5-f4 at all costs because then Black would be able to double rooks along the open f-file, thus leaving the white monarch at the mercy of all of Black's pieces.

17 ♕f1?! ♕xf1+!

No dear reader, this is not a misprint! Black is ready to enter the endgame a pawn down, which is a paradox for the Marshall Gambit. More important is the time gained by this exchange, which will enable Black to play ...f5-f4 with a strong initiative.

18 ♔xf1?

This is a serious mistake because on f1 White's king will be insecure. Better instead is 18 ♖xf1 f4 19 gxf4 ♗xf4 20 ♘d2, which was seen in a couple of games in my database. Now instead of 20...♔h8, I think Black should play 20...♖ad8!? planning the manoeuvre ...♖d8-d6-g6, with a very promising position and full compensation for the sacrificed pawn.

18...f4!

Of course!

19 gxf4 ♗xf4 20 ♔g1 ♗c7! 21 ♘d2 ♖f6 22 ♘e4 ♖g6 23 ♘g3 ♖f8 24 ♗c2 ♗f5 25 ♗xf5 ♖xf5 26 ♗d2 h5

Despite the fact that the position is some-

somewhat simplified, Black has maintained a strong initiative that means White must be careful all the time. The immediate threat is ...h5-h4 winning a piece.

27 ♖e4 ♗f4 28 ♗xf4 ♘xf4 29 ♔f1 ♖f8 30 ♖d1 ♘h3 31 ♖d2

Again this move is forced because 31 ♖e2?? would have lost on the spot after 31...h4 – White's knight cannot move due to ...♖g6-g1 mate.

31...♘g5 32 ♖e3 h4 33 ♘e4 ♘f3 34 ♖d1 ♘xh2+ 35 ♔e2 ♖f4 36 ♖h1 ♖g2

As a consequence of the lasting initiative, Black has regained his sacrificed pawn and keeps a great positional advantage due to his powerful passed h-pawn.

37 ♔d2 g5 38 ♖e2 ♖f5?!

This is not necessary; better was 38...g4 at once.

39 b3 ♔g7 40 c4 bxc4 41 bxc4 ♔g6 42 ♖b1 h3 43 ♖h1 g4 44 ♔d3 ♔g7!? 45 c5 ♔g6 46 ♖b1 ♘f3 47 ♘g3 h2 48 ♖h1

The only move because after 48 ♘xf5? ♖g1 the game is terminated.

48...♖f4 49 ♖e4

Perhaps more resistance would have been put up if White had kept all the rooks on the board.

49...♔g5 50 ♖xf4 ♔xf4 51 ♘e2+ ♔f5 52 ♔e3 ♔f6 53 ♘g3 ♔e6 54 ♘e2 ♔d7 55 ♘g3 a5 56 a4 ♔g5!

Practically leaving White in zugzwang. Black has finally found the way to break

through.

57 ♘f1 ♖g1 58 ♘g3 ♖xh1 59 ♘xh1 ♔h3! 60 f3 gxf3 61 ♔xf3 ♔e6 62 ♔g4 0-1

No, resignation is not too early because after 62...♔g1 63 ♔g3 ♔d5 64 ♔xh2 ♘f3+ 65 ♔g3 ♘xd4 66 ♘f2 ♘e6 the arising knight and pawn ending is an elementary win for Black.

Game 7

Sax-Ehlvest

Skelleftea (World Cup) 1989

1 e4 e5 2 ♘f3 ♘c6 3 ♗b5 a6 4 ♗a4 ♘f6 5 0-0 ♗e7 6 ♖e1 b5 7 ♗b3 0-0 8 c3 d5 9 exd5 ♘xd5 10 ♘xe5 ♘xe5 11 ♖xe5 c6 12 d4 ♗d6 13 ♖e1 ♕h4 14 g3 ♕h3 15 ♗e3 ♗g4 16 ♕d3 f5?!

Of course 16...♗f3? 17 ♕f1 only helps White because after ♘b1-d2 Black's bishop will be attacked.

17 f4

This is White's best reply. The thematic move ...f5-f4 has been prevented and this keeps White's kingside solid.

17...♔h8

Again harmless is 17...♗f3?! 18 ♕f1 etc.

18 ♗xd5 cxd5 19 ♘d2 g5 20 ♕f1

White should avoid the obvious trap 20 fxg5? ♗xg3!, when Black wins.

20...♕h5 21 a4!

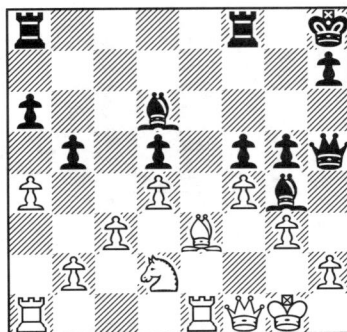

White has to seek counterplay on the opposite flank. The main point of this strong move will be obvious in another six moves.

21 a4! is much stronger than immediately taking on g5 with 21 fxg5. Play continues 21...f4 22 ♗xf4 ♖xf4! 23 gxf4 ♖f8 24 ♖e5 (the only move because otherwise Black would take on f4 with a devastating attack) 24...♗xe5 25 dxe5 h6! (another thematic move – Black tries to open the g-file along which he can endanger the white king) 26 ♖e1 hxg5 27 f5!? ♖xf5 28 ♕d3 ♖f2!? 29 ♘f1! (excellent defence; everything else loses, for example if 29 ♔xf2? ♕xh2+ 30 ♔f1 – or 30 ♔e3?? ♕f4 mate – 30...♗h3+ 31 ♕xh3 ♕xh3+ and the endgame is easily winning for Black) 29...♖xb2 30 ♕xd5 ♗f3 31 ♕d8+ ♔g7 32 ♕d7+ ♕f7 33 ♕xf7+ ♔xf7 and this ending is assessed by GM John Nunn as equal, but I think that White might even be in trouble here, for example: 34 e6+ ♔e8 35 ♘g3 ♖xa2 36 ♘f5 ♖e2 37 ♖a1 ♖e5! etc.

21...bxa4 22 fxg5 f4 23 ♗xf4 ♖xf4 24 gxf4 ♖f8 25 ♖e5!

The only move!

25...♗xe5 26 dxe5 h6 27 ♕xa6!

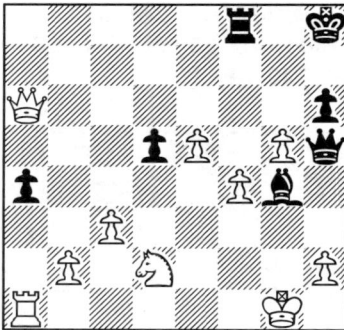

Now the importance of 21 a4! is obvious – Black's king is weak too and White's queen can potentially harass it.

27...hxg5 28 ♕d6! ♖xf4 29 ♖f1! ♗f5

Immediately losing is 29...♗h3? 30 ♖xf4 gxf4 31 ♕f8+ ♔h7 32 ♕xf4, while after 29...♖xf1+ 30 ♘xf1 ♗h3 31 ♘e3 ♕e2 32 ♕f8+ ♔h7 White has 33 ♕f2.

30 ♕xd5 ♗h3 31 ♖xf4 gxf4 32 ♕f3 ♕g5+ 33 ♔h1 ♕h4 34 ♕a8+ ♔g7 35 ♕b7+ ♔h8 36 ♕b8+ ♔h7 37 ♕c7+ ♔h6 38 ♕c6+ ♔h7 39 ♘f3 ♕g4 40 ♕e4+ ♔g7 41 ♘g1!

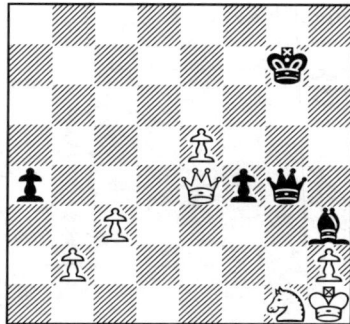

After this strong move Black's chances of swindling disappear while White's material advantage decides the game.

41...♕f5 42 ♕xf5 ♗xf5 43 ♘e2 ♗e4+ 44 ♔g1 ♔g6 45 e6 ♔f6 46 ♘xf4 ♔e5 47 e7 ♗c6 48 ♘e2 ♔d6 49 ♘d4 ♗d7 50 ♘f5+ 1-0

Game 8
Timmermans-Neil
British League 1996

1 e4 e5 ♘f3 ♘c6 3 ♗b5 a6 4 ♗a4 ♘f6 5 0-0 ♗e7 6 ♖e1 b5 7 ♗b3 0-0 8 c3 d5 9 exd5 ♘xd5 10 ♘xe5 ♘xe5 11 ♖xe5 c6 12 d4 ♗d6 13 ♖e1 ♕h4 14 g3 ♕h3 15 ♗e3 ♗g4 16 ♕d3 ♔h8?!

This move I regard as not so accurate because it stops Black from playing other plans (if he wants to play ...f7-f5 he should do so immediately, assuming he wants to avoid entering the long old main line with 16...♖ae8).

Which lines does it cut out? Well, for instance, after 16...f5?! 17 f4 g5 18 ♕f1 ♕h5 19 ♘d2, besides 19...♖ae8, Black can try the plan of 19...h6!? with the idea of tucking his king away on the safe square h7, anticipating the opening of the g-file. Against this plan White should not go in for pawn grabbing with 20 ♕g2 ♔h7 21 ♗xd5 cxd5 22 ♕xd5 ♖ad8!, which gives Black excellent attacking chances, but should continue with the same plan White plays in the text, leaving him with a comfortable advantage.

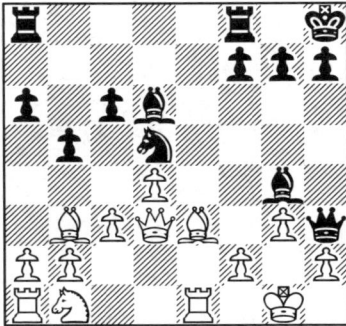

17 ♘d2 f5 18 ♕f1 ♕h5 19 ♗xd5 cxd5 20 f4 ♖ae8 21 a4! g5 22 axb5 axb5 23 ♕f2 ♖e7

White is just too solid and this is the reason why Black's attack cannot break through.

Black has also played 23...♖e6, for example: 24 fxg5 ♖fe8 25 b3 ♖8e7 26 h4 ♕e8 27 ♘f1 b4 28 c4! dxc4 29 bxc4 ♗h3 30 ♗d2 ♖e2 31 ♖xe2 ♖xe2 32 ♖e1! ♗xf1 33 ♕xf1 ♖xe1 34 ♕xe1 ♕xe1+ 35 ♗xe1 b3 36 ♗c3

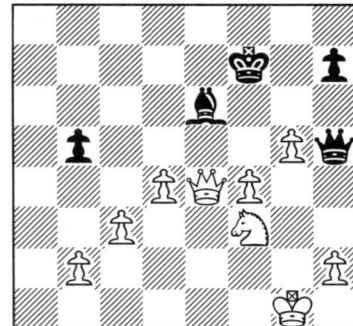

♗xg3? (this loses; with 36...♗a3 Black retained some drawing chances) 37 h5 ♗f4 38 d5+ ♔g8 39 g6 hxg6 40 hxg6 ♗c1 41 d6 ♗g5 42 d7 ♔f8 43 ♗g2 1-0, Petr-Mares, Czech Correspondence Team Ch. 1993.
24 ♖a6 ♗c7 25 fxg5 f4 26 ♗xf4 ♖xe1+ 27 ♕xe1 ♗xf4 28 gxf4 ♖e8 29 ♖a8!!

Just when it appeared that Black was getting the upper hand with his kingside attack, he has obviously overlooked this fantastic geometrical motif. The text leads to the exchange of rooks, leaving Black in a hopelessly lost position.
29...♖xa8 30 ♕e5+ ♔g8 31 ♕xd5+ ♗e6 32 ♕xa8+ ♔f7 33 ♕b7+ ♔g6 34 ♕e4+ ♔f7 35 ♘f3 1-0

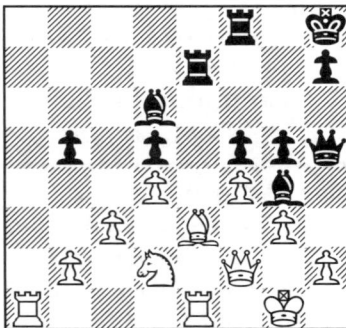

Summary

16...♖ae8 17 ♘d2 ♖e6 is very complex, but the critical line 18 a4 bxa4 19 ♖xa4 f5 20 ♕f1 ♕h5 looks okay for Black after 21 f4 and 21 ♖xa6, while 21 c4? is certainly a mistake.

It's nice to have one little line which you can use to reach a satisfactory position without learning all this opening theory, but sadly this is not the case with 16...f5?! (Game 6-8). Still, as a surprise weapon this line can occasionally serve its purpose but, all in all, I recommend playing 16...♖ae8 instead of 16...f5?!.

1 e4 e5 2 ♘f3 ♘c6 3 ♗b5 a6 4 ♗a4 ♘f6 5 0-0 ♗e7 6 ♖e1 b5 7 ♗b3 0-0 8 c3 d5 9 exd5 ♘xd5 10 ♘xe5 ♘xe5 11 ♖xe5 c6 12 d4 ♗d6 13 ♖e1 ♕h4 14 g3 ♕h3 15 ♗e3 ♗g4 16 ♕d3 (D) **♖ae8**

> 16...f5?!
>> 17 ♕f1 – *Game 6*
>> 17 f4 ♔h8 18 ♗xd5 cxd5 19 ♘d2 g5 20 ♕f1 ♕h5 21 a4 (D)
>>> 21...bxa4 – *Game 7*
>>> 21...♖ae8 – *Game 8*

17 ♘d2 ♖e6

> 17...♕h5 – *Game 5*

18 a4 bxa4

> 18...♕h5 – *Game 4*

19 ♖xa4 f5 20 ♕f1 ♕h5 (D) **21 f4** – *Game 1*

> 21 c4 – *Game 2*
> 21 ♖xa6 – *Game 3*

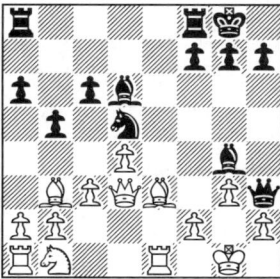
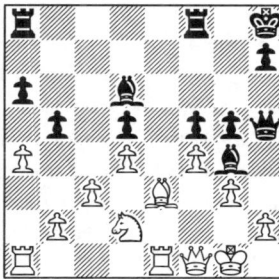
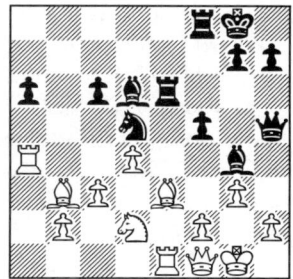

| 16 ♕d3 | 21 a4 | 20...♕h5 |

CHAPTER TWO

The Modern Method: 12 d4 and 15 ♖e4

1 e4 e5 2 ♘f3 ♘c6 3 ♗b5 a6 4 ♗a4 ♘f6 5 0-0 ♗e7 6 ♖e1 b5 7 ♗b3 0-0 8 c3 d5 9 exd5 ♘xd5 10 ♘xe5 ♘xe5 11 ♖xe5 c6 12 d4 ♗d6 13 ♖e1 ♕h4 14 g3 ♕h3 15 ♖e4

In this chapter we see the very popular rook manoeuvre ♖e1-e4, with which White prevents Black's standard attack of ...♗c8-g4 etc. It may look as if White's rook on e4 is exposed. However, in some lines the rook endangers itself even further by going to h4.

In Game 9 we shall see that 15...♗b7? stands close to being refuted. It is important to observe, despite looking awkward at first glance, how usefully placed the white rook is in an attacking role on the h-file.

In T.Ernst-Hebden (Game 10) White immediately tries to chase away Black's queen from its attacking position by playing 16 ♕f1?!. However, it will later transpire that this plan in fact helps Black's development more than it does White's.

Games 11-15 deal with the often-played 16 ♕f3. After the logical reply 16...♗f5 White has the choice between exchanging on d5 (Game 11), which gives Black control of the e4-square, and offering a positional sacrifice of the exchange by playing 17 ♗c2!? (Games 12-15). The positional exchange sacrifice is very interesting – its aim is to di-

minish Black's attacking potential on the kingside while at the same time reckoning on Black's kingside weaknesses caused by the sharp and brave 15...g5!.

17...♘f4?! (Game 12) is an attempt by Black to break up White's rock-solid kingside, but Black's kingside then becomes vulnerable so this move enjoys a dubious reputation.

Although Black lost after 17...♗f4!? (Game 13), the reader can see from the commentary of the game that Black could have improved on his play so this move can be considered a viable sideline.

Games 14-15 witness 17...♗xe4, when Black accepts the challenge by taking the offered exchange sacrifice. 20 ♗xd5? (Game 14) is a positional error because after the exchange White's compensation for the sacrificed exchange becomes minimal. The correct move is 20 ♗d3! (Game 15) leading to a complicated position with mutual chances where each side has its trumps.

16 ♕e2!? has lately been the focus of theoretical research and has been played by a couple of super-GMs. For the moment it has replaced the standard 16 ♕f3.

After 16...f5 White should firstly include 17 ♗xd5+!. It seems that after 17 ♖e6? (Game 16) White loses by force – despite his large material advantage he is unable to prevent being mated!

The initiative is a continuously important theme of the Marshall Attack and Ponomariov-Anand (Game 17) confirms this. Anand produces a study-like combination leading to perpetual check, which leads to the conclusion that 16 ♕e2 f5 is fully playable for Black.

In the final game of this chapter (Ponomariov-Adams) we see 16...♘f6. A very complicated position arises with White having a minor piece and a pawn for a rook.

Game 9
Leko-Adams
Dortmund 1999

---

1 e4 e5 2 ♘f3 ♘c6 3 ♗b5 a6 4 ♗a4 ♘f6 5 0-0 ♗e7 6 ♖e1 b5 7 ♗b3 0-0 8 c3 d5 9 exd5 ♘xd5 10 ♘xe5 ♘xe5 11 ♖xe5 c6 12 d4 ♗d6 13 ♖e1 ♕h4 14 g3 ♕h3 15 ♖e4

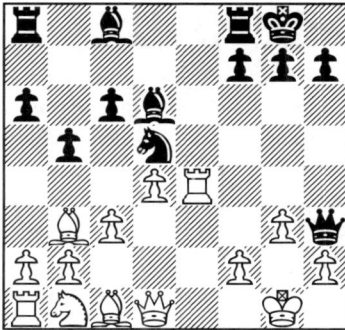

With this rook manoeuvre White is preventing both ...♗g4 and ...♗f5 (if 15...♗f5?? then 16 ♖h4! traps the queen) and sometimes, as in this game, the rook can be switched to the h-file with some threats against the black monarch.

15...♗b7?

We shall see both 15...♕d7 and 15...g5 in later games.

16 ♖h4 ♕e6 17 ♘d2 f5

Neither alternative grants Black an easy game:

a) 17...♖fe8 18 ♘e4 ♗e7 19 ♘c5 ♗xc5 20 dxc5 ♕e7 21 ♕d3! g6 22 ♕d2 h5 23 ♗xd5 cxd5 24 ♕d4 and White was a pawn up with a dominant position due to the passive bishop on b7 in Nunn-Hebden, London 1990.

b) 17...♖ae8 18 ♘e4 ♗e7 19 ♘c5 ♗xc5 20 dxc5 ♕e7 21 ♕d4 (the difference is that with the rook on f8, against 21 ♕d3 Black can answer 21...f5 avoiding the weakening of the dark squares around his king) 21...f5 22 ♗f4 ♖f7 23 ♗d6 ♕e6 24 ♕d2 h6 25 c4 bxc4 26 ♖xc4 g5 27 f4 ♕e2 28 ♕xe2 ♖xe2 29 ♖c2 and White has a clear advantage with his extra pawn in Sandipan-Yurtaev, Asian Championship, Calcutta 2001.

18 ♕h5! h6 19 ♘f3 ♗e7 20 ♖h3 c5

Black seeks the only way to get some activity but freeing his light-squared bishop also strengthens its counterpart on b3.

Very passive for Black is 20...♖ae8 21 ♗f4!, planning to follow up with ♗e5 etc.

21 dxc5 ♗xc5 22 ♗f4 ♖ae8

After 22...♕e2 White can ignore Black's threat of taking on f2 with check by playing 23 ♗xh6!, when he obtains a decisive kingside attack. Note how the seemingly awkwardly-placed rook on h3 fulfils an attacking role.

23 ♖d1

Of course not 23 ♖e1?? ♕xe1+! 24 ♘xe1 ♖xe1+ 25 ♔g2 ♔h7!, when White has no defence against the deadly discovered check on the a8-h1 diagonal.

23...♗e7

After 23...♕e2 all Black's threats are repelled by 24 ♖d2!.

24 ♗g5! ♖d7

24...♖ef7 25 ♗xh6! gxh6 26 ♘g5! ♗xf2+ 27 ♔xf2 ♕e3+ 28 ♔f1 ♕xg5 29 ♕xg5+ hxg5 30 ♗xd5 ♗xd5 31 ♖xd5 leads to a probable won ending for White.

25 ♖e1 ♕b6

Or 25...♕f7 26 ♘e5! ♕xh5 27 ♖xh5 ♖e8

28 ♗d2 ♖de7 29 ♘d3 and White retains the extra pawn for the ending.

26 ♖e2 ♔h7

Again the bishop is taboo – 26...hxg5? 27 ♕h7+ ♔f7 28 ♘xg5+ ♔f6 29 ♖h6+! ♔xg5 30 ♖g6+!! ♕xg6 31 ♕h4 is a nice mate!

27 ♖h4!

White is preparing to sacrifice his bishop on h6, which Adams overlooks.

27...a5?

The only move was 27...♖d6 but after 28 ♗c2! it is difficult to suggest any good move for Black. Here we see White attacking on the kingside which is not often the case in this opening.

28 ♗xh6! ♕xh6

Also losing is 28...gxh6 29 ♖e6! ♗xf2+ 30 ♔f1 ♘e3+ 31 ♔e2 ♗xf3+ 32 ♔xf3 ♕b7+ 33 ♔e2!

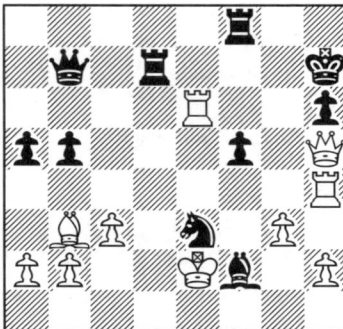

and mate follows after the capture on h6.

29 ♕g5 a4 30 ♖e6 1-0

Game 10

T.Ernst-Hebden

Gausdal 1987

1 e4 e5 2 ♘f3 ♘c6 3 ♗b5 a6 4 ♗a4 ♘f6 5 0-0 ♗e7 6 ♖e1 b5 7 ♗b3 0-0 8 c3 d5 9 exd5 ♘xd5 10 ♘xe5 ♘xe5 11 ♖xe5 c6 12 d4 ♗d6 13 ♖e1 ♕h4 14 g3 ♕h3 15 ♖e4 g5!

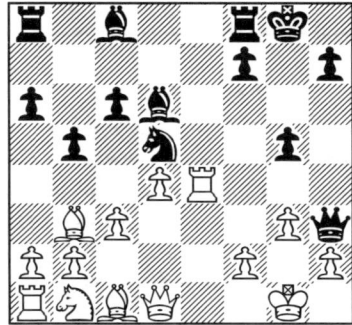

This sharp move, after many years of tournament practice, has rebuffed all challenges and is regarded as Black's most dynamic choice. The idea behind this at outwardly strange move is to deny White's rook access to the h4-square. It's based on the tactical cheapo 16 ♗xg5?? ♕f5!, attacking both the rook on e4 and bishop on g5.

16 ♕f1?!

This looks natural but we shall see that Black's queen will feel even better off on g6 from where it will be possible to control the important d3-square. So theory, with good reason, considers the text less strong than 16 ♕f3.

16...♕h5!

Stronger than 16...♕h6?! 17 f3 ♔h8 18 ♘d2 ♗h3 19 ♕e1 ♘f4!? (Black is trying at all costs to open the g-file for attack but White wisely rejects the sacrifice) 20 ♘f1! (White can draw after 20 gxf4?! gxf4 21 ♔h1 ♖g8 22 ♖e2 ♕g7 23 ♕f2 ♗e7 24 ♖xe7!

♗g2+) 20...♕g7 21 ♕f2 ♘d3 22 ♕d2 ♘xc1 23 ♖xc1 f5 24 ♖e6 ♖ad8 25 ♕f2 and Black had inadequate compensation for the pawn in Kr.Georgiev-Tseshkovsky, Moscow 1985.

17 ♕e2

Worse is 17 ♗d2?! ♗f5 (also very good for Black is 17...f5!? 18 ♖e1 f4 etc. with a strong attack) 18 ♖e1 ♗h3 19 ♕e2 ♗g4 20 ♕f1 ♖ae8 21 ♘a3 ♗h3 (avoiding 21...♗e2 22 ♗d1! with a pleasant exchange for White) 22 ♕d3 ♘f4! 23 ♗xf4 (or 23 gxf4? gxf4 24 ♔h1 f3 and it is difficult to find a defence for White) 23...gxf4 24 ♘c2 ♗g4 25 ♖xe8 ♖xe8 26 ♖e1 ♗e2! 27 ♕d2 ♕f3 28 d5 c5! (White is completely tied down and is almost in zugzwang!) 29 ♘a3 fxg3 30 ♕g5+ ♔h8 31 hxg3 ♖g8 32 ♕h4 ♗xg3 0-1 Smolensky-Heffner, correspondence 1985.

17...♕g6 18 ♖e8 ♗f5 19 ♖xa8 ♖xa8 20 ♘d2 ♗d3 21 ♖e1 ♘f4!

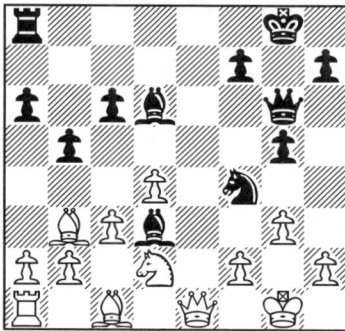

Due to the threat ...♘f4-e2+, White has no option but to accept the offered piece. This kind of sacrifice is seen both in the Marshall and the King's Indian Defence. Bearing in mind White's dormant queenside pieces, the sacrifice is completely sound. Black will gain control of the g-file and this will expose the white king.

22 gxf4 gxf4+ 23 ♔h1 ♔h8 24 ♕g1 ♕f6 25 f3 ♖e8!

Black prevents White having the opportunity to free himself by ♘d2-e4 (when ...♖e8xe4! wins at once) and is planning

...♕f6-h4 followed by ...♖e8-e1. Against this plan there is little that White can do.

26 a4

Desperation.

26...♕h4 27 ♘e4 ♖g8

White was hoping for 27...♖xe4? 28 ♗d2 and the threat of ♗b3xf7 gives him a chance.

28 ♘f2

There was nothing better because if 28 ♕f2, 28...♗xe4! 29 ♕xh4 ♗xf3 is mate while if 28 ♕d1, 28...♕h3 or 28...♗xe4 29 fxe4 ♕f2 wins for Black. After the text Black wins the queen and the rest needs no further explanation.

28...♖xg1+ 29 ♔xg1 ♕g5+ 30 ♔h1 ♗f1 31 ♘g4 h5 32 ♗d2 ♗e2 33 ♘e5 ♗xe5 34 ♗d1 ♗f1 0-1

Game 11
Jonsson-Berzinsh
Hallsberg 1993

---

1 e4 e5 2 ♘f3 ♘c6 3 ♗b5 a6 4 ♗a4 ♘f6 5 0-0 ♗e7 6 ♖e1 b5 7 ♗b3 0-0 8 c3 d5 9 exd5 ♘xd5 10 ♘xe5 ♘xe5 11 ♖xe5 c6 12 d4 ♗d6 13 ♖e1 ♕h4 14 g3 ♕h3 15 ♖e4 g5! 16 ♕f3 ♗f5 17 ♗xd5 cxd5 18 ♖e3 ♗e4

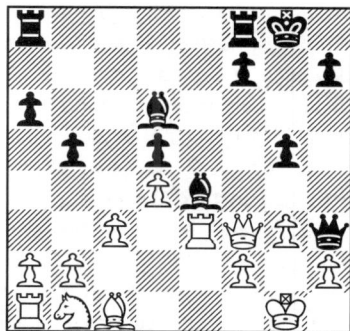

This is the more popular choice and probably stronger than the rarely seen 18...♖ad8 (used by Adams against Leko in Wijk aan Zee 2001), after which Black gets just about enough compensation for the

pawn. That game continued 19 ♘d2 ♖fe8 20 b3 ♔g7 21 ♗b2 ♗g4 22 ♕g2 ♕xg2+ 23 ♔xg2 ♖xe3 24 fxe3 ♖e8 25 ♖e1 ♗f5 26 ♔f2 ♗d3 27 ♖d1 ½-½ (it is difficult to see how White can make further progress).

19 ♖xe4 dxe4 20 ♕f6

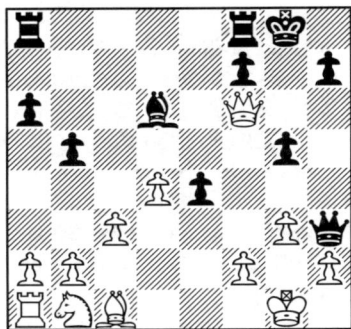

Of course not 20 ♕xe4?? ♖ae8 winning for Black.

This is the critical position arising from 17 ♗xd5 which is rightly considered as a drawing line because both sides have perpetual checks in many lines (Black using the d1-h5 diagonal after 20...♕g4 21 ♗e3 ♗e7 22 ♕xe7 ♕d1+! is one demonstration).

20...♕h5

This is slightly more accurate than 20...♕g4, which often leads, by transposition, to an ending as in the text game. However, it can also have a separate meaning after 21 ♘d2 ♗f4 (a very messy position arose after 21...♖ae8 22 ♘f1 – 22 ♕xd6? e3! is very difficult to meet – 22...♗e7 23 ♕xa6 f5 24 ♕xb5 f4 and in this hair-raising position a draw was agreed in the game Timman-Ivanchuk, Linares 1991) 22 ♘f1 ♗xc1 23 ♖xc1 ♕h5 (here we see the difference; with the queen on g4 White will win a tempo with the manoeuvre ♘f1-e3) 24 ♘e3 ♕g6 25 ♘d5 ♕g7 26 ♖e1 ♖fd8 27 ♘e7+ ♔f8 28 ♕xg7+ ♔xg7 29 ♖xe4 and White was better in the game Hernandez Molina-R.Fernandez, correspondence 1994. Two pawns usually outweigh the exchange when there are no

open files for the rook as in this game.

21 ♕xg5+

Also here there is 21 ♘d2, which is best met by 21...♖ae8! 22 ♕xd6 e3! with a strong attack – there is just enough time for White to bring both the rook on a1 and the bishop on c1 into play.

21...♕xg5 22 ♗xg5 f5 23 ♘d2 ♖ae8!

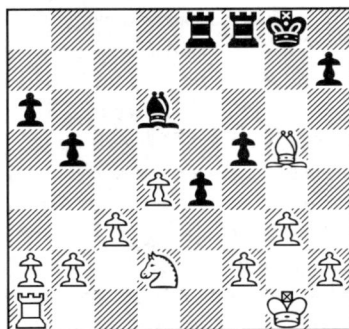

The best plan, after which it is not easy to assess who is better in the arising ending.

The other plan, bringing the king into the centre, promises less after 23...♔f7 24 a4 etc.

Black's plan is simple – play ...f5-f4 and, after the exchange of bishops, ...e4-e3, when Black's rooks will become dangerously active.

24 a4?

White's move is thematic – he opens the a-file in order to create weaknesses in the black camp. However, sometimes thematic moves, as played in this game, just don't work!

Maybe here White should try 24 ♖e1, thus preventing ...f5-f4.

24...f4 25 ♖e1

After 25 axb5 very unpleasant for White is 25...e3.

25...e3 26 fxe3 fxg3 27 hxg3 ♗xg3 28 ♖f1

In order to prevent ...♖f8-f2 but after the next move Black's pawn on a4 will become strong.

28...bxa4 29 e4 ♖xf1+ 30 ♔xf1 ♖b8 31 ♘c4 ♖xb2!!

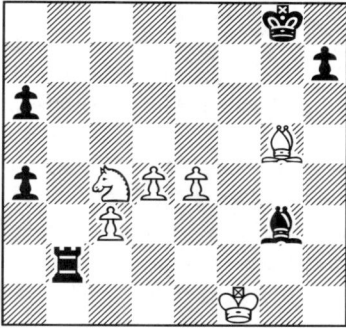

White had overlooked this tactic. After 32 ♘xb2 a3! there is nothing to stop the pawn from promoting. The rest is simple.

32 d5 ♖b3 33 d6 ♗xd6! 0-1

Game 12
Carlsson-Pedersen
Danish Junior Ch., Aarhus 1993

---

1 e4 e5 2 ♘f3 ♘c6 3 ♗b5 a6 4 ♗a4 ♘f6 5 0-0 ♗e7 6 ♖e1 b5 7 ♗b3 0-0 8 c3 d5 9 exd5 ♘xd5 10 ♘xe5 ♘xe5 11 ♖xe5 c6 12 d4 ♗d6 13 ♖e1 ♕h4 14 g3 ♕h3 15 ♖e4 g5! 16 ♕f3 ♗f5 17 ♗c2 ♘f4?!

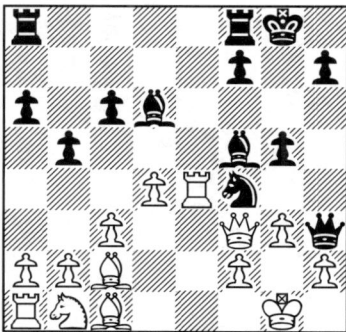

This move is considered to be a sideline against 17 ♗c2 and theory strongly condemns it. White should just stay calm and ensure his kingside remains solid. Usually White gets one or sometimes two pawns for the exchange but then Black's attack disap-

pears. The game now takes a positional turn – eventually Black's weaknesses begin to tell.

18 ♗xf4 gxf4

With this move Black has recently been trying to rehabilitate 17...♘f4?!. Old theory just considers 18...♗xe4?! 19 ♗xe4 gxf4 20 ♗xc6 fxg3 21 fxg3 with an obvious advantage to White (Harding).

19 ♘d2 ♔h8

After 19...♖ad8 White can continue 20 ♖ae1!, when his centralised pieces grant him an advantage despite the material deficit.

20 ♗b3 ♖g8

Or 20...fxg3 21 fxg3 ♗xe4 (if 21...♖g8 22 ♖e3 White keeps the advantage) and now 22 ♕f6+! followed by ♘xe4 is indeed terrible for Black.

21 ♖xf4 ♗xf4 22 ♕xf4 ♕h5 23 ♖e1 ♖ge8 24 ♖e5 ♖xe5 25 ♕xe5+ ♔g8 26 ♘e4

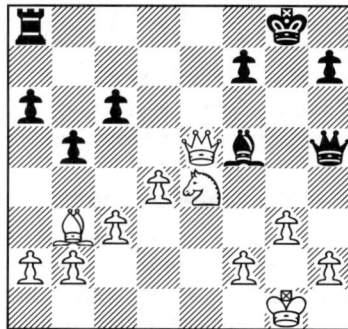

The weaknesses of the dark squares grant White a positionally won game.

26...♕g6 27 ♘f6+ ♔f8 28 ♕c5+

Very attractive looking is 28 d5 cxd5 29 ♘xd5 but Black can hold his own after 29...♗e6 30 ♕h8+ ♕g8 etc.

28...♔g7 29 ♕xc6 ♖d8 30 ♘e8+ ♔f8 31 ♕xg6 fxg6 32 ♘c7 ♖d6 33 f3

With three pawns for the exchange the win for White is but a question of time but sometimes miracles can happen in chess.

33...♖c6 34 ♘d5 a5 35 a4 b4 36 c4 ♖e6 37 ♔f2 g5 38 ♘e3 ♗d3 39 d5 ♖e5 40

c5 ♗e7 41 ♗d1 ♔d7 42 b3 ♖e8 43 ♗e2 ♗xe2 44 ♔xe2 ♖c8 45 c6+ ♔d6 46 ♔d3 ♔c5 47 ♘c4 h6 48 f4 gxf4 49 gxf4 h5 50 h4 ♖c7 51 d6 ♖xc6 52 d7 ♖c7 53 d8♕??

Surely this blunder must have been due to time trouble? The obvious 53 d8♖ or 53 ♘e5 would have forced Black to resign.

53...♖d7+!

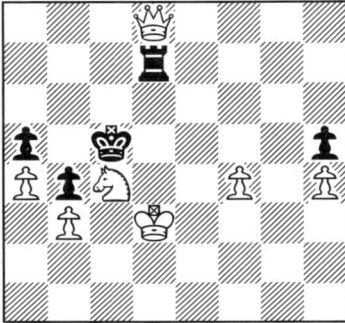

54 ♔e4

Or 54 ♕xd7 stalemate!

54...♖xd8 55 ♘xa5 ½-½

Game 13
Van Delft-Erwich
Amsterdam 2000

1 e4 e5 2 ♘f3 ♘c6 3 ♗b5 a6 4 ♗a4 ♘f6 5 0-0 ♗e7 6 ♖e1 b5 7 ♗b3 0-0 8 c3 d5 9 exd5 ♘xd5 10 ♘xe5 ♘xe5 11 ♖xe5 c6 12 d4 ♗d6 13 ♖e1 ♕h4 14 g3 ♕h3 15 ♖e4 g5! 16 ♕f3 ♗f5 17 ♗c2 ♗f4!? 18 ♗xf4

White's queenside development is retarded and 18 ♘d2 doesn't help to improve it, which is shown in the line 18...♖ae8! 19 ♖xe8 ♖xe8 20 ♘e4 g4 21 ♕e2 (bad is 21 ♕h1? ♗xc1 22 ♖xc1 ♕h6! and due to the poor position of the queen on h1 Black has good winning chances) and now 21...♗c7! grants Black promising play according to the Chinese Grandmaster Ye Jiangchuan.

18...♘xf4?!

Better is 18...gxf4!? with the intention of softening up White's kingside after the exchange on g3. Then play can continue 19 ♘d2 fxg3 20 hxg3 (worse is 20 fxg3?!, weakening the e3-square; Hursch-Leonard, correspondence 1999 continued 20...♗xe4 21 ♘xe4 f5 22 ♘f2 ♕h6! 23 ♗xf5 ♖ae8) 20...♗xe4 21 ♗xe4 ♕h6 22 ♘f1 ♖ad8 23 ♖e1 and according to American Grandmaster Leonid Shamkovich we have reached a balanced position in which Black's worse pawn structure grants White sufficient compensation for the material deficit, but not more than that.

19 ♘d2 ♗g4 20 ♕h1 ♘e2+

Or 20...f5 21 ♖ee1 ♘e2+ 22 ♖xe2 ♗xe2 23 ♕xc6 ♖ae8 24 ♖e1 (even stronger is 24 ♗b3+ ♔g7 25 ♕c7+ ♔g6 26 ♗f7+ ♔f6 27 ♗xe8 ♖xe8 28 d5 with a winning position for White, Noble-Sarfati, Auckland 1993) 24...f4 25 ♗e4 ♖xe4 26 ♕xe4 f3 27 ♕d5+ ♔h8 28 ♕e5+ ♔g8 29 ♕xg5+ ♔h8 30 ♘xf3 ♗xf3 31 ♕e5+ ♔g8 32 ♕e6+ ♕xe6 33 ♖xe6 ♔f7 34 ♖e3 ♗d5 35 b3 and with four pawns for the piece White has a clear winning advantage in Perez-de la Paz, Santa Clara 1998.

21 ♖xe2 ♗xe2 22 ♕xc6 ♗h5 23 ♕h6!

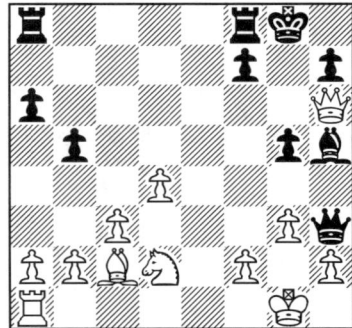

After this strong move, which gives an unpleasant pin on the h-file, Black's position falls to pieces.

23...f5 24 ♕xg5+ ♔g6 25 ♘f3 ♕h5 26 ♕f4 ♖ae8 27 ♘e5 1-0

Although White's position is indeed

dominant, Black's resignation is somewhat premature.

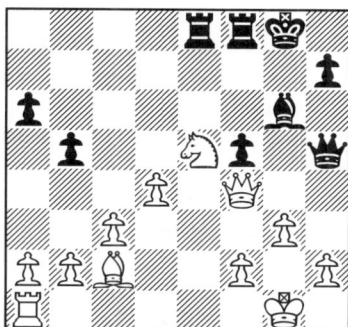

Game 14
Topalov-Adams
Sarajevo 2000

1 e4 e5 2 ♘f3 ♘c6 3 ♗b5 a6 4 ♗a4 ♘f6
5 0-0 ♗e7 6 ♖e1 b5 7 ♗b3 0-0 8 c3 d5
9 exd5 ♘xd5 10 ♘xe5 ♘xe5 11 ♖xe5 c6
12 d4 ♗d6 13 ♖e1 ♕h4 14 g3 ♕h3 15
♖e4 g5! 16 ♕f3 ♗f5 17 ♗c2 ♗xe4 18
♗xe4 ♕e6 19 ♗xg5 f5 20 ♗xd5?

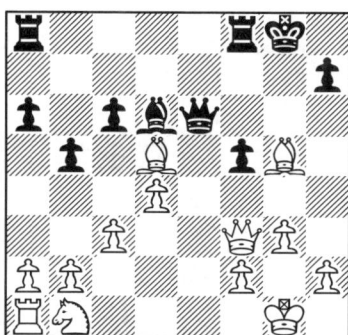

In this game Black will masterfully demonstrate the weak side of this exchange – the light squares in White's camp will become extremely vulnerable.

20...cxd5 21 ♘d2

White would like to block the f-file by playing 21 ♗f4 but there is no time because

after 21...♗xf4 22 ♕xf4 ♕e1+ 23 ♔g2 ♖ae8 would have led to a deadly pin on the first rank.

21...f4!

Thematic. Black needs space for his rooks to work in even at the cost of some material.

22 ♗xf4

White could also play 22 ♕d3 instead but after 22...fxg3 Black's advantage is obvious due to his dangerous attack on the f-file.

♗xf4 23 gxf4 ♖a7!

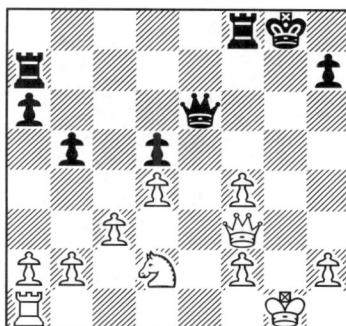

An instructive manoeuvre which occurs from time to time in this opening. The rook is switched to the kingside to put pressure on White's weak f-pawns.

24 ♔h1 ♖e7 25 ♖g1+ ♔h8 26 ♘f1 ♕e4

The ending will be very difficult for White to defend because there is no way White can get his knight to e5.

27 ♔g2

Or 27 ♕xe4 ♖xe4 28 ♘e3 ♖exf4 29 ♘xd5 ♖xf2 and Black has made a decisive intrusion along the seventh rank.

27...♕xf3+ 28 ♔xf3 ♖e1

Very accurate. This forces White to abandon the g-file. White's king is in *zugzwang*.

**29 ♖h1 ♖e4 30 ♘d2 ♖exf4+ 31 ♔e3
♖xf2 32 a4 ♖g2 33 axb5 axb5 34 b3
♖ff2 35 ♘f3 ♖b2 36 b4 ♖gc2 37 ♔d3
♖f2 38 ♔e3 ♖be2+ 39 ♔d3 ♖a2 40 ♔e3
♖ae2+ 41 ♔d3 ♖e4!**

Creating a mating net around the king.

42 ♘e5 ♖fe2! 0-1

<table>
<tr><td>

Game 15
Timmerman-Stavchev
Correspondence 1994

</td></tr>
</table>

1 e4 e5 2 ♘f3 ♘c6 3 ♗b5 a6 4 ♗a4 ♘f6
5 0-0 ♗e7 6 ♖e1 b5 7 ♗b3 0-0 8 c3 d5
9 exd5 ♘xd5 10 ♘xe5 ♘xe5 11 ♖xe5 c6
12 d4 ♗d6 13 ♖e1 ♕h4 14 g3 ♕h3 15
♖e4 g5! 16 ♕f3 ♗f5 17 ♗c2 ♗xe4 18
♗xe4 ♕e6 19 ♗xg5 f5 20 ♗d3!

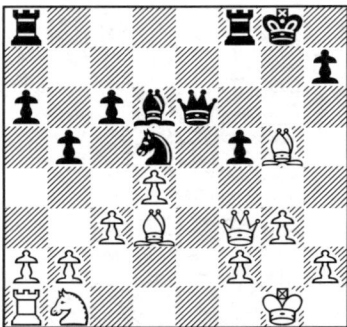

Practice has shown that White needs his light-squared bishop in order to justify the exchange sacrifice.

20...f4

The alternative is to insert 20...h6, which is a recommendation of John Nunn. It is important to mention the game Hovde-Sarink, correspondence 1991-92 which continued 21 ♗d2 ♖a7 (this position John Nunn assessed as unclear) 22 ♘a3 ♖g7 23 ♖e1 ♕f6 24 c4!? ♘e7?! 25 ♔h1 b4 26 ♘c2 a5? (Black had to play 26...c5 instead) 27 c5! ♗c7 28 ♗c4+ with an obvious advantage for White. Instead of the passive 24...♘e7, an interesting try would have been 24...♘b4!? 25 ♗xb4 ♗xb4 26 ♖e5 f4 27 ♖f5 with mutual chances in a very messy position.

Black can also play 20...♕e1+ but this doesn't yield much after 21 ♔g2 ♖ae8 22 ♗d2 ♕e6 23 ♘a3 ♗xa3 24 bxa3 ♘b6 25 ♖e1 ♕d5 26 ♖xe8 ♖xe8 27 ♗xf5 ♘c4 28 ♗h6 ♖e2 29 ♕xd5+ cxd5 30 h4!. White's

kingside pawn majority, supported by a strong pair of bishops, proved decisive in Milos-Egger, Sao Paulo 1993.

21 ♕e4

Facing Black's growing attack along the f-file, White logically seeks the exchange of queens, reckoning that two pawns for the exchange will give him the better chances.

21...♕d7

Staniszewski-Blatny, Nalenczow 1985 confirmed that the endgame favours White after 21...♕xe4?! 22 ♗xe4 ♖ae8 23 ♘d2 ♖e6 24 ♔g2 ♔g7 25 g4 h6 26 ♗h4 ♖fe8 27 ♔f3! ♗c7 28 ♗f5 ♖e1 29 ♖xe1 ♖xe1 30 ♗d7! etc.

Interesting is 21...♕f7!? (with pressure along the f-file) which, to date, has not been tested in tournament play.

For 21...♕h3 it is important to mention the game Kr.Georgiev-Lukacs, Baile Herculane 1982 which continued 22 ♗h4! ♖a7 23 ♘d2 ♖g7 24 ♗f1! ♕d7 (or 24...♕xh4?! 25 ♕e6+ followed by ♕xd6 which is clearly better for White – Black needs his dark-squared bishop in order to pressurise g3) 25 ♖e1 ♗e7 26 ♗xe7 ♖xe7 27 ♕b1 fxg3 28 hxg3 ♖fe8 29 ♖xe7 ♖xe7 30 ♘f3 and White was slightly better – he has two pawns for the exchange whilst Black's kingside on-slaught has been repelled.

22 ♘d2 ♖ae8 23 ♕h1!

Although h1 looks like an awkward square for the queen, it is in fact forced because 23 ♕g2? is refuted outright by 23...♕g4! (also worthy of consideration is 23...f3!? with the idea that if 24 ♘xf3?!, 24...♕g4! wins material) 24 ♗h4 f3 (this is the point – Black gets in ...f4-f3 with gain of tempo by attacking the white queen on g2) 25 ♕f1 ♘f4 26 ♕b1 ♖f7 27 ♗e4 ♘h3+ 28 ♔f1 ♗f4! with a winning position for Black in the game Nameth-J.Horvath, correspondence 1992.

23...♖f7

Now 23...♕g4 achieves nothing after 24 ♘e4! etc.

24 ♘e4 ♗f8 25 ♕f3 ♔g8 26 ♔h1 fxg3?!

This releases the tension on White's kingside. Black should keep up the pressure hoping to eventually play ...f4-f3, which would promise some kingside initiative.

27 ♕xg3! ♗e7?

This loses by force. Better was 27...h6 28 ♗d2 ♖g7.

28 ♕e5+ ♔g8 29 ♗h6 ♗f8 30 ♖g1+ ♖g7 31 ♗xg7!

A good assessment of the situation, reckoning that Black will not find a safe haven for his king.

31...♖xe5 32 ♗xe5+ ♔f7 33 ♘d6+! ♔e7

Forced because if 33...♗xd6 34 ♖g7+ easily wins.

34 ♗f5 ♕d8 35 ♖e1! 1-0

Black resigned because there is no decent defence against the deadly discovered check on the e-file.

> ## Game 16
> ## Smirin-Grischuk
> *European Club Cup, Crete 2001*

1 e4 e5 2 ♘f3 ♘c6 3 ♗b5 a6 4 ♗a4 ♘f6 5 0-0 ♗e7 6 ♖e1 b5 7 ♗b3 0-0 8 c3 d5 9 exd5 ♘xd5 10 ♘xe5 ♘xe5 11 ♖xe5 c6 12 d4 ♗d6 13 ♖e1 ♕h4 14 g3 ♕h3 15 ♖e4 g5! 16 ♕e2!?

It is amazing to see how opening theory can swiftly change. This move has not even been mentioned in most of the pre-2002 books on the Marshall Attack nor even in the encyclopaedias of opening theory. However, in the last couple of years it has become the point of research for most of the top players because after the usual move 16 ♕f3 Black gets enough counterplay.

As we shall see there is, in one line, a marked difference to the queen being on f3 as against e2. After ♕e2, ...♗f5-e4 doesn't win the exchange.

16...f5!?

The plan involving a kingside attack using pieces with 16...♘f6 and not pushing the f-pawn can be seen in Game 18.

17 ♖e6?

The correct 17 ♗xd5+! cxd5 18 ♖e6! is seen in Game 17.

17...♗xe6 18 ♕xe6+ ♔h8 19 ♕xd6

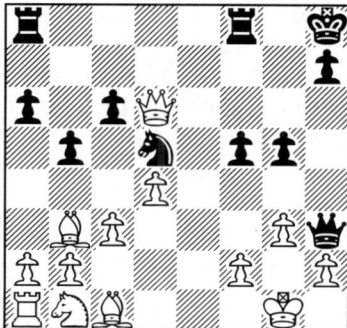

Unfortunately for White 19 ♗xd5 now loses to 19...♖ae8 while the relatively more resilient 19 ♕e2 ♖ae8 20 ♕f1 ♕xf1+! 21

♔xf1 f4! still leaves Black on top despite the queens being off the board. This is due to the dormant White queenside pieces.

19...♖ae8 20 ♗d2

Black also wins after 20 ♗e3 f4 21 ♗xd5 fxe3.

20...f4 21 ♗xd5

Or 21 ♗d1 ♖f6! 22 ♕c5 ♖h6 etc. with a mating attack.

21...cxd5 22 f3 g4! 0-1

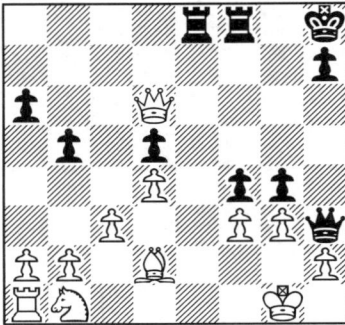

White resigned as he is unable to prevent mate in a couple of moves.

Game 17
Ponomariov-Anand
Linares 2002

---

1 e4 e5 2 ♘f3 ♘c6 3 ♗b5 a6 4 ♗a4 ♘f6 5 0-0 ♗e7 6 ♖e1 b5 7 ♗b3 0-0 8 c3 d5 9 exd5 ♘xd5 10 ♘xe5 ♘xe5 11 ♖xe5 c6 12 d4 ♗d6 13 ♖e1 ♕h4 14 g3 ♕h3 15 ♖e4 g5! 16 ♕e2!? f5!? 17 ♗xd5+! cxd5 18 ♖e6! f4!

As we have already learned, timing in the Marshall Attack is of primary importance. Black hurries with his kingside attack, ignoring the threat to his dark-squared bishop. In this game Anand proves that 16...f5!? is playable for Black and it leads to a draw by perpetual check!

'Normal' moves lead to a nearly lost position for Black, which we see from the following analysis:

a) 18...♗c7 19 ♖c6 ♖a7 20 ♕e7! with a decisive penetration into Black's position.

b) 18...♗xe6 19 ♕xe6+ ♖f7 (or 19...♔h8 20 ♗xg5 and there is no good defence against the nasty threat ♗g5-f6+) 20 ♘d2! (It is important to retain the queen on e6, thus preserving an iron grip on Black's position – just observe the poor role that Black's dark-squared bishop is playing. On the contrary 20 ♕xd6? would have turned the position around in Black's favour after 20...♖e8 21 ♗d2 f4! and suddenly Black's attack is irresistible) 20...♗c7 21 ♘f3 h6 22 ♗xg5! hxg5 23 ♕xf7+! ♔xf7 24 ♘xg5+ followed by ♘xh3 and White wins.

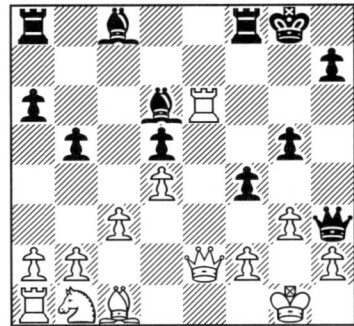

19 ♖xd6 ♗g4 20 ♕f1

Forced since after 20 f3? ♖ae8 21 ♕f1 ♕xf1+ 22 ♔xf1 fxg3 23 hxg3 ♖xf3+ 24 ♔g2 ♖e2+ 25 ♔g1 ♗h3 White will soon be mated.

20...♕xf1+!

White should not be allowed to buy necessary time for relief. Despite the exchange of queens, Black's attack is extremely strong due to the inactivity of White's queenside pieces.

21 ♔xf1 ♖ae8 22 ♗d2

Risky for White is 22 ♖h6?!, after which both 22...♔g7 and the subtle 22...♖f6!? 23 f3 (What else? 23 ♖xf6?? ♗h3+ 24 ♔g1 ♖e1 is mate) 23...♖xh6 24 fxg4 ♖xh2 and Black has at least a draw, if not more, with his rooks dominating the seventh rank.

22...♗h3+ 23 ♔g1 fxg3 24 hxg3 ♖e2 25 ♗e3

This move leads to a draw but the following variations prove that Anand's opening preparation was fantastic. In case White continues to play for a win (based on his overwhelming material advantage), he could have ended up in a lost position. For instance:

a) 25 ♖h6? g4! 26 f4 ♖g2+ 27 ♔h1 ♖e8!

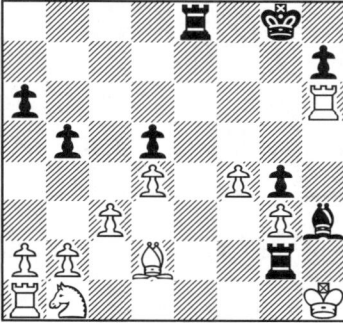

and White can do nothing against Black's rook invading the seventh rank with a mating attack to follow.

b) 25 f4 ♖fe8! 26 ♖h6 g4! leads to the previously seen scenario with White helpless to do anything against Black's mating attack.

25...♖xe3! 26 fxe3 ♖f1+ 27 ♔h2 g4!

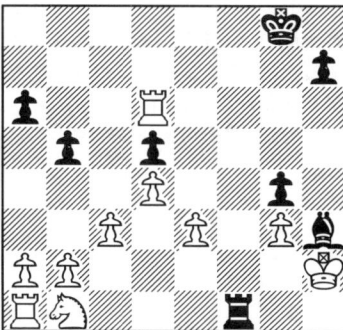

The point of the plan which started with 18...f4! – funnily enough White is unable to prevent perpetual check!

28 ♖xd5 ½-½

Although a pawn up, White is too passive to play for a win as after 28 ♘d2?! ♖xa1 29 ♖xa6 ♖e1 30 ♘b3 ♖e2+ 31 ♔g1 ♖xb2 Black is more than happy.

Game 18
Ponomariov-Adams
Linares 2002

---

1 e4 e5 2 ♘f3 ♘c6 3 ♗b5 a6 4 ♗a4 ♘f6 5 0-0 ♗e7 6 ♖e1 b5 7 ♗b3 0-0 8 c3 d5 9 exd5 ♘xd5 10 ♘xe5 ♘xe5 11 ♖xe5 c6 12 d4 ♗d6 13 ♖e1 ♕h4 14 g3 ♕h3 15 ♖e4 g5! 16 ♕e2!? ♘f6 17 ♘d2

Due to the threat ...♘f6-g4 there is no time for White to retreat his rook. However, he rightly reckons on positional compensation for the exchange due to the weaknesses created in Black's position after ...g7-g5.

17...♗f5 18 f3

The old game T.Petrosian-Averbakh, Moscow 1947 witnessed 18 ♖e5? ♗xe5 19 dxe5 ♘g4 20 ♘f3 ♖ae8 21 ♕f1 ♕xf1+ 22 ♔xf1 h6 23 h4 ♗e4 24 ♘e1 ♖xe5 25 f4 gxh4! 26 gxh4 (or 26 fxe5 h3! and Black's h-pawn is unstoppable) 26...♖e7 with a winning position for Black.

18...c5!

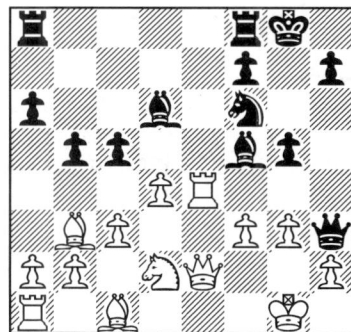

A dynamic continuation. Black is planning ...c5-c4 in order to restrict White's light-squared bishop. In the game J.Polgar-Onischuk, European Team Championship, Batumi 1999 the players agreed a draw after

18...♘xe4, which seems premature because after both 19 fxe4 and 19 ♘xe4 ♗xe4 20 fxe4, with the idea of playing e4-e5, White's position is preferable despite the small material deficit. Black's pawn weaknesses are obvious and White's light-squared bishop exerts strong pressure against f7.

19 ♕f2

An alternative is 19 ♕e3 ♗xe4 20 ♘xe4 (worse is 20 fxe4?! because of the tactical cheapo 20...♕xh2+! etc., while directly losing is 20 ♕xg5+? ♗g6 21 ♕xf6 ♗xg3! 22 hxg3 ♕xg3+ 23 ♔h1 ♖ae8 with mate to follow) 20...♘xe4 21 fxe4 ♗e7! leading to a pretty balanced position; after 22 dxc5?! Black has the strong reply in 22...♖ac8!.

19...c4 20 ♗c2 h6!?

A good positional move. Before deciding where to place his heavy pieces, Black defends the somewhat exposed g5-pawn.

21 b3 cxb3?!

I don't like this move because it frees White's dark-squared bishop. Seriously coming into consideration is 21...♖ac8!? 22 bxc4 bxc4 23 ♖b1 ♗xe4 24 ♘xe4 ♕e6 hoping for 25 ♖b6? ♘xe4 26 fxe4 ♗xg3!, which is clearly in Black's favour.

22 axb3 ♖fc8 23 ♗b2

Premature is 23 c4? ♗b4 24 c5 ♗c3 followed by ...♖d8 with strong pressure against White's centre.

23...♗b4?

This is a serious mistake after which Black will not even have the consolation of extra material compensating for his weak kingside.

Better instead was 23...♗f8!? 24 c4 bxc4 25 bxc4 ♗g7, defending his weakened kingside and later taking the exchange on e4. This would have kept the game alive.

24 ♖e5!

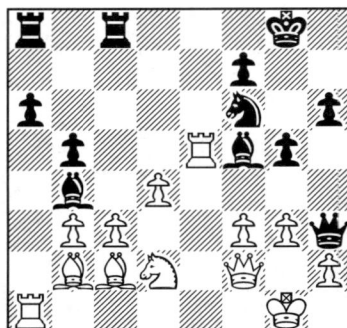

Maybe Black forgot about this simple reply.

24...♗xc2 25 cxb4 ♗g6 26 ♖c5 ♖e8 27 ♘f1 ♖ad8 28 d5

Opening up the a1-h8 diagonal is of decisive importance.

28...♘d7 29 ♘e3 h5 30 f4 h4 31 f5 hxg3 32 hxg3 ♗h5 33 d6 ♖e4 34 ♖ac1! ♘xc5 35 bxc5 ♔h7 36 ♗f6 ♖g8 37 d7 ♖h4

The last chance is a kingside attack because Black's position is already lost due to White's passed c- and d-pawns. However, White is alert and duly repels Black's attack.

38 ♕g2! ♗f3 39 ♕xh3 ♖xh3 40 ♔f2 g4 41 ♘f1 ♖h5 42 d8♕ ♖xd8 43 ♗xd8 ♖xf5 44 ♘e3 ♖h5 45 ♗h4 1-0

Summary

Firstly, it looks like 15...g5! is certainly the way for Black to play – I cannot recommend the 15...♗b7? of Game 9.

The line 15...g5! 16 ♕f3 ♗f5 17 ♗xd5 cxd5 18 ♖e3 ♗e4 19 ♖xe4 dxe4 20 ♕f6 is generally considered to be drawish, but 17 ♗c2 leads to more interesting play in which both sides have their chances.

It will be interesting to see if there are any new developments with 15...g5! 16 ♕e2!? because Ponomariov-Anand (Game 17) looks like best play and leads to a draw by perpetual check! This is important as Game 18 looks better for White, who has a strong centre and play against Black's weak pawns.

1 e4 e5 2 ♘f3 ♘c6 3 ♗b5 a6 4 ♗a4 ♘f6 5 0-0 ♗e7 6 ♖e1 b5 7 ♗b3 0-0 8 c3 d5 9 exd5 ♘xd5 10 ♘xe5 ♘xe5 11 ♖xe5 c6 12 d4 ♗d6 13 ♖e1 ♕h4 14 g3 ♕h3 15 ♖e4 g5! (D)

15...♗b7 – *Game 9*

16 ♕f3

16 ♕f1 – *Game 10*

16 ♕e2!? (D)

16...♘f6 – *Game 18*

16...f5

17 ♗xd5 – *Game 17*; 17 ♖e6 – *Game 16*

16...♗f5 17 ♗c2

17 ♗xd5 – *Game 11*

17...♗xe4

17...♗f4!? – *Game 13*; 17...♘f4 – *Game 12*

18 ♗xe4 ♕e6 19 ♗xg5 f5 (D) **20 ♗d3** – *Game 15*

20 ♗xd5 – *Game 14*

15...g5!

16 ♕e2!?

19...f5

CHAPTER THREE

12 d3 &d6 13 &e1 ♕h4 14 g3 ♕h3 15 &e4

1 e4 e5 2 ♘f3 ♘c6 3 &b5 a6 4 &a4 ♘f6
5 0-0 &e7 6 &e1 b5 7 &b3 0-0 8 c3 d5
9 exd5 ♘xd5 10 ♘xe5 ♘xe5 11 &xe5 c6
12 d3 &d6 13 &e1 ♕h4 14 g3 ♕h3 15
&e4

This chapter is very similar to the previous one. White again plays &e1-e4, but this time with a pawn on d3 rather than d4. The upshot of this is that the rook is protected on e4 and 15...g5? can simply be answered by 16 &xg5. Thus Black has to look for other ways to proceed.

We shall deal with Black's four replies:

1) 15...&d7 (Games 19-22)
2) 15...♕d7 (Games 23-24)
3) 15...♕f5 (Games 25-33)
4) 15...♘f6 (Games 34-37)

(1) 15...&d7 has never enjoyed as much popularity as the other three options – against White's best play Black cannot hope to achieve enough compensation.

In Game 19 Geller chooses 16...&ae8, allowing White to place a rook on h4. Which side profits out of this? If Murey had continued 18 ♘e4 &e7 19 &h5! (instead of the somewhat passive 18 ♘f1?! which gave Black serious counterchances), he would have achieved an excellent position.

After 16 ♘d2 we see the strange-looking 16...g5 with the idea of preventing the manoeuvre &e4-h4, even at the cost of weakening his kingside (Games 20-22). After 17 ♘f3 h6, instead of the artificial-looking 18 &d4?! of Game 20, quite promising for White is 18 ♘e5!. In the following two games, both featuring Gata Kamsky, White plays 17 &e2 with the idea of later planting, if possible, a knight on e4. However, after 17...f5, 18 ♘e4 gave Black fantastic play along the f-file following 18...fxe4 19 dxe4 &g4 20 exd5 c5! (Game 21) mainly because White's f2-square was very vulnerable. Much better is 18 c4! (Game 22).

(2) 15...♕d7 is designed to blunt White's &e4-h4 manoeuvre. In Game 23 the plan starting with ...f7-f5 does not succeed because the intended ...f5-f4 is never executed. This is prevented by the well-timed 18 f4!, which secures White a long lasting positional advantage. In Game 24 Black prefers 16...&b7 and after 17 &e1 c5 18 ♘e4 &e7 White tries to close the a8-h1 diagonal by playing 19 f3?!, which proves to have the serious drawback of weakening White's second rank and generally allowing his kingside to be pressurised.

(3) 15...♕f5 is the subject of Games 25-33. Black transfers his queen to g6 and delays

the final decision as to which diagonal his light-squared bishop belongs on.

After 16 ♘d2 ♕g6 we see, in Game 25, the rare continuation of 17 ♘f3. White eventually got into trouble after misplacing his rook on h4, which left it out of play.

Black's threat of playing ...♗c8-f5, attacking White's rook, is met by 17 ♖e1 in the following eight games. The move 17...♗c7?!, as seen in Smagin-Malaniuk (Game 26), is too slow and leaves White with a comfortable edge. Nor is 17...♗g4?! (Game 27) to be recommended. Black provokes White into playing f2-f3, hoping later to exploit the weakening of the kingside, but due to his powerful knight on e4 White keeps things firmly under control.

Stronger is 17...f5 (Games 28-33). By playing 18 c4 White forces the gain of material and the play is extremely sharp and of a forcing character. In Gara-Pokorna (Game 28), Black later committed an error which was left unpunished.

Not so impressive was Leko's invention of 18 ♘f3 against Svidler (Game 29). The idea behind this move is to transfer his knight to e5, when Black will have to trade in his dark-squared bishop. But what about the time invested? In the meantime Black manages to open the f-file, providing him with a lasting initiative.

Very original is Judith Polgar's manoeuvre against Adams when she played 18 ♕f3 followed by ♗b3-d1, intending to trade queens by playing ♕h5 (Game 30). However, Black got in a quick ...f5-f4 to prevent her plan. The game remained in the balance until she erred on move 28.

By playing 18 a4 White intends to open the a-file – see Anand-Khalifman (Game 31). In this game, instead of the usual 20 ♘f3, Anand plays the novelty 20 ♘e4!? but even in this case Black's chances are not worse.

With 18 f4 (Games 32-33) White prevents the move ...f5-f4 and gains time, albeit at the cost of giving back the pawn. Black must

constantly be careful not to end up in an unappealing ending with a bad bishop against a good knight – after playing ...f7-f5 there is no pawn left defending the weak e5-square. After the forced sequence of moves 18...♗xf4 19 ♕f3 ♗b8! 20 ♗xd5+ cxd5 Petar Popovic chooses 21 ♘f1?!, which is a passive choice because on f1 the knight has no future. Black quickly gets the better position after activating his pair of bishops.

Stronger is 21 ♘b3! (Game 33), intending to place the knight on the ideal blockading square d4. Black's key mistake in this game was putting his light-squared bishop on the passive b7-square. The commentary of the game confirms that Black could have reckoned on equality by placing the bishop on d7.

(4) The remaining four games all see 15...♘f6. After 16 ♖h4 ♕f5 17 ♗c2 the best way of parrying the threat of d3-d4 is 17...♕g6, as in Leko-Adams (Game 34).

Very popular is the critical line after 17 ♘d2 g5!? (Games 35-36). Ivanchuk's 18 ♖d4?! is the main reason why he later got into trouble. By playing the cool 18...♗c5 19 ♘f3 h6! (probably missed by Ivanchuk when he played 18 ♖d4?!), Timman emphasised the weak situation of the White rook in the centre of the board by eventually capturing it. Stronger, however, is Svidler's 18 ♖h6!.

White plays 17 ♗f4 in Game 37, which was in the past the main continuation of the line commencing 15...♘f6. I do not like the risky move 18...g5 for two reasons: firstly, it weakens the kingside and, secondly, White can force a draw by repetition. Instead I recommend 18...h6!? with the idea of ignoring the rook on h4 and concentrating on the play in the centre.

Game 19
Murey-Geller
Amsterdam 1987

1 e4 e5 2 ♘f3 ♘c6 3 ♗b5 a6 4 ♗a4 ♘f6

5 0-0 ♗e7 6 ♖e1 b5 7 ♗b3 0-0 8 c3 d5 9 exd5 ♘xd5 10 ♘xe5 ♘xe5 11 ♖xe5 ♗d6 12 ♖e1 ♗d6 13 g3 ♕d7 14 d3 ♕h3 15 ♖e4 ♗d7

Black decides to retain his bishop on the c8-h3 diagonal in order to control the important g4-square and he refrains from the traditional attack with ...f7-f5. However, this seems to me to be less dynamic so it's no wonder that in recent years black players have switched back to the above-mentioned plans.

16 ♘d2 ♖ae8 17 ♖h4!?

I quite like this rook manoeuvre. From here it guards the g4-square and prevents Black's kingside attack.

Another possibility is the natural 17 ♖xe8 ♖xe8 18 ♘e4 ♗c7 19 ♗d2 ♗b6 20 ♕f1, which still awaits further tests in tournament play.

17...♕f5 18 ♘f1?!

Better was 18 ♘e4 ♗e7 19 ♖h5 ♕g6 20 ♖e5!, keeping everything under control and retaining the extra pawn, for example: 20...f5 21 ♘d2 f4 22 ♘e4 ♔h8 23 ♕h5.

18...♕g6 19 ♗d2

White was obviously afraid to play 19 ♕f3 because of 19...♖e1, but maybe that was not so tragic for White as he can then try 20 ♖e4!?.

19...♗f5

Also good is 19...♗e7 20 ♖e4 ♗f5 21 ♖e5 ♗xd3 22 ♗xd5 cxd5 23 ♘e3 ♗d6 24 ♖xd5

♗e4! or 24 ♖xe8 ♖xe8 25 ♘xd5 ♖e2 26 ♗f4 ♕e4!? 27 ♗xd6 ♕xd5; in both cases Black has excellent play.

20 ♗xd5

Forced because 22 d4? is bad due to 20...♗e7, trapping White's rook.

20...cxd5 21 ♘e3 ♗e6!?

An alternative is 21...♗xd3 22 ♖d4 ♗e4 and now 23 f3? fails to 23...♗xg3! with a crushing attack for Black, while after 23 ♘xd5 ♗c5 24 ♘f4 ♕c6! White is losing material.

22 a4 ♗e7 23 ♖f4 ♗g5 24 ♖f3?

The position is very complicated so no wonder mutual errors occur. Much better was 24 ♖d4! ♗f6 25 ♖xd5 ♗xd5 26 ♘xd5 ♕xd3 27 ♘xf6+ gxf6 and the game would most likely have ended in a draw.

24...b4! 25 c4 ♗xe3?

Now it is Black who returns the favour. This exchange helps White to free his rook so better was 25...d4 26 ♘c2 ♗g4 27 ♗xb4 ♕h5 28 ♘xd4 ♗f6! 29 h3 ♕xh3 30 ♘c6 ♖e6! and if 31 ♗xf8? ♖e1+ 32 ♕xe1 ♗xf3 and White cannot prevent mate.

26 ♖xe3 a5 27 c5 d4 28 ♖e4 ♖d8 29 ♖c1 ♗f5 30 ♖e5 ♗d7

After 30...♗xd3 31 c6! White's passed c-pawn becomes very strong.

31 ♖g5 ♕f6 32 c6!? ♗xc6 33 ♖gc5 ♗f3 34 ♗g5!

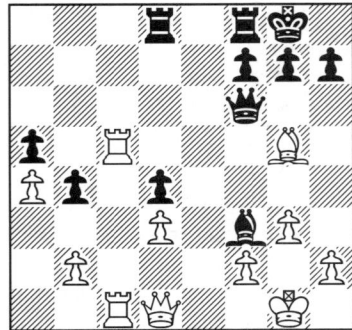

The point of White's 32nd move – with his well-centralised pieces he has a big positional advantage.

34...♕xg5 35 ♕xf3 ♕d2 36 ♖1c2 ♕e1+ 37 ♔g2 b3 38 ♖e2 ♕b4?

Better was 38...♕b1!? and if 39 ♖xa5, 39...♖c8 with some chances of survival for Black.

39 ♕c6! ♕b8 40 ♖xa5 ♖d6 41 ♕b5 ♖b6 42 ♕e5 ♕d8 43 ♕e7 ♕b8 44 ♖e4 g6 45 ♖a7 ♕d6 46 ♕xd6 ♖xd6 47 ♖b7 ♖c8 48 ♖xb3

White has a technically winning position. The game needs no further commentary.

48...♖c2 49 h4 ♖d2 50 ♔f1 ♖d7 51 a5 f5 52 ♖e2 ♖d1+ 53 ♖e1 ♖d2 54 a6 ♔f7 55 ♖c1 ♖e7 56 a7 1-0

White controls the g2-square so Black has no chances of perpetual.

Game 20
Mukhutdinov-Berzinsh
Naberezhnie Chelni 1993

---

1 e4 e5 2 ♘f3 ♘c6 3 ♗b5 a6 4 ♗a4 ♘f6 5 0-0 ♗e7 6 ♖e1 b5 7 ♗b3 0-0 8 c3 d5 9 exd5 ♘xd5 10 ♘xe5 ♘xe5 11 ♖xe5 c6 12 ♖e1 ♗d6 13 d3 ♕h4 14 g3 ♕h3 15 ♖e4 ♗d7 16 ♘d2 g5 17 ♘f3

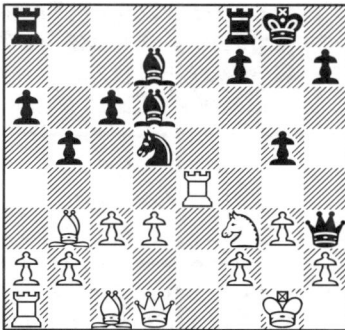

The white knight is heading towards e5 as well as attacking the pawn on g5.

Other moves are weaker:

a) 17 ♖e1 ♗g4! and now 18 f3? leads to a lost position for White after 18...♗xg3! – that's why White plays the rook to e2 in

some lines in order to protect the second rank.

b) 17 c4?! ♘f6 18 ♖e2 ♗g4 19 f3 ♗c5+ 20 ♔h1 ♖ae8! 21 fxg4 ♖xe2? (better is 21...♘xg4 and if 22 ♘e4, 22...♖xe4! 23 dxe4 ♗f2! and Black wins) 22 ♕xe2 ♖e8 23 ♘e4? (now it's White's turn to make an error; instead the simple 23 ♕f1 would have refuted Black's attack and White's material advantage would have prevailed) 23...♖xe4! 24 dxe4 ♘xe4 25 ♗f4 (of course 25 ♕xe4?? ♕f1 mate was not possible) 25...♘f2+ 26 ♕xf2 (26 ♔g1 ♘xg4+ 27 ♔h1 gxf4 28 ♖f1 ♘xh2 29 ♕g2 ♕xg2+ 30 ♔xg2 ♘xf1 wins) 26...♗xf2 27 ♗e5 ♕xg4 28 ♔g2 ♕e2 0-1 Rade-Truta, Budapest 1993.

17...h6 18 ♖d4?!

With the idea of sacrificing the exchange on d5 if the opportune moment arises. However, the move is a bit too artificial and the real acid test for Black must surely lie in 18 ♘e5!

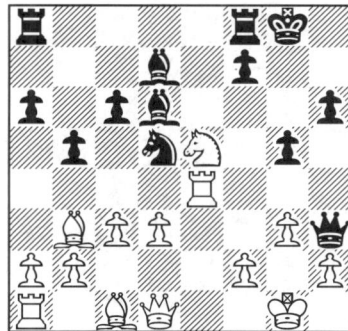

and now:

a) Exchanging the dark-squared bishops with 18...♗xe5? 19 ♖xe5 is anti-positional: 19...♖fe8 20 d4 ♗e6 21 ♕d3 ♖e7 (Liss-Computer Junior, Bikurei Haitim [rapid] 1995). Instead of 22 ♗c2?! f6 23 ♖e2 (Black has sufficient compensation after 23 ♕g6+ ♔f8! 24 ♗f5 ♗xf5 25 ♕xf5 ♕xf5 26 ♖xf5 ♖e1+ 27 ♔g2 ♔g7 because of the unpleasant pin and awkward placing of the white rook on f5) 23...♗f5! with unclear play, the simple

22 ♗d2! would have left White a pawn up and with the better position. For instance, the tactical try 22...♘f6 23 ♗xe6 ♖xe6 24 ♖xe6 ♘g4? gives nothing to Black after 25 ♖xh6! ♘xh6 (or 25...♕xh6 26 h4 etc.) 26 f3 etc.

b) 18...♗f5 with a further split:

b1) 19 ♘xc6 ♘f6. Ivanchuk assesses this as bad for White but it might be playable after 20 ♕f3!? ♗xe4 21 dxe4 ♘g4 22 ♕g2 ♕xg2+ 23 ♔xg2 ♖fe8 24 f3 – White is slightly better with two pawns for the exchange.

b2) 19 ♘g4 ♗f4! (with pressure against White's king – this an improvement over 19...♘f4?!) 20 ♘xh6+ ♕xh6 21 gxf4 ♗xe4 22 fxg5 ♕g6 23 dxe4 ♕xe4 24 ♗c2 ♕h4 25 ♕f3 ♖ae8 26 ♗d2 is slightly better for White.

b3) 19 ♖e1 ♘f6!? and Black's counterplay on the kingside must not be underestimated.

18...♗c5

It is interesting to see how 18...♖ae8? would have lost on the spot after the clever tactical resource by White – 19 ♗xd5 cxd5 20 ♖xd5 ♗c6 21 ♘xg5!.

(Black must have been hoping for a Christmas present with 21 ♖xd6?? ♗xf3 22 ♕f1 ♖e1! and White is mated) 21...♕d7 (or 21...hxg5? 22 ♖xg5+ followed by ♖g5-h5+ wins immediately for White) 22 ♘e4! etc.

19 ♖xd5

Obviously forced after 18 ♖d4?! has been played.

19...cxd5 20 ♗xd5 ♖ad8 21 d4 ♗e6?!

Black is hoping to get an attack after opening up the f-file but his aggressive possibilities will diminish after the exchange of the light-squared bishops. Much stronger was 21...♗g4!, after which I prefer Black – the main point is that after 22 dxc5 ♗e6! Black regains the sacrificed piece with interest!

22 ♗xe6 fxe6 23 ♘e5 ♗d6 24 ♘d3 ♕f5 25 ♕e2 ♖fe8 26 ♗e3 e5 27 ♘xe5 ♗xe5 28 dxe5 ♖xe5 29 a4 g4?!

Stronger is 29...♕d3!?, keeping White's advantage to a minimum.

30 axb5 axb5 31 b4 ♕e4 32 ♕a2+ ♔f8??

This spoils quite an interesting game. After 32...♕d5 it would be very difficult for White to convert his advantage into a win.

33 ♗c5+ ♔g7 34 ♗d4

Winning the exchange back and ending up with a decisive material advantage.

34...♖xd4 35 ♕a7+ ♔g6 36 ♖a6+ ♖e6 37 ♖xe6+ ♕xe6 38 ♕xd4

The queen ending is easily won for White so the rest needs no further commentary.

38...h5 39 ♕d3+ ♔g7 40 ♕xb5 ♕e1+ 41 ♕f1 ♕xc3 42 ♕b1 ♕c6 43 b5 ♕b7 44 b6 ♔f6 45 ♕c1 ♔g6 46 ♕c2+ ♔f6 47 ♕c3+ ♔g6 48 ♕d3+ ♔f6 49 ♕d6+ ♔f5 50 ♕h6 ♕d7 51 ♕xh5+ ♔e4 52 ♕g6+ ♔f3 53 ♕f6+ ♔e2 54 ♕e5+ 1-0

Game 21
Anand-Kamsky
Dortmund 1992

---

1 e4 e5 2 ♘f3 ♘c6 3 ♗b5 a6 4 ♗a4 ♘f6 5 0-0 ♗e7 6 ♖e1 b5 7 ♗b3 0-0 8 c3 d5 9 exd5 ♘xd5 10 ♘xe5 ♘xe5 11 ♖xe5 c6 12 ♖e1 ♗d6 13 d3 ♕h4 14 g3 ♕h3 15 ♖e4 ♗d7 16 ♘d2 g5 17 ♖e2 f5 18 ♘e4?!

White underestimated the strength of Black's 21st move, wrongly assessing the position to be in his favour. Better is 18 c4! which is dealt with in the next game.

The following continuations should also be mentioned:

a) 18 ♘f3!? f4! (Black must open both the f-file and the diagonal for his light-squared bishop, which means that defending the g5-pawn with 18...h6? is too slow and out of the question) 19 ♘xg5 ♛h5 20 gxf4! (better than 20 ♗xf4? ♖xf4! 21 gxf4 ♗xf4 22 f3 ♗xg5 with advantage to Black) 20...♗xf4 21 f3!, keeping open the option of playing ♘g5-e4 with unclear play because the knight on g5 is indirectly defended (21...♛xg5 22 ♖g2!).

b) 18 ♗xd5+!? cxd5 19 ♛b3 ♗c6 20 ♘f3 f4! is clearly weaker – the light squares around White's king are rather vulnerable, for instance: 21 ♘xg5 ♛g4 22 ♖e6 fxg3 and White is in deep trouble.

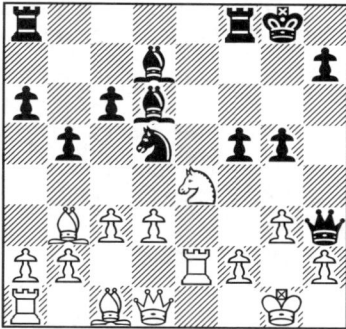

18...fxe4 19 dxe4 ♗g4 20 exd5 c5!

Shutting out the bishop on b3.

21 ♛f1 ♛h5!

Much stronger than the queen exchange which would have just led to equality.

22 ♖e3

White must cover the vulnerable g3-square because both 22 ♖e6? ♗xg3! and 22 ♖e1? c4 23 ♗c2 ♗xg3! 24 hxg3 ♗f3 lose for White.

22...c4 23 ♗c2 ♗c5 24 ♗d2

Other moves are not much better either:

a) 24 b4 ♗b6! 25 a4 ♖ad8 26 axb5 axb5.

b) 24 a4 has the idea of bringing White's rook on a1 swiftly into the game. However, this is met by 24...♖ae8! 25 ♛e1 (or 25 ♖xe8?

♛xe8! and White has difficulty in defending the f2-square) 25...♗h3 26 ♗d1 ♛f7! and it is very difficult to find a decent move for White in this position.

24...♗xe3

Even stronger was 24...♖ad8! 25 ♗e4 ♖de8! 26 ♛g2 (the only move because 26 ♖ae1? loses on the spot to 26...♖xe4! 27 ♖xe4 ♗xf2+ 28 ♛xf2 ♖xf2 29 ♛xf2 ♛xh2+ 30 ♛e3 ♛xg3+ 31 ♛d4 ♛d3+ followed by ...♛xd2) 26...♗h3 27 ♛h1 ♗xe3 28 ♗xe3 ♛e2! etc.

25 ♗xe3 ♖ae8 26 ♖e1 ♗f3 27 d6 ♗c6 28 ♛e2

After 28 ♗d1 both 28...♛f7 and 28...♛g6 leave Black with a substantial advantage.

28...♛h3 29 ♛f1 ♛e6! 30 ♗d1 ♛d5

Black doesn't allow White to activate his bishop after 30...♛xd6 31 ♗g4.

31 f3 ♛xd6 32 ♗d4

Of course the g5-pawn is taboo because 32 ♗xg5?? drops a piece to 32...♛c5+.

32...♖xe1 33 ♛xe1 g4!?

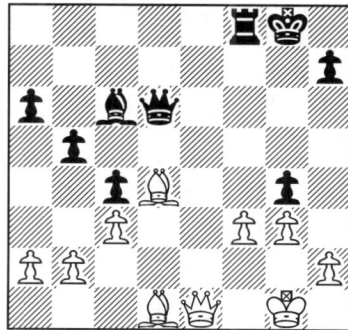

White is grovelling, the exchange down, after 33...♗xf3 34 ♗xf3 ♖xf3 35 ♛e4. A Black win is still far from easy, but with the text Black wants more and plays to continue the attack.

34 f4?!

White could have also tried 34 ♛d2!? with the idea of ♛g5+ to follow and some chances of survival.

34...♛d5 35 ♛f2 ♛g2+ 36 ♛e3 ♖e8+

37 ♗e5 ♛xb2 38 ♗xg4 ♛c2?!

Simpler is 38...♛xa2, after which the black win is just a matter of time.

39 ♔d4!

The king runs into the security of the dark squares – the best practical chance.

39...♛d3+

The situation sharply turns around after the careless 39...♛xa2? 40 ♔c5! ♛g2 41 ♛d1! – all of a sudden the white king is safe while it is Black who has to worry about the oncoming penetration of White's queen.

40 ♔c5 ♛d5+ 41 ♔b4

After 41 ♔b6?? b4! there is no retreat for White's king.

41...a5+ 42 ♔a3 ♛d3 43 ♔b2 b4 44 ♔a1

44 cxb4? axb4 45 ♛xb4 ♖xe5! 46 fxe5 ♛d4+ and Black picks up a piece and wins easily.

44...a4!

The position is more subtle than it might appear at first glance. If 44...♗e4, then 45 ♗e2 ♛d5 46 ♛f1! (but not 46 ♛d1? ♛xd1+ 47 ♗xd1 bxc3 48 ♗xc3 ♖b8 49 ♗b2 c3! and Black wins) 46...♗d3 47 ♛f3 ♛xf3 48 ♗xf3 bxc3 49 ♗xc3 ♖b8 50 a4! and White is not far from holding the ending.

45 ♗e2?!

More resilient is 45 cxb4 a3 46 ♛e2 (not 46 ♗e2? ♖xe5! 47 fxe5 ♛d4+ with mate to follow) 46...♛d5! 47 ♗f5 (or 47 ♔b1 ♛h1+ 48 ♔c2 ♗a4+ 49 ♔c3 ♛a1+! 50 ♔xc4 ♛c1+ 51 ♔d4 ♖d8+ and Black wins) 47...♛d4+! 48 ♗xd4 ♖xe2 49 ♔b1 ♖xh2 with excellent winning chances for Black.

45...♛e4 46 ♛d1 bxc3?

A blunder which saves White from defeat. After the logical 46...♗d5! 47 ♗g4 ♖xe5! 48 fxe5 ♛xe5 49 ♛d4 ♛xd4 50 cxd4 a3! 51 ♗f5 ♔g7 52 h4 h6 53 g4 ♔f6 the bishop ending would be won for Black due to the cage-like position of the white king.

47 ♗xc4+!

The thriller continues – White is alive again!

47...♔f8

The point is that after 47...♛xc4?? Black is mated: 48 ♛g4+ ♔f7 49 ♛f5+ ♔e7 50 ♛f6+ ♔d7 51 ♛d6+ ♔c8 52 ♛c7 mate!

48 ♗d6+

Wrong is the tempting 48 ♛d6+? ♖e7 49 ♛d8+ ♗e8! and Black's passed c-pawn will decide the game.

48...♖e7?!

From inertia Black plays for a win but more reasonable was 48...♔g7 49 ♛g4+ ♛g6 50 ♗e5+ ♔f8 51 ♛xg6 hxg6 52 ♗xc3 with a draw to follow.

49 ♗d3! ♛e3 50 ♗c2

White could have tried to play for a win with 50 ♗xh7!?, but after 50...♗e4! 51 ♗xe4 ♛xe4 Black's c-pawn would guarantee Black a draw.

50...♗e8 51 ♗xe7 ♔xe7 52 ♛b1 h6 53 a3 ♔f6 54 ♛d1 ♛c5

Or 54...♛d2 55 ♛xd2 cxd2 56 g4 with an immediate draw.

55 ♛d8+ ♔g7 56 ♛c7+ ♔f6 57 ♛d8+ ♔g7 58 ♛c7+ ♔f6 ½-½

Game 22
Ivanchuk-Kamsky
Tilburg 1992

---

1 e4 e5 2 ♘f3 ♘c6 3 ♗b5 a6 4 ♗a4 ♘f6
5 0-0 ♗e7 6 ♖e1 b5 7 ♗b3 0-0 8 c3 d5
9 exd5 ♘xd5 10 ♘xe5 ♘xe5 11 ♖xe5 c6
12 ♖e1 ♗d6 13 d3 ♛h4 14 g3 ♛h3 15

&e4 &d7 16 &d2 g5 17 &e2 f5 18 c4!

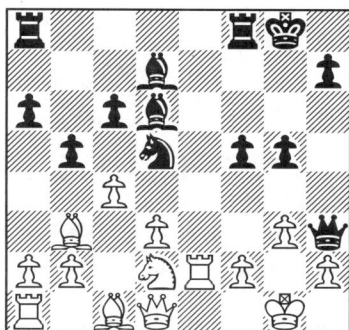

This is stronger than 18 &e4? from the previous game. However, even more accurate might be to first include 18 Wf1!? in order to avoid some variations with ...&d5-f4, and only after 18...Wh5 to play 19 c4.

18...f4!

After 18...bxc4 19 dxc4 f4 20 cxd5 fxg3 21 hxg3 &xf2!

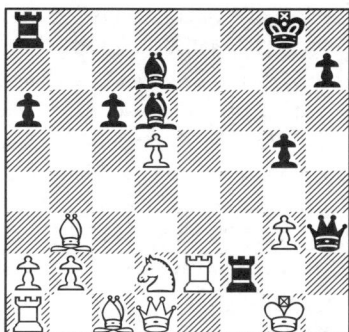

22 &xf2 Wg3+ 23 &g2 We3+ 24 &f2 Wg3+ leads to perpetual check, which White cannot avoid. For instance, 25 &f1 &h3+ 26 &e1 &e8+ 27 We2 &xe2+ 28 &xe2 We5+!? (28...&g4+ 29 &f1 is also a draw) 29 &d1 &g4+ 30 &c2 &f5+ again with perpetual check (30...cxd5?! is worse after 31 &b1! and White's piece is worth more than Black's two pawns). However, instead of 20 cxd5, White has the strong intermediate move 20 Wf1! at his disposal, which is similar to what actually happens in the game. So Black rightly prefers not to exchange on c4 in order to keep the b5-pawn alive in case he sometimes may want to play ...b5-b4 denying White's bishop the c3-square. Also Black's queen could in some lines snuff out White's d3-pawn.

19 Wf1!

Black has a draw after 19 cxd5 fxg3 20 hxg3 &xf2! 21 &xf2 Wxg3+ 22 &g2 We3+, as was shown in the previous line.

19...fxg3?!

19...Wh5!? 20 cxd5 c5! 21 f3 g4 22 gxf4 &h8 might be worth trying.

Black is well behind in material but White still has to stop Black crashing through on the g-file – the position resembles the lines of the Mar del Plata Variation of the King's Indian Defence!

20 hxg3

Worse is 20 Wxh3? gxf2+ 21 &xf2 &xh3 22 cxd5 &c5 23 &e4 &ae8! (this is stronger than 23...&xf2 24 &xf2 &f8 25 dxc6+ &g7 26 &d2 &xf2 27 &c3+ and d3-d4 to follow with roughly equal play) 24 dxc6+ &g7 25 &d2 &xe4 with a winning position for Black when he follows up with ...&f8xf2.

20...Wh5

Another interesting possibility here for Black is 20...&f4!? but it seems that Black's attack runs out of steam if White plays correctly, for instance:

a) 21 gxf4 Wh5 22 c5+ &h8 23 cxd6 &h3 24 f3! &xf1 25 &xf1 gxf4 26 &d2 &g8+ 27 &xg8 &xg8+ 28 &g2 and White has too much material for the queen.

b) 21 c5+ &h8 22 cxd6 Wh5 23 gxf4 &h3 24 Wxh3 Wxh3 25 &e3 Wh4 26 &g3! gxf4 27 &f3 Wf6 28 &g2 Wxd6 29 &d2 b4 30 &e1! and now 30...&ae8? loses to 31 &xe8 &xe8 32 &g5.

21 cxd5 &g4

21...&xg3 22 Wg2 Wxe2 23 Wxg3 We1+ 24 &f1 is also in White's favour.

22 dxc6+ &g7 23 &e4

White is also winning after 23 &e3 &c5 24 d4! &xd4 25 Wd3 &ad8 26 c7! etc.

23...&xg3 24 fxg3 &xf1+ 25 &xf1 &h3
26 &e7+ &h6 27 &d5 &f8 28 &d2 &f3
29 &xf3 &xf3 30 &e2 &g6 31 c7 &f8 32
&ae1

With a strong c7-pawn and a heavy attack against the black king, White is strategically winning.

**32...&d7 33 &e6+ &h5 34 g4+! &xg4
35 &1e4+ &f3 36 &e1 1-0**

But even more direct was 36 &h2+ &g3
37 &g4+ &h3 38 &e3+ &f3 39 &xf3 mate.

Game 23
Liang Jinrong-Peng
Chinese Championship 1992

**1 e4 e5 2 &f3 &c6 3 &b5 a6 4 &a4 &f6
5 0-0 &e7 6 &e1 b5 7 &b3 0-0 8 c3 d5
9 exd5 &xd5 10 &xe5 &xe5 11 &xe5 c6
12 &e1 &d6 13 g3 &d7 14 d3 &h3 15
&e4 &d7 16 &d2 f5?!**

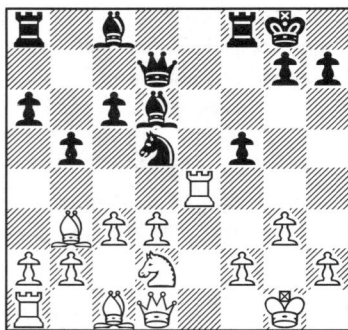

For quite a while this move has had a dubious reputation. Although Black starts the traditional f-pawn push with a gain of time by attacking White's rook, it will soon be clear that Black's king will be exposed as well later on.

17 &e1

The artificial-looking 17 &h4 was successful in the game Garbisu de Goni-Bello Figueira, Mondariz 1997 but Black's play can be improved on in various places. The game continued 17...&e7 18 &f4 &h8 19 &xd5

cxd5?! (better is 19...&xd5 keeping open the long diagonal a8-h1) 20 &b3 a5?! (also interesting here is 20...g5) 21 &e3 a4 22 &d4 &d6 23 &f3 &a6 24 &f4 with a pawn up and better position for White, who controls the important dark squares.

17...&h8

The violent 17...f4? backfires after 18 &h5! &h8 19 &e4, when it is White who is attacking. After the naïve 19...&f5? 20 &xf5! &xf5 21 &xd6 Black can resign.

18 f4!

The key strategical move – White prevents Black's traditional kingside attack of ...f5-f4, which means that in order to create some counterchances Black will have to embark sooner or later with ...g7-g5. This means weakening his king as well.

Worse is the alternative 18 &h5?!, which leaves White's queen exposed – for instance: 17...&f6 18 &h4 (probably slightly better is 19 &h3 but things are not entirely clear after 19...c5 20 &f3 c4!? 21 dxc4 bxc4 22 &xc4 &c6 23 &f1 f4 – of course not 23...&xf3? 24 &g2 etc. – 22 &d4! &b6 23 &h4 and now both 23...&g4 and 23...&g4 give Black some compensation for the sacrificed material) 19...c5 20 &f3 &b7 21 &g5 h6 22 &d2 (the planned counterattack 22 &e6? loses to 22...&c6 23 &e4!? &h7! 24 &xh6 gxh6 25 &xh6 &g8 etc.) 22...&c6 23 f3 c4! and Black took over the initiative in the game Benjamin-Kamsky, US Championship 1991.

18...&a7+

Here the queen will be somewhat far from the kingside action, but the normal 18...g5?! leads to a clearly better position for White after 19 &f3! (it is important not to let Black's c8-bishop back into the game, which happens after 19 fxg5? f4! etc.) 19...gxf4 20 &xd5 cxd5 21 &xf4 &xf4 22 gxf4 d4 23 &e2 etc.

**19 d4 &f6 20 &f3 c5 21 &e3 c4 22
&c2 g6 23 &e5**

The presence of this knight on the stronghold e5 grants White a steady advantage. Black hasn't gained the usual compensation for the sacrificed pawn.

23...♗b7 24 ♕d2 ♘e4?

After this obvious mistake Black's position becomes critical. Much better was 24...♗e4!?.

25 ♗xe4 ♗xe4 26 d5 ♕b7 27 ♘g4!

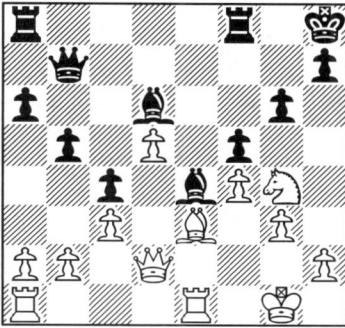

With this tactical blow, White takes complete control of the game.

27...♔g8

Or 27...fxg4 28 ♕d4+!, which transposes to the game.

28 ♕d4 fxg4 29 ♕xe4 ♖fe8 30 ♕d4 ♖ad8 31 ♗f2 ♔f7 32 b3 ♕c7 33 ♖xe8 ♖xe8 34 bxc4 ♕xc4 35 ♕xc4 bxc4 36 ♖b1 ♖d8 37 ♖b7+ ♔f6 38 ♖xh7

With his extra material, White has emerged with an easily winning ending.

38...♔f5 39 ♔g2 ♔e4 40 ♖h4 ♔d3 41 ♗d4 ♗b4 42 ♖xg4 ♗xc3 43 ♗xc3 ♔xc3 44 ♖xg6 a5 45 ♖c6 ♖xd5 46 g4 ♖d2+ 47 ♔g3 ♖xa2 48 f5 a4 49 f6 ♖a1 50 g5 a3 51 f7 ♖f1 52 g6 a2 53 ♖a6 ♖g1+ 54 ♔h3 ♖xg6 55 ♖xg6 1-0

Game 24
Leko-I.Sokolov
Groningen 1995

---

1 e4 e5 2 ♘f3 ♘c6 3 ♗b5 a6 4 ♗a4 ♘f6 5 0-0 ♗e7 6 ♖e1 b5 7 ♗b3 0-0 8 c3 d5 9 exd5 ♘xd5 10 ♘xe5 ♘xe5 11 ♖xe5 c6 12 d3 ♗d6 13 ♖e1 ♕h4 14 g3 ♕h3 15

♖e4 ♕d7 16 ♘d2 ♗b7 17 ♖e1 c5 18 ♘e4 ♗e7 19 f3?!

The intention of this move is to plug the long a8-h1 diagonal, but it allows Black a strong kingside attack by pushing the f-pawn.

Better are the following alternatives:

a) 19 ♗g5 f6 20 ♗d2 ♔h8 21 ♕h5 f5 22 ♘g5 ♗xg5 23 ♗xg5 ♕c6 24 f3 c4 25 ♗c2 b4! with counterplay for Black due to the excellently placed knight on d5, T.Ernst-I.Sokolov, European Team Championship 1992.

b) 19 a4! b4 20 ♗g5 ♗xg5 21 ♘xg5 bxc3 22 bxc3 ♖ad8 23 ♘e4 ♕c6 24 ♕h5 ♘xc3 25 ♕xc5 ♖xd3 26 ♗c4 ♕xc5 27 ♘xc5 ♖d4 28 ♗f1! ♗c8 29 ♖a3 with a white advantage in the arising ending, J.Polgar-Adams, Tilburg 1997.

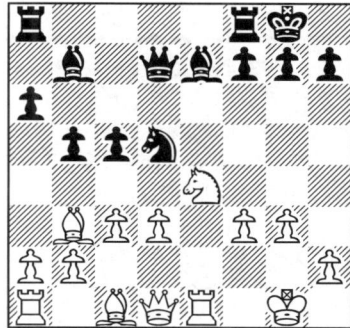

19...♔h8 20 ♗d2 f5! 21 ♘f2 f4 22 ♘e4

After 22 ♗xd5 Black has a strong intermediate move in 22...fxg3!, continuing his attack.

22...fxg3 23 hxg3 ♕h3 24 ♕e2 c4! 25 ♗c2?

White had to be brave and accept the sacrifice with 25 dxc4 ♘xc3!. Now the only defence is the hidden possibility 26 ♕g2!, which seems to lead to a drawn ending after 26...♕xg2+ 27 ♔xg2 ♘xe4 28 fxe4 ♖ad8 29 ♖ad1 bxc4 30 ♗xc4 ♗c5 31 ♗c3 etc.

25...cxd3 26 ♗xd3 ♖ad8 27 ♕f1

Black's queen on h3 is too strong to be tolerated, which is seen from the line 27

‼ad1? ♘f6! and it is difficult to meet all of black's threats on the kingside.

27...♕h5 28 g4 ♕h4 29 ‼ad1 ♘f4 30 ♗xf4 ‼xf4 31 ♕f2 ‼af8?

This lets White off the hook due to the fact that Black has missed White's 35th.

32 ♕xh4 ♗xh4 33 ‼f1 ‼xf3 34 ‼xf3 ‼xf3 35 ‼f1!

By this tactical cheapo White forces the exchange of the last rook, after which Black's advantage of the bishop pair is just of a symbolic nature.

35...‼xf1+ 36 ♔xf1 ♗e7 37 ♔e2 g6 38 ♔e3 ♔g7 39 a3 ♗c8 40 ♔f4 ♗d8 41 c4 ♗c7+ 42 ♔f3 bxc4 43 ♗xc4 ♗b7 44 b4 ½-½

Game 25
Garcia Gildardo-Bryson
Thessaloniki Olympiad 1984

---

1 e4 e5 2 ♘f3 ♘c6 3 ♗b5 a6 4 ♗a4 ♘f6 5 0-0 ♗e7 6 ‼e1 b5 7 ♗b3 0-0 8 c3 d5 9 exd5 ♘xd5 10 ♘xe5 ♘xe5 11 ‼xe5 c6 12 d3 ♗d6 13 ‼e1 ♕h4 14 g3 ♕h3 15 ‼e4 ♕f5 16 ♘d2 ♕g6 17 ♘f3

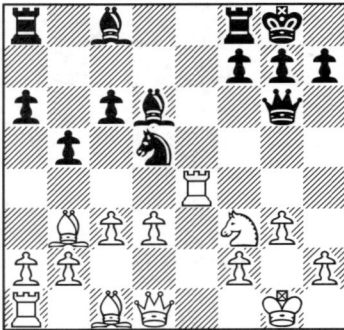

A rare move which has a bad reputation, and subsequently due to this game it has not been repeated. However, things are not so clear and indeed it might be playable.

17...f5?!

Black doesn't seem to care about the threats along the a2-g8 diagonal. Much

stronger and the acid test for 17 ♘f3 is 17...♗g4!? followed by ...♕g6-h5 with a dangerous pin.

18 ♘h4

An alternative is 18 ‼d4!? and now 18...♗e6?? drops a piece after 19 c4, while 18...♔h8?! 19 ♗xd5 cxd5 20 ♗f4! grants White a solid positional advantage due to his grip of the dark squares. So best for Black is 18...f4! 19 ‼xd5 cxd5 20 ♗xd5+ ♗e6 21 ♗xa8 ‼xa8 with quite a lot of play for the material deficit. White's kingside is under severe attack.

18...♕f6 19 ‼d4 ♗e6 20 ♘f3 ♗c5 21 ‼h4 h6 22 d4?

White had to chase away the knight from d5 with 22 c4!. Now 22...bxc4? 23 ‼xc4 followed by ‼xc6 is very bad for Black so he should settle for 22...♘e7 (threatening to trap the rook by ...♘e7-g6) 23 d4 ♗a7 (after 23...♘g6 24 cxb5 ♘xh4 25 ♘xh4 it is obvious that White has plenty for the sacrificed exchange) 24 ♕c2 ♘g6 25 ‼h5 f4 26 cxb5 fxg3 27 ‼f5. This line is interesting but I wonder how many players as White would be brave enough to try this?

22...♗d6 23 ♗f4

Or 23 ♕e2 ‼ae8 24 ♘e5 g5 25 ‼h3 f4 with an attack, but the text seriously spoils White's pawn structure on the kingside.

23...♘xf4 24 gxf4 ‼ae8

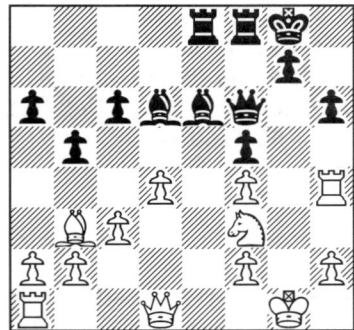

25 ♗xe6+ ‼xe6 26 d5 cxd5 27 ♕xd5 ♔h8

Worth considering is 27...♕f7!?.

28 a4 b4 29 ♖d1 bxc3 30 bxc3 ♗b8 31 ♖d4

Avoiding the trap 31 ♕d4?? ♖d6!, which wins outright for Black.

31...♗a7 22 ♖d2 ♖e4 33 c4 ♖fe8 34 ♖h3

White gives up a pawn in order to activate his poorly placed rook, but Black conserves his huge positional advantage anyway.

34...♖xf4?!

Much stronger was 34...♗b8!.

35 ♕d7 ♕e7 36 ♕d5 ♖g4+ 37 ♔g3 ♕e4 38 ♕xe4 ♖exe4 39 ♖d7 ♗c5 40 ♖d5 ♖xc4 41 ♘e5 ♖xg3+?!

More accurate was 41...♖c1+ 42 ♔g2 ♖d4! with the idea of exchanging White's other active rook. After 43 ♘g6+ ♔h7 44 ♖xf5 ♖xa4 Black would have created greater winning chances than in the game.

42 hxg3 ♖c3 43 ♔g2 ♗b4 44 ♘f7+ ♔g8 45 ♖xf5 a5 46 ♘d8!

Leading to a draw by a study-like motif.

46...♖a3 47 ♘c6 ♖xa4 ½-½

Because after 48 ♖f4! g5 49 ♖e4 Black loses his a-pawn as ♘c6xa5 follows.

Game 26
Smagin-Malaniuk
USSR Championship 1986

---

1 e4 e5 2 ♘f3 ♘c6 3 ♗b5 a6 4 ♗a4 ♘f6 5 0-0 ♗e7 6 ♖e1 b5 7 ♗b3 0-0 8 c3 d5

9 exd5 ♘xd5 10 ♘xe5 ♘xe5 11 ♖xe5 c6 12 d3 ♗d6 13 ♖e1 ♕h4 14 g3 ♕h3 15 ♖e4 ♕f5 16 ♘d2 ♕g6 17 ♖e1 ♗c7?!

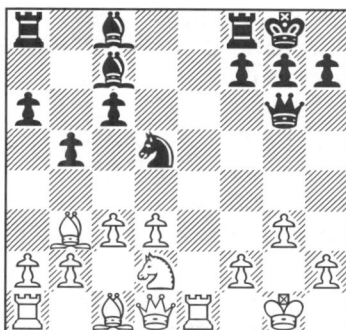

In expectation of White playing ♘d2-e4, Black removes the bishop from the attack. However, being a pawn down Black just hasn't time for such prophylactic moves. The move is simply too slow and doesn't fulfil the demands of the position because without using the f-pawn Black can hardly expect to breakthrough on the kingside.

18 ♘f3 ♗g4 19 ♘h4 ♕h5 20 f3 ♗h3

Or 20...♗e6 21 ♕e2 g5 22 ♘g2 ♖ae8 23 ♕f2 f5 24 f4 ♗b6 25 ♗e3 ♘xe3 26 ♘xe3 gxf4 27 ♕xf4 ♕f7 28 d4 ♗c7 29 ♕f3 ♗xb3 30 axb3 f4 31 ♘g4 ♕g6 32 ♘e5 ♗xe5 33 ♖xe5 and White emerged a healthy pawn to the good in De la Villa Garcia-Pablo Marin, Spanish Championship 1991.

21 ♕e2! ♖ad8 22 d4

Another possibility is 22 ♘g2 c5 23 a4 ♗c8 24 axb5 axb5 25 ♖a8 ♗e6 26 ♖xd8 ♖xd8 27 ♗c2 (also good is 27 ♘e3 with the idea of trading some pieces because 27...♘f4? loses on the spot to 28 gxf4 ♗xb3 29 ♘d5! and due to the back rank weakness Black loses material) 27...g5 28 ♘e3 b4 29 d4 cxd4 30 cxd4 ♗b6 31 ♖d1 ♘f6 32 ♘f5 (deserving of attention is 32 ♕b5!? and if 32...♗xd4, 33 ♖xd4 ♖xd4 34 ♕e5! and White is winning) 32...g4?! (better is 32...b3 33 ♗d3 ♗xf5 34 ♗xf5 ♖xd4) 33 ♘h4? (White misses 33 ♕b5! ♗xf5 34 ♕xb6 ♖e8

35 ♕xf6 ♖e2 36 h4! ♗xc2 37 ♗h6! winning)
33...♖xd4 34 ♖xd4 ♗xd4+ 35 ♔f1 ♕c5 (the
position has switched to Black's favour) 36
♔g2?? (the only move was 36 ♕d2 with
chances to survive) 36...b3 and White resigned as he loses a piece, Malar-Mikulas,
Bratislava 1991.

22...f5 23 f4

Of course White doesn't let Black play
...f5-f4, starting a kingside attack.

23...♕xe2 24 ♖xe2

After the exchange of queens Black is
committed to defend an unappealing endgame a pawn down, which is a nightmare
position for every Marshall Gambit devotee!

**24...♖fe8 25 ♖xe8+ ♖xe8 26 ♔f2 ♗g4
27 ♗e3**

This is possible because 27...♖xe3?? loses
to 28 ♗xd5+ cxd5 29 ♔xe3.

27...♔f8 28 ♖e1 ♗d8

After 28...♘f6 White plays 29 ♔g2! threatening h2-h3.

29 ♘g2 ♘f6 30 d5!?

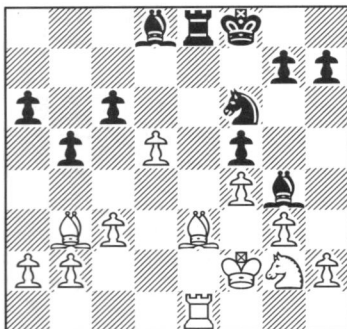

This leads to useful exchanges and a winning ending. Note how Black's light-squared
bishop is left out of play on g4. For example,
if now 30...♘e4+, 31 ♔g1 and Black is helpless.

30...cxd5

Or 30...♘xd5 31 ♗xd5 cxd5 32 ♗c5+
♔f7 33 ♖xe8 ♔xe8 34 ♘e3 g6 35 ♘xd5 and
in the long run White will win the ending.

31 ♗d4! ♖xe1 32 ♔xe1 ♔e7 33 ♘e3

♔d6 34 ♗e5+ ♔c6 35 ♗xf6 ♗xf6 36
♗xd5+ ♔d6 37 ♗g2 g5

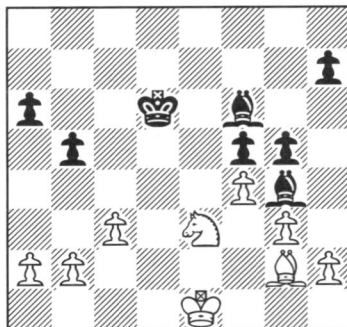

This loses a second pawn. However,
37...g6? loses a piece after 38 h3 ♗h5 39 g4.

**38 h3 gxf4 39 gxf4 ♗h5 40 ♘xf5+ ♔c5
41 ♔d2 b4?**

Accelerating defeat.

42 ♘g3! 1-0

Winning a piece after 42...♗g6 43 f5 followed by ♘g3-e4+.

Game 27
Anand-Adams
FIDE World Ch., Groningen 1997

1 e4 e5 2 ♘f3 ♘c6 3 ♗b5 a6 4 ♗a4 ♘f6
5 0-0 ♗e7 6 ♖e1 b5 7 ♗b3 0-0 8 c3 d5
9 exd5 ♘xd5 10 ♘xe5 ♘xe5 11 ♖xe5 c6
12 d3 ♗d6 13 ♖e1 ♕h4 14 g3 ♕h3 15
♖e4 ♕f5 16 ♘d2 ♕g6 17 ♖e1 ♗g4?!

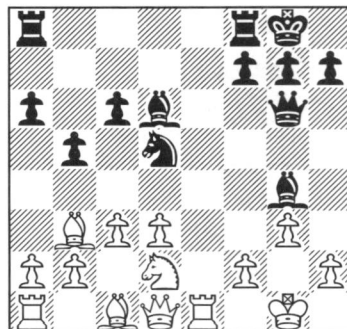

The pet line of the English super-GM Michael Adams. Black is trying to provoke f2-f3, which weakens White's vulnerable g3-pawn. Still, the move gives White enough time to protect his kingside.

It is no wonder that nobody has tried 17...Nf4? because it only helps White after 18 Ne4 Nh3+ 19 Kg2 Bg4 20 f3 Bd7. Now, amongst the many moves White can play, 21 a4! leaves him clearly on top.

18 f3 Bh3

Black has also tried the following in tournament practice:

a) 18...Bh5 19 Ne4 Rae8 20 Kg2! (it is easy to make a mistake and go for material with 20 g4? f5! 21 Nxd6 fxg4!!

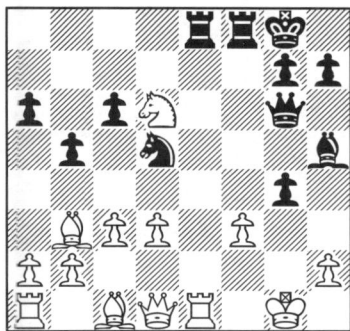

and suddenly White finds he has no defence) 20...Bb8 21 Bd2 f5 22 Nf2 (also possible is 22 Nc5) 22...Kh8 (or 22...Rxe1 23 Qxe1 Re8 24 Qf1 and Black hasn't enough compensation for the pawn) 23 Bxd5 cxd5 24 d4 f4 25 g4 Bxg4!? 26 Nxg4 (I don't see how Black can continue his attack after 26 fxg4 f3+ 27 Kf1 but White prefers a safe life, giving back some material in order to reach an ending) 26...h5 27 Qb1! Qg5 (or 27...Qxb1 28 Raxb1 hxg4 29 fxg4 with excellent winning chances for White due to his extra pawn) 28 h4 Qxh4 29 Nh2 Re3 30 Qd1 Rfe8 31 Kh1 Rxe1+ 32 Bxe1 Qh3 33 Bd2 g5 34 Qf1 Qf5 35 Re1. White has managed to repel Black's attack and he later converted his material advantage into a win,

Kr.Georgiev-Bryson, Dubai Olympiad 1986

b) 18...Bf5 19 Ne4 Bxe4 20 dxe4! (stronger than 20 fxe4 Bxg3! 21 Re2!? Nf4 22 Bxf4 Bxf4+ 23 Rg2 Qh6 24 Qg4 with only a small advantage for White, whose b3-bishop is better than Black's counterpart, Mrva-Betko, Czechoslovakian Championship 1992) 20...Bxg3 21 hxg3 Qxg3+ 22 Kf1 Qh3+ 23 Ke2 Qg2+ 24 Kd3 Nb4+ 25 cxb4 Rad8+ 26 Ke3 Rxd1 27 Rxd1 g5 28 Bd2 g4 29 Rf1 Rd8 30 Bc3 and White enjoys a huge positional advantage.

19 Ne4 Rae8

Black didn't have enough compensation for the pawn after 19...Bc7 20 Be3 Rae8 21 Qd2 in Svidler-Adams, FIDE World Championship, Groningen 1997.

20 Re2!

An important prophylactic move. White covers the second rank against a possible sacrifice on g3.

20...h5 21 Bg5

Stronger than 21 Ng5 Bf5 etc.

21...Bc7 22 Qd2 Kh8

It is not better to play 22...f5 23 Nf2 Rxe2 24 Qxe2 Qxg5 25 Nxh3 etc.

23 Rae1 f6 24 Nf2 Rxe2 25 Rxe2

Weaker is 25 Qxe2?!, which allows Black the unexpected tactical motif 25...Bxg3! 26 hxg3 Qxg5 and Black is okay.

25...Bf5 26 Bxd5 cxd5 27 Bf4!

It is important to swap dark-squared bishops, which will leave weak dark squares in Black's camp.

27...Bxf4 28 Qxf4 Bxd3 29 Rd2 Bb1

After 29...Bf5 very unpleasant for Black is 30 Qd6!.

30 Qd6 Re8 31 Qxd5?

A mistake that lets Black off the hook. With the simple 31 Qxa6! Qg5 32 Rd1 Bc2 33 Qxb5! White could have obtained a decisive material and positional advantage.

31...Qh7 32 Kg2 Re5 33 Qb3 Qe8 34 a3 Bf5 35 Qb4 Bd7! 36 Qd4 Bc6

Black's initiative gives him just enough compensation to draw.

37 ♕d3+ ♚h6 38 ♕d4 ♕a8 39 ♖d3 ♕e8 40 g4!? ♖e2 41 ♕f4+ ♚h7 42 ♕f5+ ♕g6 43 ♕xh5+ ♕xh5 44 gxh5 ♖xb2 45 ♖d6 ♗e8 46 ♖xa6 ½-½

```
Game 28
Gara-Reg.Pokorna
European Girls U18 Championship 2000
```

1 e4 e5 2 ♘f3 ♘c6 3 ♗b5 a6 4 ♗a4 ♘f6 5 0-0 ♗e7 6 ♖e1 b5 7 ♗b3 0-0 8 c3 d5 9 exd5 ♘xd5 10 ♘xe5 ♘xe5 11 ♖xe5 c6 12 d3 ♗d6 13 ♖e1 ♕h4 14 g3 ♕h3 15 ♖e4 ♕f5 16 ♘d2 ♕g6 17 ♖e1 f5

Of course 17...♕xd3?? is out of the question due to the obvious 18 ♗c2 winning the queen. The text is a standard treatment in the Marshall Gambit – Black uses her f-pawn as a battering ram in order to breakthrough White's kingside. Black should keep her attack going and not count on material – it is time that's expensive in such positions.

18 c4

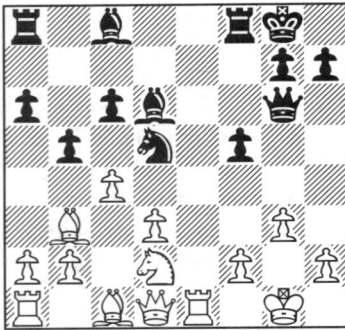

A direct attempt that in fact wins material because with her last move Black has weakened the a2-g8 diagonal. What follows is a rather forcing line in which tactical skill and memorising of the variations is of utmost importance.

18...f4

Of course there was no time for the retreat of the d5-knight because then c4-c5+ would have won Black's bishop on d6, so

Black must proceed with her attack.

19 ♘e4

White must protect the vulnerable g3-square. Weaker is the greedy 19 cxd5? fxg3 20 dxc6+ ♚h8 21 fxg3 ♗xg3 22 hxg3 ♕xg3+ 23 ♚h1 ♗g4 and Black certainly has more than a draw, such is the exposed nature of White's king.

19...fxg3 20 fxg3 ♗g4 21 ♕c2 bxc4 22 dxc4

Black has a promising position with his strong pair of bishops after 22 ♕xc4 ♗c7 23 ♕c2 ♚h8 24 ♗xd5 cxd5 25 ♘f2 ♖ac8, Hellers-Wahls, World Junior Championship 1988.

22...♖ae8!

Black sacrifices a piece but the last piece joins the attack. An important alternative is seen in Smagin-Hebden, Moscow 1986, when 22...♗b4? backfired because Black's bishop should be targeting White's kingside. White soon gained the initiative with 23 ♗d2 ♘f4 24 ♗xf4 ♗xe1 25 ♖xe1 ♗f5 26 ♕g2 ♖fe8 27 ♗c2 ♖e6 28 g4! ♗xg4 29 ♖f1 ♗e2 30 ♘g5! ♗xf1 31 ♗xg6 ♗xg2 32 ♗f7+ ♚f8 33 ♗xe6 and won because Black's bishop was trapped!

23 cxd5 ♗f3 24 dxc6+ ♚h8 25 ♗d5

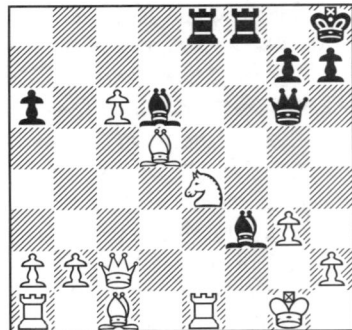

The critical position of the whole line. In the first game played in this variation White quickly lost after 25 ♗d2? ♖xe4 26 ♖xe4 ♗xe4 27 ♕c3 ♕f5 0-1 A.Ivanov-Agopov, USSR 1984. Clearly 25 ♗d2? was too slow

and no doubt it was responsible for White's quick defeat.

No better is 25 ♗f4? ♗xf4 26 c7 (or 26 ♘f2 ♕xc2 27 ♗xc2 ♗e3 and despite queens being off the board White is in trouble due to the unpleasant pin) 26...♕b6+ 27 ♔f2 ♗xc7 28 ♘c5 ♗e5 29 ♖f1 ♕d6 30 ♘e6 ♖f6 0-1 Scholis-Shkurovich, correspondence 1987.

Deserving of attention is the untried move 25 c7!?. This can lead to wild complications as demonstrated by my following analysis using *Fritz*. 25...♗xe4 26 c8♕ ♗xg3! 27 ♕xe4 ♗xh2+!

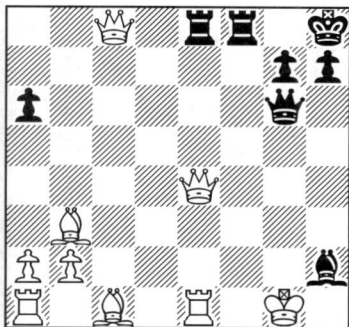

and now:

a) 28 ♔xh2 ♖f2+ 29 ♔h3 (forced since 29 ♔h1?? walks into mate after 29...♕h5+) 29...♕h5+ 30 ♕h4 (too risky is 30 ♔g3?, which seems to be losing for White because his king can end up in a mating net after 30...♕h2+ 32 ♔g4 ♖g2+ 33 ♕xg2 ♕xg2+ 34 ♔h4 ♖xc8 35 ♗f4 h6!, threatening the deadly ...g7-g5) and now Black has a choice between taking perpetual check with 30...♕f3+ or continuing the battle with chances for both sides after 30...♖h2+ 31 ♔xh2 ♕xh4+ 32 ♔g2 ♖xc8 33 ♗e3 etc.

b) 28 ♔h1 ♖f1+! 29 ♖xf1 ♕xe4+ 30 ♔xh2 ♖xc8 and this confusing position needs some practical tests.

25...♗xg3!

Using the fact that White can't take on g3 with the knight due to the pin along the b1-h7 diagonal. With this sacrifice Black softens

up White's kingside on the traditionally weak g3-square. No doubt worse is 25...♕f5?! (trying to win back some material but losing the initiative) 26 ♗e3 etc.

26 hxg3

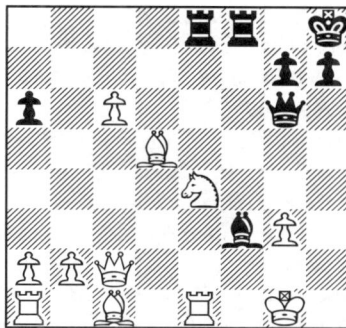

26...♗xe4?

It is strange, but this move is considered by many sources as Black's best!

Correct is 26...♖xe4! (which is even given a '??' by some authors). The main line runs 27 ♗f4!? ♖xe1+ (worse is 27...♖fxf4? 28 ♕f2 ♕h5 29 ♕h2 ♕xd5 30 gxf4 as in Andrijevic-Pavlovic, Yugoslavia 1988) 28 ♖xe1 ♕xc2 29 ♗xf3. Here a lot of authors consider White's position to be superior due to the strong passed c-pawn. I think this is wrong and after 29...♕xb2 Black's chances are by no means worse.

Instead of 26...♖xe4!, Black can also try 26...♕h5?! but White is clearly better after 27 ♕h2 ♕xd5 28 ♖xe4 ♗e4 29 ♖c1! etc.

27 ♖xe4 ♖xe4 28 ♗xe4?

Much stronger is *Fritz's* recommendation 28 ♔g2! – after the exchange of queens the arising ending with two minor pieces for a rook is an easy win for White.

28...♕xg3+ 29 ♕g2

This is an attempt to play for a win because 29 ♗g2 ♕e1+ 30 ♔h2 ♕h4+ leads to a draw.

29...♕e1+ 30 ♔h2 ♖f2 31 ♗f3 ♕e5+ 32 ♔h3 ♖xg2 33 ♔xg2 h5 34 a4 g5

After 34...h4, threatening ...♕e5-g3+,

White has the clever resource 35 ♖a3!.

35 ♗xh5 ♕e6 36 c7

Avoiding the obvious trap 36 ♗f3? g4! and suddenly it is White who is in trouble.

36...♕c6+ 37 ♗f3 ♕c2+ 38 ♔h3 ♕xc7 39 ♗xg5 ♕h7+ 40 ♔g3 ♕c7+ 41 ♗f4 ♕g7+ 42 ♗g4 ♕xb2 43 ♖h1+ ♔g7 44 ♖h5 ♕a3+ 45 ♗f3 ♕xa4 46 ♖d5 ♔f7 47 ♔g4 ♕a1 48 ♖d6 ♕g1+ 49 ♔f5 ♕c5+ 50 ♗d5+ ♔e7

It is not clear in this position whether White will win or whether Black will draw due to the reduced material left on the board. The rest is interesting only for those who are in love with endings.

51 ♖e6+ ♔d7 52 ♖e5 ♕f8+ 53 ♔e4 ♕b4+ 54 ♔f3 a5 55 ♖f5 ♕c3+ 56 ♔g4 ♕g7+ 57 ♖g5 ♕d4 58 ♗f3 ♕g1+ 59 ♗g3 a4 60 ♖d5+ ♔e7 61 ♖d3 ♕c1 62 ♗e4 ♕c4 63 ♔f3 ♕b4 64 ♗h4+ ♔e6 65 ♖e3 ♔d7 66 ♗f5+ ♔c6 67 ♗e1 ♕f8 68 ♔e4 a3 69 ♖c3+ ♔b7 70 ♖b3+ ♔c6 71 ♖c3+ ♔b7 72 ♖b3+ ♔c6 73 ♖c3+ ½-½

Game 29
Leko-Svidler
Dortmund 1998

---

1 e4 e5 2 ♘f3 ♘c6 3 ♗b5 a6 4 ♗a4 ♘f6 5 0-0 ♗e7 6 ♖e1 b5 7 ♗b3 0-0 8 c3 d5 9 exd5 ♘xd5 10 ♘xe5 ♘xe5 11 ♖xe5 c6 12 d3 ♗d6 13 ♖e1 ♕h4 14 g3 ♕h3 15 ♖e4 ♕f5 16 ♘d2 ♕g6 17 ♖e1 f5 18 ♘f3

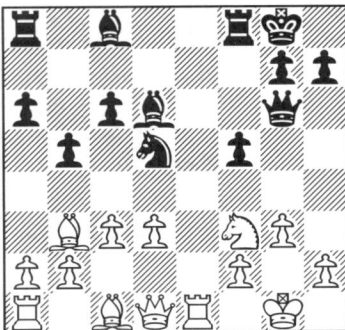

Leko's novelty hasn't been repeated in later games because Black gets relatively easy attacking chances on the kingside using the semi-open f-file.

18...f4 19 ♘e5

It is possible to play 19 ♘h4 ♕f6, when the aforementioned pressure along the f-file gives Black full compensation for the pawn.

19...♗xe5

An attempt for a brilliancy prize with the queen sacrifice 19...fxg3? backfires after 20 ♘xg6 gxf2+ 21 ♔g2! fxe1♕ 22 ♕xe1 hxg6 23 ♕e4! and White is winning.

20 ♖xe5 fxg3 21 hxg3

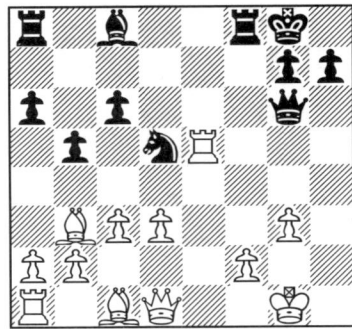

The alternative is 21 fxg3 ♗g4 (avoiding the obvious 21...♗h3? 22 ♖xd5! and White wins an important pawn) 22 ♕c2 ♖ae8 23 ♗f4 with approximately even chances.

21...♗g4 22 ♕e1

Worse is 22 ♕f1?! ♖ae8 23 ♖g5 ♕e6 24 ♗f4 h6 25 ♖e5 ♕g6 26 ♖xe8 ♖xe8 27 ♖e1 ♖xe1 28 ♕xe1 ♗f3! and White is in trouble due to the unpleasant mating threats along the h-file.

22...♗f3

A drawish alternative is 22...♖ae8 23 ♗g5 ♖xe5 (23...♗f3 24 d4 – worse is 24 ♗h4?! ♖xe5 25 ♕xe5 ♖e8 26 ♕d4 ♕e6 27 ♔h2 ♕e2! – 24...♖xe5 25 ♕xe5 ♖f5 26 ♕b8+ ♖f8 also leads to a draw) 24 ♕xe5 ♖f5 25 ♕b8+ ♖f8 26 ♕e5 ♖f5 etc.

23 ♗d2

The alternative is 23 ♗d1!? in order to exchange Black's deadly light-squared bishop: 23...♗xd1 24 ♕xd1 ♖xf2!? 25 ♔xf2 ♕f6+ 26 ♗f4 ♘xf4 and now 27 ♖e4!? looks dangerous for White but it is a great question how Black should use the discovered checks on offer. Maybe 27...♘xd3+ 28 ♔e3 ♖d8 29 ♖d4 ♖xd4 30 cxd4 ♘xb2 with a balanced position despite the unbalanced material!

23...♖ae8 24 a4

Safer is 24 c4!? bxc4 25 dxc4 ♘f6 (Black can draw at will by 25...♖xe5 26 ♕xe5 ♖f5 27 ♕b8+ ♖f8 28 ♕e5 ♖f5 with a repetition) 26 c5+ ♔h8 27 ♕e3! ♘e4 (or 27...♕g4 28 ♖xe8 ♖xe8 29 ♕f4 ♕h5 30 ♕h4 and White defends against the mate) 28 ♖xe8 ♕xe8 29 ♗d1 ♗xd1 30 ♖xd1 ♕h5 (surprisingly 30...♖xf2? loses to 31 ♗a5! with the deadly threat of ♖d1-d8) 31 ♖f1 ♕g4 32 ♕d4! and the position is about equal – White is a pawn up which is compensated by Black's strong pressure on the light squares.

24...h6 25 ♗d1?

Just when White wanted to exchange Black's strong f3-bishop, along comes the decisive error. Better was 25 d4 with the point that after 25...♖xe5 26 ♕xe5 ♖f5 White has 27 ♗c2! ♕h5 28 ♕e6+! and suddenly Black's king has no good squares because White takes the rook on f5 with check. So it wasn't White's mistake on move 24 that was the decisive error (as stated by some commentators), but his next move!

25...♖xe5 26 ♕xe5 ♗xd1 27 ♖xd1 ♕xd3 28 ♕d4 ♕f3 29 ♗e1?

This definitely loses to a nice tactic. The only chance was 29 ♖e1 ♖f5 30 ♖e8+ ♔f7 31 ♖e5 ♖xe5 32 ♕xe5 ♕d1+ 33 ♗e1 bxa4, when Black has much the better position due to the strong knight on d5.

29...♘e3! 30 fxe3 ♕e2!

White's bishop has no good squares to retreat to!

31 ♗f2 ♕xf2+ 32 ♔h1 ♕xg3 33 axb5 ♖f5 34 ♕d8+ ♔h7 35 ♕d3 ♕g6 0-1

But quicker was 35...♕h3+ 36 ♔g1 ♕g4+ 37 ♔h2 ♕h5+ 38 ♔g1 ♕g6+ followed by

...♖f5-h5 mate.

Game 30
J.Polgar-Adams
Dos Hermanas 1999

1 e4 e5 2 ♘f3 ♘c6 3 ♗b5 a6 4 ♗a4 ♘f6 5 0-0 ♗e7 6 ♖e1 b5 7 ♗b3 0-0 8 c3 d5 9 exd5 ♘xd5 10 ♘xe5 ♘xe5 11 ♖xe5 c6 12 d3 ♗d6 13 ♖e1 ♕h4 14 g3 ♕h3 15 ♖e4 ♕f5 16 ♘d2 ♕g6 17 ♖e1 f5 18 ♕f3

At the time this game was played this was a new move. White immediately tries to prove that Black's 17th move has weakened the a8-h1 diagonal and, if necessary, the text enables White to exchange queens by ♕f3-h5 after ♗b3-d1 has been played.

18...♔h8 19 ♗d1

The logical continuation after her previous move. Instead, grabbing a second pawn with 19 ♗xd5?! cxd5 20 ♕xd5 ♖b8 would have been very risky – although White is two pawns to the good, her task is not easy because of the problems on the a8-h1 diagonal.

19...f4 20 g4

Black wins back a pawn with an excellent position after 20 ♕h5?! fxg3 21 fxg3 ♗xg3 22 ♕xg6 ♗f2+! followed by ...hxg6.

20...h5 21 h3 ♘f6 22 ♕g2!

A reasonable decision. White gives back a pawn but fortifies her kingside. Computers would certainly consider 22 ♕xc6?! winning material, claiming that White is winning.

However, Black gets an enormous attack, for example: 22...hxg4 23 ♕xa8? f3! (from now on White's king will be in a cage) 24 h4 (obviously the only move) 24...♗f5 and now:

a) 25 ♕a7 ♗xd3! 26 ♕d4 (or 26 ♖e6 g3! 27 ♖xd6 gxf2++ 28 ♔xf2 ♘g4+ 29 ♔g3 ♕xd6+ 30 ♔xg4 ♕f4+ winning) or 26...g3 27 ♗xf3 gxf2+ 28 ♔xf2 ♗g3+ 29 ♔e3 ♖e8+ with a winning attack.

b) 25 ♕c6 g3 26 ♕xf3 gxf2+ 27 ♔xf2 ♗xd3 with numerous threats.

True, instead of the greedy 23 ♕xa8?, better is 23 hxg4 ♗xg4 24 ♕g2 ♖ae8 25 ♘e4 ♕h5 26 ♕h1 ♕xh1+ 27 ♔xh1 ♘xe4 28 dxe4 f3!, although even here after the exchange of queens White's position looks very dangerous because Black can start a mating attack using the g- and h-files!

22...hxg4 23 hxg4 ♗xg4

Slightly worse is 23...♘xg4?! 24 f3!, when White obtains the better ending due to her superior pawn structure.

24 ♖e6 ♕h5 25 ♗xg4

Worse is 25 ♖xf6? ♗xd1 26 ♖xd6 ♖ae8 27 ♘e4 ♗f3 28 ♕h2 ♖e5! 29 ♕xh5+ ♖xh5 30 ♘g3 fxg3 31 fxg3 ♖h1+ 32 ♔f2 ♖h2+ 33 ♔e3? c5! and White is mated!

25...♘xg4 26 ♖xd6

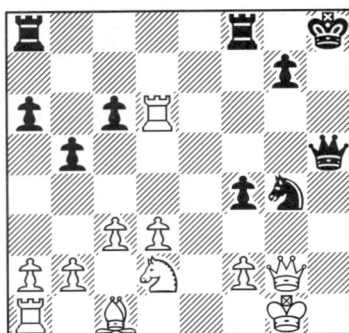

White takes the offered material and plays for a win, otherwise she could have settled for a probable drawn ending after 26 ♕h1!? ♕xh1+ 27 ♔xh1 ♖f6 28 ♖xf6 ♘xf6 29 f3 followed by ♘d2-e4.

26...♖ae8 27 ♘e4

An alternative was 27 ♘f3!? ♖e2 28 ♗d2 ♖xf2 29 ♕xf2 ♘xf2 30 ♔xf2 g5 31 ♖e1 ♕h3! 32 ♖ee6! ♕g3+ 33 ♔e2 ♕g2+ 34 ♔e1 ♕xf3 35 ♖h6+ with perpetual along the sixth rank.

27...♘e5 28 f3?

But this is too optimistic. Did she really think that White is better with an extra piece despite the exposed position of her king?

The normal 28 ♗d2 ♘f3+ 29 ♔f1 ♘h2+ would have led to a draw.

28...♘xf3+ 29 ♔f2 ♘h4 30 ♕h1

White has other alternatives:

a) 30 ♕h3 g5!, followed by ...g4, and if 31 ♕d7, 31...♘f5! is good for Black.

b) 30 ♕g5 ♕f3+ 31 ♔g1 (or 31 ♔e1 ♕h1+ – but not 31...♖xe4+?! 32 dxe4 ♘g2+ 33 ♔d2 ♕f2+ 34 ♔d1 ♕g1+ 35 ♔d2 f3 36 ♔c2 f2 37 ♕h5+ ♔g8 38 ♗d2! ♕xa1 39 ♖h6!! ♕b1+!? 40 ♔b3! and Black cannot avoid perpetual check! – 32 ♔f2 ♕h2+ 33 ♔f1 ♘f5! 34 ♕g2 ♘e3+ 35 ♗xe3 fxe3+ and Black wins) 31...♖e5!! 32 ♕xh4+ ♖h5

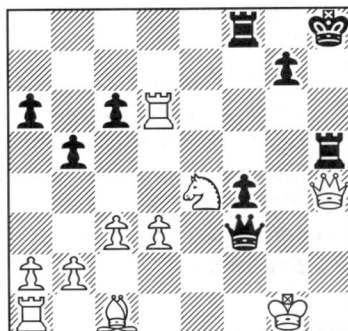

and now:

b1) 33 ♕xh5+ ♕xh5 34 ♗d2 f3 35 ♘f2 ♖f6! 36 ♖xf6 gxf6 and White's king is not defensible.

b2) 33 ♖d8!? ♕d1+ 34 ♔f2 ♖xh4 35 ♖xf8+ ♔h7 36 ♘g5+ ♔g6 37 ♘f3 ♖h1 38 ♖xf4 ♕c2+ 39 ♔g3 ♖xc1 with a technically winning ending for Black.

c) 30 ♕g1 ♕f3+ 31 ♔e1 ♘f5 32 ♕h2+

&g8 33 &d7 &g3 with numerous threats.

d) 30 ₩h2 &e5! (with the idea of ...₩h5-f3+ followed by ...&e5-h5) with an easy win for Black. This virtually refutes 30 ₩h2.

30...g5 31 b4

The best. White must complete the development of her queenside and at the same time generate some counterplay along the a1-h8 diagonal.

31...g4 32 &b2 g3+ 33 &g1 &f3+ 34 &g2

The tactical attempt 34 ₩xf3? doesn't yield the desired effect after 34...₩xf3 35 c4+ &g8 36 &g6+ &h7 37 &g5+ &xg6 38 &xf3 &e2! and Black is winning.

34...&h2! 35 c4+ &g8 36 ₩d1?

This loses quickly. The most stubborn defence was hidden in 36 &g1!. Now Black can force a draw with 36...&f3+ or play the much stronger 36...₩g4! (worse is 36...f3? 37 &xg3 f2+ 38 &g2 f1₩+ 39 ₩xf1! and White wins, but certainly not 39 &xf1?? &e2+! 40 &xe2 ₩xe2+ and White will soon be mated!) 37 &h6 f3 38 &h8+ &f7 39 &h7+ &e6! 40 &e1! &f5! and now:

a) 41 &d6+ &g6 42 &g7+ &h6! – a fantastic position!

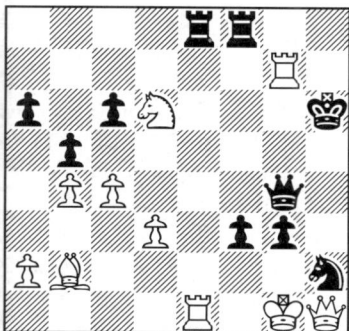

Black loses material but the white king is defenceless!

b) 41 &xh2 gxh2+ 42 &f1 f2! 43 &xf2 &g6+! 44 &e3 ₩f4+ 45 &e2 ₩f2+ 46 &d1 ₩xb2 and Black wins.

36...f3+

Now it is all very easy for Black.

37 &xg3 ₩g4+ 38 &f2 ₩h4+ 39 &e3

Or 39 &g1 ₩g4+ 40 &f2 ₩h4+ 41 &e3 (also losing is 41 &g1 f2+ 42 &xf2 &xf2) 41...₩g5+ 42 &f2 &g4+ 43 &g1 &xe4! and Black wins.

39...₩f4+ 40 &d4 ₩e5+ 41 &e3 &g4+ 42 &d2 ₩xb2+ 43 ₩c2 ₩xa1 44 &g6+ &h7 45 &xg4 f2 0-1

Game 31
Anand-Khalifman
FIDE World Ch., New Delhi 2000

1 e4 e5 2 &f3 &c6 3 &b5 a6 4 &a4 &f6 5 0-0 &e7 6 &e1 b5 7 &b3 0-0 8 c3 d5 9 exd5 &xd5 10 &xe5 &xe5 11 &xe5 c6 12 d3 &d6 13 &e1 ₩h4 14 g3 ₩h3 15 &e4 ₩f5 16 &d2 ₩g6 17 &e1 f5 18 a4!?

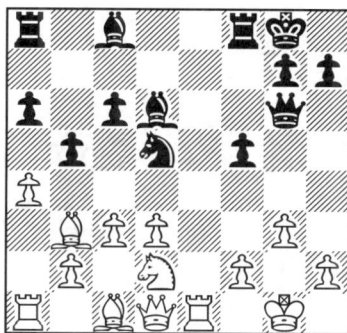

This discovery, made by Anand, is the latest fashion in the Marshall Gambit! White hurries to open up the a-file which will in many variations enable him to play &a1-a6 with strong counterplay to compensate for Black's kingside pressure.

18...&b8

If Black plays 18...f4, White shouldn't take on b5 allowing Black to sacrifice a piece on g3 with a strong attack, but should settle for 19 &e4. After 19...fxg3 20 fxg3 &g4 21 ₩d2, with the idea of playing ₩d2-g5, he would maintain the advantage.

19 axb5 axb5 20 &e4!?

The alternative is 20 ♘f3 f4 21 ♘e5 ♗xe5 22 ♖xe5 fxg3 23 fxg3 ♗g4 24 ♕e1 ♗h3 and now, instead of 25 ♗e3?! ♖f1+ 26 ♕xf1 ♗xf1 27 ♖xf1 ♖f8 (or 28...♕xd3 and Black is slightly better) 28 ♖xf8+ ½-½ as in Anand-Adams, Dos Hermanas 1999, better looks 25 ♖g5!? followed by ♗c1-f4.

Too optimistic for White is 20 c4?! f4! 21 cxd5 fxg3 22 fxg3 ♗xg3 23 ♔h1 (or 23 hxg3 ♕xg3+ 24 ♔h1 ♗g4 25 dxc6+ ♔h8 26 ♖e2 ♗xe2 27 ♕xe2 ♖f2 28 ♕xf2 ♕xf2 – White has enough material for the queen but the very bad coordination of his pieces gives Black a clear advantage) 23...♗g4 24 ♖e6 ♗xe6 25 dxe6 ♖f2!, when the situation looks rather grim for White.

20...fxe4 21 dxe4 ♗g4 22 ♕d4 ♗f3!

The best move. Weaker are both 22...♖be8?! and 22...♗c7?! because in each case White can respond with 23 ♖a6!, threatening to take on c6, after which Black's position crumbles like a sand castle.

23 exd5 c5

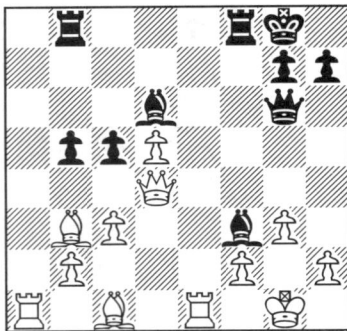

The whole point of Black's play initiated with his 22nd move. White is two pawns up but his light-squared bishop has been blocked, while Black's menacing bishop on f3 reminds White to be very careful against various mating threats.

24 ♕h4

White transfers his queen to the kingside in order to prevent the intrusion of Black's queen to h3. The alternative, awaiting further

tests, is 24 ♕d2 ♗f4 25 ♕xf4 (the queen sacrifice is forced because after the careless 25 ♕c2? ♕g4! suddenly White is left without any good defence!) 25...♖xf4 26 ♗xf4 ♖f8 27 d6+ (or 27 ♖e3?! ♖xf4 28 d6+ c4 29 d7 ♖f8 30 ♖xf3 ♖d8! and Black is much better) 27...c4 28 ♗d1 ♗c6 29 ♖a6 ♖e8 30 ♖f1 (White can draw by 30 ♖xe8+ ♕xe8 31 ♔f1 ♕e4 32 f3 ♕b1 33 ♖xc6 ♕xd1+ 34 ♔g2 etc.) 30...♕e4 31 f3 ♕d5 with a balanced position.

24...♖be8 25 ♗d2

Worth consideration is 25 ♖xe8+ ♖xe8 26 ♗f4 ♕e4 27 ♖f1 and now:

a) 27...♗h1 28 ♕h3! (28 f3 ♗xf3 29 ♗xd6 ♕e3+ 30 ♖f2 and Black hasn't got more than a draw by perpetual check) 28...♗xf4 29 gxf4 ♗f3 (forced because after 29...c4? 30 ♗d1 ♕xd5 31 f3! Black's bishop is suddenly trapped!) 30 d6+ c4 31 d7 ♖d8 32 ♗d1 and despite White's weakened kingside Black is fighting for a draw due to his deficit of material.

b) 27...c4!? might be better: 28 ♗xd6 ♕xh4 29 gxh4 cxb3 followed by ...♗f3xd5 is a probable draw but White might instead try 28 ♗a2!? with the point that 28...♗h1 29 ♕h3 ♗xf4 is met by 30 ♗b1! targeting h7.

All those variations await further testing but it is clear how dangerous 18 a4!? is for Black.

Besides 25 ♖xe8+, White has played 25 ♗e3 (as in the Anand-Adams, Dortmund 2000) with the idea of closing the e-file. Now Black should have continued 25...♖e5!, threatening to win the white queen by ...♖e5-h5, and after the forced 26 ♕h3 c4 27 ♗a2 ♖a8!? Black would have had enough compensation for the material deficit.

25...♗e4 26 ♖e2 ♕f5!

With the deadly threat ...♕f5-f3!.

27 ♗f4 c4 28 ♖xe4!

Forced because 28 ♗xd6 ♕f3! 29 ♖xe4 ♕xf2+ 30 ♔h1 ♕f3+ 31 ♔g1 ♖xe4 is winning for Black.

28...♖xe4 29 ♗c2 ♗xf4 30 ♗xe4 ♕xe4

31 gxf4 ½-½

31...♕xd5 32 ♕g5 ♖f5 33 ♖a8+ ♕xa8 34 ♕xf5 ♕a1+ 35 ♔g2 ♕xb2 is clearly equal.

Game 32

P.Popovic-M.Pavlovic

Cetinje Team Championship 1993

---

1 e4 e5 2 ♘f3 ♘c6 3 ♗b5 a6 4 ♗a4 ♘f6 5 0-0 ♗e7 6 ♖e1 b5 7 ♗b3 0-0 8 c3 d5 9 exd5 ♘xd5 10 ♘xe5 ♘xe5 11 ♖xe5 c6 12 d3 ♗d6 13 ♖e1 ♕h4 14 g3 ♕h3 15 ♖e4 ♕f5 16 ♘d2 ♕g6 17 ♖e1 f5 18 f4

White decides to give back the pawn to slow down Black's ...f5-f4 break. He will be able to gain the necessary time to consolidate his kingside by attacking the black bishop on f4.

18...♗xf4 19 ♕f3

Rarely seen is 19 ♘f3 and now, instead of the poor 19...♗c7? 20 ♘e5 ♗xe5 21 ♖xe5 ♗e6 22 c4 bxc4 23 dxc4 ♘b6 24 ♗e3 ♖ab8 25 ♕d6 ♗f7 26 ♕xg6 hxg6 27 ♖c5 which leaves Black with a bad ending, much better is 19...♗xc1! 20 ♖xc1 f4 21 ♘e5 (worse is 21 c4? ♘e3! 22 cxb5+ ♔h8 23 ♕d2 ♕h5! 24 gxf4 ♕g4+ 25 ♔f2 ♖xf4 26 ♖xe3 ♗g4 27 ♗d1 ♖ae8! and it is obvious that White is not going to survive all the pressure) 21...♕h6 22 ♕f3 with a near level position.

19...♗b8!

The best move. As we shall see, Black's rook on a8 is indirectly defended by tactics.

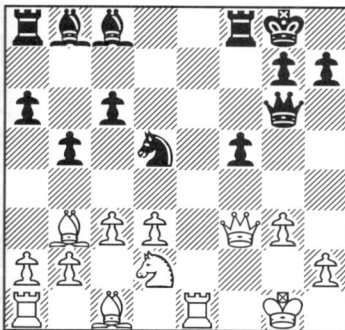

20 ♗xd5+ cxd5 21 ♘f1?!

This is too passive. Better is 21 ♘b3!, which is shown in the next game.

What happens if White takes on d5 with check? Well, after 21 ♕xd5+ ♔h8 White has two possibilities:

a) 22 ♕xa8? ♕b6+ 23 d4 ♗b7 (here is the obvious point behind 18...♗b8!) 24 ♖e6! ♕c7! and White has to give up his queen after which he has to struggle for a draw.

b) 22 ♘f3 ♗xg3! and now:

b1) 23 ♖e2? ♗c7+ 24 ♔g2 ♕b6+ 25 d4 ♗b7 26 ♕d7 ♖g8 27 ♘g5 ♖af8 wins for Black.

b2) 23 hxg3? ♕xg3+ 24 ♔f1 (24 ♔h1? ♖a7! with ...♗c8-b7 to follow is winning for Black) 24...f4 25 ♘g5 h6! 26 ♘f7+ ♖xf7 27 ♖e8+ ♔h7 28 ♕xf7 ♗h3+ 29 ♔e2 ♖xe8+ 30 ♕xe8 f3+ 31 ♔d2 f2 32 ♕e4+ ♕g6!! 33 ♕xg6+ ♔xg6

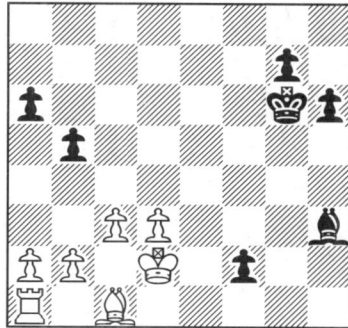

with a beautiful win for Black which well demonstrates his attacking potential.

b3) 23 ♕xa8! (forced) 23...♗xe1+ 24 ♔f1 f4 25 ♔xe1 ♖e8+ 26 ♔f2 ♗h3 27 ♕xe8+ ♕xe8 28 ♗xf4 is one long line in which Black is slightly better but the most likely outcome is a draw.

21...♗b7 22 ♖e7 ♗c6 23 ♕e3 f4?!

With this move Black loses the lions share of the advantage. Much stronger was 23...♖f6! with the idea of controlling the important e6-square. After 24 ♕g5 ♗d6 25 ♕xg6 ♖xg6 followed by ...f5-f4 Black's pair of bishops would have become very strong in the open position.

24 ♕e6+ ♕xe6 25 ♖xe6 ♗d7 26 ♖e7 ♗h3 27 ♗xf4 ♗xf4 28 gxf4 ♖xf4 29 ♖e3

The game soon fizzled out into a draw.

29...♗g4 30 ♖g3 d4 31 ♘d2 ♖af8 32 cxd4 ♖xd4 33 ♘e4 ½-½

Game 33
Am.Rodriguez-L.Perez
Cuban Championship 1998

1 e4 e5 2 ♘f3 ♘c6 3 ♗b5 a6 4 ♗a4 ♘f6 5 0-0 ♗e7 6 ♖e1 b5 7 ♗b3 0-0 8 c3 d5 9 exd5 ♘xd5 10 ♘xe5 ♘xe5 11 ♖xe5 c6 12 d3 ♗d6 13 ♖e1 ♕h4 14 g3 ♕h3 15 ♖e4 ♕f5 16 ♘d2 ♕g6 17 ♖e1 f5 18 f4 ♗xf4 19 ♕f3 ♗b8! 20 ♗xd5+ cxd5 21 ♘b3!

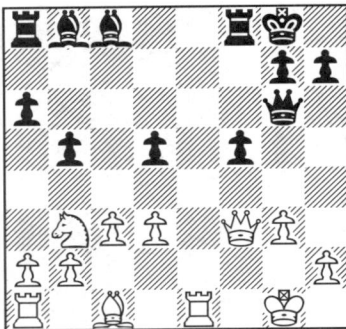

Much stronger than 21 ♘f1?! as in the previous game. The knight is now striving to occupy the excellent d4-square. Black must avoid at all costs the exchange of the dark-squared bishops because, due to the pawn structure, his light-squared bishop will be no match for White's knight.

21...♗b7?!

The bishop hurries to occupy the long diagonal but it is still not clear on which diagonal the bishop stands better. White may be able to close the diagonal the bishop is now on. Much better for Black is 21...♕f7!, for

example: 22 ♘d4 ♗a7 23 ♗f4 ♗d7 24 ♖e5 b4! 25 ♖ae1 ♖ae8 26 ♔f1 ½-½ Leko-Adams, Linares 1999.

22 ♗f4 ♗a7+ 23 d4 ♖ae8 24 ♕f2 ♖e4 25 ♘d2 h6!?

In order to avoid grovelling in an unappealing position, Black sacrifices the exchange to activate his light-squared bishop. This is his best practical chance.

26 ♘xe4 dxe4 27 h4 ♕g4 28 ♕e2 ♕h3 29 ♖f1 ♗b8 30 ♕h2 ♕g4 31 ♗xb8 ♖xb8 32 ♖f4 ♕g6 33 ♕f2 e3 34 ♕h2

34 ♕xe3 ♖e8 35 ♕f2 ♖e2! 36 ♕xe2 ♕xg3+ 37 ♔f1 ♕xf4+ gives some counterplay for Black.

34...♖e8 35 ♖e1 e2?

A grave positional mistake giving White the f2-square for his queen after which the game is virtually won.

36 ♕f2 ♕c6 37 ♔h2 g6 38 h5!

White has managed to defend against the threats along the a8-h1 diagonal and now the time is ripe for his decisive counterattack!

38...gxh5 39 ♖xf5 h4 40 gxh4 ♔h7 41 ♖f7+ 1-0

Game 34
Leko-Adams
Madrid 1998

1 e4 e5 2 ♘f3 ♘c6 3 ♗b5 a6 4 ♗a4 ♘f6 5 0-0 ♗e7 6 ♖e1 b5 7 ♗b3 0-0 8 c3 d5 9 exd5 ♘xd5 10 ♘xe5 ♘xe5 11 ♖xe5 c6 12 d3 ♗d6 13 ♖e1 ♕h4 14 g3 ♕h3 15 ♖e4 ♘f6

Black's knight is re-routed towards the kingside, possibly g4. Also, in some variations Black avoids lines where White exchanges on d5.

16 ♖h4 ♕f5 17 ♗c2

17 ♘d2 is the subject of Games 35-36, while 17 ♗f4 is discussed in Game 37.

17...♕g6!

The most reliable reply. Black is ready to meet d3-d4 with ...♗c8-f5 and simultaneously he intends to play ...♗c8-g4 with a creeping kingside initiative.

Another interesting possibility at this point is 17...♖e8!? and now White can choose between the following:

a) 18 d4 ♕d5 19 ♗b3 ♕f5 leads to repetition which is a recurring theme in the lines after 17 ♗c2.

b) 18 ♗e3 ♖xe3! 19 fxe3 g5 20 ♖d4 ♗c7 and now:

b1) 21 e4 ♕h3 22 ♕f1 ♕xf1+ 23 ♔xf1 c5 24 ♖d5 ♘xd5 25 exd5 ♗h3+

followed by ...♖e8 with more than sufficient compensation for the pawn in the ending due to his strong pair of bishops.

b2) 21 ♘d2 c5 22 ♖e4 ♘xe4 23 ♘xe4 ♗b7 with a very promising position for Black in Darga-Jimenez, Havana 1964.

c) 18 ♗f4?! g5! (now the point behind 17...♖e8!? becomes clear – the rook on f8 will not hang after White takes on d6) 19 d4 (better was 19 ♗xd6 gxh4 with only a small advantage for Black) 19...♘e4 20 f3 ♗xf4! 21 ♗xe4 ♖xe4! 22 ♖xf4 gxf4 23 fxe4 ♕xe4 24 ♘d2 ♕e3+ 25 ♔g2 c5! with clear advantage for Black in Poletaev-Sadomskij, correspondence 1956-57.

d) 18 ♘d2 ♗g4 (clearly worse is 18...g5? 19 ♘e4! leaving Black with a rotten kingside) 19 ♘f3 (the only move since 19 ♘e4? ♖xe4 20 f3!? – or 20 dxe4 ♕xf2+ 21 ♔h1 ♗e7! – 20...♗xg3! 21 hxg3 ♕e5! leaves White without a good defence) 19...♕g6 and now White can try either 20 ♘g5!? or 20 d4 ♗f5. Black

has sufficient compensation for the pawn because he has control of both the e-file and the light squares.

18 ♘d2

Dubious is 18 ♗f4?! ♗e7! (of course Black doesn't swap his dark-squared bishop; instead he leaves White's badly placed rook on h4) 19 d4 ♗f5 20 ♗xf5 ♕xf5 21 ♗e5 ♘d5 22 ♖g4 g5! and White's rook is trapped.

18...♗g4 19 ♘f3

This leads to an unpleasant pin but White doesn't want to weaken his second rank with the alternative 19 f3 ♗f5.

19...♖fe8 20 ♔g2 ♘d5

Also worth consideration is 20...h6!? and if 21 d4, then 21...♗f5 22 ♗xf5 ♕xf5 23 ♗f4 g5.

21 d4

Here it is White who can play differently with 21 h3 ♗f5 22 ♘d4!? etc.

21...♗f5 22 ♗xf5 ♕xf5 23 ♗d2 ♘f6

Black is ready to meet the manoeuvre ♕d1-b1 with ...♘f6-e4. Weaker is 23...h6 24 ♕b1! etc.

24 ♗f4 ♗f8 25 ♗d2

Possibly playable is 25 ♗e5 g5 26 ♗xf6 gxh4 27 ♗xh4 while another alternative is 25 ♕b1!? ♘e4 26 ♗e5 ♕xf3+! 27 ♔xf3 ♘d2+ 28 ♔g2 ♘xb1 29 ♖xb1 f6 followed by ...♖e2 entering the White camp. White is a pawn up but the out-of-play rook on h4 gives Black adequate compensation.

25...♗d6 26 ♗f4 ♗f8 27 ♗d2 ♗d6 ½-½

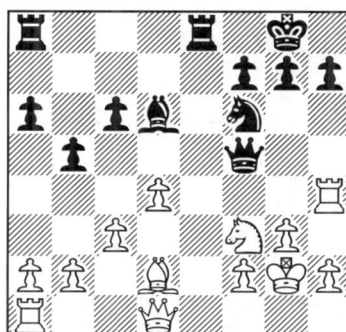

It might be a disappointing end for the reader but such is a scientific top level game nowadays. The position is in the balance because Black has excellent control of the light squares while White's rook on h4 is out of play.

> # Game 35
> ## Ivanchuk-Timman
> *Wijk aan Zee 1999*

1 e4 e5 2 ♘f3 ♘c6 3 ♗b5 a6 4 ♗a4 ♘f6 5 0-0 ♗e7 6 ♖e1 b5 7 ♗b3 0-0 8 c3 d5 9 exd5 ♘xd5 10 ♘xe5 ♘xe5 11 ♖xe5 c6 12 ♖e1 ♗d6 13 d3 ♕h4 14 g3 ♕h3 15 ♖e4 ♘f6 16 ♖h4 ♕f5 17 ♘d2 g5!?

Black is not tired of harassing White's rook. It should be mentioned that White's d3-pawn was taboo again, this time due to 17...♕xd3?? 18 ♖d4! and Black loses a piece.

18 ♖d4?!

White continues to be stubborn and willingly sacrifices the exchange. We shall see the stronger continuation 18 ♖h6! in the next game.

18...♗c5 19 ♘f3 h6!

A subtle idea that casts doubts over White's artificial eighteenth move – Black calmly protects his g5-pawn.

Also interesting is 19...♗e6!?, continuing with his development while White's rook still cannot escape. On the contrary, weaker is the greedy 19...♗xd4?! 20 ♘xd4 ♕h3 (forced

because both 20...♕c5? 21 ♕f3! and 20...♕d7? 21 ♗xg5 looks pretty bad for Black, who has his kingside completely ruined) 21 ♗xg5 ♘g4 22 ♘f3 ♗e6 (even worse is 22...♗f5? 23 ♗e7! and White nets the third pawn; after Black removes the rook from f8 White plays ♗xf7+! and the bishop is taboo due to ♘g5+ with a fork) 23 ♕f1 and White is slightly better because he has two pawns for the exchange and a healthy pawn structure.

20 ♗f4?

This is the decisive mistake. White intends to exchange the dark-squared bishops with the manoeuvre ♗f4-d6 but this original idea just will not work. White could have tried to justify his eighteenth move by 20 h4!? and then Black has the following choices:

a) 20...♗xd4 21 ♘xd4 ♕h3 22 hxg5 ♘g4 23 ♘f3 hxg5 24 ♗xg5 leads to a very unclear position where both sides have pluses and minuses – note how both kings are exposed.

b) 20...♗e6 21 hxg5 ♗xb3 22 axb3 hxg5 23 ♕d2 ♘h7 is about equal.

c) 20...♘g4 21 ♖xg4!? ♕xg4 22 d4 ♗d6 23 hxg5 ♗xg3 24 ♘e1! ♖e8!? needs further testing, for example:

c1) 25 ♕xg4?! ♖xe1+ 26 ♔g2 ♗xg4 27 ♔xg3 h5! 28 g6 ♗e6 is better for Black due to the unpleasant pin along the first rank.

c2) 25 ♘g2 seems best, against which Black can start a very strong attack by sacrificing a piece with 25...♗h2+!? 26 ♔xh2 ♕h3+ 27 ♔g1 ♗g4 28 ♕c2 ♔h8!. The threat of ...♗g4-f3 is very annoying for White – certainly it is food for thought!

20...♗b7

Later it was discovered that even stronger is 20...♖e8! with the deep idea of avoiding the exchange of dark-squared bishops. After 21 ♗d6 ♗b6! it would be very difficult for White to defend against the imminent ...c6-c5. In the case of 20...♗xd4?! 21 ♘xd4 ♕h3 22 ♗d6 ♘g4, besides 23 ♘f3, White can also try 23 ♕f3!? with good counterplay.

21 ♗d6 ♗xd6 22 ♖xd6 c5 23 ♘d2 ♖ad8

24 ♖xd8

The alternative was 24 ♖b6 ♖xd3 25 ♖xb7 ♘e4 26 ♘xe4 ♖xd1+ 27 ♖xd1 ♕xe4 28 ♖dd7 c4 (after 28...♕b1+?! 29 ♔g2 c4 30 ♗d1 ♕xb2 31 ♗h5! White gets reasonable drawing chances) 29 ♗d1 g4! and Black is much better.

24...♖xd8 25 ♗c2

Or 25 ♕e2? c4! 26 dxc4 ♖xd2! 27 ♕xd2 ♕f3 and Black wins.

25...♘g4 26 ♕e2

White's situation is worse than it might look at first glance. After 26 ♕e1 c4 27 ♗d1 ♖xd3 28 ♗xg4 ♕xg4 29 ♕e8+ ♔g7 30 ♕e5+ ♔h7 31 ♕e7 ♗d5 32 ♕e1 there comes the well known sacrifice 32...♖xd2! 33 ♕xd2 ♕f3 34 ♔f1 ♗e6! 35 ♔g1 ♗h3 with mate to follow.

26...c4! 27 ♗d1

27 ♘e4 doesn't save White after 27...cxd3 28 ♕xg4 ♕xg4 29 ♘f6+ ♔g7 30 ♘xg4 dxc2 31 ♘e3 ♖d2 32 ♖c1 ♗e4 33 ♔f1 ♗d3+ and the ending is pretty hopeless.

27...♖xd3 28 ♕xg4 ♕xg4 29 ♗xg4 ♖xd2 30 ♖b1 ♗e4 31 ♖e1 ♗d3 32 b4 ♖xa2 33 ♖c1 f5 34 ♗h3 ♔f7 35 ♗f1 ♗e4 36 ♗g2 ♔f6 37 ♗xe4 fxe4 38 ♖e1 ♔f5 39 ♔f1 ♖a3

The rook and pawn ending is easily winning for Black, who is a pawn up with an active king. It only needs good endgame technique which Timman will demonstrate.

40 ♖e3

Or 40 ♖c1 e3! 41 fxe3 ♔e4! and Black's king will pick up the white pawn on c3 and there is nothing White can do about it.

40...a5 41 bxa5 ♖xa5 42 ♖e2 ♖a1+ 43 ♔g2 ♖a3 44 ♖c2

Forced because after 44 ♖e3? b4! Black's c-pawn is unstoppable.

44...♔e5 45 ♔f1 b4! 46 cxb4 c3 47 ♔e2

White could have tried to activate his rook but it would not have changed the result of the game. After 47 ♖c1 ♔d4 48 ♖d1+ ♔c4 49 ♖d8 c2 50 ♔e2 ♖c3! the e-pawn promotes.

47...♔d4 48 b5 ♖b3 49 ♖xc3 ♖xc3 50 b6 ♖b3 51 b7 ♖xb7 0-1

Game 36
Svidler-Adams
Elista Olympiad 1998

1 e4 e5 2 ♘f3 ♘c6 3 ♗b5 a6 4 ♗a4 ♘f6 5 0-0 ♗e7 6 ♖e1 b5 7 ♗b3 0-0 8 c3 d5 9 exd5 ♘xd5 10 ♘xe5 ♘xe5 11 ♖xe5 c6 12 d3 ♗d6 13 ♖e1 ♕h4 14 g3 ♕h3 15 ♖e4 ♘f6 16 ♖h4 ♕f5 17 ♘d2 g5!? 18 ♖h6!

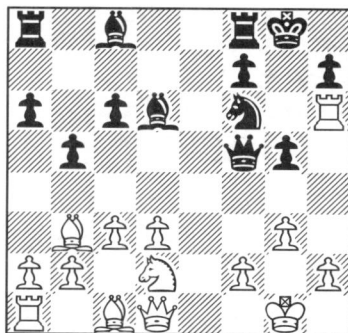

This leads to another exchange sacrifice but under much better conditions for White. The weak side of the aggressive 17...g5!? will be revealed – Black's kingside is like White's, vulnerable to attack as well!

It should also be mentioned that 18 ♘e4 is not as strong as the text: 18...gxh4 19

②xd6 ♕g6 planning ...♗c8-g4 etc.

18...②g4 19 ②e4 ②xh6 20 ②xd6 ♕g6

The attempt of counterattacking with 20...♕h3? doesn't achieve much after 21 ♕e2 (better than 21 ②xc8 ♖axc8 22 ♗xg5? ②g4 23 ♕f3 ♕xh2+ 24 ♔f1 ♕h5 25 ♕f4 ♕h1+ 26 ♔e2 ♖ce8+ 27 ♔d2 ♕xa1 28 ♕xg4 ♕e1+ 29 ♔c2 h5 30 ♗xf7+ ♖xf7 0-1 Valko-Egri, Nyiregyhaza 1994 – obviously not an exemplary game by White) 21...♗f5 22 ♗xg5 ②g4 23 f3 ♗xd3 24 ♕d2 ②e5 25 ♕e3!

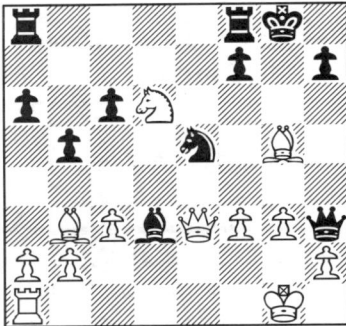

and White keeps everything under control, while it is difficult to give Black any good advice since his minor pieces are under attack and he will lose some material.

21 ②e4!

Gaining time by attacking Black's pawn on g5. This is far stronger than 21 ②xc8?! ♖axc8, when Black is at least equal.

21...②g4

With the text Black gives up a pawn in order to get some activity for his pieces.

21...g4?! 22 ♗g5! ♗f5 23 ♕d2 results in a dominating position for White.

After 21...♗f5 22 ②xg5 ♗xd3 23 ②f3! ♗c4 24 ②e5 ♕e6 25 ♗xh6 ♕xh6 26 ②xc4 bxc4 27 ♗xc4 we reach the position where there is little doubt that White is better – two pawns for the exchange and a healthy pawn structure. Compare this to Black's shattered pawns.

22 ♗xg5 ♗f5 23 ♗f4 ♖ad8 24 ♕e2

This is stronger than 24 f3 ♖fe8! 25 ♕e2

②e5 etc.

24...♖fe8 25 ♖e1 ♔g7?!

Covering the vital f6-square, which is visible in the line 25...②e5? 26 ♗xe5 ♖xe5 27 ②f6+! and White is winning. However, better was 25...♗xe4 26 fxe4 ②f6 planning ...②f6-d5, although the advantage is still with White.

26 f3 ②e5 27 ♗c2 c5 28 ♕e3! f6

Despite all efforts Black's position is very difficult because White firmly keeps control of the e4-square. Thus hopeless for Black is 28...c4? 29 d4 ②d3 30 ♗xd3 cxd3 31 ♕xd3 ♖e7 32 d5!, with ♕d3-d4+ following.

29 ♔h1 ♗xe4?!

Perhaps a result of time trouble. Maybe Black should have gone in for a slightly improved version of the previous line with 29...c4!? 30 d4 ②d3 31 ♗xd3 cxd3 32 ♕xd3 ♖e7 with some chances to save the game, although materially White should be winning with three pawns for the exchange. However, Black would still have some slight chances due to the pin down the e-file.

30 fxe4 ②d7 31 d4 cxd4 32 cxd4 ②b6

White's central pawns have started to roll and there is nothing for Black to do. After 32...f5 33 g4! fxg4 34 ♗d3 White gets an irresistible kingside attack.

33 ♕f2 ②d5 34 ♗d2!

Avoiding a trap. After 34 exd5? ♖xe1+ 35 ♕xe1 ♕xc2 36 ♕e7+ ♔g6 37 ♕xd8 ♕d1+ 38 ♔g2 ♕e2+ it's perpetual check because the winning try 39 ♔h3?? ♔h5!!

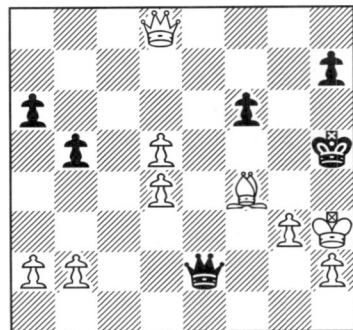

suddenly turns out to be a study-like loss – White is unable to prevent mate despite the extra piece and reduced material!

34...♘e7 35 e5 f5 36 e6! ♕f6 37 ♗b3 ♔g8 38 ♖e5 ♔g7 39 d5 ♕xe5 1-0

Black resigned as White is clearly winning after 40 ♗c3 ♕xc3 41 bxc3 ♘xd5 42 ♕xf5 ♘e7 43 ♕f7+ ♔h6 (43...♔h8 44 ♗c2 ♘g6 45 e7 ♖xe7 46 ♕f6+) 44 ♕f6+ ♘g6 45 h4!.

Game 37
Hulley-Allenby
Correspondence 1994

---

1 e4 e5 2 ♘f3 ♘c6 3 ♗b5 a6 4 ♗a4 ♘f6 5 0-0 ♗e7 6 ♖e1 b5 7 ♗b3 0-0 8 c3 d5 9 exd5 ♘xd5 10 ♘xe5 ♘xe5 11 ♖xe5 c6 12 ♖e1 ♗d6 13 d3 ♕h4 14 g3 ♕h3 15 ♖e4 ♘f6 16 ♖h4 ♕f5 17 ♗f4

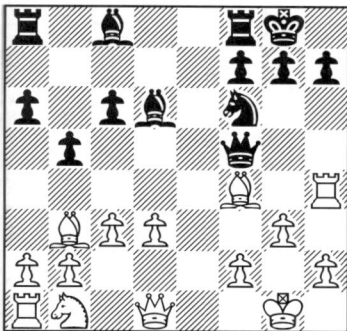

Certainly the move which tests 15...♘f6 the most. White intends to exchange dark-squared bishops, which would greatly diminish Black's kingside initiative.

17...♗e7

This move is considered the best at Black's disposal because 17...g5? led to a position without prospects for Black after 18 ♗xd6 gxh4 19 ♗xf8 ♔xf8 20 ♕e2 ♗b7 21 ♘d2 c5 22 f3 hxg3 23 hxg3 ♕g5 24 ♕f2 ♖d8 25 ♗c2 ♘h5 26 ♘f1. Now the game Anand-L.Cooper, British Championship 1988 ended abruptly after 26...♕d5 27 ♖e1 ♕xf3?? 28 ♕xc5+ and Black resigned; after

28...♔g7 29 ♕g5+ Black loses his rook.

18 ♗c2 g5

An interesting new idea was tried in Ariskin-Gorbunov, Kstovo 1998, where the continuation was 18...h6!? 19 d4 ♕d5 20 ♗e5 ♗b7 21 ♗b3 ♕d7 22 ♘d2 c5 23 f3 c4 24 ♗c2 ♘d5 25 ♕e2 ♗xh4 26 ♕e4 f5 27 ♕xh4 ♘e3. Surely White's play can be improved upon, but Black's idea is interesting in any case because after the text move, the mainline continuation after 17 ♗f4, White has a guaranteed draw, which sometimes Marshall devotees like to avoid!

19 d4 ♕d5 20 ♗b3 ♕f5 21 ♗c2 ♕d5 22 c4!?

The winning try – White will sacrifice a couple of pawns or even a piece in order to achieve a strong kingside attack.

22...bxc4 23 ♘c3 ♕a5 24 b4!

Continuing with sacrificial play.

24...♗xb4?

After 24...♕xb4?! 25 ♗xg5 ♕xc3 26 ♕c1! things would not have been any rosier for Black than in the game. The critical line is 24...cxb3 25 axb3 ♕xc3 26 ♗xg5 ♖e8 (or 26...♖d8 27 ♗xh7+ ♘xh7 28 ♗xe7 with a strong attack) 27 ♕c1 ♔h8!? 28 ♗xf6+ ♗xf6 29 ♖xh7+ ♔g8 30 ♖h8+!? ♗xh8 31 ♗h7+. White wins the queen but Black will have enough material as compensation so it is a big question whether White has more than a draw in this line.

25 ♗e5! ♖e8

Black desperately frees the f8-square for his king. The alternatives do not save Black from defeat:

a) 25...♗xc3 26 ♖xh7! ♕xe5 27 dxe5 ♘xh7 28 ♗xh7+ with an overwhelming advantage to White, but not 28 ♕h5? f5 29 exf6 ♖a7! and Black is still alive and kicking.

b) 25...gxh4 26 ♕c1!! ♘e4 27 ♘xe4 f6 28 ♘xf6+ ♖xf6 29 ♕g5+ and Black is mated.

26 ♘e4! ♖xe5 27 ♘xf6+ ♔f8 28 dxe5 gxh4 29 ♘xh7+ ♔g7 30 ♕h5 1-0

A game played in the best attacking style reminiscent of the early 19th century.

Summary

Those interested in playing 15...♗d7 should take a closer look at Game 22, which led to a complex struggle with some advantage to White, but Black certainly had counterchances.

In Game 24, better was the possibility of 19 a4! as indicated in the game commentary. This would have given White a small but lasting advantage, which means the plan with 15...♕d7 does not yield Black full equality.

After 15...♕f5 16 ♘d2 ♕g6 17 ♖e1 the critical move is certainly 17...f5, after which White has quite a few interesting ways forward but Black looks to be okay.

Finally, after 15...♘f6 16 ♖h4 ♕f5 17 ♘d2 g5 18 ♖h6! (Game 36), White obtains two pawns for the exchange and, with Black's weakened kingside, White clearly has the better play. So, at the moment, the ball is in Black's court here.

1 e4 e5 2 ♘f3 ♘c6 3 ♗b5 a6 4 ♗a4 ♘f6 5 0-0 ♗e7 6 ♖e1 b5 7 ♗b3 0-0 8 c3 d5 9 exd5 ♘xd5 10 ♘xe5 ♘xe5 11 ♖xe5 c6 12 d3 ♗d6 13 ♖e1 ♕h4 14 g3 ♕h3 15 ♖e4 (D) ♕f5

    15...♕d7 16 ♘d2

       16...f5 – *Game 23*; 16...♗b7 – *Game 24*

    15...♗d7 16 ♘d2

       16...♖ae8 – *Game 19*

       16...g5

          17 ♘f3 – *Game 20*

          17 ♖e2 f5: 18 c4 – *Game 22*; 18 ♘e4 – *Game 21*

    15...♘f6 16 ♖h4 ♕f5

       17 ♗c2 – *Game 34*; 17 ♗f4 – *Game 37*

       17 ♘d2 g5!?: 18 ♖d4 – *Game 35*; 18 ♖h6! (D) – *Game 36*

16 ♘d2 ♕g6 17 ♖e1

    17 ♘f3 – *Game 25*

17...f5

    17...♗g4 – *Game 27*; 17...♗c7 – *Game 26*

18 f4 (D)

    18 ♘f3 – *Game 29*; 18 ♕f3 – *Game 30*; 18 a4 – *Game 31*; 18 c4 – *Game 28*

18...♗xf4 19 ♕f3 ♗b8 20 ♗xd5+ cxd5 21 ♘b3 – *Game 33*

    21 ♘f1 – *Game 32*

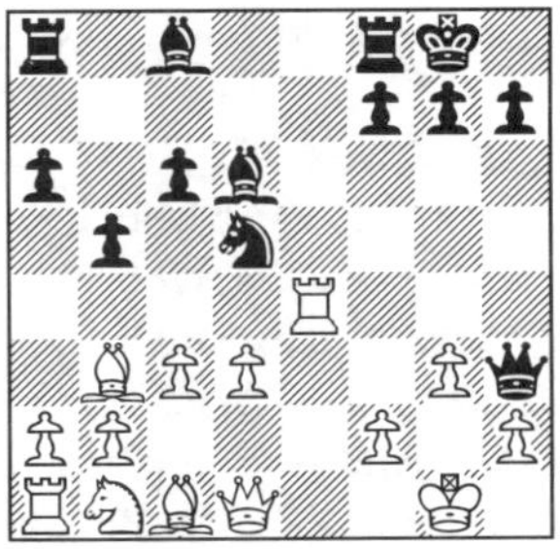

15 ♖e4

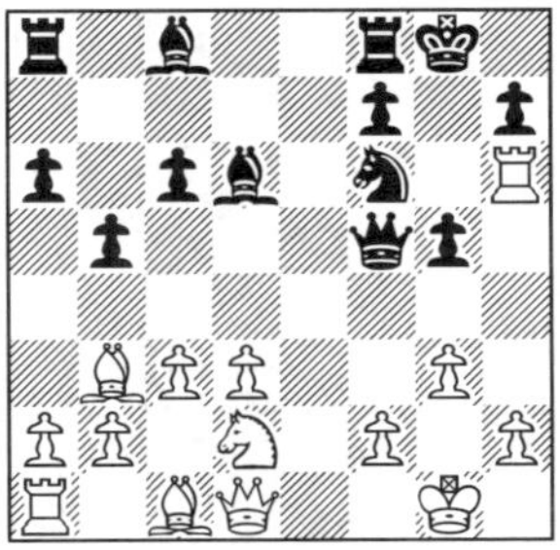

18 ♖h6!

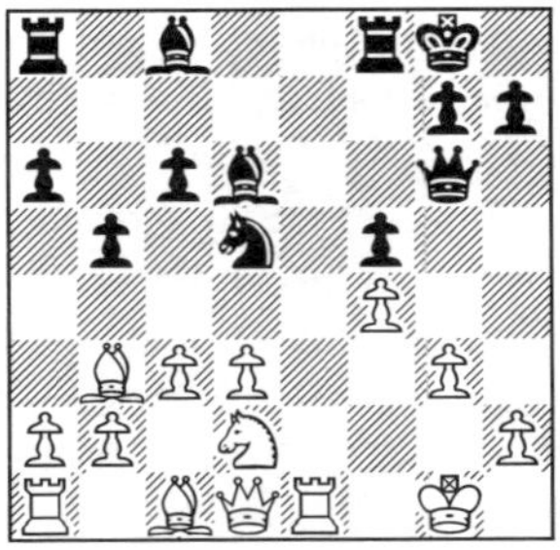

18 f4

CHAPTER FOUR

12th and 13th Move Options for White

1 e4 e5 2 ♘f3 ♘c6 3 ♗b5 a6 4 ♗a4 ♘f6
5 0-0 ♗e7 6 ♖e1 b5 7 ♗b3 0-0 8 c3 d5
9 exd5 ♘xd5 10 ♘xe5 ♘xe5 11 ♖xe5 c6

In this chapter we will deal with the main alternatives for White on the twelfth and thirteenth moves. These are the following:

1) 12 d4 ♗d6 13 ♖e2 (Games 38-40)
2) 12 g3 (Games 41-45)
3) 12 ♗xd5 (Games 46-51)

(1) White's set-up using the rook on e2 is chiefly for defensive purposes. This rook move was considered some twenty years ago as an important finesse but has recently gone out of fashion due to the fact that Black has several good plans at his disposal.

In Game 38 we see a pet line of the English GM John Nunn. However, nowadays after 14 f3, instead of retreating the bishop to h5 (which was Nunn's original idea), Black has started to develop his bishop on f5 where it is indeed more actively placed.

The main line after 13 ♖e2 goes 13...♕h4 14 g3 ♕h3 15 ♘d2 ♗f5 and now White is at the crossroads: does he exchange Black's light-squared bishop by playing 16 ♗c2 (Game 39) which allows Black a kingside attack after 16...♗xc2 17 ♕xc2 f5!; or does he seek counterplay on the opposite flank by

playing 16 a4, as in Game 40?

(2) 12 g3 used to be a pet line of former World Champion Bobby Fischer, which only confirms its strategical value. The move is aimed at preventing Black's queen from joining in the kingside attack via h4. However, it weakens some important squares around the king, notably h3. Although nowadays white players are not so attracted by this move as they used to be in the past, every Marshall devotee still should be prepared to meet it.

The positional approach 12...♗f6 is seen in Games 41-42. An excellent example of Black's counterplay is the game F.Braga-Geller (Game 41), in which Black sacrifices a piece and in return obtains some lasting strategical gains (in particular the pin along the d-file). The similar positional piece sacrifice is seen in Game 42.

Transferring the knight to the kingside by 12...♘f6?! is seen in Game 43, while the other choice for Black is 12...♗d6 (Games 44-45).

(3) 12 ♗xd5 is the so-called Kevitz Variation, in which White exchanges his light-squared bishop for Black's knight on d5. Players who prefer clear-cut positions rather than wild complications usually adopt this line. It enjoys a very solid reputation but it doesn't put enough pressure on Black, so

with correct play Black will not have too many problems in achieving equality.

After the sequence 12 ♗xd5 cxd5 13 d4 ♗d6 14 ♖e3 ♕h4 15 h3 Black chooses 15...f5?! in Game 46 and 15...g5!? in the following game.

Games 48-51 witness Black's main move, 15...♕f4. The reader should study Gufeld-Blatny (Game 48) where, after a repetition of moves (a common occurrence when Black chooses 15...♕f4), Black decides to play on with ...♕f6-g6.

Game 49 witnesses the line 15...♕f4 16 ♖e5 ♕f6 17 ♖e1 ♕g6 18 ♕f3, which was at its peak during the 1965 Tal-Spassky match in Tbilisi.

In the last two games in this chapter Black's threat of ...♗c8xh3! is parried by 18 ♔h1. after which Black can choose either 18...♗f5 (Game 50) or 18...♗d7 (Game 51).

Game 38
Djurhuus-D.Pedersen
Gausdal 1994

---

1 e4 e5 2 ♘f3 ♘c6 3 ♗b5 a6 4 ♗a4 ♘f6 5 0-0 ♗e7 6 ♖e1 b5 7 ♗b3 0-0 8 c3 d5 9 exd5 ♘xd5 10 ♘xe5 ♘xe5 11 ♖xe5 c6 12 d4 ♗d6 13 ♖e2

The idea behind this move is to defend the potentially vulnerable second rank. This might seem too abstract, but one variation can confirm it. If Black continues 13...♗g4

and White responds with 14 f3, then 14...♕d8-h4? is a mistake because of 15 g3 ♗xg3 16 hxg3 ♕xg3+ and now White has 17 ♖g2! refuting Black's sacrificial play.

13...♗g4

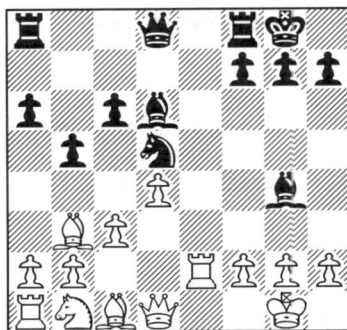

This rare continuation is a favourite of English GM John Nunn, who has adopted it on several occasions. Black is provoking f2-f3, hoping in the future to exploit the slight weakening of the kingside.

14 f3 ♗h5?!

Recently Black started to rehabilitate the variation by playing 14...♗f5 and indeed Black's light-squared bishop stands well on the b1-h7 diagonal: 15 ♗xd5 cxd5 16 ♘d2 ♗d3 17 ♖f2 (wrong is 17 ♖e3? ♕h4! 18 ♖xd3 ♗xh2+ 19 ♔f1 ♗g3 20 ♖e3 ♖ae8! and White has no defence) 17...b4 18 cxb4 ♖e8 (also good is 18...♕c7 19 ♘f1 ♗xf1 20 ♔xf1 ♗xh2 21 ♖c2 ♕b6 22 ♕d3 ♕f6 23 ♗e3 ♗g3 with full compensation for the sacrificed pawn because White's king is not safe, Kotronias-I.Sokolov, Elenite 1992) 19 ♘f1 ♗xf1 20 ♕xf1 ♕b8! 21 g3 ♕xb4 22 ♔g2 ♕xd4 with equal play, Kotronias-De Vreugt, Kavala 2002.

15 ♗xd5

Even stronger is 15 ♕f1! ♗g6 16 ♕f2 ♕f6 17 g3 ♗d3 18 ♖e1 ♕g6 19 ♘d2 f5 20 f4 ♔h8 21 ♘f3 ♗e4 22 ♘e5 ♗xe5 23 dxe5 h6 24 ♗c2 ♗xc2 25 ♕xc2 ♕e6 26 ♗d2 g5 27 ♖f1 g4 28 b3! ♖ac8 29 c4 and White was a clear pawn up in the game Kindermann-

Nunn, Dortmund 1991.

15...cxd5 16 ♘d2 f5 17 ♘f1

An alternative is 17 ♕b3 ♖e8!? 18 ♖xe8+ ♕xe8 19 ♘f1 (but not 19 ♕xd5+? ♗f7 20 ♕xd6 ♕e3+ 21 ♔f1 ♖e8 22 g3 ♕e1+ 23 ♔g2 ♖e2+ 24 ♔h3 ♕f2 25 ♕b8+ ♗e8 26 g4 fxg4+ with a winning attack for Black) 19...♗f7 20 ♗d2 f4 21 a4 ♖b8 22 axb5 ♖xb5 23 ♕c2 ♗g6 24 ♕c1 ♗d3 25 ♗xf4 ♗xf4 26 ♕xf4 ♖xb2 27 ♕g5 ♗c4 28 ♘g3 h6 29 ♕c1 ♕b8 30 ♕e1 a5 and White, due to his extra pawn, was slightly better in Kotronias-Nunn, Kavala 1991.

17...f4 18 ♕b3 ♕g5?

On g5 the queen will be exposed to some cheapos due to the pin on the c1-h6 diagonal.

19 g4!

An elegant way of meeting the threat ...♗h5xf3.

19...♖ae8?

Black had to retreat his bishop by playing 19...♗f7, although even then he would have stood worse. The text, however, loses by force.

20 h4! ♕xh4 21 ♖h2 ♕e1 22 ♖xh5

White plays accurately. Black was hoping for 22 gxh5? ♖f5! with the deadly threat ...♖f5-g5+ etc.

22...♖e2 23 ♗e3!

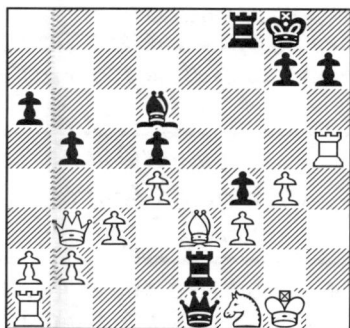

23...♕xa1 24 ♕xd5+ ♔h8

Or 24...♗f7 25 ♖f5! and White wins.

25 ♕xd6 ♖a8 26 ♕g6 h6 27 g5! 1-0

Black cannot avoid being mated after 27...♖e1 28 gxh6 ♖xg1+ 29 ♔g2 etc.

Game 39
Ljubojevic-Nunn
Szirak 1987

---

1 e4 e5 2 ♘f3 ♘c6 3 ♗b5 a6 4 ♗a4 ♘f6 5 0-0 ♗e7 6 ♖e1 b5 7 ♗b3 0-0 8 c3 d5 9 exd5 ♘xd5 10 ♘xe5 ♘xe5 11 ♖xe5 c6 12 d4 ♗d6 13 ♖e2 ♕h4

The main move and surely the most natural one. By threatening mate on h2, Black forces White to weaken the light squares around his king by playing g2-g3.

The idea of Czech GM Pavel Blatny, 13...♗c7 intending to play ...♕d8-d6, hasn't for some reason attracted other Marshall devotees but it might be playable. After 14 ♘d2 ♕d6 15 ♘f1 f5 16 a4 ♔h8 17 ♗d2 f4 18 f3 g5 19 axb5 g4!? 20 ♖e5 ♕g6 21 ♖xd5 gxf3 22 ♕xf3 ♗g4 23 ♕f2 cxd5 24 ♖xa6 ♕f5 we get a messy position which is difficult to evaluate.

14 g3 ♕h3

Sometimes Black plays 14...♕h5 with the idea of keeping the h3-square reserved for Black's bishop. Then play can continue 15 ♘d2 ♗h3 (worse is 15...♗f5? 16 ♖e1 ♗g4 17 f3 ♗h3 18 ♘e4 ♗c7 19 a4! ♕g6 20 axb5 axb5 21 ♖xa8 ♖xa8 22 ♘g5 ♗f5 23 ♕e2! ♗d7 24 ♖xd5 cxd5 25 ♕e7 ♕f5 26 g4 1-0 Kindermann-Steinbacher, Biel 1991) 16 f3 ♗c7 17 ♘e4!? ♕xf3 18 ♘g5 ♕h5 19 ♘xh3 ♕xh3 20 ♗d2 ♖ae8 21 ♕f1 ♕d7 22 ♖ae1 ♖xe2 23 ♕xe2 with a tiny advantage for White due to his pair of bishops.

15 ♘d2 ♗f5 16 ♗c2

The simple strategy with 16 ♗xd5 cxd5 17 f3 ♖ae8 18 ♘f1 is best met by 18...h5!, intending ...h5-h4, granting Black a long lasting initiative on the kingside.

16...♗xc2 17 ♕xc2 f5 18 c4

White can prevent ...f5-f4 only by playing 18 f4?!, against which Black can continue with either 18...♕g4 19 ♘f1 ♗xf4 or

18...♗xf4!, when 19 gxf4? ♕g4+ 20 ♖g2 ♕xg2+! 21 ♔xg2 ♘e3+ followed by ...♘xc2 is winning for Black.

18...♕g4!

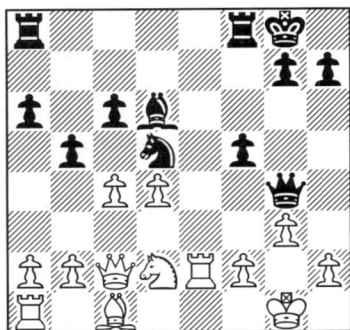

An important intermediary move that brings disharmony into the white camp.

19 ♖e6?!

White plays optimistically. The safer option was 19 ♖e1, against which there can follow 19...f4! (a thematic breakthrough in the Marshall Attack by which Black kills two birds with one stone – both the f-file will be opened and the critical square g3 will be undermined; for achieving such aim the sacrifice of the d5-knight is a small price to pay) 20 f3 ♕h3 21 cxd5 fxg3 22 ♘f1 gxh2+ 23 ♔h1 ♖f6 24 f4! (the only defence because White is losing after both if 24 ♕e4? ♖g6! and 24 ♕g2? ♖g6!) 24...♖h6 25 ♕f2 ♖f8 26 ♖e6 ♖xe6 27 dxe6 ♕xe6 28 ♗d2 ♗xf4 29 ♗xf4 ♕e4+ 30 ♕g2 ♕xf4 31 ♘xh2 ♕xd4 with roughly equal chances, Mokry-Panczyk, Polanica Zdroj 1984.

19...♘f4!?

This looks very spectacular but in fact it only leads to perpetual check. Later it was found that a stronger continuation was 19...f4! (Black cheekily continues with his plan regardless of the fact that with his last move White has attacked the bishop on d6) 20 ♕e4 (the only move since 20 ♖xd6? fxg3 21 hxg3 ♖xf2! or 20 fxg3 ♘e3 is equally hopeless for White) 20...♘e3! 21 ♘f3 (again

forced because after 21 fxe3? ♕d1+ Black's attack breaks through) 21...fxg3 22 ♕xg4. Here Dr John Nunn gives 22...gxf2+ 23 ♔xf2 ♘g4+ 24 ♔g2 ♖f6 as slightly better for Black, but I like 22...gxh2+! 23 ♘xh2 ♗xh2+ 24 ♔xh2 ♘xg4+ followed by ...♘g4xf2 even more, when Black keeps his extra pawn and has the better ending.

20 ♖xd6?

Later a defence was found in 20 f3!, after which Black has nothing better than to settle for a draw by perpetual check with 20...♘h3+ 21 ♔g2 ♘f4+ 22 ♔g1 ♘h3+, Hübner-Timman, Tilburg 1987.

20...♖ae8!

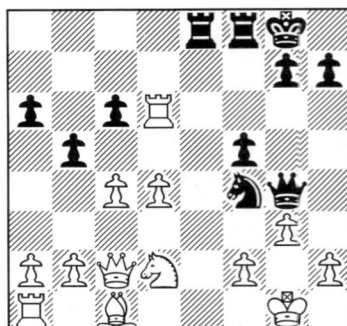

Now White is defenceless against both ...♖e1+ and ...♖e2.

21 cxb5

This loses but what doesn't?

21...♖e2 22 ♕c4+ ♔h8 23 ♕xe2 ♘xe2+ 24 ♔g2 f4 25 bxc6 fxg3 26 hxg3 ♘f4+ 0-1

1 e4 e5 2 ♘f3 ♘c6 3 ♗b5 a6 4 ♗a4 ♘f6 5 0-0 ♗e7 6 ♖e1 b5 7 ♗b3 0-0 8 c3 d5 9 exd5 ♘xd5 10 ♘xe5 ♘xe5 11 ♖xe5 c6 12 d4 ♗d6 13 ♖e2 ♕h4 14 g3 ♕h3 15 ♘d2 ♗f5 16 a4

With this move White opens up the a-file

with the aim of weakening Black's back rank in the event of an exchange of rooks.

16...罝ae8!?

For Black it is more useful to exchange off the rook on e2, which defends White's position, rather than the idle one on a1.

17 罝xe8

Bad is 17 axb5? ♘f4!! 18 gxf4 ♛g4+ 19 ♔f1 ♗d3 20 ♘e4 ♛f3! 21 ♔e1 ♗e2 22 ♛xe2 ♛h1+ 23 ♔d2 罝xe4 24 ♛d1 ♗xf4+ 25 ♔d3 罝e1 26 ♗xf4 ♛e4+ 0-1 Enders-Goldberg, Bundesliga 1992.

17...罝xe8 18 ♘f1 h5!

Stronger than 18...b4 19 c4 ♘f6 20 c5 ♗c7 21 ♗c4 etc.

19 axb5 axb5 20 罝a6?

The threat to Black's c6-pawn is just an illusion – with this move White loses precious time. Correct was 20 ♗xd5! cxd5 21 ♘e3, which would have kept the game in the balance.

20...♘c7!

White has obviously overlooked this strong move because now 21 罝xc6? drops a rook after 21...♗e4! due to the mortal threat of mate on g2.

21 罝a7 h4

Onwards towards the white king!

22 ♘e3 hxg3 23 fxg3 ♗xg3! 24 hxg3 罝xe3! 25 ♗xe3 ♛xg3+ 26 ♔f1

White is forced to give up his queen because if 26 ♔h1?, 26...♗e4+ forces mate on the next move.

26...♗h3+ 27 ♔e2 ♗g4+ 28 ♔d2 ♗xd1 29 ♗xd1 ♘d5 30 罝a8+ ♔h7 31 罝e8 f5

The battle is over.

32 ♔e2 ♛h2+ 33 ♔d3 ♛xb2 0-1

Game 41
F.Braga-Geller
Amsterdam 1986

---

1 e4 e5 2 ♘f3 ♘c6 3 ♗b5 a6 4 ♗a4 ♘f6 5 0-0 ♗e7 6 罝e1 b5 7 ♗b3 0-0 8 c3 d5 9 exd5 ♘xd5 10 ♘xe5 ♘xe5 11 罝xe5 c6 12 g3

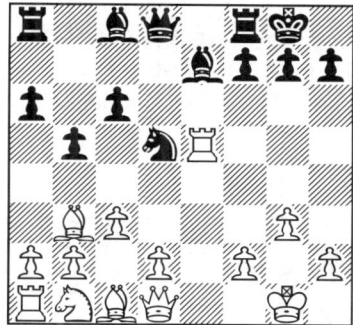

This move is nowadays rarely seen, although it was employed a couple of times by the great Robert Fischer. White denies the h4-square to Black's queen but weakens the light squares (in particular h3) around his king, which is obviously a drawback.

12...♗f6

This is the positional treatment. With this set-up (with the bishop on f6), Black renounces a direct attack against the white king but prefers to seek long-term positional compensation for the sacrificed pawn. The bishop might exert very unpleasant pressure against White's undeveloped queenside. This can be seen in many lines where Black plays the thematic ...b5-b4! opening up the a1-h8 diagonal.

13 罝e1 c5

Unclear is 13...罝a7 with the idea of exchanging rooks via e7. Then play could con-

tinue 14 d4 ♗e7 15 ♖xe7 ♕xe7 16 ♘a3!
(Black has sufficient compensation for the
pawn after 16 ♗xd5 cxd5 17 ♗e3 ♖e8 18
♘d2 ♗h3 19 ♕f3 ♕e6 20 ♖e1 ♗g4 21 ♕g2
♗h3 22 ♕f3 ♗g4 23 ♕h1 h5 24 h4 ♕f5,
Fischer-O'Kelly, Havana 1965) 16...♗h3 17
♘c2 ♖e8 18 ♗d2 ♕e4 19 ♘e1 ♕g6 20 ♗c2
♗f5 21 ♗xf5 ♕xf5 22 ♕f3 ♕g6 23 ♕d3
♕g4 24 ♘g2 g6 25 f3. White has managed to
repel Black's pressure and the extra pawn
soon told in Decsi-Angelov, correspondence
1984.

14 d4

Black obtains very active play after 14 d3
♗b7 15 ♘d2 b4! 16 cxb4 ♘xb4 17 ♘e4
♗e7 18 ♗c4 ♘c6 19 ♗f4 ♘d4 20 ♖c1 ♔h8
21 ♕h5 f5 22 ♘d2 ♗d6 23 ♗e5 ♗xe5 24
♖xe5 ♕c7 25 ♗e3 f4, Sirontisnj-Rapoport,
correspondence 1974.

14...♗b7!?

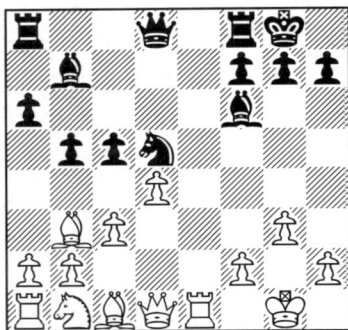

Maybe this move doesn't grant Black full
compensation for the sacrificed material but
it has been scoring quite well in tournament
practice. Rather than trading on d4, when
following cxd4 White can occupy the c3-
square with his knight, Black sacrifices a second pawn.

It is also possible to play the normal
14...cxd4 15 cxd4 ♗b7 16 ♘c3 ♘xc3 17
bxc3 ♕d7, planning ...♕d7-c6 in some lines,
but then White is at least slightly better so
why give up a pawn and then struggle to get
it back?

Not so logical is 14...c4?!, trying to fortify
his well placed knight on d5 but on the other
hand leaving the f6-bishop with nothing to
do on the a1-h8 diagonal. This move was
successful in the old game Glienke-Matthaus,
correspondence 1956 in which White lost
badly after 15 ♗c2 ♖a7 16 ♗e4? ♖e7 17
♗g2 ♗g4! 18 f3 ♖xe1+ 19 ♕xe1 ♖e8 20
♕f1 ♗f5 21 ♘d2 ♗d3 22 ♕d1 ♘e3 0-1.
However, White's play could clearly have
been improved upon. In particular, 16 ♘d2
with ♘d2-e4 to follow gives White a huge
advantage.

15 dxc5

Less convincing for White are the following alternatives:

a) 15 ♗c2?! ♖e8 and now:

a1) 16 dxc5 ♕d7 17 ♗e4 ♖ad8 18 ♘d2
♘xc3! 19 c6 (an interesting tactical solution
which, however, does not solve all of White's
problems; after the natural 19 bxc3 ♗xe4
Black is at least slightly better) 19...♗xc6 20
♗xc6 ♘xd1 21 ♖xe8+ ♕xe8 22 ♗xe8 ♖xe8
and due to the double threat ...♖e1+ and
...♘xb2 it is obvious that White is in trouble.

a2) 16 ♖xe8+ ♕xe8 17 dxc5 ♖d8 18 ♕d3
g6 19 ♕f1 b4!

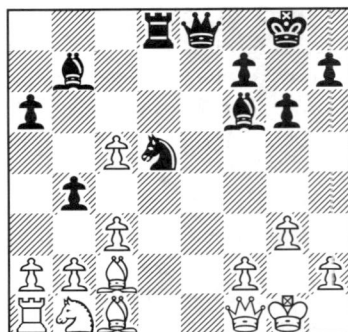

(again this thematic move – Black
strengthens the influence of his dark-squared
bishop while White lags behind in development) 20 ♗h6 (or 20 ♗d2 ♕c5! etc.)
20...bxc3 21 bxc3? (already a decisive mistake
after which White loses material; he should

have played 21 ♘xc3 although White still keeps an inferior position) 21...♗b4! 22 cxb4 ♗xa1 23 ♗e3 ♕c6 24 f3 ♖e8 25 ♘d2 ♖xe3 26 ♕xa1 ♕e6 27 ♗e4 ♗xe4 28 fxe4 ♗e2 29 ♘f3 ♕xe4 30 ♕f6 ♕b1+ 0-1 Cappellani-Lagumina, Catania 1991.

b) 15 ♗e3?! ♖e8 16 ♕d2 ♘xe3 17 fxe3 ♕d7 18 ♕f2 cxd4 19 exd4? (correct is 19 cxd4 but after 19...a5! 20 a4 bxa4 21 ♖xa4 ♕c6 22 d5 ♕b5 Black's initiative is clear due to his powerful pair of bishops and the lack of coordination of White's pieces – in particular the a4-rook is misplaced) 19...♖xe1+ 20 ♕xe1 ♖e8 21 ♕f2 ♗g5! 0-1 Paes de Lira-Mendes de Prado, Brazil 1994. There is no good remedy against the oncoming ....♗e3.

15...♖e8

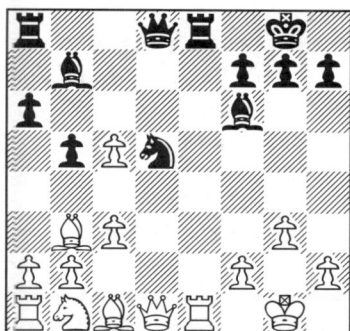

This was an original idea first played by Geller. The compensation for the two pawns is obvious but it is difficult to assess whether it is sufficient or not. However, under tense tournament conditions playing this position as White is not easy, especially with his underdeveloped queenside. On the other hand, Black's moves are not difficult to find. – note in particular ...♕d7 connecting the rooks. Black will also have the options of ...♕d7-c6 or ...b5-b4.

16 ♘d2

White can avoid the sacrifice which comes next with the following moves:

a) 16 a4 ♖xe1+ 17 ♕xe1 ♕d7 18 ♕d1 ♖e8 19 ♗e3 ♕f5 20 ♗xd5 ♗xd5 21 ♘d2 ♗c6 22 axb5 axb5 23 ♕e2 ♕d5 24 f3 b4! 25 c4 (or 25 ♘e4 ♖xe4! 26 fxe4 ♕xe4 when Black has at least a draw by perpetual check) 25...♕e6 26 ♘f1 ♗d4 27 ♖a6 ♕c8 28 ♖a5 ♕c7 29 ♖a6 ♕c8 and White should have taken the draw after 30 ♖a5 in Bierenbroods-Helle, correspondence 1996.

b) 16 ♗d2?! doesn't solve the problem of queenside development. Black has 16...♕d7 17 ♗e3 ♖ad8 18 ♗xd5 ♗xd5 19 ♘d2 and, instead of 19...♗b7?!, much better is 19...♕h3 20 f3 h5! with an initiative.

c) 16 ♗e3 ♘xe3 17 ♕xd8 (with the queens remaining on the board White is even worse: 17 fxe3? ♕e7!, threatening ...♕e4 or capturing on c5, gives Black a substantial advantage) 17...♖axd8 18 fxe3 ♗e7 followed by ....♗xc5 with a clear advantage to Black, whose rampant bishop pair begins to tell. The weak pawn on e3 now becomes very vulnerable.

d) 16 ♖xe8+ ♕xe8 17 ♗xd5? ♖d8! and Black regains his piece and has a near-crushing attack on the a1-h8 diagonal.

16...♘xc3!? 17 bxc3 ♗xc3

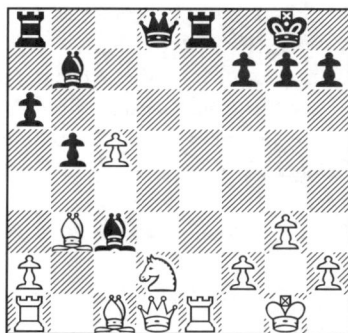

With this piece sacrifice Black's dark-squared bishop becomes the most important piece on the board!

18 c6!?

White returns a pawn in order to take away the c6-square from the black queen. The alternative and possibly critical continuation is 18 ♖b1. Now Black should not play the slow 18...♕d7? 19 ♖xe8+ ♖xe8, when both 20 ♗c2 (Assmann-Hansel, Germany 1995) and 20 ♘f1 ♕c6 21 f3 ♕xc5+ 22 ♔g2 (Van Asperen-McCorry, correspondence 1999) repelled Black's attack, but the aggressive 18...♕d3!.

I guess Geller must have had this in mind before playing the piece sacrifice. A possible continuation after 18...♕d3! could be 19 ♖xe8+ (the threat was ...♖xe1+ followed by ...♕xb1 so this exchange is practically forced) 19...♖xe8 20 ♗c2 (20 ♘f1 with the plan to go for a counterattack is not sufficient either after 20...♕xb1 21 ♕d7 ♖f8 22 ♕xb7 ♕xc1 etc.) 20...♕d5 21 f3 ♕xc5+ 22 ♔g2 ♖d8! and it is not easy to see how White can get out of the pin on the d-file because after 23 ♖b3 there comes the very strong 23...b4 etc. Despite being a piece up, White's task is by no means easy.

18...♗xc6 19 ♖xe8+ ♕xe8 20 ♖b1 ♖d8 21 ♕c2

Or 21 ♗c2 ♕d7 and Black regains his piece with advantage.

21...♗xd2

The tempting 21...♕e1+? 22 ♘f1 ♗e4 is refuted by 23 ♗g5! winning for White.

22 ♗xd2 ♗e4 23 ♗xf7+

This is forced because White loses after 23 ♖e1? ♗xc2 24 ♖xe8+ ♖xe8 25 ♗xc2 ♖e2!, picking up one of the bishops.

23...♔xf7 24 ♕b3+ ♗d5 25 ♕b4 ♕e4

Otherwise White plays ♖e1 with unclear

play, so Black heads into the ending. Then, even with opposite coloured bishops, White's weaknesses on the a8-h1 diagonal and the pawn on a2 grant Black considerable winning chances.

26 ♕xe4 ♗xe4 27 ♖b2 ♖d4 28 h3?

White wants to control the light squares on the kingside by playing g3-g4 and later bringing his king to g3. However, this plan is too slow. He should have tried to bring his king into the centre by first pushing his pawn to f4 instead. After the text White is lost.

28...♗d5 29 ♖c2

Or 29 a3 ♖d3! and the a3-pawn drops.

29...♖a4 30 ♖c7+ ♔e6 31 g4 ♖xa2 32 ♗e3 b4

Black's pair of passed pawns on the queenside decide. The rest requires no further explanation.

33 ♗d4 g5 34 ♖xh7 ♖d2 35 ♗h8 ♖d1+ 36 ♔h2 ♖h1+ 37 ♔g3 ♖g1+ 38 ♔h2 ♖g2+ 39 ♔h1 ♖xg4+ 40 ♔h2 ♖h4 41 ♖xh4 gxh4 42 f4 a5 0-1

Game 42
T.Ernst-Dam
Lugano 1988

---

1 e4 e5 2 ♘f3 ♘c6 3 ♗b5 a6 4 ♗a4 ♘f6 5 0-0 ♗e7 6 ♖e1 b5 7 ♗b3 0-0 8 c3 d5 9 exd5 ♘xd5 10 ♘xe5 ♘xe5 11 ♖xe5 c6 12 g3 ♗f6 13 ♖e1 c5 14 d4 ♗b7 15 dxc5 ♕d7

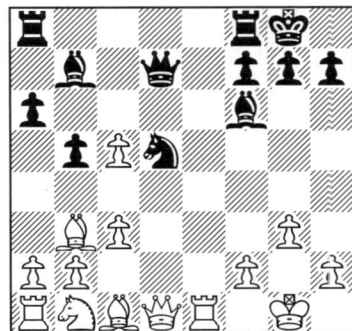

Black hurries to connect his rooks – soon one of them will appear on e8 – and the queen can go to c6 creating mating threats on the a8-h1 diagonal.

16 ♘d2 ♘xc3!? 17 bxc3 ♗xc3 18 ♖b1 ♖ad8 19 ♖e2 ♕c6 20 f3 ♕xc5+ 21 ♔g2 ♗xf3+!?

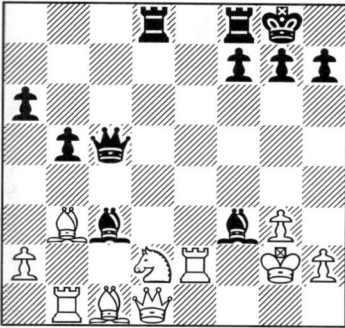

A spectacular sacrifice of a second piece with which Black is trying to force a draw by perpetual check!

22 ♔xf3

Deserving of attention is John Nunn's recommendation of 22 ♘xf3!? ♖xd1 23 ♗xd1 ♕d5 and now White does not play 24 ♗b3? ♕d3 25 ♖c2 ♖e8, when his forces would be tied up, but 24 ♗c2!, when the position is difficult to assess. Although the material is roughly equal, White probably stands better.

22...♖d3+ 23 ♔g2 ♕c6+ 24 ♔g1

Or 24 ♔h3 ♕d7+ with an immediate perpetual check.

24...♗d4+ 25 ♖f2 ♗xf2+ 26 ♔xf2 ♕b6+ 27 ♔f1 ♕f6+ 28 ♔e2?

This is just suicide. White stubbornly continues to play for a win by avoiding the perpetual check, but now he ends up in a lost position.

28...♕f5!

White must have underestimated this strong centralising move, after which he must shed a great deal of material and his position becomes hopeless.

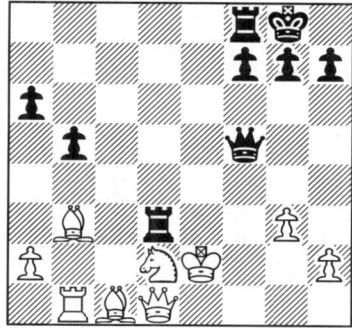

29 ♕h1

The only move that can be made in order to find an escape route for the white king.

29...♖e8+ 30 ♔d1 ♖xd2+ 31 ♔xd2 ♕f2+! 32 ♔c3 ♖c8+ 33 ♔d3

Or 33 ♔b4 ♕c5+ 34 ♔a5 b4+ 35 ♔xa6 ♕d6+ 36 ♔b5 ♖c5+ 37 ♔xb4 ♕d4+ with imminent mate to follow.

33...♖d8+ 34 ♗d5 ♕f5+ 35 ♔e2 ♕xb1 36 ♗d2 ♖e8+ 37 ♔f2 ♕d3! 0-1

Game 43
Fischer-Spassky
Santa Monica 1966

1 e4 e5 2 ♘f3 ♘c6 3 ♗b5 a6 4 ♗a4 ♘f6 5 0-0 ♗e7 6 ♖e1 b5 7 ♗b3 0-0 8 c3 d5 9 exd5 ♘xd5 10 ♘xe5 ♘xe5 11 ♖xe5 c6 12 g3 ♘f6?!

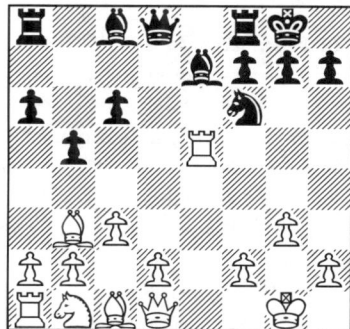

The point of this manoeuvre is to transfer

the knight to the kingside. This, however, appears somewhat slow and is insufficient for Black to obtain full equality.

13 d4 ♗d6 14 ♖e1 ♗g4 15 ♕d3!

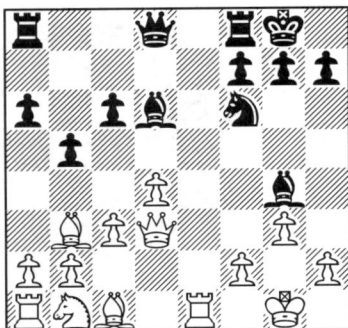

White is not obliged to play the more natural 15 f3, which would have weakened White's kingside and the g3-square in particular. Then Black has the choice between the following:

a) 15...♗f5 16 ♗e3 ♕c7 17 ♗f2 ♖ad8 18 ♘d2 ♖fe8 19 ♘f1 h5 20 ♕d2 ♘d5 21 ♕g5 with a clear advantage to White as in Bauerndistel-Laschek, correspondence 1978.

b) 15...♗h5 16 ♗e3 ♖e8 17 ♘d2 ♕c7 18 ♗f2 c5 19 d5?! ♖xe1+ 20 ♕xe1 ♖e8 21 ♕f1 c4 22 ♗c2 ♘xd5 23 ♕h3 ♗g6 24 ♗xg6 hxg6 25 ♘e4 ♗e7 with equal play, Kremer-Sadowo, correspondence 1976.

c) 15...♗h3! is Black's best reply. 16 ♗g5 ♕c7 17 ♗xf6 gxf6 18 f4 ♗xf4! and now:

c1) 19 ♕h5 ♗xg3 20 ♖e2 ♖fe8 21 ♔h1 ♖xe2 22 ♕xe2 ♗f4 23 ♘d2 f5 with advantage for Black, Yudovich-Zapletal, correspondence 1972-76.

c2) Even worse is the acceptance of the sacrifice with 19 gxf4? ♔h8! (but not the impulsive 19...♕xf4? due to 20 ♕d3! with a double threat to Black's bishop and exchanging the queens via g3, thus repelling Black's attack) 20 ♔h1 ♖g8 21 ♕f3 ♗g2+ 22 ♕xg2 ♖xg2 23 ♔xg2 ♕xf4 with a winning position for Black.

15...c5 16 dxc5

The recommendation of GM Lev Gutman, 16 ♗c2 c4 17 ♕f1 ♕d7 18 f3 ♗h3 19 ♕f2, is quite possible but the text move is more clear-cut. In the ending it will be more difficult for Black to find compensation for the pawn.

16...♗xc5 17 ♕xd8 ♖axd8 18 ♗f4

Even stronger is 18 ♗g5! ♖fe8 19 ♘d2 and Black has absolutely no compensation for the pawn. This variation casts serious doubts over the whole line starting with 12...♘f6?!.

18...h6! 19 ♘a3

White is obliged to place his knight on this awkward square since the more obvious move 19 ♘d2? loses material to 19...g5!.

19...g5 20 ♗e3 ♗xe3 21 ♖xe3 ♖d2 22 ♘c2?!

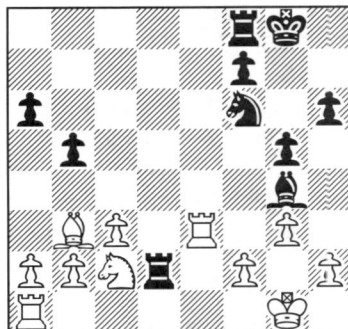

Black has succeeded in getting his rook to the seventh rank, thus largely improving his chances. It is strange that Fischer played this somewhat passive move when he had the chance of gaining the advantage by 22 c4! b4 23 ♘c2 a5 24 ♖e5.

22...♖e8 23 ♖xe8+ ♘xe8 24 ♘e3 ♗f3 25 ♗c2 ♘d6 26 b3 ♔f8

Black's strong rook on d2 is paralysing White's position and thus White's winning attempts are in vain.

27 a4 ♘e4 28 ♗xe4 ♗xe4 29 axb5 axb5 30 b4 ♖b2 31 g4 ♔g7 32 ♔f1 ♔f6 33 ♖a5 ♖b1+ 34 ♔e2 ♖b2+ 35 ♔f1 ½-½

Game 44
Contini-Adinolfi
Correspondence 1998

---

1 e4 e5 2 ♘f3 ♘c6 3 ♗b5 a6 4 ♗a4 ♘f6 5 0-0 ♗e7 6 ♖e1 b5 7 ♗b3 0-0 8 c3 d5 9 exd5 ♘xd5 10 ♘xe5 ♘xe5 11 ♖xe5 c6 12 g3 ♗d6 13 ♖e1 ♖e8

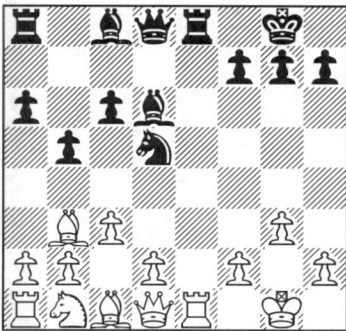

With this move Black goes for the exchange of White's only active piece – the rook on e1. White's other rook, still on a1, will take some time to join in and in the meantime White must defend accurately especially as Black will have control of the e-file.

This line is extremely popular amongst correspondence players.

14 d4

White has other continuations at his disposal:

a) 14 d3 ♖a7!

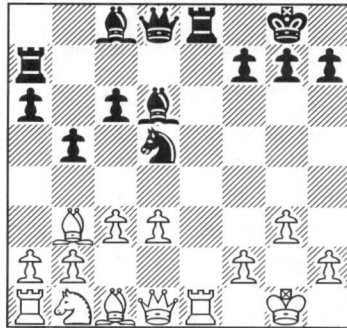

(this rook manoeuvre is important in many lines of the Marshall Gambit – it is the quickest means for Black to get this rook transferred to the e-file) 15 ♘d2 ♗f5 16 ♘e4 ♖ae7 17 ♗c2? ♗c5 18 ♗d2 ♗b6 19 ♔g2 ♕d7 20 f3 ♗h3+ 21 ♔h1 f5 22 ♗b3 fxe4 23 dxe4 ♔h8 24 exd5 ♖xe1+ 25 ♗xe1 ♕f5 26 ♗c2?? (losing) 26...♖xe1+ 27 ♕xe1 ♕xf3 mate (0-1) De Souza-Barbosa, correspondence 1992.

b) 14 a4 and now Black should not go in for 14...♗g4? 15 ♖xe8+ ♕xe8 16 ♕xg4 ♕e1+ 17 ♔g2 ♕xc1 18 ♕d1!, when Black must exchange queens and enter into a poor ending a pawn down since after 18...♕xb2??, 19 ♖a2! White traps the black queen. Instead of 14...♗g4?, Black should play 14...♖xe1+ 15 ♕xe1 ♗f5!, when he will have excellent play for his pieces.

c) White can remove the unpleasant knight by exchanging it with 14 ♗xd5 cxd5 15 d4 ♖xe1+ 16 ♕xe1 and now:

c1) 16...♖a7 17 ♗e3 ♖e7 18 ♘d2 ♗g4 19 ♕f1 ♕d7 20 ♖e1 ♗h3 21 ♕e2 ♗g4 22 ♕f1 ♗h3 23 ♕e2 f5 24 f4 g5?! 25 ♕f2 (even stronger is 25 ♕f3! hitting the pawn on d5) 25...gxf4? (maybe Black had to play 25...g4 but in any case his position is worse) 26 ♗xf4 ♗xf4 27 ♖xe7 ♕xe7 28 gxf4 with clear advantage to White, Kang-Weissieder, correspondence 1991.

c2) Deserving of attention is 16...♗f5!? 17

♗e3 ♕d7 18 ♘d2 ♖e8 19 ♕e2 ♗g4 20 f3
(White avoids a draw by repetition with 20
♕f1 ♗h3 or 20 ♕d3 ♗f5 etc.) 20...♗h3 21
♖e1 h5 with compensation for the sacrificed
pawn.

14...♗g4?

This tempting move backfires and allows
a forced refutation. For 14...♖xe1+ see the
next game.

Another possibility was 14...♖a7!? with the
idea of transferring the rook to e7 as has
been played in a couple of games. I believe
this alternative to be quite playable for Black.

**15 ♖xe8+ ♕xe8 16 ♕xg4! ♕e1+ 17
♔g2 ♕xc1 18 ♕e2 ♘f4+**

Planned when Black played 14...♗g4?, but
it does not work. By now there was no way
back, not even after the variation 18...a5 19
♗xd5 cxd5 20 ♕d2! ♕xd2 21 ♘xd2 a4 22
a3 f5 23 f4 ♔f7 24 ♘f1 ♖e8 25 ♔f3 ♖e4 26
♘e3 (Hellers-J.Howell, New York 1990), or
18...♗e7 19 ♗xd5 cxd5 20 ♕d2 ♕xd2 21
♘xd2 when Black enters a poor ending a
pawn down. This explains the piece sacrifice
in the game.

19 gxf4 ♕xf4 20 ♔f1!

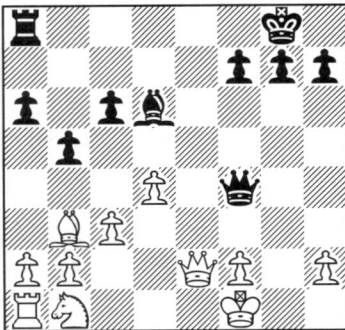

Much stronger than the previously played
20 ♕f3 ♕g5+ 21 ♔f1 ♕c1+ and 20 ♕h5
♕e4+ 21 ♕f3 ♕g6+ 22 ♔h1 ♕h6, when
Black draws by perpetual check.

20...♕c1+ 21 ♗d1! ♗xh2 22 ♕d2 1-0

The ending after 22...♗f4 23 ♕xc1 ♗xc1
24 a4 is technically winning for White.

---

1 e4 e5 2 ♘f3 ♘c6 3 ♗b5 a6 4 ♗a4 ♘f6
5 0-0 ♗e7 6 ♖e1 b5 7 ♗b3 0-0 8 c3 d5
9 exd5 ♘xd5 10 ♘xe5 ♘xe5 11 ♖xe5 c6
12 g3 ♗d6 13 ♖e1 ♖e8 14 d4 ♖xe1+ 15
♕xe1 ♗h3 16 ♕e4

After this Black's initiative is of almost decisive proportions. White had to play 16 ♘d2
♕d7 17 ♘f1 ♖e8 18 ♘e3 ♕f5 19 ♕e2!?
with a complicated struggle ahead where it is
not easy to see how Black can retain his initiative. In the meantime, White has good
chances to consolidate his position.

16...♕d7 17 ♗e3 ♖e8 18 ♕d3 ♗f4!

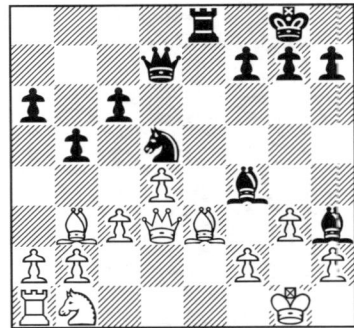

The bishop is taboo since if the g-file is
opened White will get mated after ...♕g4+.

19 ♘d2?

This definitely loses but White's position
was very difficult anyway, It was a big question whether he could have saved the game
because after 19 ♗d2 ♕e6 20 ♘a3 ♗f5
Black wins a piece.

19...♘xe3 20 fxe3 ♖xe3 0-1

---

1 e4 e5 2 ♘f3 ♘c6 3 ♗b5 a6 4 ♗a4 ♘f6

---

5 0-0 &e7 6 &e1 b5 7 &b3 0-0 8 c3 d5 9 exd5 &xd5 10 &xe5 &xe5 11 &xe5 c6 12 &xd5

This is known as the Kevitz Variation of the Marshall Attack.

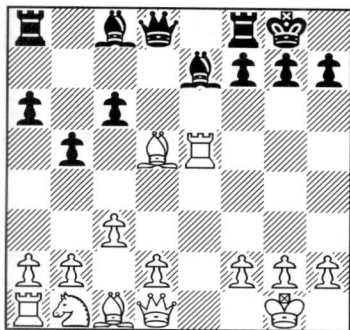

12...cxd5

It is obvious that Black's d5-knight is a powerful piece which controls some important squares (in particular f4). However, it is not clear if White's light-squared 'Spanish' bishop is worth less than Black's knight. One thing is clear: after the exchange White's plan of playing a2-a4 and opening the a-file is not so attractive anymore. Besides, Black does not have to consider an attack against his knight – compare this with lines in which White plays a2-a4, Black takes on a4 and White follows up with c3-c4.

The good side of the exchange on d5 is that White clarifies the situation in the centre. Black has to be careful not to allow White to swap the dark-squared bishops after the manoeuvre &d1-f3 and &c1-f4. In this case he would be left a pawn down with a weak light-squared bishop against the strong knight due to the weakness of the dark squares, e5 in particular. So Black must react actively on the kingside in order to destroy the pawn shelter around White's monarch.

13 d4 &d6 14 &e3

The alternative is 14 &e1 &h4 15 g3 &h3 16 &f3 etc.

14...&h4 15 h3 f5?!

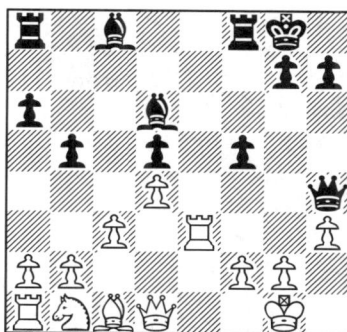

This game will show that from the three main moves at Black's disposal in this position (15...f5?!, 15...&f4 and 15...g5!?), this move is the worst and this has been proven through tournament practice.

As we shall see, 15...&f4 (Games 48-51) is a solid option with the only practical drawback being that when a stronger player plays Black against inferior opposition, he must avoid the drawing continuations and after 15...&f4 there is a possibility for White to repeat moves.

16 &f3!

That White needs his queen on f3 in order to cover White's vulnerable kingside, namely the h3- and g2-squares, could be seen from the following example: 16 &b3? &b7 17 &d2 f4 18 &f3 &h5 19 &e6 &ad8 20 &e1 &c8! 21 &e5. The old game Polyak-Olifer, Kiev 1960 continued logically with 21...&xe5 22 &xe5 (worse is 22 dxe5? &xh3! and there is no way White can defend here) 22...&g6 23 &h2 f3 and now:

a) 24 &g5 &d3! with a dangerous initiative due to White's weakened light squares.

b) 24 g4? &xg4! 25 hxg4 (or 25 &g5 &d6+ with a positionally won game for Black) 25...&xg4 26 &g5 &h4+ 27 &h1 &f5! 28 &xf5 &g4+ 29 &f1 &g2+ 30 &e1 &g1+ 31 &d2 &xf2+ and 32...&e2 mate.

16...&b7 17 &d2

The alternative is the odd-looking but not necessarily bad 17 &a3!?. Although 'the knight on the rim' rule is well known, Black could not prove its drawbacks in Perenyi-Wegner, Balatonbereny 1988: 17...g5 18 ♖e6 g4 19 ♕e2 ♖ad8 20 g3 ♕h5 21 ♗h6 ♖fe8 22 ♖e1 ♗c6 23 hxg4 fxg4 24 ♕d2 ♕f5 25 ♕g5+ ♕xg5 26 ♗xg5 and in the later stages of the game White managed to convert his material advantage into a win.

17...g5 18 ♕e2 g4

Black is trying to improve on the well-known game Hübner-Nunn, Skelleftea (World Cup) 1989, in which Black played 18...f4? allowing the tactic 19 ♘f3 ♕h5 20 ♘xg5!!

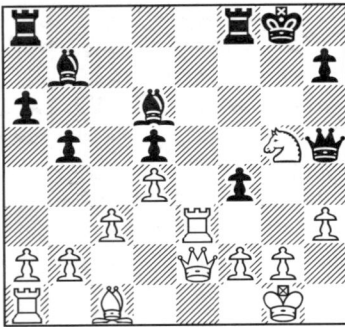

with a winning position for White since after 20...♕xg5, 21 ♖g3! wins Black's queen.

19 ♖e6 ♖ad8 20 ♘f1

This is not bad but even stronger is the nice idea found by Polish grandmaster Marcin Kaminski: 20 g3! ♕xh3 21 ♘e4!!

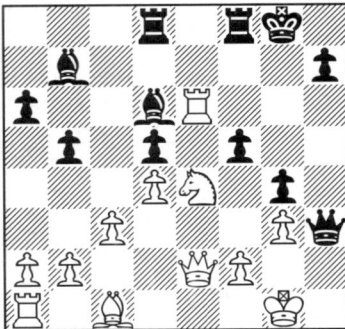

when both 21...dxe4 and 21...fxe4 lose to 22 ♖h6! trapping Black's queen! The game Kaminski-Panczyk, Lubniewice 1989 continued 21...f4 22 ♘xd6 fxg3 23 fxg3 ♖xd6 24 ♗f4! ♖xf4 25 ♖e8+! and Black resigned because after the forced 25...♖f8 26 ♖xf8+ ♔xf8 27 ♖f1+ wins.

20...gxh3 21 ♖h6?!

Surprisingly this natural move lets Black off the hook! 21 g3! ♕g4 22 f3 ♕h5 23 ♗h6 with a clear advantage to White was later found to be more accurate. It is not often that you see White attacking in the Marshall!

21...♕g4 22 ♕e6+ ♔h8 23 ♖xh3 ♗c8 24 ♕h6 ♖f7 25 ♗g5 ♖g7! 26 ♕xg7+

Black's threats along the g-file were about to become deadly so White is practically forced into this exchange.

26...♔xg7 27 ♗xd8 f4 28 ♖e1 ♕g6

From the materialistic point of view, Black is doing quite badly but a closer look into the position reveals that Black's powerful pair of bishops grants him sufficient counterplay.

29 ♖h4 f3 30 g3 h5 31 a3 ♗g4 32 ♘h2 ♕f5 33 ♘xg4 hxg4 34 ♔h2 ♕d7 35 ♗g5

Due to the possible intrusion of Black's queen to h3, White's rook must be idly left on the h-file, which means he doesn't objectively have any winning chances.

35...♕f5 36 ♗d8 ½-½

Game 47
Hübner-Nunn
European Team Ch., Haifa 1989

1 e4 e5 2 ♘f3 ♘c6 3 ♗b5 a6 4 ♗a4 ♘f6 5 0-0 ♗e7 6 ♖e1 b5 7 ♗b3 0-0 8 c3 d5 9 exd5 ♘xd5 10 ♘xe5 ♘xe5 11 ♖xe5 c6 12 ♗xd5 cxd5 13 d4 ♗d6 14 ♖e3 ♕h4 15 h3 g5!?

This sharp continuation is considered to be the main line for Black. The expert on the Marshall Attack, English Grandmaster John Nunn, has adopted it in quite a few games.

The aim of the g-pawn advance is to soften up White's kingside by means of ..g5-g4.

This is an attractive option considering that White's queen usually goes to f3 in order to defend the kingside.

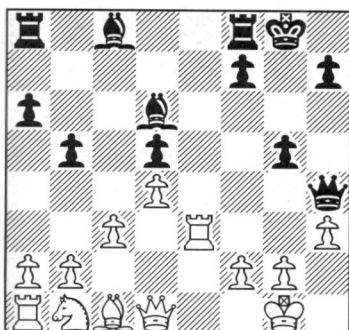

As usual, besides advantages, there are also drawbacks. With the text Black has weakened the f6-square, a reason for White's next logical idea.

16 Wf3 ♗e6 17 Wf6 ♖fe8

The alternatives are weaker:

a) 17...♖ae8? is the usual story of 'wrong rook's move'. It transpires that Black will need rooks on d8 and e8 in order to chase away White's queen as necessary with ...♗d6-e7 and, if Wf6-e5, ...♗e7-d6 with a draw by repetition. The game Hübner-Pinter Budapest 1989 continued 18 ♘a3 (or 18 ♘d2 Wf4! 19 Wxf4 ♗xf4 20 ♖e1 ♗xh3! 21 ♖xe8 ♖xe8 22 ♘f3 – of course not 22 gxh3?? ♖e1+ followed by ...♗xd2 and Black wins – 22...♗xc1 23 ♖xc1 ♗g4 24 ♘xg5 h6 25 ♘h3 ♗xh3 26 gxh3 ♖e2 27 b4 ♖xa2 with a dead draw; Black should know this tactical cheapo because if he doesn't then he is simply a pawn down for nothing) 18...Wh5 19 ♗d2 h6 20 ♘c2 ♗f4 21 ♖d3 We2 22 ♗xf4 gxf4 23 ♘e1 Wxb2 24 ♖ad1 and, due to bad pawn structure and weak dark squares in Black's camp, White's advantage is indisputable.

b) 17...Wh5 is not seen so much nowadays:

b1) An instructive game is Yermakov-Sikov, correspondence 1965/66: 18 ♖e1? h6

19 ♗e3 ♔h7!

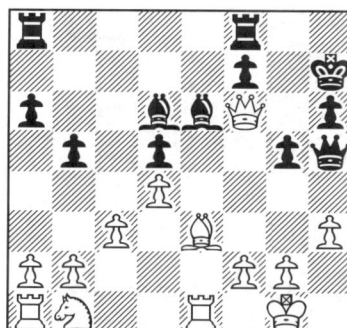

(the Marshall student should remember this king manoeuvre – Black builds up a deadly attack along the g-file by doubling rooks and there is not much that White can do to prevent it – White's queen merely helps Black execute his plan) 20 ♘d2 ♖g8 21 ♘f1 ♖g6 22 Wf3 g4! 23 hxg4 ♖xg4 24 ♘g3 Wg6 25 ♘e2 ♖g8 26 g3 Wh5 27 ♔g2? (a mistake which accelerates defeat) 27...Wh3+!! 0-1.

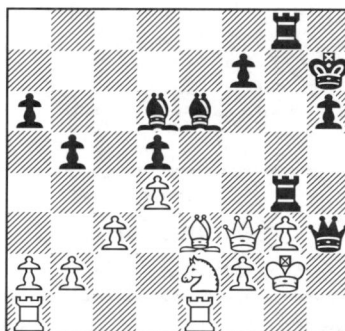

b2) 18 ♘d2 g4 19 ♖xe6! fxe6 20 Wxe6+ Wf7 21 ♖xd6 Wxf2+ 22 ♔h2 ♖ae8 23 Wg3. We are now following the analysis of the late World Champion Mikhail Tal, who assessed the position as slightly better for White. The game Kuhnikanno-Matthe, correspondence 1984 continued 23...♖e1 24 Wxg4+ ♔h8 25 ♘f3 ♖g8 and in this position White should have played 26 ♗g5! ♖xg5 27 Wxg5 ♖xa1 28 Wxd5 with advantage because White's king is safe whilst on the contrary Black's naked king will bring him lots of headaches. The material, an exchange for two pawns, is roughly balanced.

18 ♘a3

Galkin-Jenni, Yerevan 1999 saw 18 ♘d2 ♗e7? 19 ♕e5 h6 20 g4! ♖ad8 21 ♕h2 ♗xg4 (there was no good defence against ♘d2-f3 trapping the black queen) 22 hxg4 ♕xg4+ 23 ♕g2 ♕d1+ 24 ♘f1 g4 25 ♖xe7 ♖xe7 26 ♗xh6 1-0.

18...♕h5 19 ♗d2 ♗e7 20 ♕f3

An extremely complicated struggle arose in Wolff-Hellers, New York 1990 after 20 ♕e5!? ♖ad8 21 f4 ♕g6 22 fxg5 ♗f5 23 ♕g3 ♗e4 24 ♖f1 ♗d6 25 ♕h4 ♗e6 26 ♖e2 ♖de8 27 ♖fe1 f6!?. Black enjoys adequate compensation due to White's inactive knight on a3 – the game later ended in a draw.

20...♕g6 21 ♖ae1 g4 22 ♕g3 gxh3 23 gxh3 ♗d6! 24 ♕xg6+ hxg6 25 ♘c2 ♔g7 26 ♘b4 ♗xb4 27 cxb4 ♖h8

Black is threatening to double rooks on the h-file to pick up the h3-pawn. If anyone is better in the endgame then it is Black, but the opposite-coloured bishops guarantee a peaceful end.

28 ♖c1 ♗xh3 29 ♖c7 ♖ac8 30 ♖xc8 ½-½

Game 48
Gufeld-Blatny
Honolulu 1996

---

1 e4 e5 2 ♘f3 ♘c6 3 ♗b5 a6 4 ♗a4 ♘f6 5 0-0 ♗e7 6 ♖e1 b5 7 ♗b3 0-0 8 c3 d5 9 exd5 ♘xd5 10 ♘xe5 ♘xe5 11 ♖xe5 c6 12 ♗xd5 cxd5 13 d4 ♗d6 14 ♖e3 ♕h4 15 h3 ♕f4 16 ♖e5

The old analysis of the great Estonian grandmaster Paul Keres reminds us that 16 ♖g3?! is weaker due to 16...♕f6! 17 ♖f3 ♕h4 18 ♕d3 ♗g4! with a strong initiative for Black.

16...♕f6 17 ♖e3 ♕f4 18 ♖e5 ♕f6 19 ♖e3 ♕g6!?

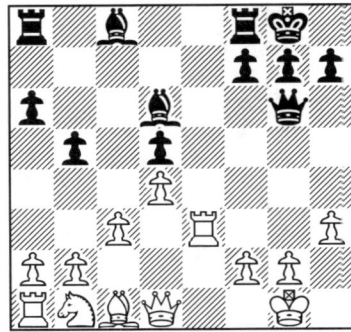

The problem of modern day tournament chess of how to avoid a draw when the stronger player has the black pieces also applies to the Marshall Attack. Black could have taken the draw with 19...♕f4 but he decides to play for the win.

20 ♘d2 f5 21 ♕f3 f4!? 22 ♖e1

A wise choice – White rejects the option of swallowing up the hot pawn by 22 ♕xd5+ ♔h8, which would merely help Black opening the a8-g2 diagonal for his light-squared bishop. The g2-square would clearly have become vulnerable.

22...♔h8 23 ♘b3 ♗f5 24 ♗d2 h5!

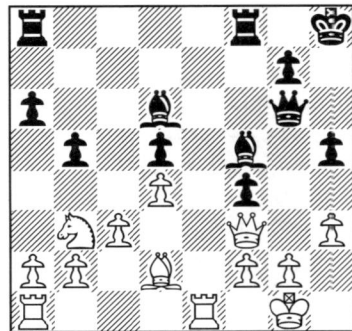

Preparing ...♗f5-e4 which, played immediately, would have led to nothing after 25 ♕g4.

25 ♕xd5 ♗xh3 26 ♕f3 ♗g4 27 ♕e4 ♗f5 28 ♕f3 ♖ad8

Perhaps a wiser choice would have been

to settle for a draw by 28...♗g4 instead?

29 ♘a5 ♗c8 30 ♘c6 ♗b7 31 d5 ♗xc6 32 dxc6 ♗c7 33 ♖ad1 ♖d3 34 ♕e4 ♕xe4 35 ♖xe4 ♖f6

On 35...♖fd8?!, White has the strong reply 36 ♖e7!.

36 ♖d4 ♖d6 37 ♖xd3 ♖xd3 38 ♔f1 ♖d6 39 ♔e2 ♖xc6 40 ♗c1

Deserving of attention is 40 ♖h1!? g6 41 ♖h3 in order to prevent the advance of Black's kingside pawn majority.

40...♖e6+ 41 ♔d3 ♖d6+ 42 ♔e2 ♖xd1 43 ♔xd1 ♔h7 44 ♔e2 ♔g6 45 b3 ♔f5 46 c4 bxc4 47 bxc4 g5

The ending should be drawn but White was getting short of time.

48 ♗a3 ♔e4 49 ♗c5 ♔e5 50 f3 g4 51 ♗f2 ♗a5 52 ♔d3 ♔f5 53 c5 ♔e5 54 ♔c4 gxf3 55 gxf3 ♗d8 56 c6 ♔d6 57 ♔d4 ♔xc6 58 ♔e4 ♔b5

Or 58...h4 59 ♗g1! (avoiding the trap 59 ♔xf4? h3 60 ♔g3 ♗h4+! 61 ♔xh4 h2 and Black wins) 59...h3 60 ♗h2 ♗c7 61 ♔f5 ♔b5 62 ♔g4 ♔a4 63 ♔xh3 ♔a3 64 ♔g4 ♔xa2 65 ♗xf4 ♗xf4 66 ♔xf4 a5 67 ♔g5 a4 68 f4 a3 69 f5 drawing.

59 ♔xf4 ♔b4 60 ♔g3 ♔a3 61 f4 ♔xa2 62 f5 ♔b3 63 ♔h3 ♔c4 64 ♗h4 ♗c7 65 f6 ♔d5 66 ♗e1 ♗d8 67 ♔h4 ♗xf6+ 68 ♔xh5 ♔c4 69 ♗a5 ♗c3 70 ♗d8 ♔b5 71 ♔g4 ♗a5 72 ♗f6 ♗b6 73 ♗c3 ♔c4 74 ♗e1 ♗c5 75 ♔f3??

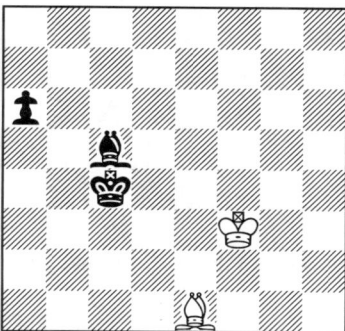

A fatal mistake letting Black's a-pawn pro-

promote. The bookish draw was hidden in 75 ♗a5! ♔b5 76 ♗d8 ♗b6 77 ♗xb6 ♔xb6 78 ♔f3 a5 (or 78...♔b5 79 ♔e2 ♔b4 80 ♔d2 ♔b3 81 ♔c1) 79 ♔e2 a4 80 ♔d2 a3 81 ♔c2.

75...♗b4 76 ♗h4 a5 77 ♔e2 ♔b3 78 ♔d1 ♔b2! 79 ♗f6+ ♔b1 80 ♔e2 ♔c2 0-1

Game 49
J.Polgar-Z.Almasi
Groningen 1997

---

1 e4 e5 2 ♘f3 ♘c6 3 ♗b5 a6 4 ♗a4 ♘f6 5 0-0 ♗e7 6 ♖e1 b5 7 ♗b3 0-0 8 c3 d5 9 exd5 ♘xd5 10 ♘xe5 ♘xe5 11 ♖xe5 c6 12 ♗xd5 cxd5 13 d4 ♗d6 14 ♖e3 ♕h4 15 h3 ♕f4 16 ♖e5 ♕f6 17 ♖e1 ♕g6 18 ♕f3 ♗e6

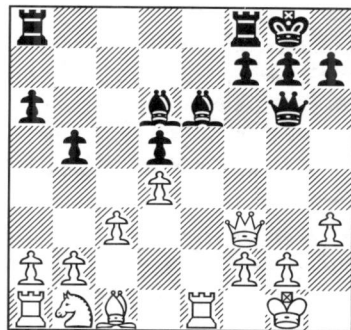

Since the match Tal-Spassky, Tbilisi 1965, in which the former World Champion Boris Spassky adopted the Marshall Attack in order to blunt Tal's play with the white pieces, this move has been considered the best for Black. Still, from time to time we see Black developing his light-squared bishop on other squares. For example:

a) 18...♗d7 is played with the idea of keeping the e-file open for active operations. At the same time the move contains a trap: 19 ♕xd5? ♗c6! 20 ♕g5 (forced because 20 ♕xc6?? ♗h2+ wins the queen) 20...♖ae8 21 ♖d1 ♕e4 22 f3 (22 ♘d2 ♕e2 23 ♖f1 ♖e6 with the idea of following up with ...♖g6 is certainly no improvement for White) 22...♕e2 23 ♕d2 ♗xf3! 24 ♕xe2 (forced because 24 gxf3? ♗h2+! 25 ♔h1 ♕xf3+ 26 ♔xh2 ♖e2+ wins immediately for Black) 24...♗xe2 25 ♖d2 ♗g3 26 ♘a3 ♗e1 27 ♖c2 ♗d3 is an amusing winning line for Black.

After 18...♗d7, A.Sokolov-Geller, New York 1990 continued 19 ♗e3 ♖ae8 20 ♘d2 h5 21 ♔h1 ♗b8 22 ♗f4 ♕c2 23 ♗xb8 ♕xd2 (or 23...♖xe1+ 24 ♖xe1 ♕xd2 25 ♖e7 and White is again on top) and now White missed the strong reply 24 ♖ed1! with a big advantage because if 24...♕xb2?, 25 ♗d6 wins the exchange.

b) 18...♗f5 19 ♗e3 ♖ae8 20 ♘d2 ♖e4?! is an ambitious try which, however, backfired after 21 a4 ♗b8 22 axb5 axb5 23 ♘xe4 dxe4 24 ♕e2 ♗xh3 25 f4! repelled Black's attack in J.Howell-M.Heidenfeld, Groningen 1989.

19 ♗e3

Equal is 19 ♗f4 ♗xf4 20 ♕xf4 ♗xh3 21 ♕g3 ♕c2! (stronger than going for the ending after 21...♕xg3, which is better for White) 22 c4! ♗e6 23 cxd5 ♗xd5 24 ♘c3 ♖ad8 25 ♖e2 ♕g6 26 ♕xg6 hxg6, Kholmov-Tal, Kislovodsk 1966.

Judit decides to play for the win by keeping her extra pawn, although Black will have adequate compensation due to his strong pair of bishops.

19...♖ac8!

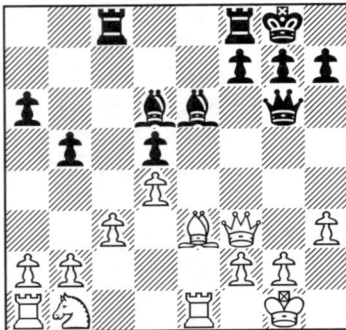

Since Black has developed his bishop on e6 there is nothing for the black rook to do

on the e-file any more. Black now creates active play along the c-file.

20 ♘d2 b4 21 cxb4 ♗xb4 22 a3 ♗d6 23 ♖ac1 ♖c2 24 b4 ♖xc1 25 ♖xc1 ♕d3

Attacking White's weakened a-pawn, thus keeping the game balanced.

26 ♖c6 ♗b8 27 a4 ♗d7?

After this error White will get her b-pawn moving, possibly as far as b7, which will give Black a headache. Stronger was 27...♕a3 28 ♖xa6 ♕b4! with an imminent draw.

28 ♖c1! ♕a3 29 ♖b1 ♗e6 30 b5 ♕xa4 31 b6 ♕a3 32 b7 h6 33 h4

I prefer 33 ♘b3! ♕a2 34 ♕d1 ♗f5 35 ♖a1 ♕b2 36 ♘c5.

33...♕e7 34 ♗f4?

Why give up the h-pawn? Better was 34 g3 and if 34...♕d7 35 ♗f4 ♗g4 36 ♕e3 ♖e8, White has 37 ♗xb8! ♖xe3 38 fxe3 and the b7-pawn decides the game.

34...♕xh4 35 ♗xb8 ♖xb8 36 ♕d3 ♕f4 37 ♕c3 ♔h7 38 ♖b6 a5 39 g3 ♕g4 40 ♘f3 ♗f5

Due to her kingside weaknesses it is now White who is fighting for survival.

41 ♘e5 ♕d1+ 42 ♔g2 f6 43 ♘c6 ♗e4+ 44 f3 ♕e2+ 45 ♔g1 ♗xf3 46 ♖b2 ♕d1+ 47 ♔f2 ♖xb7!

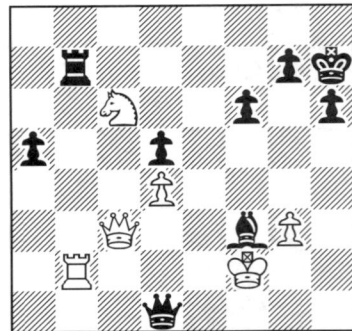

The b7-pawn drops and White is lost.

48 ♖d2

The rook is taboo – 48 ♖xb7? ♕e2+ 49 ♔g1 ♕g2 mate.

48...♖b3 0-1

Game 50
Van der Wiel-Nunn
Amsterdam 1990

1 e4 e5 2 ♘f3 ♘c6 3 ♗b5 a6 4 ♗a4 ♘f6 5 0-0 ♗e7 6 ♖e1 b5 7 ♗b3 0-0 8 c3 d5 9 exd5 ♘xd5 10 ♘xe5 ♘xe5 11 ♖xe5 c6 12 ♗xd5 cxd5 13 d4 ♗d6 14 ♖e3 ♕h4 15 h3 ♕f4 16 ♖e5 ♕f6 17 ♖e1 ♕g6 18 ♔h1 ♗f5

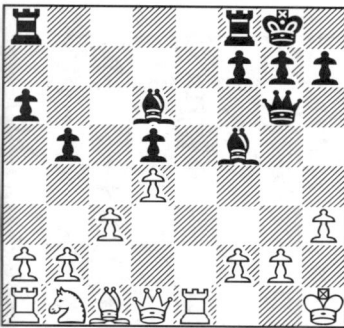

As we shall see, the only difference between this move and 18...♗d7 is that in some lines it will be useful for Black to include ...♗f5-c2. Generally it is considered nowadays that this line leads to a draw, with White having no chance whatsoever to extract even the slightest opening advantage.

19 ♗e3

Awkward for White is 19 ♘d2?! ♖ae8 20 ♘f3 ♗c2! 21 ♕d2 ♗e4 and if 22 ♘h4? ♕f6! White is suddenly in trouble.

19...♗c2

An alternative is 19...♗e4 20 ♕g4 ♕xg4 21 hxg4 f5! 22 gxf5 ♖xf5. Now, instead of the correct 23 ♘d2 leading to a draw by perpetual check after 23...♖h5+ 24 ♔g1 ♗h2+ etc., in the game Tempestini-Tinture, correspondence 1991 White chose the weaker 23 f3? ♗g3! 24 ♖f1 (after 24 fxe4 Black has 24...♖h5+! winning) 24...♖e8 25 ♗f2 ♗d3 26 ♗xg3 ♖xf1 27 ♘d2 ♗xg2+! and White was forced to resign.

20 ♕g4

After 20 ♕f3?! the surprising 20...f5! 21 ♕xd5+ ♔h8, with the nasty threat ...♗c2-e4, is very strong for Black.

20...♕xg4 21 hxg4 f5!

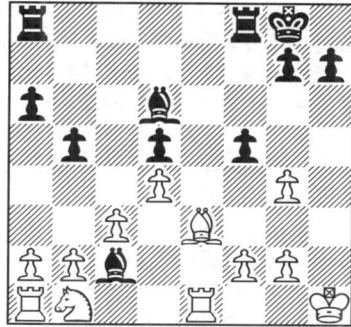

Despite the exchange of queens, White's king is not completely safe on h1.

22 gxf5 ♖xf5 23 ♔g1

White can try to avoid perpetual check with 23 g4, which looks slightly risky. The game Wendehals-Stock, correspondence 1993 continued 23...♖f3 24 ♘d2 ♖h3+ 25 ♔g2 ♖h2+ 26 ♔g1 ♖f8 27 b3 ♖h4 28 f3 ♖h3 29 a4 ♖g3+ 30 ♔h1 ♖h3+ 31 ♔g1 ♖g3+ ½-½.

23...♖h5 24 ♘d2

Only Black will have winning chances after the weakening move 24 f3? ♗g3 etc.

24...♗h2+ 25 ♔h1 ♗b8+

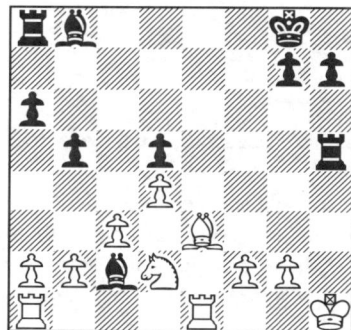

26 ♔g1 ♗h2+ 27 ♔h1 ½-½

Game 51
Abdelnnabi-A.Kuzmin
Dubai 2000

1 e4 e5 2 ♘f3 ♘c6 3 ♗b5 a6 4 ♗a4 ♘f6
5 0-0 ♗e7 6 ♖e1 b5 7 ♗b3 0-0 8 c3 d5
9 exd5 ♘xd5 10 ♘xe5 ♘xe5 11 ♖xe5 c6
12 ♗xd5 cxd5 13 d4 ♗d6 14 ♖e3 ♕h4
15 h3 ♕f4 16 ♖e5 ♕f6 17 ♖e1 ♕g6 18
♔h1 ♗d7

This seemingly modest move has the following ideas behind it:

1) Black leaves the e-file open along which the black rook(s) will be able to exert strong pressure, reckoning that White will develop his dark-squared bishop on e3.

2) Black retains the option of playing ...f7-f5, which is naturally out of the question with the bishop on f5.

19 ♗e3 f5

Worthy of attention is 19...♖ae8 20 ♘d2 ♖e6!? 21 ♘f1 ♖fe8 22 ♕d2 f5 23 f4 ♖8e7! 24 ♕f2 ♕e8 with very active play for Black, Viaud-Slavchev, correspondence 1991.

20 f4 ♖ae8 21 ♘d2 ♖xe3!?

An incredible exchange sacrifice based purely on positional grounds. In return, Black's pair of bishops will control a lot of important squares. Also his light-squared bishop comes to life after ...f5-f4. It is difficult to tell whether the sacrifice is 100 percent sound but in a tournament game it has great practical value.

22 ♖xe3 ♗xf4 23 ♖e2 ♗g3 24 ♘f3

Passive is 24 ♘f1?! ♗d6 followed by ...f5-f4.

24...♕h6

Keeping an eye on the potentially vulnerable h3-pawn, where Black can sacrifice a piece.

25 ♖e7 ♕d6 26 ♕e2 h6 27 ♖e1!

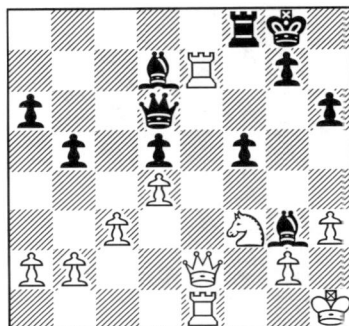

Although White has managed to invade the black camp with his rook, there is no real target to be attacked since Black's pair of bishops (especially the one on g3) is very strong. Hence it is understandable for White to give back the exchange to reduce Black's pressure. From now on Black will have to watch out for his weakened dark squares.

27...♗xe1 28 ♕xe1 f4 29 ♕e5 ♕xe5 30 ♖xe5

Or 30 ♘xe5 ♗f5 31 ♖a7 ♖f6 32 ♖a8+ ♔h7 33 ♖d8 ♗e4 34 ♘d7 and despite the initial reaction that Black is in trouble, he has the cold-blooded 34...♖f7 35 ♘f8+ ♔g8 when the discovered check doesn't give White more than a draw.

30...♖f5 31 ♖e7 ♖f7 32 ♖e5 ♖f5 33 ♖e7 ♖f7 34 ♖e5 ½-½

Summary

Ljubojevic's overoptimistic play, starting with 19 ♖e6?!, led to his demise in Game 39. However, after best play, starting with 19 ♖e1 etc., all White can hope for is a draw. After 16 a4 (Game 40) both 16...♗d3 and 16...♖ae8!? grant Black sufficient counterplay but I prefer 16...♖ae8!?. One must take into consideration that two white pieces from the queenside (the a1-rook and the c1-bishop) do not participate in the fight.

In the encounters with 12 g3, Game 42 should have ended in a draw; White only loses after overestimating his position. Transferring the knight to the kingside by 12...♘f6?! (Game 43) is too slow and leaves White with an indisputable edge. The final option, 12...♗d6, grants him sufficient compensation for the pawn if he exchanges on e1 on move fourteen (Game 45). On the contrary, Black should avoid embarking on the combination which contains a hole with 14...♗g4?, as illustrated in Game 44.

15...f5?! (Game 46) is clearly Black's worst choice of the three possible moves. However, the viable option 15...g5!? (Game 47), despite looking dubious at first glance, leads to enough counterplay for Black, who can hope to play...g5-g4 at a later stage.

In Game 48 one should remember the importance of Blatny's 24...h5!, the main aim of which is to prevent White playing the ♕f3-g4 manoeuvre to trade queens. After this strong move Black achieves sufficient counterplay.

In Game 49 Almasi plays actively with 19...♖ac8! followed by ...b5-b4, looking for counterplay along the c-file which is unusual in the Marshall Gambit – normally Black is more interested in the e-file. Still, the position is kept in the balance and any mistake proves costly. Indeed, the game saw the advantage switching back and forth.

In the last two games, both 18...♗f5 and 18...♗d7 grant Black equality due to activity along the e-file.

1 e4 e5 2 ♘f3 ♘c6 3 ♗b5 a6 4 ♗a4 ♘f6 5 0-0 ♗e7 6 ♖e1 b5 7 ♗b3 0-0 8 c3 d5 9 exd5 ♘xd5 10 ♘xe5 ♘xe5 11 ♖xe5 c6 12 ♗xd5

> 12 g3
>> 12...♘f6 – *Game 43*
>> 12...♗f6 13 ♖e1 c5 14 d4 ♗b7 15 dxc5
>>> 15...♖e8 – *Game 41*; 15...♕d7 – *Game 42*
>> 12...♗d6 13 ♖e1 ♖e8 14 d4
>>> 14...♗g4 – *Game 44*; 14...♖xe1+ – *Game 45*
> 12 d4 ♗d6 13 ♖e2
>> 13...♗g4 – *Game 38*
>> 13...♕h4 14 g3 ♕h3 15 ♘d2 ♗f5
>>> 16 ♗c2 – *Game 39*; 16 a4 – *Game 40*

12...cxd5 13 d4 ♗d6 14 ♖e3 ♕h4 15 h3 ♕f4

> 15...g5!? – *Game 47*; 15...f5?! – *Game 46*

16 ♖e5 ♕f6 17 ♖e1

> 17 ♖e3 – *Game 48*

17...♕g6 18 ♔h1

> 18 ♕f3 – *Game 49*

18...♗f5 – *Game 50*

> 18...♗d7 – *Game 51*

CHAPTER FIVE

Alternatives to the Main Line 11...c6

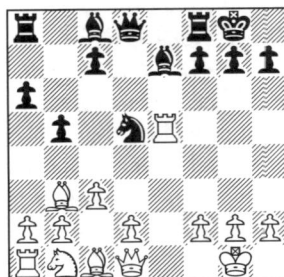

1 e4 e5 2 ♘f3 ♘c6 3 ♗b5 a6 4 ♗a4 ♘f6 5 0-0 ♗e7 6 ♖e1 b5 7 ♗b3 0-0 8 c3 d5 9 exd5 ♘xd5 10 ♘xe5 ♘xe5 11 ♖xe5

In this chapter we look at less common alternatives for Black on move eleven: 11...♘f4?!, 11...♘b6?!, 11...♗b7 and 11...♘f6. Playing these moves has the advantage of not having to learn the reams of theory that accompany the main move 11...c6.

In Games 52-53 Black chooses the very rare 11...♘f4?! and 11...♘b6?!. On the contrary, the move 11...♗b7 (Games 54-59) is played far more and is in fact becoming a serious alternative to the main move 11...c6.

In Games 54-55 we see the positional treatment starting with 12 ♕f3, when White must choose between 13 ♖xd5? and 13 ♗xd5.

Games 56-59 deal with 12 d4, which is the most frequently played move by White. The old continuation is 12...♕d7?! (Games 56-57), with the idea of quickly connecting the heavy pieces and starting action along the e-file or on the kingside. In Games 58-59 Black plays 12...♗f6, with which he abandons the idea of a kingside attack and intends to seek compensation for the sacrificed pawn using other factors such as having a bishop on f6 exerting strong pressure along the long diagonal. Also, moves like ...c7-c5 and ...b5-b4

often come in handy. In short, Black reckons on quick development and active piece play.

Games 60-62 deal with 11...♘f6, which was preferred by Frank Marshall in his historic encounter with Capablanca, the debut of the Marshall gambit. With 11...♘f6 Black, without hesitation, starts a kingside attack and aims for the ...♘f6-g4 manoeuvre.

Games 61 and 62 are very instructive. Black follows the long forcing line 12 d4 ♗d6 13 ♖e1 ♘g4 14 h3 ♕h4 15 ♕f3 ♘xf2 16 ♖e2 ♗g4 17 hxg4 ♗g3 18 ♖xf2 ♕h2+ 19 ♔f1 ♕h1+ 20 ♔e2 and tries to improve upon the stem game Capablanca-Marshall.

Game 52
Comp. Zugzwang-Wehmeier
Lippstadt 1993

---

1 e4 e5 2 ♘f3 ♘c6 3 ♗b5 a6 4 ♗a4 ♘f6 5 0-0 ♗e7 6 ♖e1 b5 7 ♗b3 0-0 8 c3 d5 9 exd5 ♘xd5 10 ♘xe5 ♘xe5 11 ♖xe5 ♘f4?!

This rare continuation can still be seen in correspondence games (the Swedish player Jan Lind often uses it) and it can also be used as a surprise weapon. However, theory, not without good reason, considers this move inferior to the standard 11...c6 because Black loses time in transferring his knight to g6 which in turn gives White time to catch up with the development of his queenside.

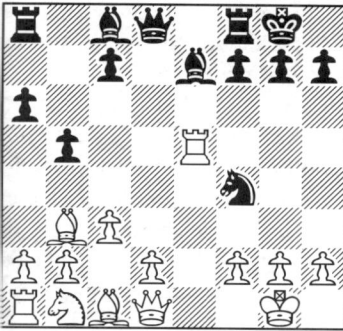

12 d4

Weaker is 12 ♕f3 ♗d6! 13 d4 (13 ♕xf4? ♗xe5 14 ♕xe5? ♖e8! etc. wins for Black) 13...♗xe5 14 dxe5 ♘d3 15 ♕xa8 ♘xc1 etc.

12...♘g6 13 ♖h5

On h5 the white rook seems to be somewhat awkwardly placed so it is not entirely clear whether this move or 13 ♖e1 is better. I would say that it might simply be a matter of taste and that both moves are of equal strength.

Let us see some examples with 13 ♖e1 ♗b7:

a) 14 ♗e3 ♔h8 15 ♘d2 f5 16 f3 ♘h4?! (this is suspicious; better is 16...♗d6!?) 17 a4 ♕d6 18 axb5 ♕g6 19 g3 ♗d6 20 f4 ♖ae8 21 bxa6 ♗a8 22 d5 ♖xe3 23 ♖xe3 ♗c5 24 ♘c4 ♖e8 25 ♔f2 ♕h6 26 ♕d3 ♘g6 27 ♔g2

♗xe3 28 ♘xe3 ♘xf4+ 29 gxf4 ♕b6 and Black has managed to regain some of the sacrificed material but White's chances are still preferable, Hermansson-Lind, correspondence 1996.

b) 14 ♘d2 with a further split:

b1) 14...♘h4 15 ♘e4 ♔h8 16 f3 ♕d7 17 ♗f4 ♖ae8 18 a4 f5 19 ♘g5 ♗xg5 20 ♗xg5 ♗xf3?! (Black had absolutely no compensation at all for the pawn so he tries this desperate move that surprisingly wins, thanks to his generous opponent) 21 ♖xe8 ♕xe8 and now in Zolotonos-Barenboim, USSR 1968 White could have punished his opponent with 22 gxf3 ♕g6 23 f4 h6 24 axb5 axb5 25 ♖a6! ♕xa6 26 ♗xh4, when the two bishops clearly outweigh the black rook. Instead he played the weaker 22 ♕e1? ♘xg2 23 ♕xe8 ♖xe8 24 axb5, overlooking 24...h6! 25 ♗d2 axb5 26 ♔f2 ♘h4 27 ♗e3 g5 after which Black later managed to convert his extra pawn into a win.

b2) 14...c5 15 ♘f3 c4 16 ♗c2 f5 17 ♘e5 (or 17 ♕e2 ♔h8 18 ♘e5 ♘xe5 19 dxe5 ♕d5 20 f3 ♗c5+ 21 ♔h1 ♖ae8 22 ♗f4 ♕f7 23 ♖ad1 ♖e6 24 b3 ♕h5 25 bxc4 g5 26 ♗g3 f4 27 ♖d7 – 27 ♗f2 ♖h6 28 h3 ♗xf3! 29 ♕xf3 ♕xf3 30 gxf3 ♗xf2 is good for Black – 27...fxg3 – weaker is 27...♖h6? 28 ♖xb7 fxg3 29 h3 etc. – 28 ♖xh7+ ♕xh7 29 ♗xh7 ♖h6 30 h3 ♖xh3+!? 31 gxh3 ♗xf3+ 32 ♕xf3 ♖xf3 33 ♗e4 ♖xc3 34 cxb5 axb5 35 ♔g2 ♔g7 36 ♖e2 ♔f8 and the ending in Jonsson-Lind, Sollentuna 1995 was later drawn) 17...♕d5 18 f3 ♘xe5 19 dxe5 (even stronger is 19 ♖xe5!, not weakening the a7-g1 diagonal, after which Black has no compensation for the sacrificed pawn) 19...♕e6 (the old analysis of the late former World Champion Mikhail Tal's runs 19...♗c5+ 20 ♔h1 f4! 21 b3 ♕xd1 22 ♗xd1 ♗c6 and Black is okay – food for thought) 20 ♕e2 g5 21 ♗e3 h5 22 ♕f2 ♖f7 23 ♗c5 with clear advantage for White in Kondali-Dalko, correspondence 1972. Obviously Black's play was not great, but even after better play I don't think he should have enough for the pawn.

13...♗b7

13...♗d7!? had success in Gromer-Van den Bosch, Hamburg Olympiad 1930 after 14 ♗e3 ♘h4 15 ♗f4 ♕c8 16 ♕e2? ♘g6 17 ♕e4 ♗g4 18 ♖e5 ♘xe5 19 dxe5 ♕f5 etc. However, instead of the poor 16 ♕e2?, much stronger is 16 ♕d3! ♘g6 17 ♗g5 ♗d6 18 h3 with some advantage to White.

14 ♕g4!?

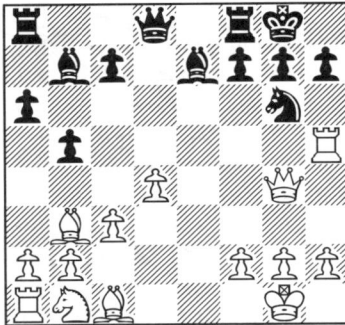

This is an improvement over 14 ♕d3 and now:

a) 14...♖e8?! 15 ♗e3 c5 16 ♕f5 c4 17 ♗c2 ♕c7 18 ♘d2 ♖ad8 19 ♕h3 h6 20 ♗xg6! (wrong is 20 ♗xh6? gxh6 21 ♗xg6 fxg6 22 ♖xh6 ♗f6 23 ♖xg6+ ♗g7 24 ♘f3 ♕f7 25 ♖g3 ♖e2, which ended up in Black's favour in Kurtesch-Balogh, correspondence 1966) 20...fxg6 21 ♕e6+ ♔h7 22 ♖xh6+!

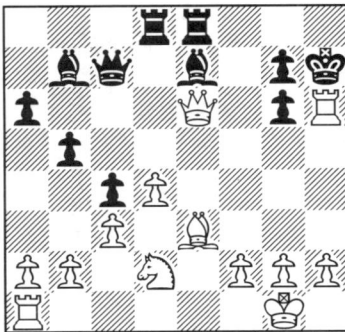

22...gxh6 23 ♕f7+ ♔h8 24 d5! with a de-

cisive advantage for White in the game Kuhnert-Holzvoight, correspondence 1983/84. After the forced 24...♗d6 25 ♗d4+ ♖e5 26 ♕xg6 ♕g7 (also forced) 27 ♕xg7+ ♔xg7 28 f4 White regains all the sacrificed material with interest.

b) Better is 14...c5!? 15 ♗c2 cxd4 16 cxd4 ♖e8 17 ♗e3 ♕d6! 18 ♘c3 ♗f6 19 ♗b3 ♖ad8 and Black has some compensation due to his active pieces. After 20 ♖d1 there follows 20...♗xd4! with complications because Black's bishop is taboo due to White's weak back rank and there is no obvious way White can make use of the pin on the d-file.

14...♕d6 15 ♗e3 ♖ae8 16 ♘d2 ♗c8 17 ♕f3 ♕d7

After 17...♘h4 White has the strong reply 18 ♕e4! etc.

18 a4 ♘h4 19 ♕e4

Also possible is 19 ♕e2!?.

19...♘f5 20 ♘f3 g6 21 ♘e5 ♕d6 22 ♗xf7+!?

This leads to both a positional and material advantage for White, although the weaker 22 ♖h3 is also adequate.

22...♖xf7 23 ♘xf7 ♔xf7 24 ♖xh7+ ♔g8 25 ♖h3 ♕f6 26 ♕d5+?!

Even stronger was 26 ♗f4! etc.

26...♗e6 27 ♕c6 ♖f8 28 d5 ♗c8 29 ♕xf6 ♗xf6 30 axb5 axb5 31 ♗c5 ♖e8 32 ♖d3 ♗b7 33 f3 ♖a8 34 ♖xa8+ ♗xa8 35 b3 ♗b7 36 ♔f2 ♔f7 37 ♔e2 ♔e8 38 ♗b4 ♗d7 39 ♖d1 ♗e5 40 g3 ♗d6 41 ♗xd6 ♔xd6 42 g4 ♘e7 43 h4 ♔e5 44 d6?

An unexplicable blunder of pawn. Perhaps the computer was getting tired! With the simple 44 c4! a win for White would have been just a matter of time.

44...cxd6 45 ♖e1 ♔f6 46 ♔d3 ♘c6 47 f4 ♗c8 48 ♖g1 ♘a5 49 b4 ♘c6 50 ♔e4 ♘e7 51 h5 ♗b7+ 52 ♔d3?!

More active was 52 ♔d4!, which still retains some winning chances.

52...gxh5 53 gxh5 ♘f5

Stronger was 53...♘d5! with an easy draw.

54 ♖g6+ ♔f7 55 ♖g5 ♔f6 56 c4 bxc4+ 57 ♔xc4 ♗e4 58 b5 d5+ 59 ♔b4 d4 60 ♖g6+ ♔f7 61 ♖a6 ♔g7 62 b6 ♘e3 63 ♖a7+ ♔h6 64 ♖d7

White cannot win after 64 b7 ♗xb7 65 ♖xb7 ♘d5+ followed by ...♘d5xf4 etc.

64...♔xh5 65 ♔c5 ♘f5 66 ♖xd4 ♘xd4 67 ♔xd4 ♗b7 68 f5 ½-½

Game 53
Olivier-Montavon
Geneva 1997

---

1 e4 e5 2 ♘f3 ♘c6 3 ♗b5 a6 4 ♗a4 ♘f6 5 0-0 ♗e7 6 ♖e1 b5 7 ♗b3 0-0 8 c3 d5 9 exd5 ♘xd5 10 ♘xe5 ♘xe5 11 ♖xe5 ♘b6?!

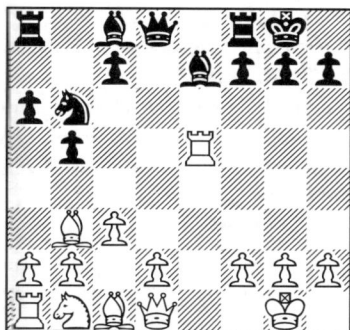

From time to time we come across this rarely seen move. With the text Black keeps the a8-h1 diagonal open. However, bearing in mind that Black removes his knight to the queenside, he can hardly expect to justify his pawn sacrifice. I am sure that Frank Marshall would not have been happy with 11...♘b6. It is mainly used as a surprise weapon but has poor results in competitive play.

12 d4 ♗d6 13 ♗g5

White tries to prevent Black from playing ...♕d8-h4. However, this move is not compulsory and the following alternatives are possible as well:

a) 13 ♖e1 ♕h4 14 g3 ♕h3 15 ♕f3!? ♗g4 16 ♕g2 ♕h5 17 ♗e3 ♗f3 18 ♕f1 ♔h8 19

♘d2 ♗b7 20 ♗d1 ♕f5 21 f3 ♕g6 22 ♘e4 f5 23 ♘xd6 cxd6 24 ♕g2 ♖ae8 25 ♗b3 ♗a8 26 ♖e2 f4 27 gxf4 ♕h5 28 ♔f2 ♖f6 29 ♗c2 ♘d5 30 ♖ae1 ♖ef8 31 f5 and Black's attack was not sufficient to justify the deficit of material, Am.Rodriguez-Mendoza, Bogota 1990.

b) 13 ♖e3!? is a move I quite like because the rook fulfils a good defensive role on the third rank: 13...♕h4 14 g3 ♕h3 15 ♘d2 ♗b7 16 ♕f1 ♕d7 17 ♘e4 (this is better than 17 ♗c2 f5 18 f4 g5 19 ♗d1 ♘d5 20 ♗b3 ♔h8 21 ♗xd5 ♗xd5 22 ♘b3 ♖ae8 with compensation for the pawn because White was weak along the a8-h1 diagonal, Boese-Montavon, Leipzig 1998) 17...♔h8 18 ♗d2 ♘d5 19 ♖e2 f5 20 ♘xd6 cxd6 21 f3 f4 22 g4 ♖f6 23 ♖ae1 ♖af8 24 ♗d1 g5? 25 ♕h3 ♖8f7 26 ♗c2 h6 27 ♗f5 ♕c7 28 ♖e6 ♔g7 29 ♕h5 a5 30 h4 with a winning position for White who, besides being a pawn up, has a kingside attack as in the game Klovans-Montavon, Leipzig 1998.

13...♕d7 14 ♖e1 ♗b7 15 ♘d2 ♖ae8

Sometimes Black prefers 15...♖fe8, which might be a bit more accurate – this can be seen later on when we analyse White's eighteenth move. Note that the f8-square would then be freed for the black king.

16 ♗h4

White can also try 16 f3 closing the long diagonal. It is simply a matter of taste which of 16 f3 and 16 ♗h4 to choose. Both moves are of equal strength – with the text White hurries to bring his bishop to g3 in order to reinforce his kingside.

16...♘d5

Or 16...♖xe1+ 17 ♕xe1 ♖e8 18 ♕d1 ♘d5 19 ♗g3 ♘f4 20 ♗xf4 ♗xf4 21 ♘f1 g6 and a draw was agreed in the old game Bertok-Stein, Stockholm 1962. However, in the final position I think White should have played on with little risk as he had the extra pawn, although it's true that Black's two bishops would have made it very difficult to win.

17 ♕f3 c5 18 ♘e4?!

Stronger is 18 dxc5! ♗xc5 (if 18...♘f4 19 ♘e4 ♖xe4 20 ♖xe4 ♗xe4 21 ♕xe4 ♕g4 22 ♔h1 ♗xc5 23 ♗g3 White is a pawn ahead) 19 ♘e4 with a clear advantage for White because Black will have to retreat his bishop to e7 putting an end to his activity. 19...♗b6? loses by force to 20 ♗xd5 ♕xd5 21 ♘f6+!

21...gxf6 22 ♕g3+ and to avoid mate Black must give up his queen.

18...♖xe4!

Black sacrifices the exchange rather than allow his dark-squared bishop to be exchanged for White's knight. This is one more example confirming that the initiative is of vital importance in the Marshall Attack.

19 ♕xe4 ♘f4 20 d5 f5 21 ♕e3 c4 22 ♗c2 ♗xd5 23 f3

Interesting is the following sharp variation: 23 ♕d2? ♗xg2 24 ♗g3 ♗a8! 25 ♗xf4 ♕b7! 26 ♗e4 fxe4 and White will be slaughtered on the long diagonal!

23...♘xg2!

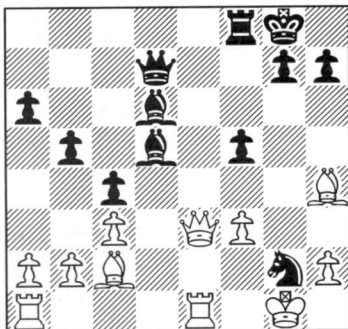

This sacrifice shows that Black has a good positional feeling for the initiative. Objectively this move should have led to a draw by perpetual check.

24 ♔xg2 f4 25 ♕f2 ♕g4+ 26 ♔f1 ♗xf3 27 ♗e7 ♕h3+ 28 ♔g1 ♗c7!?

Black continues to play for the win rather than accepting the draw with 28...♕g4+.

29 ♗c5

Also deserving of attention was 29 b4, which would have led to a draw.

29...♖d8?

Wrong – this is overoptimistic. This was the last chance for Black to take the draw.

30 ♖e7 ♖d5 31 ♖e8+ ♔f7 32 ♖f8+ ♔e6 33 ♖e1+ ♔d7 34 ♖e7+ ♔c6 35 ♖f5?

Simpler was 35 ♖xg7 after which White easily wins with his extra material.

35...♕g4+ 36 ♔f1 ♕h3+ 37 ♔g1

White is still winning after 37 ♔e1!, not fearing 37...♕xf5 because after 38 ♕xf3 (of course the black queen is taboo because of mate on d1) 38...♕xc2 39 ♖xc7+ ♔xc7 40 ♕xd5 ♕b1+ 41 ♔d1 ♕xd1+ 42 ♔xd1 g5 43 ♗f8! g4 44 ♗h6 f3 45 ♔e1 ♔d6 46 ♔f2 ♔e5 47 h3 ♔f5 48 ♔g3! the ending is a straightforward win for White.

37...♕g4+ 38 ♔f1 ♗d8 39 ♖xd5

Or 39 ♖e6+ ♔b7 40 ♖f7+ ♗c7 41 ♖ee7 ♖xc5 42 ♗f5!, not falling for the trap of taking the rook which allows perpetual check.

39...♗xd5 40 ♗e4??

An incredible blunder, dropping a rook, in what is assumed to be time trouble. White was naturally still winning after 40 ♖a7 etc.

40...♕d1+ 41 ♔g2

Or 41 ♕e1 ♕xe1+ 42 ♔xe1 ♗xe7 43 ♗xe7 (43 ♗xd5+ ♔xc5 would not save White) 43...♗xe4 with a winning endgame for Black.

41...♗xe7 0-1

Game 54
V.Ivanov-Vuori
Correspondence 1986

1 e4 e5 2 ♘f3 ♘c6 3 ♗b5 a6 4 ♗a4 ♘f6 5 0-0 ♗e7 6 ♖e1 b5 7 ♗b3 0-0 8 c3 d5 9 exd5 ♘xd5 10 ♘xe5 ♘xe5 11 ♖xe5 ♗b7

Black develops his bishop on the long diagonal. This move is seen from time to time and could prove successful if White is not prepared for it.

12 ♕f3

12 d4 is seen in Games 56-59.

12...♗d6 13 ♖xd5?

This is wrong – the correct continuation will be seen in our next game. With the text White gains a huge material advantage but he will have to pay a high price for it – his first rank is badly weakened. Also, his queenside is well behind in development.

13...♖e8

This is the move that is usually played but I think 13...♕e7!?, in order not to give White the opportunity to take on f7, might be even stronger, for example:

a) 14 ♕e3 ♖ae8! 15 ♕xe7 ♖xe7 16 ♔f1 ♖fe8 and we have reached a curious position when after the exchange of queens White is still helpless to defend his back rank!

b) 14 ♔f1 ♖ae8! (Black should put this rook on e8 and not the other one) 15 ♕d1 ♗xd5 16 ♗xd5 ♕e5 17 ♗f3 ♕xh2 18 g3 ♖e6! 19 d4 ♖fe8 20 ♗d2 ♗xg3! 21 fxg3 ♕xg3 followed by ...♖f6 and Black wins.

14 ♔f1

In some games White has tried 14 ♕xf7+!? but the results have been incredibly poor for White – Black has actually won all the games! For instance:

a) 14...♔xf7 15 ♖xd6+ ♔f8 16 ♖xd8 ♖axd8 17 ♔f1 ♗e4 (White has two pieces for a rook but his undeveloped queenside makes his position untenable) 18 f3 ♗d3+ 19 ♔f2 ♖e2+ 20 ♔g3 ♖d6 21 ♘a3 ♖g6+ 22 ♔h3 ♖exg2 23 ♗c2 ♖g1 0-1 Kettner-Kountz, Ladenburg 1992.

b) 14...♔h8!? might also be winning for Black but is more complicated. 15 ♔f1 ♕h4 and now both 16 d4 ♖f8 (Black also wins with 16...♕e4!) 17 ♖h5 ♕e4 18 ♖xh7+ ♕xh7 19 ♕e6 ♗xg2+ (0-1 Nowrouzy-Wenger, Graz 1993) and 16 ♖h5 ♕e4! lose immediately for White. After 16 ♕f3 ♕xh2 17 g4 (17 g3 ♕h3+ 18 ♕g2 ♖e1+ wins the queen) 17...♗g3! 18 ♘a3 ♗xf2 19 ♕xf2 ♕h1+ 20 ♕g1 ♖e1+! Black again has managed to breakthrough. So White's most resilient defence is 16 d3 ♖f8! 17 ♖h5 (or 17 ♗g5 ♕xh2 and White is helpless), but after 17...♕g4! Black is still winning.

14...♕e7

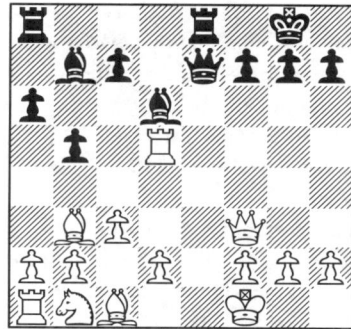

15 ♕xf7+?

The only try is 15 ♕e3 ♕h4 and now:

a) 16 ♖d4? loses after 16...♗xg2+ 17 ♔xg2 ♕xh2+ 18 ♔f3 ♕h1+ 19 ♔e2 ♖xe3+ 20 dxe3 ♕xc1 21 ♖d2 ♕g1 22 ♗d5 ♖e8 23 ♖d1 ♕g4+ 24 ♗f3 ♕c4+ 25 ♖d3 ♕h4 26 ♘d2 f5 27 ♖h1 ♕f6 28 ♗d5+ ♔h8 29 ♖d4 g5 30 f3 c5 31 ♖d3 c4 32 ♖d4 ♗c5 33 ♔f2 ♗xd4 34 cxd4 f4 35 ♘e4 fxe3+ 36 ♔xe3 ♕f4+ 37 ♔e2 g4 38 ♖f1 gxf3 0-1 Nebel-Abicht, Ruhr Championship 1996.

a) 16 ♕f3 ♕xh2 17 g4 and now 17...h5 looks very promising for Black.

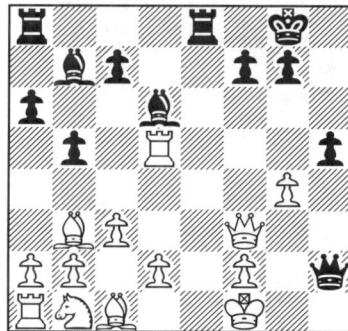

White has the choices between the following:

a1) 18 gxh5? ♗c8! 19 ♖d3 ♗g4! 20 ♗xf7+ ♔h8 21 ♕xg4 ♕h1+ 22 ♕g1 ♖e1+ 23 ♔xe1 ♕xg1+ 24 ♔e2 ♕xc1 and Black wins.

a2) 18 ♕xf7+!?, however, might just be

holding the position for White after 18...♔xf7 19 ♖xh5+ ♔g6 20 ♗c2+ ♗e4 21 ♖xh2 ♗xh2 22 d3 ♗f3 23 d4+ ♗e4 24 ♘a3 – Black has only a slightly better ending. This gives the impression that after 13 ♖xd5?, 13...♖e8 is not the best move for Black and that 13...♕e7!? is even stronger.

15...♔xf7 16 ♖e5+ ♔f6 17 ♖xe7 ♖xe7 18 d4 ♗e4

Black has both a positional and material advantage. With his dormant queenside, White is unable to put up any resistance.

19 ♗e3 ♗d3+ 20 ♔e1 ♗xh2 21 ♔d2 ♗e4 22 f3 ♗f5 23 d5 ♖ae8 24 ♗d4+ ♔g6 25 c4 b4! 0-1

Denying the c3-square for the knight on b1.

Game 55
Anand-Short
Manila Olympiad 1992

---

1 e4 e5 2 ♘f3 ♘c6 3 ♗b5 a6 4 ♗a4 ♘f6 5 0-0 ♗e7 6 ♖e1 b5 7 ♗b3 0-0 8 c3 d5 9 exd5 ♘xd5 10 ♘xe5 ♘xe5 11 ♖xe5 ♗b7 12 ♕f3 ♗d6 13 ♗xd5

Obviously the strongest reply. After the forced 13...c6 followed by capturing on d5 with a pawn, Black will close the a8-h1 long diagonal. In some ways this helps White because in many variations he is obliged to make a concession by playing g2-g3 – this would have catastrophic consequences if the long diagonal were opened.

13...c6 14 ♖e2

Basically there is not much difference whether White places his rook on e1 or e2 because White, later on, often exchanges on e8 so the two rook moves may transpose. Worth considering is 14 ♖e1 cxd5 15 d4 ♕c7 16 g3 ♖fe8 17 ♗e3 b4 18 cxb4 ♕c2 19 a3 ♕xb2 20 ♘d2 ♖ac8 21 ♘f1 ♕c2 22 ♗f4 ♖xe1 23 ♖xe1 ♗f8 24 ♖e8 ♕xd4 25 ♗e3 ♕b2 26 ♗c5 ♖xc5 (forced) 27 bxc5 and White is the exchange up in Gross-Svatos, Czech League 1997.

Of course White can't afford to take the hot pawn with 14 ♗xf7+?? ♖xf7 15 ♖f5 ♕e7!, after which he could resign because of his vulnerable back rank.

14...cxd5 15 d4 ♕c7 16 g3

There is a tactical reason why 16 h3? is bad – after 16...♖ae8 we have:

a) 17 ♘d2 b4! (Black can keep White worrying about his queenside before he completes normal development with ♘b1-d2) 18 ♘b3 ♖xe2 19 ♕xe2 bxc3 20 bxc3 ♕xc3 21 ♗e3 ♖e8 22 ♖c1 ♕b4 with advantage for Black in Szelag-Stern, Poznan 1999 because Black has managed to regain the sacrificed pawn and has retained the presence of his pair of bishops.

b) Even worse is 17 ♖xe8 ♖xe8 18 ♗e3 b4! and now 19 cxb4?? leads to a forced mate after the brilliant 19...♕c1+!!

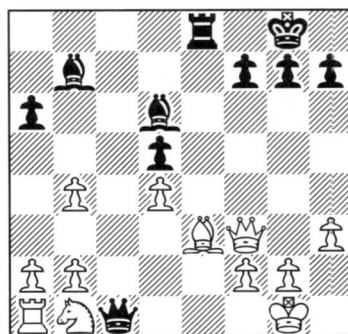

20 ♗xc1 ♖e1 mate.

16...♖ae8

Usually Black places this rook on e8 because if White doesn't exchange on e8, then Black's rook can be useful on f8 as Black can later play ...f7-f5.

Premature is 16...f5? 17 ♗f4!, when Black is weak on the dark squares.

17 ♘d2

The alternative is 17 ♖xe8 ♖xe8 18 ♗e3 b4 19 a3 a5 but tournament practice has shown that White's extra pawn is not important since White's pieces are very restricted.

Also deserving of attention is 17 ♗e3!? b4 18 cxb4 ♗xb4 19 ♘c3 ♗xc3 20 ♖c1! ♕a5 21 bxc3 ♖e7? 22 ♗h6! ♖xe2 23 ♕g4! g6 24 ♕xe2 with a winning position for White in Viljanen-Perho, correspondence 1989. However, instead of the poor 21...♖e7?, the logical continuation 21...♖e4! would have kept White's advantage to a minimum.

17...b4 18 cxb4 ♕c2 19 ♖e3 ♗c8!

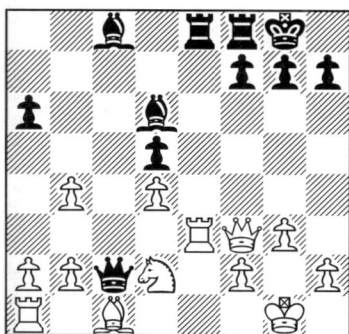

The bishop has nothing to do on the long a8-h1 diagonal so Black transfers it to the c8-h3 diagonal in order to pressurise the white kingside (h3 in particular). This is an improvement over the earlier 19...♗xb4?! 20 ♘f1 ♖e4 21 ♖b3! a5 (the piece sacrifice 21...♖e1? 22 ♖xb4 ♗c8 seen in Haba-Pirrot, Germany 1992 didn't prove to be correct – 23 ♔g2 ♗f5 24 ♘e3 ♖xe3 25 ♕xe3 ♗e4+ 26 ♔h3 and White was winning) 22 ♗e3 (worse is 22 ♗f4?! ♗a6 23 ♘e3 ♕c6 24 a3 ♗d2 25 ♘f5 ♕c2 26 ♗e5? ♗c1! 0-1 Pinter-

nagel-Borchert, correspondence 1989) 22...♗a6 23 ♖c1 ♕e2 24 ♕xe2 ♗xe2 25 a3 ♗c4 26 axb4 ♗xb3 27 ♘d2! with material advantage to White in B.Müller-Karlsch, correspondence 1989.

20 ♘f1 ♗xb4 21 a3 ♗a5 22 b4

Nice is the forcing variation 22 ♕xd5? ♗e1! 23 ♕f3 ♗b7 24 ♕f4 ♖e6!, with the idea of playing ...♖f6 against which White has no decent reply.

22...♗b6 23 ♖xe8 ♖xe8 24 ♗e3 ♗e6

Black has improved the placement of his light-squared bishop – in some lines he may create mating threats with ....♗h3. Black's pair of bishops fully compensate for White's extra pawn. Anand realises that any winning try could backfire and reconciles himself to a peaceful result.

25 ♕d1 ♖c8 26 ♘d2 ½-½

Game 56
Rogers-Djuric
Brocco 1988

1 e4 e5 2 ♘f3 ♘c6 3 ♗b5 a6 4 ♗a4 ♘f6 5 0-0 ♗e7 6 ♖e1 b5 7 ♗b3 0-0 8 c3 d5 9 exd5 ♘xd5 10 ♘xe5 ♘xe5 11 ♖xe5 ♗b7 12 d4 ♕d7?! 13 ♘d2

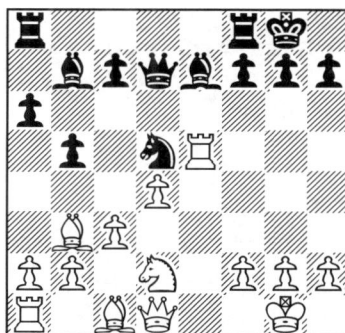

There are many other possibilities for White but it seems most logical to continue with the development of his queenside.

The fourth edition of *ECO* (2002) gives as the main line for White the simple continuation 13 &xd5 &xd5 14 &f4 (or 14 ♘d2 ♖ad8 15 a4? b4! 16 ♘f1 c5 17 dxc5 &f6 18 ♖e3 ♕c6 19 ♕g4 h5 20 ♕xb4 &xg2 with clear advantage to Black, Wikner-Berzinsh, Hallsberg 1993) 14...&b7 15 ♖e1 c5 16 dxc5 ♕c6 17 ♕g4 &xc5 18 ♘d2 ♖ae8 19 ♘f3 (worse is 19 ♘b3?! ♖xe1+ 20 ♖xe1 ♖e8 21 ♖xe8+ ♕xe8 22 &d2 h5! 23 ♕d1 – 23 ♕xh5? ♕e4! – 23...♕e4 24 ♕f1 &d6 25 ♘d4 ♕e5 26 f4 ♕e4 27 h3 b4! and Black had more than sufficient compensation for the sacrificed pawn due to White's vulnerable f4-pawn and Black's powerful pair of bishops, Dvoirys-Yermolinsky, Vilnius 1984) 19...♖xe1+ 20 ♖xe1 ♖e8 21 &e5 f6 22 &d4 and assesses the position as slightly better for White. However, I doubt if White can convert his material advantage into a win and I consider this position as drawish.

Also it should be mentioned that after 13 ♕f3 ♖ad8 14 ♘d2 (14 ♕f5 ♖xf5 15 ♖xf5 ♖fe8 16 &e3 g6 17 ♖e5 f6 18 ♖e4 &g7 – the awkward position of the white rook grants Black sufficient compensation – 19 &d2 c5 20 ♘a3 ♘c7 21 ♖e2 cxd4 22 ♖ae1 &f8 23 ♖xe8 ♘xe8 24 cxd4 ♖xd4 25 &c3 ♖d8 is equal, Harley-Hebden, Hastings 1988/89) 14...c5! 15 dxc5 &f6 16 ♖e1 ♘xc3 Black stands well.

13 ♕h5 is similar to lines with 13 ♕f3: 13...♘f6 14 ♕f5 ♕xf5 15 ♖xf5 &e4 and:

a) Inferior is 16 ♖g5? &d6 17 f4 ♖fe8 18 ♘d2 &b7 19 ♘f1 ♖e1 20 ♔f2 ♖xc1!

and White resigned in Gardner-Harding, correspondence 1975 because after 21 ♖xc1 &xf4 Black emerges a whole rook up.

b) 16 ♖e5 &d6 17 ♘d2 &b7 (of course the rook on e5 was taboo) 18 ♖e1 ♖fe8 19 ♖xe8+ ♖xe8 20 ♘f1 ♖e1 (again we come across the motif of White's weak back rank) 21 f3 &f4 22 &xf4 ♖xa1 23 &xc7 ♘d5 with clear advantage to Black, Beikert-B.Schneider, Germany 1988.

Note that 13 a4?! needs to be mentioned, although it must be wrong considering White is behind in development.

13...♘f4 14 ♘e4

This is safer than 14 ♘f3 against which Black can venture an unclear piece sacrifice with 14...♘xg2!? 15 ♖xe7 (obviously this is forced since 15 ♔xg2?? ♕g4+ and Black wins) 15...♕xe7 16 ♔xg2 ♖ad8 17 d5 ♕e4 18 ♕d4 ♕g6+ 19 ♔f1 ♕h5 20 ♕f4 ♖d6 with an unclear position, Tukmakov-Ma.Tseitlin, Odessa 1972. White has the extra material but Black has plenty of play against White's weakened king, which makes it very difficult to evaluate the position.

14...♘g6 15 ♘c5 &xc5 16 ♖xc5 ♖ae8 17 &e3 ♔h8

Black removes his king from the a2-g8 diagonal in order to play ...f7-f5 preparing for a kingside attack. Objectively speaking, White's chances are much the better since there is no weakness in the white camp (White has only to be careful with his king's rook) and, besides, White has a pair of bishops and an extra pawn. Black's only hope consists of rapid development and pressure along the e-file. White's weak back rank should also be noted.

18 ♖h5! &e4

Obviously 18...f5?? fails to the well known tactic 19 ♖xh7+! ♔xh7 20 ♕h5 mate.

The alternative 18...h6 was seen in Hartmann-Vodep, correspondence 1996 in which White won quickly after 19 a4 (in his commentary to the text game Grandmaster Ian Rogers recommends 19 h3 for White but the text is also good because we can reach the same position but with White's pawn on a4 rather than on a2, which cannot be bad for White) 19...f5 20 ♗xh6! gxh6 21 ♖xh6+ ♔g7 22 ♕h5 ♕d6 23 ♖h7+ ♔f6 24 h4! ♕f4 (obviously the only move since there was no other way to defend the mate on g5) 25 ♖h6 ♖g8 26 ♗xg8 ♖xg8 27 axb5 axb5 28 ♖e1! 1-0. In this game Black lost quickly without making any obvious mistakes which shows that the whole variation starting with 12...♕d7 is not playable for Black and that only 12...♗f6 can revitalise the line with 11...♗b7.

19 h3 ♘e7 20 ♖e5! f5 21 d5 ♘g6 22 ♖e6!

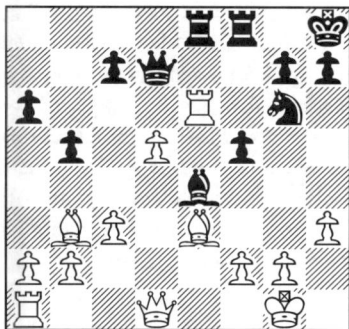

Very strong indeed. Black's kingside initiative has come to an end since his minor pieces, especially the knight, are not active enough. After 22 ♖e6 Black has an unpleasant choice – either to suffer the presence of White's powerful rook on e6 or to eliminate it, thus giving White a strong passed e-pawn. In short, White is a pawn up with the better position.

22...♖d8 23 ♗g5! ♗xd5 24 ♗xd8 ♗xe6 25 ♕xd7 ♗xd7 26 ♗xc7

With the bishop pair and an extra pawn, the win is simply a matter of technique.

26...♖c8 27 ♗d6 h6 28 ♖d1 ♔h7 29 f3 a5 30 ♗g3 ♗c6 31 ♗c2 ♖f8 32 ♗c7 a4 33 ♖d6 ♗e8 34 ♖d8 h5 35 ♗b6 f4 36 ♗c5 ♖h8 37 ♗d3 ♔h6 38 ♖b8 h4 39 a3

♔h7 40 ♔f2 ♔h6 41 ♖b6 1-0

Game 57
Kudrin-Hebden
Las Palmas 1989

1 e4 e5 2 ♘f3 ♘c6 3 ♗b5 a6 4 ♗a4 ♘f6 5 0-0 ♗e7 6 ♖e1 b5 7 ♗b3 0-0 8 c3 d5 9 exd5 ♘xd5 10 ♘xe5 ♘xe5 11 ♖xe5 ♗b7 12 d4 ♕d7?! 13 ♘d2 ♘f4

Rarely seen is 13...c5 14 ♘f3 cxd4 15 cxd4 ♗f6 16 ♖e1 ♖fe8 17 ♖xe8+ ♖xe8 18 ♗d2 ♕d6 19 h3 ♘f4 20 ♘e5! ♗xe5 21 dxe5 ♕c6 (bad is 21...♕xe5? 22 ♗xf4 ♕xf4 23 ♕d7! with a double attack on b7 and e8) 22 ♕g4 ♘d3 23 e6! with advantage to White, Klovans-Ma.Tseitlin, Novosibirsk 1986.

14 ♘e4 ♗d6

Black tries to improve over 14...♘g6 from the previous game but, as we shall see, it is not enough for reaching full equality.

15 ♘xd6 cxd6 16 ♖g5 ♘g6 17 ♖g3

White rightly understands that Black's main compensation for the pawn is the misplaced rook on g5.

Also possible is 17 ♕g4!? ♖ae8 18 ♗e3 ♕e7? 19 h4! ♔h8 20 h5 f5 21 ♖xf5 ♖xf5 22 ♕xf5 ♘h4 23 ♕g5 ♗xg2 24 ♕xe7 ♖xe7 25 ♗g5 ♘f3+ 26 ♔xg2 ♘xg5 27 a4 1-0 Wolff-Leisebein, correspondence 1991. White played more weakly in the game Henao-Djuric, Saint John 1988 with 17 ♗e3 ♖ae8 18 a4 ♗e4 19 axb5 axb5 20 ♗c2? (better is

20 d5 f5 21 ♖a7 with complicated play)
20...d5 21 ♗xe4 ♖xe4 22 ♕c2 f5 23 g3 ♕e6
24 ♖e1? ♘e7! (also good was the simple
24...h6 25 ♖xg6 ♕xg6 26 ♕b3 ♕c6 with a
material advantage for Black but with the text
Black wants to control the position even
more than that) 25 ♕d1 g6 26 ♕d2 ♕f6 27
f3 ♖e6 28 g4 (an ugly move but there is
nothing else as otherwise the rook on g5 is
trapped) 28...h6 29 gxf5 ♘xf5 30 ♖xf5 ♕xf5
31 ♗xh6 ♖xe1+ 32 ♕xe1 ♗f7 33 f4 ♕g4+
34 ♔h1 ♖a7 35 ♗g5 ♔f7 36 ♕f1 ♖a2 37
♕b1 ♕e2! 0-1.

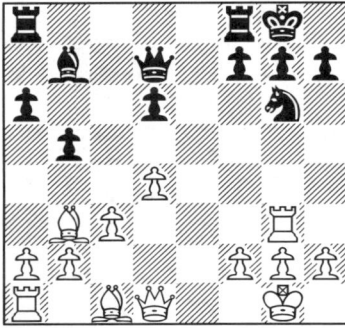

17...♖ae8 18 ♗g5 ♕f5 19 ♗c2 ♗e4 20
♗xe4 ♖xe4 21 a4!? bxa4?

Black counts on the weakening of White's
back rank after a recapture on a4. However,
it will transpire that the pawn on a6 is very
weak and will fall.

22 ♖xa4 ♕e6 23 ♖e3 d5 24 ♖xe4 ♕xe4
25 ♖xa6 ♖e8 26 h3 h6 27 ♗e3 ♔h7

With two extra pawns White is easily winning.

28 ♕f3 ♕b1+ 29 ♔h2 f5 30 ♕h5 f4 31
♗xf4 ♘xf4 32 ♖xh6+! gxh6 33 ♕f7+
♔h8 1-0

Game 58
C.Hansen-Hector
Malmö 1997

1 e4 e5 2 ♘f3 ♘c6 3 ♗b5 a6 4 ♗a4 ♘f6
5 0-0 ♗e7 6 ♖e1 b5 7 ♗b3 0-0 8 c3 d5

9 exd5 ♘xd5 10 ♘xe5 ♘xe5 11 ♖xe5
♗b7 12 d4 ♗f6

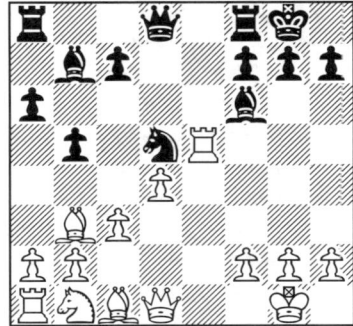

Dissatisfied with the results after
12...♕d7?!, Black has recently switched to
this move in an attempt to rehabilitate the
11...♗b7 line. Black's idea is clear – with the
eventual ...c7-c5 he will open up the long a1-
h8 diagonal for his dark-squared bishop.
However, I would like to emphasise that with
the placement of the bishop on f6 instead of
d6, Black will try to achieve positional compensation for the pawn rather than go all out
for the usual kingside offensive.

13 ♖e1

The most logical continuation. Sometimes
White plays 13 ♗xd5 instead, which I think
is unnecessary since White's light-squared
bishop is at least as strong as the black knight
on d5. The game Sisniega-Milos, São Paulo
1991 continued 13...♗xd5 14 ♖e1 ♖e8 15
♗e3 ♕d6 16 ♘d2 ♖e7 17 ♘f1 ♖ae8 18
♕d2 ♕c6 19 f3 ♗h4 20 ♗f2 ♗xf2+ 21
♔xf2 ♖xe1 22 ♖xe1 ♗xa2. Taking the pawn
restored the material balance and a level ending arose.

13...♖e8

The more active 13...c5 can be seen in the
next game.

14 ♘a3

The alternative 14 ♘d2 doesn't promise
any advantage to White, for example:

a) Bad is 14...b4? 15 c4 ♘f4 16 d5 ♘d3 17
♖xe8+ ♕xe8 18 ♗c2 ♘xb2 (the piece sacri-

fice 18...♘xf2? was refuted in De Firmian-Kreiman, US Championship 1994 after 19 ♔xf2 ♝d4+ 20 ♔f1 ♕e3 21 ♕e1 ♕g1+ 22 ♔e2 ♕xg2+ 23 ♔d3! ♝f2 24 ♕e4 ♕xh2 25 ♘f3 ♕h3 26 ♝e3 ♝xe3 27 ♔xe3 c6 28 d6! g6 29 ♔f2 ♕h5 30 ♕e5 ♕xe5 31 ♘xe5 c5 32 ♖d1 ♖d8 33 ♝a4 1-0) 19 ♝xb2 ♝xb2 20 ♖b1 ♝c3 21 ♘e4 ♕e5 22 ♕d3! ♖e8 23 ♘xc3 bxc3 24 f4! ♕e2 25 ♕xh7+ ♔f8 26 h3 with a technically winning position for White, who has both the extra pawn and the attack in De Firmian-Crawley, Lugano 1989.

b) 14...♘f4 15 ♘f3 ♝xf3 16 ♖xe8+ ♕xe8 17 gxf3 ♝g5 18 ♝xf4 ♝xf4 (with White's weakened kingside Black has sufficient compensation for the pawn) 19 ♕d3 ♕e7 20 ♕f5 ♝d6 21 ♕e4 (White played poorly in Joecks-Stern, Germany 1998, which continued 21 f4? ♖e8 22 ♝d5 g6 23 ♕g4 ♔h8! 24 a4 bxa4 25 ♖xa4 ♕e1+ 26 ♔g2 ♖e2 27 ♕f3 ♖xb2 28 ♝a2 ♖c2 29 ♖xa6 ♖c1 30 ♖a8+ ♔g7 31 ♕e3 ♕h1+ 0-1) 21...♖e8 22 ♕xe7 ♖xe7 23 a4 g6 24 axb5 axb5 25 ♖a8+ ♔g7 26 ♖b8 ♖e2 27 ♖xb5 and here the players agreed a draw in Koch-Hauchard, French Championship 1993.

14...b4 15 ♘c4

The text is stronger than 15 cxb4?! ♘xb4 16 ♝e3 c5! 17 ♕h5 ♕d7 18 ♘c4 g6 19 ♕h3 ♕xh3 20 gxh3 cxd4 21 ♝d2 ♖xe1+ 22 ♖xe1 ♘d3 23 ♖f1 ♖d8 24 f3 ♝d5 with a clear advantage to Black due to his better pawn structure in J.Howell-Pirrot, Bad Wörishofen 1991.

15...bxc3 16 ♘a5!

Harmless is the continuation 16 ♘e5 ♕d6 17 ♕e2 ♖e7 18 bxc3 ♘xc3 19 ♕c4 ♕d5 20 ♕xd5 ♝xd5 21 ♝a3 ♖e6 22 ♝xd5 ½-½ as in the old game Mukhin-Romanishin, Vilnius 1971.

16...♝xd4 17 ♖xe8+!

This is an improvement over 17 ♘xb7 from the game Servat-Adla, Buenos Aires 1990 and is in fact the greatest problem for 12...♝f6 devotees and the whole line starting with 11...♝b7.

Black was just about okay after 17 ♘xb7 ♕f6 18 ♖f1 cxb2 19 ♝xb2 ♝xb2 20 ♝xd5 ♝xa1 21 ♕xa1 as in Servat-Adla, Buenos Aires 1990. Best is then 21...♖e5! after which White's small material advantage is compensated by Black's strong centralised pieces.

17...♕xe8 18 ♘xb7 cxb2 19 ♝xb2 ♝xb2 20 ♝xd5 ♝xa1 21 ♕xa1 ♕b5 22 ♕d1! ♖e8 23 g3 g6 24 a4 ♕e2 25 ♕b3 ♔g7 26 ♔g2

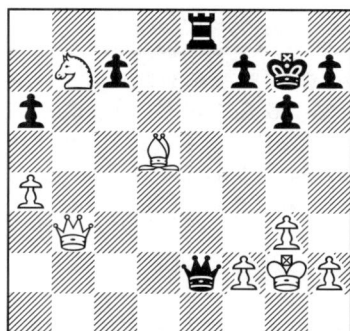

In this position, which is of a technical nature, the two minor pieces clearly outweigh the rook and pawn. White improves the position of his king against any possible unpleasant checks on his back rank. The position can be assessed as close to winning for White.

26...♕e5 27 ♕c4 ♕a1? 28 ♕xc7 ♕f6 29 ♕c4 ♖e1 30 ♘c5 ♕a1 31 ♕f4 ♖g1+ 32 ♔h3

White's king is safe enough on h3 as Black has insufficient pieces to create serious mating threats.

32...f5 33 ♕c7+ ♔h6 34 ♕f4+ ♔g7 35 ♘e6+ ♔f6 36 ♘d4! ♕e1 37 ♘f3

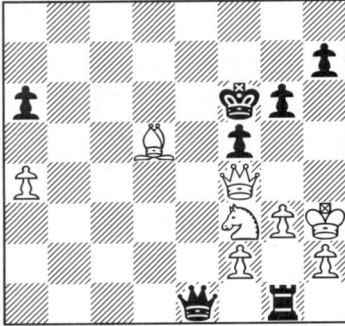

With multiple threats. The rest is easy.

37...♕f1+ 38 ♔h4 ♔e7 39 ♕c7+ ♔e8 40 ♗c6+ ♔f8 41 ♕d8+ 1-0

Game 59
Kulaots-Giorgadze
Wichern 1999

---

1 e4 e5 2 ♘f3 ♘c6 3 ♗b5 a6 4 ♗a4 ♘f6 5 0-0 ♗e7 6 ♖e1 b5 7 ♗b3 0-0 8 c3 d5 9 exd5 ♘xd5 10 ♘xe5 ♘xe5 11 ♖xe5 ♗b7 12 d4 ♗f6 13 ♖e1 c5!?

An active continuation trying to justify 12...♗f6.

14 dxc5 ♖e8 15 ♘a3

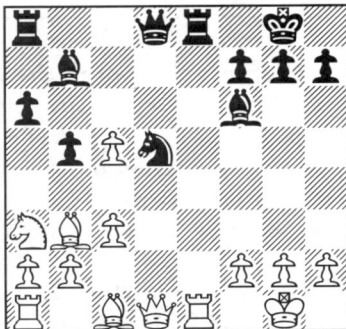

Although at first glance it looks rather awkward, White must play this move since after the reckless 15 ♘d2? ♘f4! Black's initiative would become extremely dangerous.

15...♕c7 16 ♘c2

Anand-Short, Amsterdam 1993 saw 16 ♖xe8+ ♖xe8 17 ♗xd5 ♖d8 18 ♗f4! (of course White is so far behind in development that there is not even time to consider the possibility of 18 ♗xf7+? ♕xf7 19 ♕f1, after which his position becomes very difficult regardless of his advantage in material) 18...♕xf4 19 ♕f3 ♕xf3 20 ♗xf3 ♗xf3 21 gxf3 b4 22 ♘c2 bxc3 23 bxc3 ♖c8 24 ♖b1 h6 25 c4 ♖xc5 26 ♘e3 ♗d4 27 ♖c1 ♗xe3 28 fxe3 ♔f8 and the ending, despite the material imbalance, is drawish. White could have tried the queen sacrifice with 19 ♗xb7!? ♖xd1 20 ♖xd1, which appears to be somewhat advantageous for White, but I think Black can save himself as he can soon play ...♗f6-e5 blocking White's passed c-pawn.

16...♗xc5 17 ♗d2 ♘b6

The knight is heading for c4 in order to put pressure on the b2-pawn. Black has sufficient compensation for the pawn as both his bishops are very active. Indeed, his compensation resembles that which Black obtains in the Benko Gambit.

18 ♕g4 h5 19 ♕h3 ♘c4 20 ♗e3

White must be a player with strong nerves in order to play the alternative 20 ♗xc4 ♕xc4 21 ♕xh5?! ♕d3! 22 ♕d1. Black's initiative looks threatening but I cannot find anything forced here. Perhaps Black should settle for 22...♕g6 23 f3 (23 g3? weakening the long diagonal is ugly) 23...♗xf3 24 ♕xf3 ♕xc2 and Black regains his sacrificed material and has the better position.

20...♘xe3 21 ♖xe3 ♖ad8 22 ♖ae1 ♖xe3 23 ♕xe3 ♕c6 24 f3 a5 25 ♘d4

After 25 a3 Black can play 25...♕d6, having in mind the possibility of ...♕d2. It is obvious that in this position, despite the pawn deficit, Black with his powerful pair of bishops doesn't run the risk of losing.

25...♕c5 26 ♗c2 g6 27 ♘b3 ♕xe3+ 28 ♖xe3 a4 29 ♘d4

White decides to give back his extra pawn after which the game fizzles out into a draw. The text is practically forced since after 29 ♘c5?! ♖d2! 30 ♗e4 ♗c8! Black will pick up a queenside pawn with excellent chances.

29...♗xd4 30 cxd4 ♖xd4 31 ♔f2 ♔f8 ½-½

Game 60
Eslon-Barczay
Kecskemet 1983

---

1 e4 e5 2 ♘f3 ♘c6 3 ♗b5 a6 4 ♗a4 ♘f6 5 0-0 ♗e7 6 ♖e1 b5 7 ♗b3 0-0 8 c3 d5 9 exd5 ♘xd5 10 ♘xe5 ♘xe5 11 ♖xe5 ♘f6

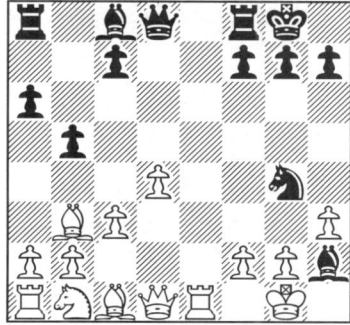

Marshall's original continuation.

12 d4 ♗d6 13 ♖e1 ♘g4

Premature is the piece sacrifice 13...♗xh2+? 14 ♔xh2 ♘g4+ and now:

a) 15 ♔g3? ♕d6+ 16 ♗f4 ♕g6! and the threatened discovered check on e3 is very unpleasant for White. 17 ♔f3 ♘f6!? threatens ...♕g4+, or 17 ♗c2 f5 18 ♔f3 (with or without including ♗b3+ ♔h8) 18...♗b7+ 19 d5 ♖ae8 threatening ...♘g4-h2+ with a strong attack for Black.

b) 15 ♔g1! ♕h4 16 ♕f3 ♗b7 17 ♕g3 ♖ae8 (this is supposed to be the idea behind the line starting with 13...♗xh2+? but, as we shall see, the sacrifice can be refuted) 18

♖xe8 ♖xe8 19 ♗d2! ♕xg3 20 fxg3 ♖e2 21 d5 with ♗b3-d1 to follow, when Black's attack comes to an end and White's material advantage is decisive.

14 h3 ♗h2+?

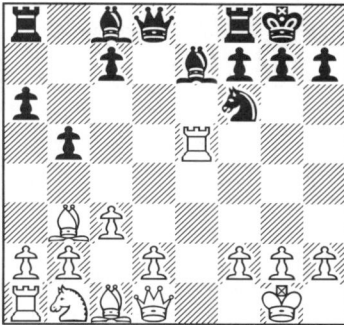

This tempting move is a direct mistake, which will be demonstrated in this game. White will be able to refute Black's attack with accurate play. The more critical 14...♕h4 will be discussed in Games 61-62.

15 ♔f1 ♘xf2

This is the natural follow up to Black's previous move. The alternative is 15...♕h4 against which, of course, White does not take the poisoned knight but quietly continues 16 ♕f3 ♗d6 17 ♗f4! ♗xf4 18 ♕xf4 g5 19 ♕g3 ♕h5 20 ♘d2 ♘h6 21 ♘e4 ♕g6 22 ♕xg5, which won for White in Crapulli-Sage, German NATO Championship 1989.

16 ♕f3!

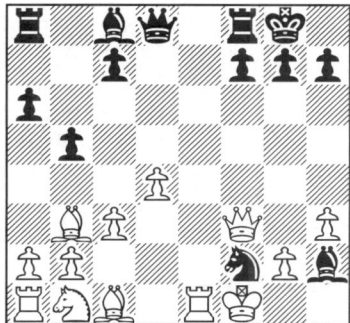

This is the refutation of 14...♗h2+?. Of course White is not obliged to accept the sacrifice with 16 ♔xf2??, which would have led to a winning attack for Black after 16...♕h4+ followed by ...♗c8xh3. Instead White strengthens his kingside and in the meantime a black minor piece will eventually fall.

16...♘h1

Unfortunately for Black the knight has no better square to go to. If 16...♘xh3 17 gxh3 ♕h4 18 ♖e4 ♗xh3+ 19 ♔e2 ♕xe4+ 20 ♕xe4 ♖ae8 21 ♕xe8 ♖xe8+ 22 ♔f2 (Dudukin-Trofimov, Russian Under-18 Championship 2001) White has a clear advantage in the ending with bishop against two pawns. Although the pawns look dangerous, it is not actually easy to advance them as they are still on their initial squares.

17 ♗f4

White shouldn't be greedy and go for material with 17 ♕xa8?, which was ruthlessly punished in the game Kamphuis-Berkvens, Hengelo 1996: 17...♕h4 18 ♕f3 ♘g3+ 19 ♔f2 g5! 20 ♗e3 g4 21 ♕c6 gxh3 22 ♕h6 ♘e4+! 23 ♔e2 ♗g4+ 24 ♔d3 ♕xe1 25 ♘d2 ♘f2+ 0-1.

17...♗b7 18 d5 ♗xf4 19 ♕xf4 g5 20 ♕f3 ♕d6 21 ♔g1 ♖ae8 22 ♘d2 ♘g3 23 ♔f2!

23...♕f4 24 ♕xf4 gxf4 25 ♔f3 ♔g7 26 c4?!

After a forced sequence of moves, in or-

der to save his knight Black was obliged to enter into an endgame in which the fall of his f-pawn is imminent. However, White had to play accurately and this move allows Black to diminish the advantage to a minimum. The correct move was 26 ♖ad1! in order to defend the d5-pawn. Only later should the f4-pawn be captured safely with a winning position.

26...bxc4 27 ♗xc4 ♘f5 28 ♔xf4 ♘e7! 29 ♘f3 ♘xd5+ 30 ♔g3 ♘e3

Black has managed to win back a pawn and White's advantage is not as big as before.

31 ♗b3 ♖e7?

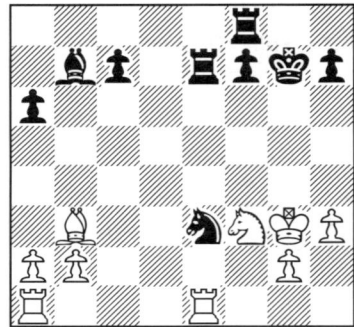

A blunder. Better was 31...♘f5+.

32 ♔f2 ♖fe8 33 ♗a4! c6 34 ♘d4 ♔f8

Due to the nasty threat ♖xe3 followed by ♘d4-f5+ winning a piece, Black had no time to defend his c6-pawn.

35 ♗xc6 ♗xc6 36 ♘xc6 ♖e4 37 ♖ac1 ♖8e6 38 ♔g1 ♘c4 39 ♖xe4 ♖xe4 40 ♖c2 ♘e5 41 ♘xe5 ♖xe5 42 ♔f2 ♖a5 43 b3 ♔e7 44 ♔e3 ♔d6 45 ♔d4 ♖f5 46 ♔e4 ♖f1 47 ♔e3 f5 48 ♖c4! ♖e1+ 49 ♔f3 a5 50 ♖a4 ♖e5 51 g3 ♖d5 52 ♔f4 ♔e6 53 ♖c4 ♖d2 54 ♖a4 ♖d5 55 h4 h5 56 a3 1-0

Game 61
Firt-Cempel
Konik 1995

1 e4 e5 2 ♘f3 ♘c6 3 ♗b5 a6 4 ♗a4 ♘f6

5 0-0 &e7 6 &e1 b5 7 &b3 0-0 8 c3 d5 9 exd5 &xd5 10 &xe5 &xe5 11 &xe5 &f6 12 d4 &d6 13 &e1 &g4 14 h3 &h4

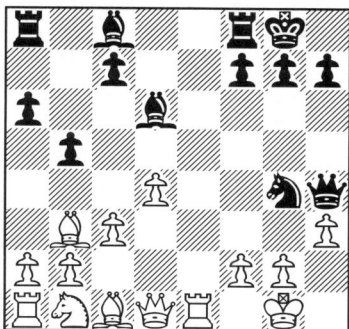

After 14...&xf2 White transposes to the game with 15 &f3! (of course taking the knight with 15 &xf2? would allow Black a winning attack after 15...&h4+ etc.).

15 &f3

White defends the vulnerable f2-square. It is easy to see that the knight on g4 is taboo.

15...&xf2

It was this piece sacrifice that the godfather of the Marshall attack Frank Marshall had in mind when inventing his Gambit.

Very rarely seen are the following continuations:

a) 15...&d7? and now:

a1) 16 &d2! (White continues with the development of his queenside; once White manages to consolidate he will be a pawn up for nothing) 16...&h8 17 &a3 f5 18 &f4! &f6 19 &xd6 cxd6 20 &e7 and White still has his extra pawn and dominant position in Kubis-Ren.Pokorna, Slovakia 1997.

a2) White also has 16 &e4!? &h8? (this is overoptimistic but after the better 16...h5 White continues with his plan by playing 17 &f4!, exchanging the dark-squared bishops and retaining a big advantage) 17 &xg4 &ae8 18 &d2 &xg4 19 &xg4 &e7 20 &a3 (preventing mate on the back rank) 20...f5 21 &f3 &xa3 22 bxa3 &xa3 23 &f4 with a winning position for White in Zaragatski-

Sobolevsky, Bad Zwesten 2000.

b) 15...&e6?! hasn't yielded good results for Black in tournament play either. White has several strong options at his disposal:

b1) 16 &e4!

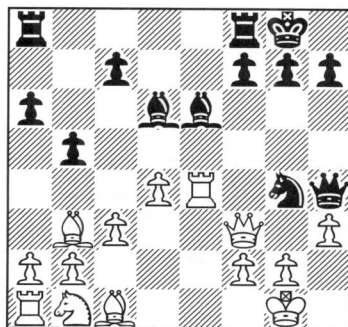

might be the simplest way for obtaining the advantage: 16...&h2+ (or 16...&ae8 17 &xe6 &xe6 18 &e3 &h2+ 19 &f1 &xe3+ 20 &xe3 &f6 21 &e2 &g3 22 &f3 and White has successfully managed to retain the extra pawn with his king's position still being safe, Sigurdsson-Morel, Helsinki Olympiad 1952) 17 &f1 &xb3 18 axb3 f5 19 &e2 &d6 20 &f4! &ae8 21 &xe8 &xe8 22 &d2 &xf4 23 &xf4 &e6 24 &g1 and Black's attack no longer exists. White has both a positional and material advantage, Grischuk-Gromadin, Moscow 1996.

b2) 16 &f4 is not so clear after 16...&xf2!? 17 &xd6 (17 &xf2 &xf2+ 18 &xf2 &xf4 19 &xe6 fxe6 led to an equal ending in Rojas-Vogel, correspondence 1994) 17...&xh3+ 18 &f1 (obviously forced) 18...cxd6 19 &e4 &h6! and the threat of ...&h6-c1+ followed by taking on b2 gives Black counterchances.

b3) 16 hxg4 &h2+ 17 &f1 &xg4 18 &e4! (18 &d5? led to disaster in Vlcek-Rachela, Zvolen 2000 after 18...&f4 19 g3 &h3+ 20 &e2 &g4+ 21 &d3 &xc1 22 &xc1 &ae8 23 f3 &g6+ 24 &d2 &xg3 25 &d1 &f4+ 0-1, whilst the ending is roughly equal after 18 g3 &h5 19 &xf7+ &xf7 20 &xa8+ &f8 21 &e5 &h3+ 22 &e1 &xe5+ 23 dxe5 &xa8 24 &e3

h5, Valcarcel-Pacini, correspondence 1972; White also has at his disposal 18 ♖e4 ♗f4 19 ♗xf4 ♗xf3 20 gxf3 ♕h1+ 21 ♔e2 ♖fe8 22 ♗c2 ♖xe4+ 23 fxe4 f5 with chances for both sides, Krivic-Deretic correspondence 1980) 18...♖ae8 19 ♕xe8 ♗d6 20 ♗xf7+ ♔h8 21 ♕xf8+ ♗xf8 22 ♔g1! ♗d7 23 ♘d2 ♕f6 24 ♗d5 1-0 Hadzi-Deretic, correspondence 1980.

16 ♖e2

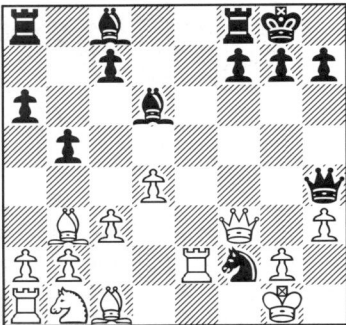

An instructive and well-known mistake is 16 ♕xf2? because after 16...♗h2+! (16...♗g3?? loses on the spot to 17 ♕xf7+! ♖xf7 18 ♖e8 mate so 16...♗h2+! is essential as it prevents the winning sacrifice on f7) 17 ♔f1 ♗g3 18 ♕e2 (now 18 ♕xf7+?? ♖xf7+ and the difference with the white king sitting on f1 is that Black takes the queen with check so White has no time to deliver mate on e8) 18...♗xh3! with a mating attack.

There is, however, another good defence in 16 ♗d2!. The following complications work in White's favour: 16...♗b7!? 17 ♕xb7 ♘d3 18 ♖e2 ♕g3 19 ♔f1 ♘f4 20 ♖f2! ♕d3+ 21 ♔g1 ♘e2+ 22 ♖xe2 ♕xe2 23 ♕f3 and according to the Swedish GM Tom Wedberg Black no longer has an attack.

16...♗g4

Black's attack comes to an end after 16...♘xh3+? 17 gxh3 ♗xh3 18 ♖e4! ♕g3+ (obviously tactical attempts like 18...♗h2+ or 18...♗g4 backfire) 19 ♕xg3 ♗xg3 20 ♗g5! and if 20...h6, then 21 ♖e3 gives White a

winning ending.

Sometimes Black tries 16...♘g4.

In the position above Black has been scoring well, although White's chances are clearly better (16...♘g4 has more often than not been played when Black was the stronger player).

a) 17 ♕xa8? ♕g3! 18 hxg4 ♕h2+ 19 ♔f1 ♗g3 20 ♗e3 (this is the only playable move for White) 20...♕h1+ 21 ♗g1 ♗h2 22 ♗xf7+ ♔h8! (but not 22...♖xf7+?! 23 ♔e1 with unclear play) with an amusing position where, despite a huge material advantage, it is difficult to find a move for White.

b) White can also play the quiet move 17 ♗f4 which only leads to equality after 17...♗b7 18 d5 ♘f6 19 ♗xd6 cxd6 20 ♘d2 ♖ae8 etc.

c) The thematic reply 17 ♖e4? was strongly answered by 17...h5! 18 hxg4 ♗b7 19 d5 ♖ae8 and White had no defence in Leger-Veile, correspondence 1991.

d) White's best reply seems to be 17 g3! and now Black is in trouble as is demonstrated by the following examples:

d1) 17...♕xg3+ 18 ♕xg3 ♗xg3 19 hxg4 ♗b7 20 ♘d2 ♖ae8 21 ♗d1 ♖xe2 22 ♗xe2 ♖e8 23 ♔f1 ♖e6 24 ♘f3 ♖g6 25 g5 and White is clearly winning with his extra material but in fact actually managed to lose in Sorensen-Hintikka, correspondence 1984.

d2) 17...♕xh3 18 ♕xa8 ♕g3+ 19 ♕g2 and Black's attack is not worth the sacrificed rook.

17 hxg4 &g3

The same position arises after 17...&h2+ 18 &f1 &g3 (18...&h1? is even worse for Black after 19 &e3 &g3+ 20 &e1 &xe2+ 21 &xe2 &ae8 22 &d2 h5 23 &e4! hxg4 24 &f5 &d6 25 &f1 &e7 26 &d5 &h7 27 &g5 1-0 Sammalvuo-Nyysti, Vammala 1995) 19 &xf2 etc.

18 &xf2 &h2+ 19 &f1 &h1+ 20 &e2 &xf2

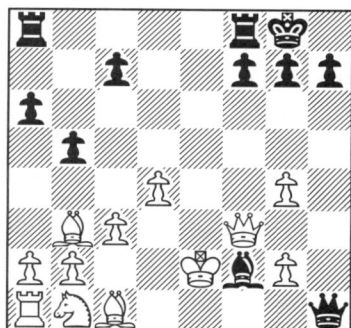

20...&xc1 is seen in the next game.

21 &d2!

Less accurate is 21 &a3?! &ae8+ 22 &d3 &f1+ 23 &c2 &e2+ 24 &d2 &xd2+ 25 &xd2 &xa1 26 &xf2 &xb2+ 27 &c2 c5 with unclear play, Holmsten-Ketonen, Finnish Team Championship 1991.

21...&h4 22 &d3

White's king must run to the queenside in order to find a safe haven, after which his material advantage will prevail.

22 &h3 was the start of an excellent defence in the famous game Capablanca-Marshall, New York 1918 (which we also mentioned in the introduction to this book). The game concluded 22...&ae8+ 23 &d3 &f1+ 24 &c2 &f2 25 &f3 &g1 26 &d5 c5 27 dxc5 &xc5 28 b4 &d6 29 a4! (this brings the rook on a1 into play) 29...a5 (this is a desperate attempt for counterplay as he was losing anyway) 30 axb5 axb4 31 &a6 bxc3 32 &xc3 &b4 33 b6 &xc3 34 &xc3 h6 35 b7

&e3 36 &xf7+! 1-0.

22...&ad8 23 &c2 c5

Black must open the d-file in order to expose White's king.

24 dxc5 &xd2+ 25 &xd2 &xa1 26 &b1!

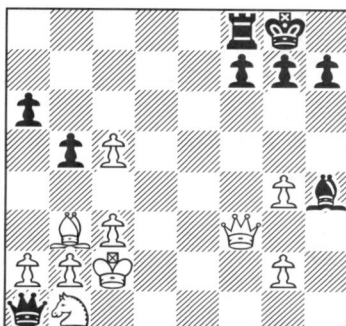

From a material viewpoint Black is not doing badly but in order to free his queen from its prison on a1 he will have to shed some material. Black also has to worry about White's strong passed c-pawn.

26...a5 27 c6 a4 28 &d5 b4 29 cxb4 &f6 30 &c3 a3 31 bxa3 h6 32 &e3 &g5 33 &c5 &c1+ 34 &b3 &f4 35 c7 &c8 36 &xf7+!

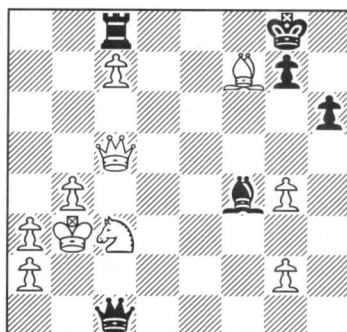

36...&h8

White is also winning after 36...&xf7 37 &f5+, picking up the rook on c8.

37 &e6 &xc7 38 &f8+ &h7 39 &g8+ 1-0

It's mate in two.

will hold up Black's kingside pawn majority.

Game 62
J.Bird-Beckett
Correspondence 1993/94

---

1 e4 e5 2 ♘f3 ♘c6 3 ♗b5 a6 4 ♗a4 ♘f6
5 0-0 ♗e7 6 ♖e1 b5 7 ♗b3 0-0 8 c3 d5
9 exd5 ♘xd5 10 ♘xe5 ♘xe5 11 ♖xe5
♘f6 12 d4 ♗d6 13 ♖e1 ♘g4 14 h3 ♕h4
15 ♕f3 ♘xf2 16 ♖e2 ♗g4 17 hxg4
♗h2+ 18 ♔f1 ♗g3 19 ♖xf2 ♕h1+ 20
♔e2 ♕xc1

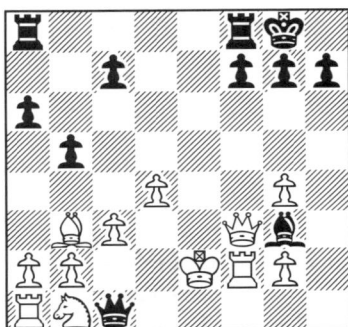

In short, this move is not much better than 20...♗xf2 from the previous game.

21 ♕xg3 ♕xb2+ 22 ♔d3!

This is even stronger than 22 ♘d2, which was also in White's favour after 22...♕xa1 23 ♖xf7 ♔h8 (or 23...♖xf7 24 ♗xf7+ ♔xf7? 25 ♕f3+, winning the rook on a8) 24 ♖e7 ♖fe8 25 ♕e5 ♖xe7 26 ♕xe7 ♕g1 27 ♗d5, Pletanek-J.Rodrigues, correspondence 1994.

22...♕xa1 23 ♔c2 b4 24 g5!

In the oncoming ending White's two minor pieces will clearly outweigh Black's rook and this move will be very useful because it

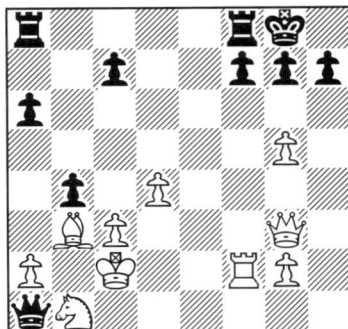

24...bxc3 25 ♕xc3 ♕xc3+ 26 ♘xc3 ♖ad8 27 ♘e2?!

This is a bit passive. Stronger was the more natural 27 ♔d3! and if 27...c5, then 28 d5 with a technically winning position.

27...g6 28 ♗c4 a5 29 ♖f3 ♔g7 30 ♖a3 ♖a8

Maybe a better practical chance was to sacrifice a pawn by playing 30...f6 but White, with best play, should still be winning.

31 ♗d5 ♖a7?

The rook has nothing to do on a7 and this loses easily. The only chance was 31...♖a6.

32 ♖e3 h6

This move shows the strength of 24 g5!. In order to get rid of this blockading pawn, Black must play ...h7-h6 sooner or later.

33 gxh6+ ♔xh6 34 a3 f5?! 35 ♘f4 ♖f6 36 ♖h3+ ♔g7

36...♔g5 37 ♘e6+ is winning for White because after 37...♔g4? 38 ♗f3 is actually mate!

37 ♘e6+ ♔g8 38 ♘xc7+ ♔f8 39 ♖h7 1-0

Summary

With regard to 11...♘f4?! and 11...♘b6?!, such a 'quick fix' repertoire could be successful in a single game (one must also count on the effect of surprise!) but in general I do not recommend it. With 11...♘b6?! Black does not generate enough play on the kingside (Black's knight is far away from the scene of the action on the kingside), whilst with 11...♘f4?! Black invests in several tempi in order to transfer the knight to g6. Indeed, it is not clear whether the knight is better placed on d5 or on g6.

After 11...♗b7 12 ♕f3 ♗d6, the move 13 ♖xd5? (Game 54) almost loses by force mainly due to White's weak back rank which allows Black all sorts of cheapos. Game 55 is food for thought. The first impression is that Black has not been able to demonstrate full equality.

After 11...♗b7 12 d4, the move 12...♕d7?! (Games 56-57) is currently under a cloud and is definitely not playable for Black if White plays correctly. That is why Black is currently putting all his hopes on 12...♗f6. Although from the theoretical point of view the pawn sacrifice might not be perfect, this line is absolutely fine for Black in modern day tournament play.

Marshall's 11...♘f6 was initially popular but in subsequent years White found the method to obtain an advantage in this variation and nowadays this old-fashioned treatment has been replaced by the modern 11...c6.

The straightforward 14...♗h2+? (Game 60) does not work. The cool defence 15 ♔f1 ♘xf2 16 ♕f3! refutes Black's assault.

In the forcing line 12 d4 ♗d6 13 ♖e1 ♘g4 14 h3 ♕h4 15 ♕f3 ♘xf2 16 ♖e2 ♗g4 17 hxg4 ♗g3 18 ♖xf2 ♕h2+ 19 ♔f1 ♕h1+ 20 ♔e2, tournament practice has shown that neither 20...♗xf2 nor 20...♕xc1 are playable for Black. White's king feels absolutely safe on the queenside since Black hasn't enough forces left to attack it. In the long run White's material advantage (often two minor pieces against a rook) should prevail, so the general assessment is that White is clearly better if not close to winning.

1 e4 e5 2 ♘f3 ♘c6 3 ♗b5 a6 4 ♗a4 ♘f6 5 0-0 ♗e7 6 ♖e1 b5 7 ♗b3 0-0 8 c3 d5 9 exd5 ♘xd5 10 ♘xe5 ♘xe5 11 ♖xe5 ♗b7

11...♘b6?! – *Game 53*; 11...♘f4?! – *Game 52*

11...♘f6 12 d4 ♗d6 13 ♖e1 ♘g4 14 h3

14...♗h2+ – *Game 60*

14...♕h4 15 ♕f3 ♘xf2 16 ♖e2 ♗g4 17 hxg4 ♗g3 18 ♖xf2 ♕h2+ 19 ♔f1 ♕h1+ 20 ♔e2

20...♗xf2 – *Game 61*; 20...♕xc1 – *Game 62*

12 d4

12 ♕f3 ♗d6

13 ♖xd5 – *Game 54*; 13 ♗xd5 – *Game 55*

12...♗f6

12...♕d7 13 ♘d2 ♘f4 14 ♘e4

14...♘g6 – *Game 56*; 14...♗d6 – *Game 57*

13 ♖e1 c5 – *Game 59*

13...♖e8 – *Game 58*

CHAPTER SIX

The Steiner Variation: 9...e4

1 e4 e5 2 ♘f3 ♘c6 3 ♗b5 a6 4 ♗a4 ♘f6 5 0-0 ♗e7 6 ♖e1 b5 7 ♗b3 0-0 8 c3 d5 9 exd5 e4?!

This gambit line was introduced into tournament practice in 1929 by Herman Steiner. However, with best play, as we shall see, White retains a clear advantage. This variation has for a long time been out of fashion and is virtually only seen in correspondence games, although it is occasionally (and only occasionally) used as a surprise.

In Games 63-64 we deal with 10 ♘g5?!, which is clearly not White's best choice. After 10...♗g4! White has to make an early concession – either to weaken his kingside by playing 11 f3 or to fall even further behind in development by playing 11 ♕c2, which is perhaps the lesser of the two evils.

Better is 10 dxc6 exf3 and now 11 ♕xf3 is seen in games 65-67. Very instructive is the game in which the late Hungarian GM Laszlo Szabo managed to refute White's plan involving the exchange sacrifice on e5. Yes, Game 65 is well worth playing through.

In Bargel-Valenta (Game 66) we study the critical position arising after 11...♗g4 12 ♕g3 ♗d6 13 f4 ♖e8 14 d4.

In Fischer-Bernstein (Game 67) the former World Champion rejects playing f2-f4, considering it as an important weakening of his kingside, and settles instead for f2-f3. Finally in this chapter we see the strongest reply against Steiner's 9...e4?!, which is 11 d4! (Game 68).

Game 63
Van Linden-S.Bernstein
New York 1974

1 e4 e5 2 ♘f3 ♘c6 3 ♗b5 a6 4 ♗a4 ♘f6 5 0-0 b5 6 ♗b3 ♗e7 7 ♖e1 0-0 8 c3 d5 9 exd5 e4?! 10 ♘g5?! ♗g4!

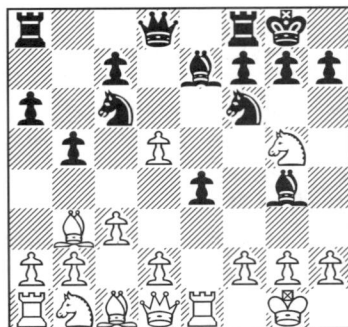

The other continuations are clearly worse:
a) 10...♘a5?! 11 ♘xe4 ♘xe4 12 ♖xe4 ♘xb3 13 axb3 ♗f5 14 ♖e5 ♗d3 15 ♕f3 ♗d6 16 ♖e3 ♖e8 17 h3 and Black still has to demonstrate that he has sufficient compensa-

tion for the sacrificed material. However White should, of course, avoid 17 ♖xe8+ ♕xe8 18 ♕xd3?? (better is 18 ♕e3 but after 18...♕e5! Black is okay) 18...♕e1+ 19 ♕f1 ♗xh2+! and Black wins.

b) 10...♘e5?! 11 ♘xe4 ♘d3 12 ♘xf6+ ♗xf6 13 ♖e3 ♗f5? (better is 13...♘xc1 14 ♕xc1 ♗b7 with a clear advantage to White) 14 ♕f3! (wrong is 14 a4? ♗g5 15 ♖e2 ♖e8! and White's weak back rank begins to tell) 14...♕d7 15 ♖xd3 ♗e4!? 16 ♕e2 ♕f5 17 ♖e3 ♗xb1 18 d3 with a decisive advantage for White, Fox-Steiner, Bradley Beach 1929.

11 f3 exf3 12 gxf3

White can play more quietly with 12 ♘xf3 but after 12...♘a5!? 13 ♗c2 ♖e8! 14 d4 ♕xd5 15 ♕d3 ♗d6 Black's position should be preferred due to White's undeveloped queenside, Morley-Harding, Teeside 1972.

12...♘xd5 13 ♘xh7

White loses material after 13 ♖xe7? ♕xe7! 14 ♗xd5 ♕xg5 etc.

13...♗f5!?

The alternative is 13...♗d6!? 14 ♗xd5 ♗xh2+ 15 ♔xh2 ♕h4+ 16 ♔g1 ♕g3+ and now correct is 17 ♔h1 after which Black has no more than a draw. However, in the game Pfeiffer-Rothmund, Oberschwaben 1992 White played 17 ♔f1? and lost after 17...♖h3+ 18 ♔e2 ♖fe8+ 19 ♗e4 ♖xe4+! 20 fxe4 ♗g4+ 21 ♔f1 ♗xd1 22 ♖xd1 ♕f3+ 23 ♔e1 ♕xe4+.

14 ♘xf8 ♗d3!

A picturesque position, White is a whole rook up but things are not so clear because White's entire queenside is frozen and his kingside is seriously weakened.

15 ♖e4?

After this White ends up in a lost position. No better was 15 a4 due to 15...♘f4! but the following alternatives deserve attention:

a) 15 ♘g6!? fxg6 16 f4 intending ♕d1-f3, when White gets counterplay on the long a2-g8 diagonal.

b) 15 f4!?, again intending ♕f3, with unclear play after 15...♗xf8 16 ♕f3. Note that 16...♕h4? loses to 17 ♕g3!.

15...♗xf8 16 ♕e1 ♕g5+ 17 ♖g4 ♕f5 18 ♗xd5 ♕xd5 19 ♖e4 ♖d8 20 b4 ♖d6!

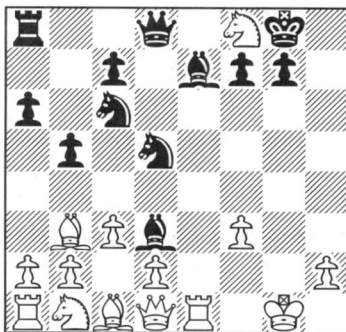

The rook is heading towards g6, leaving White's monarch virtually without any proper defence.

21 ♗b2 ♖g6+ 22 ♔f2 ♕h5 23 ♕h1 ♗xe4 24 fxe4 ♘e5 25 ♔e3 ♖g3+ 26 ♔f2 ♖h3 0-1

Game 64
Frank-Schuchardt
Bruchkoebel 1993

1 e4 e5 2 ♘f3 ♘c6 3 ♗b5 a6 4 ♗a4 ♘f6 5 0-0 ♗e7 6 ♖e1 b5 7 ♗b3 0-0 8 c3 d5 9 exd5 e4?! 10 ♘g5?! ♗g4! 11 ♕c2

In contrast to 11 f3 where White weakens his kingside, here he keeps his kingside solid but Black achieves colossal development.

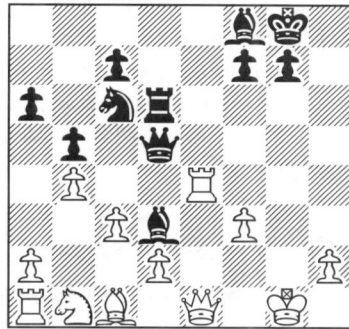

11...♘e5! 12 ♘xe4 ♘xe4 13 ♕xe4 ♗d6 14 f4

An alternative is 14 d4 f5 and now White has a choice between the following:

a) 15 ♕c2?! ♘f3+! 16 gxf3 ♕h4 17 fxg4 ♕xh2+ 18 ♔f1 fxg4 19 ♗e3 ♖ae8! 20 ♔e2 (the only move because after 20 ♘a3 g3! White has no good reply) 20...♖xf2+ 21 ♔d3 ♖xc2 22 ♗xc2 ♗g3 23 ♖e2 ♕h1 with a clear advantage to Black.

b) 15 ♕e3? f4 16 ♕e4 ♗f5 17 ♕e2 ♘d3 18 ♖d1 ♖e8 19 ♕h5 g6 20 ♕h6 ♗f8 21 d6+ ♔h8 22 dxc7 ♕f6 and White resigned because his queen is trapped, Campbell-Dillinger, US Amateur Team Championship 1990.

c) The queen sacrifice with 15 ♕xe5!? ♗xe5 16 dxe5 (D.Popovic-Paramentic, Yugoslavia Women's Championship 1993) might be White's best chance but Black is obviously okay here. For instance, instead of 16...♔h8 as played in the game, Black can try 16...f4 at once.

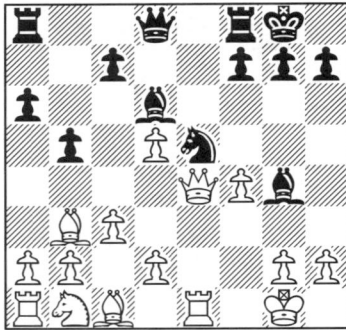

14...f5 15 ♕e3 ♘g6 16 g3

Worse is 16 h3? ♕h4! 17 hxg4 ♗xf4 18 ♕e6+ ♔h8 after which White is defenceless.

16...♖e8 17 ♕f2

Or 17 ♕xe8+ ♕xe8 18 ♖xe8+ ♖xe8 19 ♔f1 and now 19...♗e2+! is strong.

17...♖xe1+ 18 ♕xe1 ♕f8

Overoptimistic is 18...♗xf4? 19 gxf4 ♘xf4 20 d3 ♘e2+ 21 ♔g2 ♕d6 22 h3 ♕g6 23 hxg4 ♕xg4+ 25 ♔h2 ♕h5+ 25 ♔g2 ♕g6+

26 ♔h2 ♕d6+ 27 ♔g2 ♖e8 and now 28 ♗g5! would have refuted Black's sacrificial play. In the game Virostko-Valenta, Frydek Mistek 1996 White continued 28 ♗d1? ♕g6+ 29 ♔h2 ♕h5+ 30 ♔g2 ♕g4+ 31 ♔h2 f4! 32 d4 f3 0-1.

19 d3

Also worth considering is 19 d4 ♖e8 20 ♕f1 ♖e7 21 a4 ♕e8 threatening ...♖e1 with better play for Black.

19...♖e8 20 ♕f1

After 20 ♗e3, 20...♘xf4! 21 gxf4 ♗xf4 is very strong.

20...♗e2 21 ♕h3?

This loses by force because here White's queen is too far away from the main battleground. More resilient was 21 ♕f2.

21...♗xd3 22 ♘d2 ♖e1+ 23 ♔f2 ♕e7 0-1

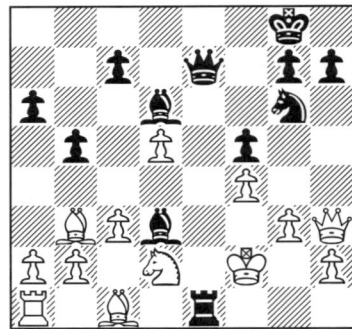

White is unable to prevent the upcoming mate.

Game 65
Van den Berg-Szabo
Haifa 1958

---

1 e4 e5 2 ♘f3 ♘c6 3 ♗b5 a6 4 ♗a4 ♘f6 5 0-0 ♗e7 6 ♖e1 b5 7 ♗b3 0-0 8 c3 d5 9 exd5 e4?! 10 dxc6 exf3 11 ♕xf3

10 dxc6 exf3 11 ♕xf3 is regarded by modern day opening theory as better than 10 ♘g5?! but, as we shall see, Black will obtain just enough compensation in exchange for

his material deficit largely due to his lead in development. After the text Black will gain important time by attacking White's queen.

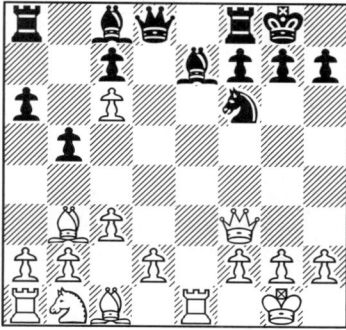

11...♗g4 12 ♕g3

Very rarely seen is 12 ♕f4 ♗d6 13 ♕d4 ♖e8 14 ♖e3, after which Black can continue 14...♗f5! 15 h3 ♘e4 with very active play.

12...♗d6

Often Black plays 12...♖e8, which is just a transposition after 13 d4 ♗d6 14 f4 etc.

13 f4 ♖e8 14 ♖e5?

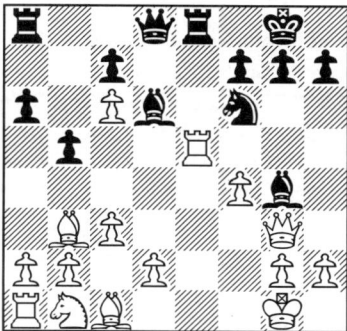

With this exchange sacrifice White intends to take the initiative away from his opponent. Black's next move is practically forced otherwise White will play d2-d4 supporting his rook on e5.

14 d4 is the subject of the next game.

14...♗xe5

Not so convincing is 14...♗e6, but the well-known game Boleslavsky-Pirc, Saltsjo-

baden 1948 ended in a draw after 15 d4 ♗xb3 16 axb3 ♗xe5 17 fxe5 ♘e4 18 ♕f3 ♕h4 19 g3 ♘g5 20 ♕f5 ♕e4! 21 ♕xg5 ♕e1+ 22 ♔g2 ♕e2+ 23 ♔g1 ♕e1+.

15 fxe5 ♘h5!

Much better than 15...♕e7? 16 d4 ♗h5 17 ♘d2! (not so clear is 17 ♗g5?! ♘e4! 18 ♗xe7 ♘xg3 etc.) 17...♘g4 18 ♘e4 and White is dominating the whole board.

16 ♕xg4 ♖xe5 17 ♘a3?

After this mistake White is decidedly lost. A better choice was 17 ♕f3!?, although I think that even in this case Black should be better.

17...♖e1+ 18 ♔f2 ♘f6!

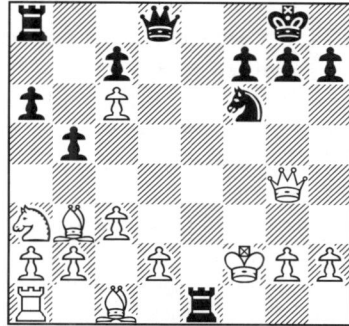

This is the move that White obviously missed when playing 17 ♘a3?. Black only draws after the tempting continuation 18...♖xc1? 19 ♖xc1 ♕xd2+ 20 ♔f3 ♕d3+ 21 ♔f2 ♕d2+ etc.

19 ♕f4?

This loses immediately – slightly better was 19 ♕d4.

19...♕e7

This wins but even quicker was 19...♖e4! and if 20 ♕f3 or 20 ♕f5, then 20...♘g4+ wins, while if 20 ♕g3, then 20...♘h5! 21 ♕h3 ♕f6+ is decisive.

20 ♕f3 ♖h1 21 ♘c2 ♘e4+ 22 ♔e2 ♘xc3+ 23 ♔d3 ♖d8+ 24 ♘d4

Or 24 ♔xc3 ♕c5+ with mate on the next move.

24...♘e2 0-1

Game 66
Bargel-Valenta
Chrudim 1993

1 e4 e5 2 ♘f3 ♘c6 3 ♗b5 a6 4 ♗a4 ♘f6
5 0-0 ♗e7 6 ♖e1 b5 7 ♗b3 0-0 8 c3 d5
9 exd5 e4?! 10 dxc6 exf3 11 ♕xf3 ♗g4
12 ♕g3 ♗d6 13 f4 ♖e8 14 d4 ♖xe1+!?

This move is rare but I checked the arising endgame with the help of *Fritz* and the move is quite playable – Black achieves an equal ending.

More frequently played is 14...♘h5 15 ♖xe8+ ♕xe8 16 ♕f2 ♕xc6 and now White has a choice between the following:

a) 17 h3 ♗e6 18 ♗e3 ♖e8 19 ♘d2 ♗xb3 20 axb3 g5! (a quite unusual way of regaining back the sacrificed pawn because if 21 fxg5? ♗g3! the bishop on e3 is lost) 21 ♘f3 ♘xf4 22 ♘e5 ♗xe5 23 dxe5 ♖xe5 24 ♗xf4 gxf4 25 ♕xf4 ♖e6 with an equal position, Matanovic-Milic, Beverwijk 1958.

b) 17 ♗e3 ♖e8 18 ♘d2 and here I believe Black should have continued 18...♖e7! with the hidden idea of playing ...♕c6-e8 exploiting the unpleasant pin along the e-file. This gives Black sufficient compensation for the sacrificed pawn due to his active pieces.

15 ♕xe1 ♕e8

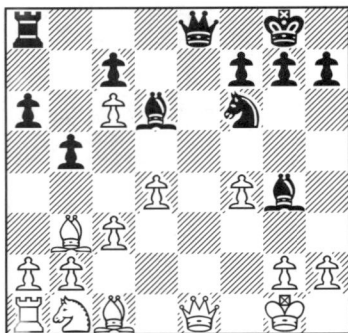

Even after the exchange of queens Black will continue to dominate the e-file.

16 ♕xe8+ ♖xe8 17 ♘a3 ♖e1+ 18 ♔f2

♖h1 19 ♘c2 ♗f5 20 ♗e3

After 20 ♘e3 ♗e4! White is kept under serious pressure due to the pin along the first rank.

20...♘g4+ 21 ♔f3 ♘xh2+ 22 ♔e2 ♖xa1
23 ♘xa1 ♗e4

With this move Black restores the balance in material.

24 g3 ♗xc6 25 d5 ♗d7 26 ♘c2 ♘g4 27 ♗d4 g5!? 28 ♔f3?

This is an error which allows Black to create a very dangerous passed h-pawn. Correct is 28 fxg5 ♗xg3 29 ♔f3 and the game would most probably end up as a draw.

28...gxf4 29 gxf4 h5 30 ♘e3 ♘xe3 31 ♔xe3?

But after this last mistake Black's h-pawn becomes unstoppable. White should have continued 31 ♗xe3 with reasonable chances of a draw.

31...♗g4!

Cutting off White's king from f3 where Black's passed pawn could be controlled.

32 ♗f6 ♗c5+ 33 ♔e4 ♗f2! 34 ♗e5

White saw too late that his intended 34 ♗d8 h4 35 ♗xc7 h3 36 f5 ♗g1! loses because he would be forced to sacrifice his bishop for Black's h-pawn.

34...h4 35 f5 ♗g3 36 ♗xg3 hxg3 37 ♔e3 ♔g7 38 ♗c2 ♔f6

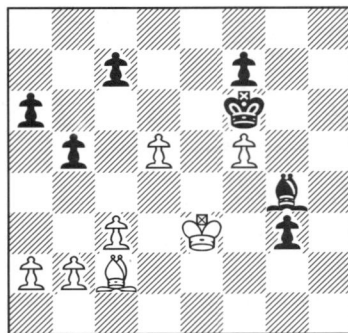

With the fall of the pawn on f5 the game is over because Black creates passed f- and g-pawns. The rest needs no explanation.

39 ♗e4 ♗xf5 40 ♗g2 ♔e5 41 b4 ♗b1
42 a3 f5 43 d6 f4+ 44 ♔e2 cxd6 45
♗b7 ♗e4 46 ♗xa6 f3+ 47 ♔f1 ♗d3+
0-1

Game 67
Fischer-S.Bernstein
New York 1959

---

1 e4 e5 2 ♘f3 ♘c6 3 ♗b5 a6 4 ♗a4 ♘f6
5 0-0 ♗e7 6 ♖e1 b5 7 ♗b3 0-0 8 c3 d5
9 exd5 e4?! 10 dxc6 exf3 11 ♕xf3 ♗g4
12 ♕g3 ♗d6 13 ♕h4 ♖e8 14 f3

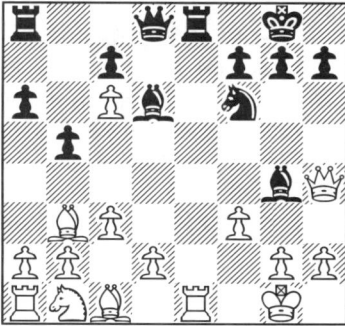

White intends to avoid any unnecessary weakening, which is the case when White plays d4 and f4, but after the text White's lag in development will be obvious. The other question is whether Black is capable of taking advantage of this fact.

14...♗f5

There is the funny sacrifice 14...♗xh2+!? 15 ♔xh2 ♕d6+ 16 ♔g1 ♖xe1+ 17 ♕xe1 ♖e8 18 ♕f2 ♗xf3!? 19 gxf3 ♕d3 20 ♗d1 ♘h5, which was seen in a 1963 correspondence game Petursson-Johansson. After 21 ♘a3 ♖e6! Black had a really dangerous attack. No better for White is 21 ♕h4 as Black can offer a third piece with 21...♘f4!!. Then after 22 ♕xf4 ♖e1+ and 23...♕f1 White is struggling. Instead White could try 22 ♔f2 ♖e2+ 23 ♔g3 (worse is 23 ♗xe2? ♕xe2+ 24 ♔g3 ♕e1+ 25 ♔g4 f5+ and Black wins) 23...♖g2+ 24 ♔xf4 and now after the quiet move

24...h6! Black has at least a draw.

15 d4 ♗xh2+ 16 ♔xh2 ♘g4+ 17 ♔g3 ♕xh4+ 18 ♔xh4 ♖xe1 19 fxg4 ♖xc1 20 gxf5

After the complications we have a very difficult position to assess. My first impression is that Black should not be worse here due to the pin along the first rank, but with the next move Black goes astray.

20...♖d8?

Missing the golden opportunity for 20...♔f8!, which after 21 a4 bxa4 22 ♗xa4 ♖e8!

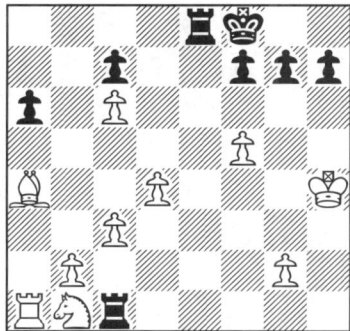

would have led to a quite promising position for Black according to the analysis of Gutman and Vitomskis. After the text Black virtually loses an important tempo.

21 a4!

Now Black must be careful not to fall prey to a back rank mating cheapo.

21...b4 22 d5 ♖b8 23 d6!

Creating a dangerous passed c-pawn which will decide the issue of the game.

23...cxd6 24 ♗c4 ♖c8 25 ♗xa6 ♖xc6 26 ♗b5 ♖b6 27 c4 d5

A desperate attempt to create some mating threats, but Black just hasn't got sufficient forces.

28 a5 g5+ 29 ♔xg5

Not fearing any ghosts. Fischer's greatest virtue, shown in this game, was that he strived for the simplest possible solutions.

29...h6+ 30 ♔g4 ♖b8 31 a6

White has clearly been winning for some time.

31...dxc4 32 a7 ♖a8 33 ♗c6 h5+ 34 ♔g5 ♖xb1 35 ♖xb1 ♖xa7 36 ♖c1 ♖a2 37 ♖xc4 ♖xb2 38 f6 1-0

Game 68
Browne-Bisguier
Oberlin 1975

---

1 e4 e5 2 ♘f3 ♘c6 3 ♗b5 a6 4 ♗a4 ♘f6 5 0-0 ♗e7 6 ♖e1 b5 7 ♗b3 0-0 8 c3 d5 9 exd5 e4?! 10 dxc6 exf3 11 d4!

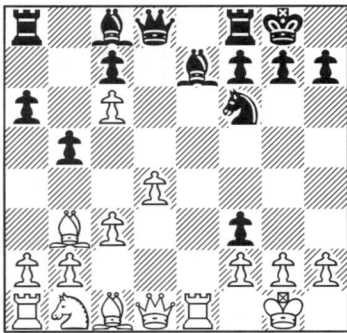

This is the strongest continuation, which casts a doubt over the Steiner Variation. White simply continues with his development, thus allowing his kingside to be weakened after Black takes on g2. However, it will transpire that Black's chances of creating a serious kingside attack are not so great due to the excellently placed and centralised white pieces.

11...fxg2

Alternatives are clearly weaker:

a) 11...♗g4? 12 gxf3 ♗h5 13 ♗f4 ♗d6 14 ♗g3! completely secures the safety of White's kingside.

b) 11...♗d6 12 ♗g5 ♗xh2+ 13 ♔xh2 ♘g4+ 14 ♔g1 ♕xg5 15 ♕xf3 h5 16 ♘a3 ♗f5 17 ♘c2 ♖ae8 18 ♘e3 ♗e4 19 ♕g3 ♗xc6 20 ♕xc7 ♘xe3 21 ♕xc6 ♖c8 22 ♕f3 and White keeps his extra pawn. He also has the better position due to his strong light-squared bishop on b3.

12 ♗g5

Not so clear is 12 ♕f3 ♗e6! 13 ♗f4 (very risky is 13 ♗xe6?! fxe6 14 ♖xe6 ♘d5 15 ♕xg2 ♗h4! with powerful play along the f-file) 13...♘d5 14 ♗g3 a5! 15 ♘d2 a4 16 ♗c2 ♕e8! 17 ♕d3 g6 18 ♕xb5 ♖b8 followed by ...♖b8xb2.

12...♗g4 13 ♕d3 ♖e8 14 ♘d2 ♘d5

Or 14...♘h5 15 ♖xe7! ♖xe7 16 h3! (an important move because it is only equal after 16 ♗xe7? ♕xe7 17 ♕e3 ♖e8! etc.) 16...♗e6 17 ♕e3! with a clear advantage to White.

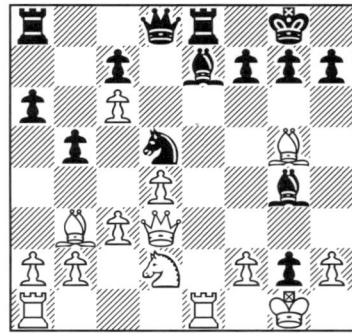

15 ♗xe7

Deserving of attention is 15 ♘f3! ♗xf3 (even worse is 15...♗xg5? 16 ♖xe8+ ♕xe8 17 ♘xg5 and White wins) 16 ♗xe7 ♖xe7 17 ♕xf3 with nearly a winning advantage for White.

15...♖xe7 16 ♖xe7 ♘xe7 17 ♕e4 ♗f5

18 ♕f3

Black achieves some counterplay after 18 ♕xg2?! ♘g6 etc.

18...♕d6 19 ♖e1 ♗g6 20 ♘e4 ♕xc6 21 ♘f6+!

With this combination White converts into a winning ending.

21...gxf6 22 ♕xc6 ♘xc6 23 ♗d5 ♖b8 24 ♗xc6 b4 25 c4 b3 26 a3 ♗d3 27 c5 ♖d8 28 d5 ♗b5

Or 28...♗f1 29 ♖e3 ♗c4 30 ♖c3! ♗xd5? 31 ♖d3! and Black loses due to the pin along the d-file, while after 28...♗c4 29 ♖c1 ♗xd5? 30 ♖d1! is also decisive for exactly the same reason.

29 ♗xb5 axb5 30 ♖d1 ♔f8 31 ♖d3 ♔e7

If Black tries to free himself with 31...c6, White has 32 dxc6! ♖xd3 33 c7 and the pawn will queen.

32 ♔xg2 ♖g8+ 33 ♔f3 ♖g5 34 ♖xb3 ♖xd5 35 ♖xb5 ♖h5 36 ♔g3?!

Stronger was 36 a4! ♖xh2 37 a5 and White should win. The sloppy technique shown by White lets his opponent off in what is a lost rook and pawn ending.

36...♖g5+ 37 ♔f3 ♖f5+ 38 ♔g2 ♖g5+ 39 ♔f1 ♖h5 40 ♔g2 ♖g5+ 41 ♔f1 ♖h5 42 ♖a5? ♖xh2 43 ♖a6 ♖h6 44 b4 ♖g6!

It is important to cut off White's king from the g-file, which means Black's passed h-pawn will give him some drawing chances.

45 ♖a8 h5 46 ♖h8 ♖g5 47 ♔e2

It is not possible to advance the queenside pawn because if 47 a4 Black has 47...♖g4!.

47...f5 48 f4?

A decisive mistake which throws away the win for White. With the logical 48 ♔f3! White was still winning.

48...♖g3 49 ♖xh5 ♖xa3 50 ♖xf5 ♖b3 51 ♖e5+ ♔d7 52 ♖e4 ♔c6 53 f5 ♔d5 54 ♖e7 ♖xb4 55 ♖xc7 f6 56 ♔f3 ♔e5 57 ♖e7+ ♔xf5 58 c6 ♖c4 59 c7 ♖c3+ 60 ♔e2 ♔f4

Now a draw is on the cards.

61 ♔d2 ♖c6 62 ♔d3 f5 63 ♔d4 ♖c1 64 ♔d5 ♖d1+ 65 ♔e6 ♖e1+ 66 ♔d7 ♖d1+ 67 ♔e8 ♖c1 68 ♔d8 ♔g3 69 ♖g7+ ♔f3 70 ♖f7 f4 ½-½

The game could continue 71 c8♕ ♖xc8+ 72 ♔xc8 ♔e3 73 ♔d7 f3 74 ♔e6 f2 75 ♔e5 ♔e2 etc.

Summary

In Game 64 Black is really doing fine after the forceful sequence 11...♞e5! 12 ♞xe4 ♞xe4 13 ♛xe4 ♝d6 14 f4 f5 15 ♛e3 ♞g6 etc.

In Game 66 theory regards that Black has enough compensation for the sacrificed pawn but not any more than that. Valenta adopts the very interesting plan with the exchange of queens(!), which looks illogical but leads to a drawn ending. However, he manages to win the game but only with the help of his opponent.

The ending in Game 67 with White having two minor pieces for a rook is by no means better for White since it is not easy to see how he can disentangle himself from the unpleasant pin along the first rank. Even earlier in the game it is possible that Bernstein could have tried 14...♝xh2+!?, which may have caused serious problems. Fischer, in any case, only won the game because Bernstein blundered with 20...♜d8?, He should have played 20...♚f8!, which would have given him at least a good position, if not more.

11 d4! is the main reason why the world's top players like Adams and Svidler never play the Steiner. In Game 68 the shock value fails as Walter Browne transforms his positional advantage into a clear technically winning ending by playing ♞e4-f6+!. However, later on his sloppy technique lets his opponent off the hook and he fails to win the rook and pawn ending.

1 e4 e5 2 ♞f3 ♞c6 3 ♝b5 a6 4 ♝a4 ♞f6 5 0-0 b5 6 ♝b3 ♝e7 7 ♜e1 0-0 8 c3 d5 9 exd5 e4 10 dxc6

      10 ♞g5 ♝g4 (D)
            11 ♛c2 – *Game 64*; 11 f3 – *Game 63*

10...exf3 11 ♛xf3

      11 d4! (D) – *Game 68*

11...♝g4 12 ♛g3 ♝d6 13 f4

      13 ♛h4 –*Game 67*

13...♜e8 14 d4 (D) – *Game 66*

      14 ♜e5 – *Game 65*

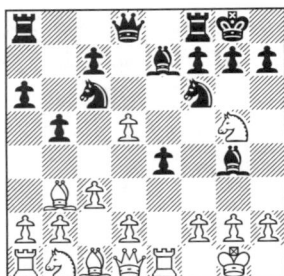 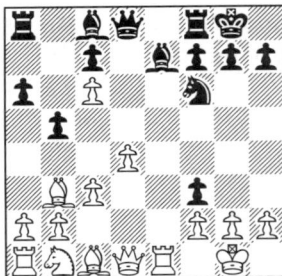 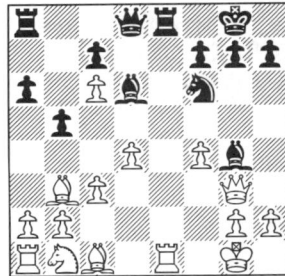

    10...♝g4   *11 d4!*   *14 d4*

CHAPTER SEVEN

Anti-Marshall with 8 h3 ♗b7 9 d3 d6 10 a3

1 e4 e5 2 ♘f3 ♘c6 3 ♗b5 a6 4 ♗a4 ♘f6 5 0-0 ♗e7 6 ♖e1 b5 7 ♗b3 0-0 8 h3 ♗b7 9 d3 d6 10 a3

It is amazing just how quickly the theory of this modern Anti-Marshall set-up has developed. With his tenth move White simply creates an escape square on a2 for the b3-bishop in case of ...♘a5, but without creating tension on the queenside with a2-a4 (see Chapter 8).

In Game 69 Black avoids the main lines by playing 10...♘a7!?. Black can also play in the spirit of the Breyer Variation of the Closed Ruy Lopez if he chooses 10...♘b8, as seen in Games 70-71.

The speciality of Czech GM Pavel Blatny, 10...♘d4, is seen in Jansa-P.Blatny (Game 72) and A.Kovacevic-Berzinsh (Game 73).

The popular 10...♘a5 followed by ...c7-c5 is the subject of Games 74-78. After 10...♘a5 11 ♗a2 c5 12 ♘c3, Adams chooses 12...h6 in Game 74, while 12...b4?!, with the sacrifice ...b4-b3 in mind, is seen in Game 75.

The main continuation for Black after 10...♘a5 11 ♗a2 c5 12 ♘c3 is 12...♘c6. In Game 76 Gelfand plays 13 ♘e2?! against Adams, while Game 77 sees Kasparov try 13 ♗g5 against the same opponent. In Game 78 White plays the logical 13 ♘d5.

Games 79-83 deal with the line 10...♕d7

11 ♘c3 ♖ae8, after which White has many different possibilities: 12 ♗e3, 12 ♘d5, 12 ♗a2, 12 ♗d2 and 12 a4. These moves are all dealt with in turn.

Finally, in Game 84 Black delays moving his d6-pawn and instead plays 9...♖e8.

Game 69
Korneev-B.Lalić
Seville 2002

---

1 e4 e5 2 ♘f3 ♘c6 3 ♗b5 a6 4 ♗a4 ♘f6 5 0-0 ♗e7 6 ♖e1 b5 7 ♗b3 0-0 8 h3 ♗b7

8...d6 9 c3 would transpose to the mainline Closed Spanish.

9 d3 d6 10 a3

White creates a pawn chain (d3, e4) against Black's b7-bishop which might be annoying for the black-sided Marshall player. White often develops his knight to c3 from where it can either be transferred to g3 (via e2) or simply stay put to guard the d5-square. As this system has grown in popularity in the past decade, Black will need some knowledge to counter it.

10...♘a7!?

An interesting idea introduced into tournament play by English Grandmaster Mark Hebden. With the text Black makes it hard for White to execute his main manoeuvre ♘c3-d5 since Black can then simply exchange on d5 to achieve a strong position in the centre. The difference between this, at first glance, strange move and 10...♘b8 is that here Black can quickly play ...c7-c5 and ...♖a8-c8. However, Black must be wary of his knight being stranded away from the centre.

11 c4

A theoretical novelty played after 45 minutes thought, which shows that 10...♘a7!? came as a thunderbolt for the usually well prepared Russian Grandmaster Oleg Korneev. Before this White had always been playing 11 ♘c3 c5 but Black had experienced no problems as can be seen from the following examples:

a) 12 ♘h2 ♖c8 13 ♘g4 ♘c6 14 ♘xf6+ ♗xf6 15 ♗d5 ♖c7 16 ♗e3 ½-½ Luther-Hebden, Cappelle la Grande 1998.

b) 12 ♗g5 ♘e8! 13 ♗xe7 ♕xe7 14 ♗d5 (or 14 ♘d5 ♕d8 followed by ...♘e8-f6 and Black has no problems in reaching equality) 14...♘c6 15 ♘e2 ♘c7 16 ♗a2 ♔h8 17 ♘g3 g6 18 ♕d2 f5 19 exf5 gxf5 20 ♕g5 ♕xg5 21 ♘xg5 d5 and Black had the initiative in Boudre-Hebden, French League 2000.

11...bxc4 12 ♗xc4 c5 13 ♘c3 a5

Preventing any possibility of White playing b2-b4.

14 ♘g5!? ♖b8

Protecting the bishop because the threat

was 15 ♗xf7+ ♖xf7 16 ♘xf7 ♔xf7 17 ♕b3+ and 18 ♕xb7.

15 f4 ♘c6

A good defence. Weaker is 15...exf4?! 16 ♗xf4 h6 17 ♘f3 and Black must reckon with the unpleasant threat of e4-e5, when Black's rook on b8 can easily become a target for White's bishop on f4.

16 ♘f3

The alternative was 16 f5 ♘d4 17 ♘f3 ♘d7 planning ...♘d4xf3+ followed by ...♗e7-g5 with very complicated play ahead.

16...exf4 17 ♗xf4 ♘d7 18 ♘d5 ♘ce5 19 ♘xe5 ♘xe5 20 ♗xe5 dxe5 21 b3 ♗xd5 22 ♗xd5 g6 23 ♖a2 ♔g7 24 ♗c4 ♖b6 25 ♖f1 ♖f6 26 ♖xf6 ♗xf6 27 g3 ♗e7 28 ♖f2 ♕d4?!

The opposite-coloured bishops promise Black an easy draw. However, this is the first inaccuracy. If I wanted to free myself with ...f7-f5 it was more appropriate to do it immediately with 28...f5!? 29 exf5 ♖xf5. We shall see that, with Black's queen on d4, White's manoeuvre ♖f2-e2 gains in strength because later White can play ♖e2-e4 attacking Black's queen and gaining a tempo.

29 ♔g2 f5!? 30 exf5 e4?

I didn't like the look of 30...♖xf5 31 ♖e2!, when White is just a tiny bit better. If White plays 31 ♖xf5 (instead of 31 ♖e2!) 31...gxf5 32 ♕h5 Black has an easy draw after 32...♕b2+ 33 ♔f3 e4+! etc.

31 ♕e1!

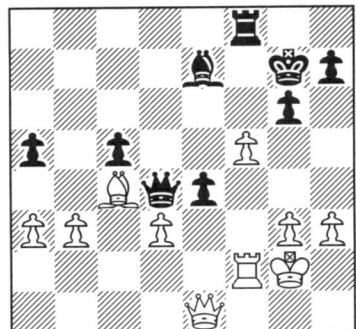

This is what I overlooked.

31...gxf5 32 dxe4 fxe4

Neither is 32...♕xe4+ 33 ♕xe4 fxe4 34 ♖e2 very pleasant for Black – to defend a pawn down despite the opposite-coloured bishops is not great fun.

33 ♖e2 ♗d6 34 ♖xe4 ♕b2+

Only now did I see that the planned 34...♖f2+ loses after the cold-blooded 35 ♔h1! ♕b2 36 ♖g4+! and White mates first!

35 ♖e2 ♕f6 36 ♖e3 ♕b2+ 37 ♖e2 ♕f6 38 h4

Stronger was 38 ♗d5! ♕g5 39 ♕c3+ ♖f6 40 ♗c4 etc.

38...♕f3+ 39 ♔h3 ♕f5+ 40 ♔h2 ♕g4 41 ♔g2 ♕f3+ 42 ♔h2 ♕g4 43 ♖e7+

After 43 ♖e4 ♖f2+ 44 ♕xf2 ♕xe4 45 ♕f7+ ♔h6 46 ♕f6+ ♕g6 Black just manages to defend the position.

43...♔h8 44 ♕c3+ ♕d4 45 ♖e3

Maybe a better winning try was hidden in the ending after 45 ♕xd4+ cxd4 46 ♖d7 ♗xa3 47 ♖xd4 etc. It is difficult to say – probably White's chances to win this game and Black's to draw are 50-50. Who knows?

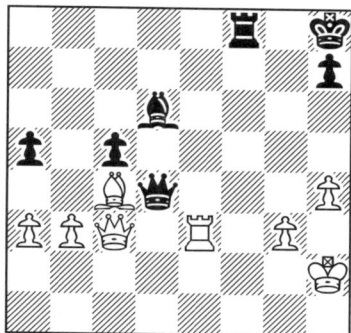

45...♔g7 46 a4 ♕xc3 47 ♖xc3 ♗e5 48 ♖e3 ♖e8 49 ♔h3 ♖e7 50 ♖f3 ♗f6! 51 ♖f5

51 ♔g4 is worth considering.

51...♖e5 52 ♖f4 h5!? 53 ♖f3 ♖e7 54 ♖d3?!

Better is 54 ♔g2.

54...♗d4 55 ♔g2 ♖e3 56 ♖d1 ♔g6

Worse is 56...♗e5?! 57 ♖d5! etc.

57 ♖f1 ♗e5 58 ♗f7+ ♔g7 59 ♖f5 ♖xg3+ 60 ♔f2 ♖c3 61 ♔e2

White's sloppy endgame technique has allowed me to reach a drawn position. I also have an easy draw after 61 ♖xe5 ♔xf7 62 ♖xh5 ♖xb3 63 ♖xc5 ♖b4 64 ♖xa5 ♖xh4.

61...♗d4 62 ♗c4 ♖e3+ 63 ♔d2 ♖h3 64 ♖xh5 ♔g6 65 ♖g5+ ♔f6 66 ♖h5 ♔g6 67 ♖g5+ ♔f6 68 ♖d5 ♖xh4 69 ♔d3 ♗e7 70 ♖g5 ♔d6 71 ♖g6+ ♔e5 72 ♖e6+ ♔f5 73 ♖a6 ♖h3+ 74 ♔e2 ♖h2+ 75 ♔f3 ♗c3 76 ♖d6 ♗b4 77 ♖d5+ ♔f6 78 ♖d8 ♖h4 79 ♔e3 ♖d4 80 ♖xd4 ½-½

Game 70
Ponomariov-Ivanchuk
FIDE World Ch., Moscow 2002

1 e4 e5 2 ♘f3 ♘c6 3 ♗b5 a6 4 ♗a4 ♘f6 5 0-0 ♗e7 6 ♖e1 b5 7 ♗b3 0-0 8 h3 ♗b7 9 d3 d6 10 a3 ♘b8 11 ♘bd2 ♘bd7 12 ♘f1 ♖e8 13 ♘g3

13 ♗a2 is discussed in the next game.

13...c6

13...♘c5 is not enough for equality after 14 ♗a2 ♘e6 15 ♘g5! ♘xg5 16 ♗xg5 h6 17 ♗e3 d5 18 ♕f3 ♗f8 19 ♖ad1 ♕d6 (Black could have released a tension in the centre by playing 19...d4 but in that case the scope of activity for White's light-squared bishop would have been increased to the maximum) 20 exd5 ♗xd5 21 ♘e4 ♗xe4 22 dxe4 ♕c6 23 ♕f5 ♖e7 (the seventh rank must be defended because if 23...♕xc2?, 24 ♖d7! is very strong) 24 c3 with steady positional advantage for White due to the pair of bishops, Shirov-Svidler, European Club Cup, Halkidiki 2002.

14 ♘h2 d5 15 ♕f3

Or 15 ♘f5 ♗f8 16 ♕f3 and now instead of the poor reply 16...♔h8? 17 ♗g5 h6 18 ♗h4 g6 19 ♘e3 g5 20 ♗g3, when Black's kingside was seriously weakened in the game Shirov-Adams, Wijk aan Zee 1998, Black should start counterplay in the centre with

16...dxe4 17 dxe4 c5 18 c4 (the only move otherwise black plays ...c5-c4 shutting out the light-squared bishop) 18...♕b6 19 ♘g4 ♘xg4 20 ♕xg4 ♕g6 with equality.

15...g6 16 ♗a2?!

This is a prophylactic move against the ...♘d7-c5 manoeuvre attacking White's bishop. However, more forceful was 16 ♗h6 ♘c5 17 ♗a2 ♕d6 18 ♘g4 with a small but lasting advantage for White because White's bishop on h6 is a thorn in Black's position.

16...♗f8 17 ♗g5 h6 18 ♗d2 ♗g7 19 ♘g4 ♘xg4 20 hxg4 ♘c5 21 ♖ad1 ♖c8 22 ♘f1 ♘e6 23 ♕g3 ♔h7 24 ♘h2 f6!

A nice move which prevents White's attempt at a kingside attack commencing with g4-g5. Black's dark-squared bishop will emerge into play via the a3-f8 diagonal if necessary.

25 ♘f3 c5 26 ♕h2 ♘d4 27 ♘xd4?!

It might have been better to play 27 c3, not opening the c-file for Black.

27...cxd4 28 c3 dxc3 29 bxc3?

This leaves the a-pawn defenceless. Better was 29 ♗xc3 d4 30 ♗d2 ♖c2 31 ♗c1 and Black's rook will later be ejected from c2 by ♗a2-b1. It's true that in that case Black would maintain the advantage due to having the larger control of space.

29...dxe4 30 dxe4 ♕e7 31 a4

White should have tried 31 ♕h3!?, hoping for 31...♕xa3?! 32 ♗xh6!! ♗xh6 33 ♖d7+ ♖e7 34 g5 fxg5 35 ♖xb7 ♖xb7 36 ♕xc8 and

it is not clear who is better. Of course Black is not obliged to fall into this with 31...♕xa3?!.

31...bxa4 32 ♕h3 ♖ed8 33 ♕f3 ♖c7 34 ♗c1 ♖cd7 35 ♗b1 ♕e6 36 ♖xd7 ♖xd7 37 ♗c2 ♗c6 38 ♖d1 ♕a2 39 ♖xd7 ♗xd7 40 ♕d1 ♗b5

Black should keep his dangerous passed a-pawn alive so this is better than 40...♗xg4 41 f3 ♗e6 42 ♗xa4 etc.

41 ♗e3 ♕c4 42 ♔h2 ♗c6 43 ♕a1 ♗f8

43...♗xe4?! 44 ♕xa4 is obviously worse than the text.

44 ♗b1 a3?

This grave error lets slip a deserved win for Black. One down with just four games to go in a world title match, it is not just the chess that proves decisive but also chess psychology! After the simple 44...♗xe4 45 ♗a2 ♕c6 46 f3 ♗d3 followed by 47...e5-e4 White could resign.

45 f3 ♕b3 46 ♕a2 ♗a4 47 ♔g3 ♔g7?

One error causes another, which is often the case. It is really hard to imagine that Black will even lose this game and with it virtually the match! After the correct 47...g5 Black would still preserve some winning chances.

48 ♕d2!

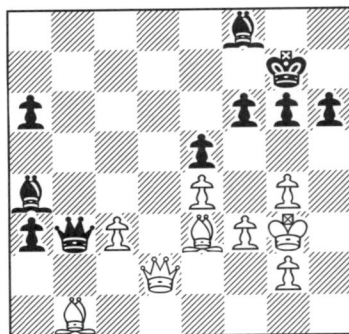

This is what Black had overlooked. Now if 48...♕xb1, then 49 ♗xh6+ ♔g8 (49...♔f7 50 ♕d5+ ♔e8 51 ♕e6+ ♗e7 52 ♕c8+ leads to perpetual check) 50 ♕d5+ ♔h8 51 ♗xf8

a2 52 ♕f7 ♕e1+ and it is Black who takes the draw by perpetual check.

48...g5

A desperate try to win but, bearing in mind that Black was now in time trouble, a wiser choice would have been to take the draw.

49 ♗a2 ♕b7 50 ♕d3

50 ♕d5 immediately is also worthy of attention.

50...♗e8 51 ♕d5 ♕xd5 52 exd5

Now White has dangerous passed c- and d-pawns that make the result uncertain – White is certainly no longer worse!

52...a5 53 c4 ♗b4 54 c5 ♔f8 55 ♔f2 ♗b5 56 c6 ♔e7 57 ♗a7 ♔d8 58 ♗b6+ ♔c8 59 ♔e3 a4??

A final mistake. Black can draw by 59...♗f1! 60 g3 (or 60 ♔e4 ♗xg2 61 ♗c4 ♗d6 62 ♗xa5 ♗h1 and White can't win) 60...a4 61 ♔e4 ♗e2 62 ♔f5 ♗xf3 63 ♗c4 ♗d6 64 ♔e6 ♗c7 65 ♗c5 ♗e2 66 ♗a2 ♗xg4+ 67 ♔f6 e4 68 d6 e3! 69 dxc7 e2 70 ♗b4 ♗xc7 71 ♔g6 ♗f3 72 ♔xh6 ♗xc6 73 ♗c4 a2 74 ♗xa2 ♗d5 75 ♗b1 a3 76 ♔xg5 a2 77 ♗xa2 ♗xa2 etc.

60 ♔e4 ♗e2

Or 50...♗f1 61 ♔f5 ♗xg2 62 ♗c4 ♗d6 63 ♔e6 ♗c7 64 ♗xc7 ♔xc7 65 d6+ ♔xc6 66 d7 and the passed d-pawn queens.

61 ♔f5 e4 62 ♔e6 exf3 63 d6 ♗xd6 64 ♔xd6 1-0

Game 71
Kasparov-Kramnik
Linares 2003

1 e4 e5 2 ♘f3 ♘c6 3 ♗b5 a6 4 ♗a4 ♘f6 5 0-0 ♗e7 6 ♖e1 b5 7 ♗b3 0-0 8 h3 ♗b7 9 d3 d6 10 a3 ♘b8 11 ♘bd2 ♘bd7 12 ♘f1 ♖e8 13 ♗a2 c6 14 ♘g3 ♗f8 15 ♘f5 d5 16 d4!?

A very sharp continuation. Black now has to be careful because both White's bishops can become increasingly active.

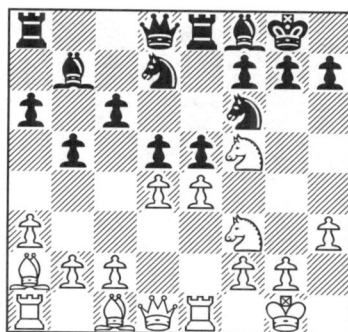

16...c5!

White's idea would become transparent after 16...exd4? 17 e5! ♘e4 18 ♖xe4! dxe4 19 ♘g5 ♘xe5 20 ♕h5 and Black will soon be mated.

17 dxc5 ♘xc5 18 exd5 e4 19 ♘3d4 ♗xd5 20 ♗xd5 ♕xd5

Also possible was 20...♘xd5 21 ♕g4 ♕f6 22 ♗g5 ♕g6 etc.

21 ♗g5 ♘fd7

21...♘cd7!? 22 ♕d2 ♖e5 also deserves attention.

22 ♕g4 ♘e5 23 ♕g3 ♘e6 24 ♖ad1 ♘xg5 25 ♕xg5 ♕b7 26 ♘g3 ♘c4 27 ♘df5 ♖e6

From this square Black's rook defends the kingside. 27...♘xb2 28 ♖d4 f6 29 ♕g4 would have been dangerous for Black.

28 b3 ♘xa3 29 ♖xe4 ♖xe4

Bad is 29...♘xc2? 30 ♖xe6 fxe6 31 ♘h5! exf5 32 ♖d7! ♕xd7 33 ♘f6+ and White wins.

30 ♘xe4 ♕xe4 31 ♘h6+ ♔h8 32 ♘xf7+ ♔g8 33 ♘h6+ ♔h8 ½-½

Game 72
Jansa-Blatny
Czech Championship 1998

1 e4 e5 2 ♘f3 ♘c6 3 ♗b5 a6 4 ♗a4 ♘f6 5 0-0 ♗e7 6 ♖e1 b5 7 ♗b3 0-0 8 h3 ♗b7 9 d3 d6 10 a3 ♘d4

♗d6 18 ♗d2?!

After 18 ♗xd6 ♕xd6 Black is slightly better, so best was 18 ♗e3! pressurising the c5-pawn and keeping the game balanced.

18...♕f6 19 ♗c3 ♕f5 20 ♕g4 ♕xg4 21 hxg4 ♖fd8 22 ♗a5?!

White should have realised the forthcoming danger and avoided it by playing 22 d4!? c4 23 ♗b4 ♗xb4 24 axb4 f6 (of course not 24...♖xd5? 25 ♖xa6! using Black's back rank weakness) 25 ♖e6 ♖xd5 26 ♖exa6 ♖xa6 27 ♖xa6 ♖xd4 with a probable draw.

22...♖d7 23 b4 ♗f8 24 bxc5 ♗xc5 25 ♗b4 ♗f8 26 ♗xf8 ♔xf8 27 a4?

After this Black will obtain a strong passed b-pawn. Better was 27 ♖ac1 ♖xd5 28 ♖c3.

27...b4! 28 a5

Now White will have to worry about his a5-pawn, but this had to be played, otherwise Black would have played ...a6-a5 supporting his strong passed b4-pawn with excellent winning chances.

28...♖xd5 29 ♖eb1 ♖b8 30 ♖b3 ♖d4 31 f3 ♔e7 32 ♔f2 ♔d6 33 ♔e3 ♔d5 34 ♔d2 ♔c5 35 ♖h1

Also after 35 ♖c1+ ♔b5 36 ♖c7 ♖f4 White's a5-pawn is doomed.

35...♔b5 36 ♖a1 ♖e8 37 ♖bb1 g6 38 ♖b3 h5 39 gxh5 gxh5 40 ♖h1 ♖e5 41 ♖a1 f5!

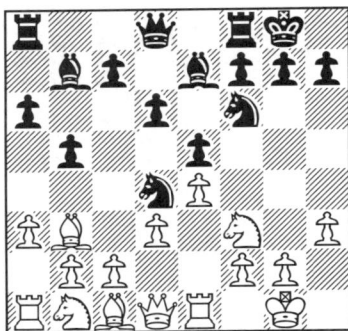

This pet line of the Czech Grandmaster Pavel Blatny surprisingly does not have too many followers even though a refutation has not been found. Probably what deters the black-sided players is that after the exchange on d4 White gets a kingside pawn majority (the e5-pawn has been removed) and thus White has potential attacking chances. However, Black also has his own trump card – by playing ...♘c6-d4 and ...c5-c4 he keeps White's light-squared bishop out of play for some time.

11 ♘xd4 exd4 12 c3 dxc3 13 ♘xc3 c5 14 ♗f4 d5!

A good pawn sacrifice by which Black frees himself. White will have doubled d-pawns so his extra pawn is rather weak and lacks the support of other pieces. Once Black regains one of them, he will be better.

15 ♘xd5 ♘xd5 16 ♗xd5 ♗xd5 17 exd5

White has to content himself with a waiting policy while Black plans to play ...f5-f4 followed by ...♖e5-g5 winning White's g2-

pawn. White's next move is practically forced.

42 g3 f4 43 gxf4 ♖xf4 44 ♖c1 ♔xa5 45 ♖c4 ♖xc4 46 dxc4 h4

With the fall of White's a5-pawn, the game is virtually over. Black's 'a' and 'b' connected passed pawns are decisive. The rest needs no explanation.

47 ♖b1 h3 48 ♔d3 h2 49 ♖h1 ♖h5 50 f4 ♔b6 51 f5 ♔c5 52 f6 ♖h7 53 f7 ♖xf7 54 ♖xh2 ♖d7+ 55 ♔c2 ♔xc4 56 ♖h5 ♖d5 57 ♖h4+ ♔b5 0-1

Game 73
A.Kovacevic-Berzinsh
Interlaken 2001

---

1 e4 e5 2 ♘f3 ♘c6 3 ♗b5 a6 4 ♗a4 ♘f6 5 0-0 ♗e7 6 ♖e1 b5 7 ♗b3 0-0 8 h3 ♗b7 9 d3 d6 10 a3 ♘d4 11 ♘xd4 exd4 12 ♘d2

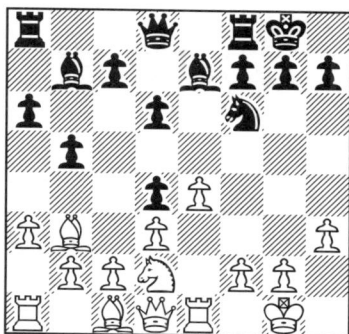

As we have seen from the previous game, Black gets a satisfactory position after 12 c3 dxc3 13 ♘xc3 c5 14 ♗f4 d5!. In this game White hurries to bring his knight to the kingside where he obviously has an advantage.

12...c5 13 ♘f1!?

White tries to improve over the game Lanka-Blatny, European Team Championship, Debrecen 1992, in which Black had no problems after 13 ♘f3 ♘d7 14 a4 ♘e5 15 ♗f4 ♗f6 16 ♘h2 ♘g6 17 ♗d2 ♗g5! etc.

13...d5

Passive is 13...♘d7?! 14 ♘g3 ♗g5 15 f4 ♗h4 16 ♕g4 ♗xg3 17 ♕xg3 ♔h8 18 f5 and White has the advantage of the two bishops and a promising attack, Konigova-Hodova, Czech Championship 1999.

14 e5 ♘e8 15 ♘g3 f5?

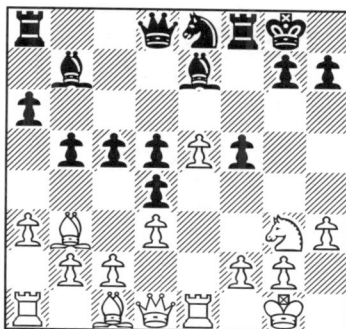

A serious positional mistake which both leaves White with a strong passed e-pawn. and weakens Black's kingside. There was no need for panicking by playing this move because once White's knight lands on f5 it is not the end of the world. Better instead was 15...c4 16 ♗a2 ♗c5 17 ♘f5 ♗c8! 18 ♕f3 ♗xf5 19 ♕xf5 ♘c7 with an approximately equal position as White's light-squared bishop is away from the main scene of the action.

16 ♕f3 g6

Maybe Black was hoping to continue 16...f4 17 ♘e2 g5 but after the strong reply 18 h4! his kingside would have been left shattered.

17 ♗h6 ♘g7 18 c3 dxc3 19 bxc3 ♖f7 20 ♘e2 c4 21 dxc4 dxc4 22 ♕xb7 cxb3 23 ♖ad1 ♕c8 24 ♕d5

The consequences of weakening the a2-g8 diagonal by playing 15...f5? have become obvious – White's queen dominates the board while Black can do very little to stop White's powerful passed e-pawn.

24...♗xa3

This loses but 24...b2 in order to confuse the matter would not have saved the game

either.
25 ♘d4!

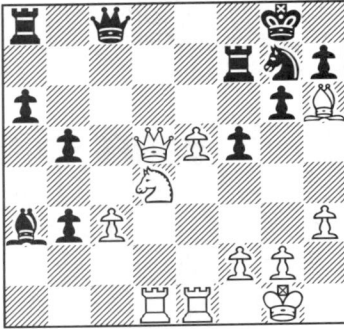

**25...♗e7 26 e6 ♖f8 27 ♘c6 ♖e8 28
♕d7! 1-0**

Black resigns as if 28...♗f8, then 29 ♕f7+
♔h8 30 e7 clearly wins.

Game 74
Murey-Adams
European Club Cup, Hilversum 1993

**1 e4 e5 2 ♘f3 ♘c6 3 ♗b5 a6 4 ♗a4 ♘f6
5 0-0 ♗e7 6 ♖e1 b5 7 ♗b3 0-0 8 h3
♗b7 9 d3 d6 10 a3**

Finnish Grandmaster Heikke Westerinen
first introduced this innocent-looking system.
However, it was only after this game that
suddenly many white players started taking it
up.

10...♘a5 11 ♗c2 c5 12 ♘c3 h6?!

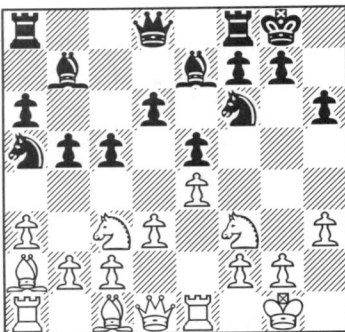

Nowadays this move is regarded as a bit
too slow and it doesn't grant Black full equality.

13 b4

With the text White aims to seize control
over the d5-square. However, recently this
move has been replaced by the more ambitious 13 ♘e2!.

White transfers the knight to the kingside,
which seems to undermine 12...h6?!. The
point is that once the white knight lands on
f5, Black would prefer his pawn to be on h7
rather than on h6, especially as there are unpleasant sacrifices on h6 in the air. Here are a
few examples of 13 ♘e2!:

a) 13...d5? 14 exd5 ♘xd5 15 ♘xe5 ♗d6
16 ♘f4! ♘xf4 17 ♗xf4 ♕c7 18 ♕h5 leads to
a horrible version of the Marshall for Black,
Konguvel-Montauon, Biel 2000.

b) 13...♖e8?! (weakening the f7-square) 14
♘g3 c4 15 ♗d2! cxd3 16 cxd3 ♗f8 17 ♘h2
♘c6 18 ♘h5! ♘d4 19 ♖e3 ♘e6 20 ♖g3 and
all White's pieces are attacking the black
monarch, Korneev-V.Rodriguez, Mislata
1999.

c) 13...♕c7 14 ♘g3 ♘h7 15 ♘f5 ♗f6 16
♘h2 ♗c8 17 ♕f3 ♘c6 18 c3 ♘e7 19 ♘xe7+
♕xe7 20 ♘g4 ♗g5 21 ♘e3 ♗e6 22 ♘d5
♗xd5 23 ♗xd5 ♖xc1 24 ♖axc1 ♖ac8 25
♕e2 ♘f6 26 ♗a2 ♖fd8 27 ♖cd1 ♕c7?! 28
f4! with pressure for White due to his strong
light-squared bishop, Berzinsh-Pedersen,
Aarhus 1993.

d) Apparently never tried in practice is 13...♘c6 14 ♘g3 ♘d4 15 ♘xd4 exd4 (or 15...cxd4 16 f4 with better play for White) 16 ♘f5 ♗c8 17 ♘xe7+ ♕xe7 18 ♗f4 ♗e6 19 e5! and again White has the better chances due to his pawn structure.

13...♘c6 14 ♘d5 ♘xd5

Worth consideration is 14...♘d4!? 15 ♘xe7+ ♕xe7 16 c3 ♘xf3+ 17 ♕xf3 a5! 18 bxc5 dxc5 19 ♕g3 ♔h8 and Black appears to be okay.

15 ♗xd5 ♕c7 16 c3 ♘d8

Or 16...a5 17 bxc5 dxc5 18 ♖b1 b4 19 ♗d2 with a slight but steady advantage for White.

17 ♕b3 ♖c8 18 ♗e3 cxb4

After 18...♗xd5 19 ♕xd5 ♘e6 20 a4! etc. White retains his pressure on the queenside.

19 cxb4 ♕c3?

After defending accurately Black misses White's strong 21st move. Instead he could have drawn easily with 19...♗xd5 20 ♕xd5 ♕c6! 21 ♕xc6 ♘xc6 22 ♖ec1 ♗f6 23 ♖c3 ♘e7 followed by exchanges on the c-file.

20 ♕xc3 ♖xc3 21 ♖ec1!

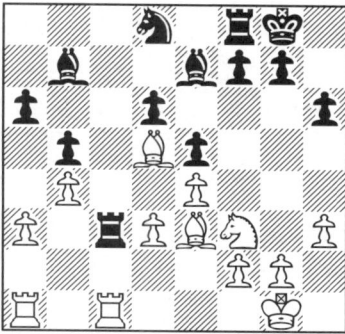

After this strong move White seizes control of the c-file.

21...♖xc1+

21...♖xd3? would have lost a piece to 22 ♗xb7 ♘xb7 23 ♖c7 etc.

22 ♖xc1 ♗xd5 23 exd5 f5 24 ♖c7 ♗f6 25 g4!

White secures control of the vital e4-

square. Going for a material advantage with 25 ♖a7?! ♘f7 26 ♖xa6 ♖c8! would have been wrong because Black gets counterplay.

25...f4 26 ♗b6 ♘f7 27 ♖c6

Again White prefers to retain an iron grip on the position, which is far stronger than 27 ♖a7 ♖c8 etc.

27...♖a8 28 ♘d2 ♔f8 29 ♘e4 ♗e7 30 ♗c7 ♖c8 31 ♗a5 ♖a8

After 31...♖xc6 32 dxc6 ♔e8 White continues with 33 ♘c3 followed by ♘d5 with a winning position.

32 ♘c3 ♔e8 33 a4 bxa4 34 ♘xa4 ♘g5 35 ♔g2 e4

As the battle on the queenside is lost for Black (the pawn on a6 is lost), he searches desperately for play elsewhere.

36 h4! ♘f3 37 dxe4 ♘xh4+ 38 ♔f1 ♘f3 39 ♘b6 ♖b8 40 ♘c4 ♘h2+ 41 ♔g2 ♘xg4 42 ♘xd6+ ♔f8 43 ♘c4 ♗f6 44 ♔f3 ♘e5+ 45 ♘xe5 ♗xe5 46 ♔g4 ♔f7 47 ♔f5 ♖e8

In this ending all White's pieces are on dominating squares. Grandmaster technique sees White home.

48 ♖xa6 ♗b8 49 d6 g6+ 50 ♔xf4 ♔e6 51 ♗c7 ♔d7 52 e5 ♖f8+ 53 ♔e4 ♗xc7 54 ♖a7 1-0

Game 75
Bologan-Zaitsev
Moscow 1998

---

1 e4 e5 2 ♘f3 ♘c6 3 ♗b5 a6 4 ♗a4 ♘f6 5 0-0 ♗e7 6 ♖e1 b5 7 ♗b3 0-0 8 h3 ♗b7 9 d3 d6 10 a3 ♘a5 11 ♗a2 c5 12 ♘c3 b4?!

With this rather impulsive move Black intends, at an early stage, to seize the initiative. Black has in mind, in some lines, to throw in the typical pawn sacrifice ...b4-b3 in order to shut in White's light-squared bishop. However, as we shall see, White's chances are still to be preferred.

13 ♘d5

An alternative which might be even

stronger is 13 axb4 cxb4 14 ♘d5 ♘xd5 15 ♗xd5 ♘c6 16 c3. This gave White clearly the better chances in Lanka-Reichwehr, Schwabisch Gmund 1994 after 16...♕c7 17 d4 a5 18 ♗e3 bxc3 19 bxc3 ♖ab8 20 ♖c1 h6 21 ♘h2! ♘d8 22 c4 ♗c8 23 f4 ♘e6 24 dxe5 dxe5 25 f5 ♘f4 26 ♔h1 ♖b2 27 ♗xf4 exf4 28 ♕h5 with strong pressure on the kingside. Obviously this is only an example of what can happen to Black if he treats the opening in a passive manner as in this game.

13...b3!? 14 ♘xe7+ ♕xe7 15 cxb3 ♘c6 16 ♗e3 a5

Black has some compensation for the sacrificed pawn because the activity of White's light-squared bishop has been seriously diminished.

17 ♘h4 ♗c8 18 f4!? ♘xe4?

Tempting, but it turns out to be an error. Correct was 18...♘g4! 19 hxg4 ♕xh4 20 f5 ♗a6 (but not 20...♘d4?!, when 21 b4! cxb4 22 axb4 axb4? 23 ♗xf7+! decides the outcome of the game) with ...♘c6-d4 to follow, giving Black reasonable compensation for the pawn.

19 ♘f3 ♘f6 20 fxe5 ♘xe5

White's chances are also to be preferred after 20...dxe5 21 ♖c1 because Black's c5-pawn is rather weak.

21 ♗xc5! dxc5 22 ♖xe5 ♗e6 23 ♖c1 ♘d7 24 ♖e1 ♕d6 25 d4!

Lets take stock of what is happening. White has managed to clear up the position

in the centre, leaving him a safe pawn to the good. Soon White's pawn majority on the queenside will start rolling forward.

25...♕g3 26 dxc5 ♗xh3 27 ♕d2 ♗e6 28 ♗b1 ♘f6 29 b4 axb4 30 axb4 ♖fd8 31 ♕g5 ♕b8

The same reply follows after 31...♘g4, rejecting Black's 'attack'.

32 ♕h4 ♖a4 33 ♘g5 ♖xb4 34 ♗xh7+ ♔f8 35 ♘xe6+ fxe6 36 ♕h3 ♖d2 37 ♖xe6 ♖f4 38 ♗g6 1-0

Game 76
Gelfand-Adams
Wijk aan Zee 2002

---

1 e4 e5 2 ♘f3 ♘c6 3 ♗b5 a6 4 ♗a4 ♘f6 5 0-0 ♗e7 6 ♖e1 b5 7 ♗b3 0-0 8 h3 ♗b7 9 d3 d6 10 a3 ♘a5 11 ♗a2 c5 12 ♘c3 ♘c6 13 ♘e2?!

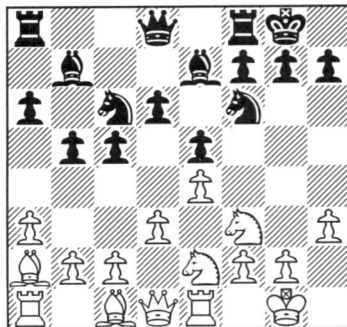

White intends to transfer his knight to g3 in order to support his kingside attack but, as we shall see, this plan is rather unconvincing. The fact that White loses control of the d5-square is of the utmost importance.

13...♗c8! 14 ♘g3 ♗e6 15 ♘f5?!

After this White will achieve the advantage of having the bishop pair but, more importantly, Black will gain control over the centre. White would have done better by playing simple chess with 15 ♗xe6 fxe6 16 c3, although even then Black would have a very pleasant position.

15...♗xf5 16 exf5 ♕d7 17 g4 h6 18 c3

Probably after playing 15 ♘f5?! White's first intention was to continue with 18 ♘h2 ♖fe8 19 h4, but then he noticed 19...♘h7! 20 ♘f3 ♗f8 followed by ...d6-d5 and White's attack grinds to a halt as Black seizes control of the centre.

18...♖fe8 19 b4 cxb4 20 cxb4

Slightly better was 20 axb4 but White is pinning his hopes on the opening of the a1-h8 diagonal by playing ♗c1-b2 and d3-d4.

20...♗d8?!

Black seems to forget about the safety of his kingside. Better was 20...a5! with a strong initiative on the queenside.

21 ♗b2?

This is consistent with 20 cxb4 but, as we shall see, White's dark-squared bishop will play no great role on the long diagonal. Much stronger was 21 ♗e3! a5 22 ♕d2 and Black has to watch out for a possible sacrifice on h6.

21...a5! 22 bxa5

Black is also much better after 22 d4 e4 23 d5 ♘xb4! 24 axb4 exf3.

22...♗xa5 23 ♖e2 ♗b6 24 ♕b3?

White overlooks the next move and loses precious time. Better was 24 ♖c2.

24...♕b7!

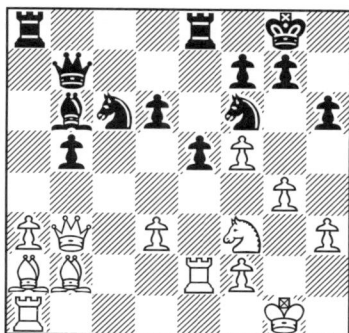

With the obvious threat of ...♘c6-a5 winning a piece.

25 ♕d1 ♖a4

Also deserving attention was 25...♘b4!?

with a clear advantage to Black.

26 ♖c2 ♘e7 27 ♘h2?!

After this White will end up in a position where he is virtually out of moves. After 27 ♗c1?! very promising for Black is the piece sacrifice 27...♘xg4! 28 hxg4 ♖xg4+ 29 ♔f1 ♘xf5 30 ♗b2 ♖f4!. So White had to play 27 d4!? e4 28 ♘e1 etc.

27...♘ed5 28 ♕f3 ♖f4 29 ♕g2

Or 29 ♕g3 ♖c8 30 ♖ac1 ♖xc2 31 ♖xc2 b4! and White is in deep trouble.

29...e4 30 ♖e1

The alternatives are not rosy for White:

a) 30 dxe4 ♘xe4 31 ♘f3 ♘xf2! 32 ♖xf2 ♖e2 winning outright for Black.

b) 30 d4 ♕a7 31 ♖d1 b4 32 ♗xd5 ♘xd5 33 axb4 ♘xb4 with ...♘b4-d3 to come and Black will dominate the board.

30...♖xf2!

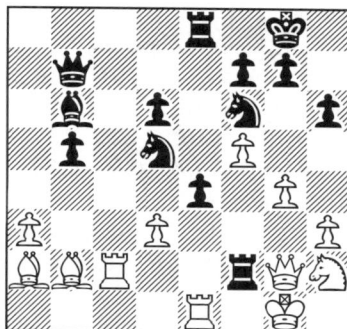

31 ♖xf2 ♘f4 32 ♕g3 ♗xf2+ 33 ♔xf2 ♘xd3+ 34 ♔f1 ♘xb2 35 h4

A desperate attempt to avoid inevitable defeat. 35 ♕xd6 ♘d3 followed by either ...♕b7-a7 or ...♖e8-c8 also leaves White without a decent reply.

35...♕d7 36 ♔g2 ♘d3 37 ♖f1 e3 38 g5 hxg5 39 hxg5 ♘h5 0-1

Game 77
Kasparov-Adams
Linares 1999

1 e4 e5 2 ♘f3 ♘c6 3 ♗b5 a6 4 ♗a4 ♘f6

5 0-0 &e7 6 &e1 b5 7 &b3 0-0 8 h3 &b7 9 d3 d6 10 a3 &a5 11 &a2 c5 12 &c3 &c6 13 &g5

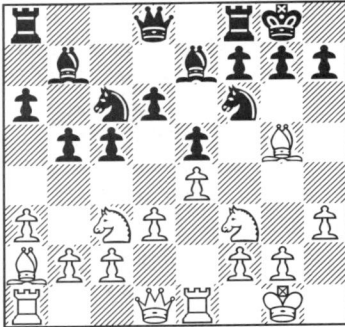

With this move White's idea is crystal clear – he intends to exchange on f6 in order to eliminate one of the pieces defending the d5-square.

13...&d7

Less logical although possible is 13...h6 14 &xf6 &xf6 15 &d5 &d7 16 &h2 &d8 17 &g4 &h8 18 &e3 &g5 19 &g4 &xg4 20 hxg4 &ab8 21 &f5 &d4 22 &xb7 &xb7 23 &xd4 (of course not 23 &xd6? &d7 and White loses material) 23...cxd4 24 &d5 g6 25 g3 f5 26 &g2 f4 with a slightly better ending for White in J.Polgar-Adams, Frankfurt (rapid) 1999.

Black can also play 13...&e8 to avoid the exchange on f6. The game Golod-Van den Doel, London 1999 continued 14 &d2 &c7 15 &d5 &xd5 16 &xd5 &d7 17 c3 &d8 18 &xb7 (stronger is 18 a4! &xd5 19 exd5 &b8 20 axb5 axb5 21 &b3 with a small but steady positional advantage for White due to his pressure on the queenside) 18...&xb7 19 d4 &c6 20 d5 &a5 21 b3 c4! 22 b4 &b3 23 &b1 f5 24 exf5 &xf5 (worse is 24...&xd5 25 &g5! &xd1 26 &bxd1 &xg5 27 &xg5 &xf5 28 &e4! and White regains his pawn with advantage) 25 &e3 and here the players agreed a draw.

14 &h2

Also worthy of a mention is 14 &xf6!?,

fighting for control over d5.

14...&e8!

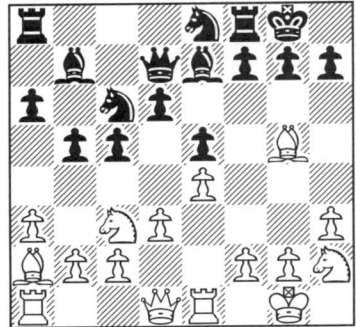

With this excellent move Black solves all his opening problems because after 15 &xe7 &xe7 Black would adequately control the d5-square.

15 &d2 &c7 16 &f1 &h8 17 &g3 &d4

As a result of accurate play, Black has achieved a very promising position.

18 &ce2 &de6 19 b4 d5 20 bxc5 &xc5 21 &b4 &fe8 22 &xc5 &xc5 23 &c3 &ad8 24 &h5

Maybe White should have realised the danger and started to play for a draw by 24 exd5 &xd5 25 &xd5 &xd5 26 &xd5 &xd5 etc.

24...f6 25 d4?

This is over-ambitious; better here was 25 exd5.

25...exd4

Or 25...&xe4 26 &cxe4 dxe4 27 &f7!? with unclear play.

26 &xd5 &e5

An alternative was 26...&xe4!? 27 &f4 g5 28 &h6!? &g7! 29 &xg7+ &xg7, repulsing White's temporary threats and retaining the extra pawn.

27 &h4 &xd5 28 exd5 &xd5 29 &xe5 fxe5 30 &xd5 &xd5 31 &e1 &e6?!

Black misses a chance for the activation of his pieces by 31...d3! 32 exd3 &xd3 33 &d1 &d4 34 &e4 h6 with a clear advantage.

32 &f5 &f4 33 &g5 &d7 34 &h4 h6 35

♕g4 g5?

A typical time trouble move that weakens the kingside.

36 ♘f3 e4?

Black's position also becomes fraught with danger after 36...♖e7 37 ♕f5! but the text is a blunder which loses a pawn.

37 ♖xe4!

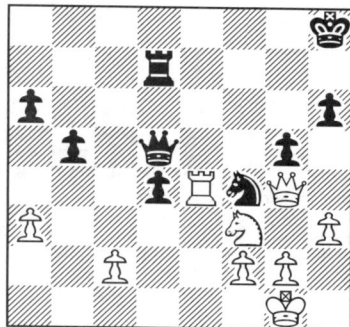

37...♕xe4 38 ♕xd7 d3

Or 38...♕xc2 39 ♕xd4+ ♔g8 40 ♕d8+ ♔g7 41 ♕e7+ ♔g8 42 ♘e5 ♕d1+ 43 ♔h2 ♕d5 with reasonable drawing chances for Black.

39 cxd3 ♕xd3 40 ♕c8+ ♔g7 41 ♕b7+ ♔g8 42 ♕xa6 ♘e2+

White preserves good winning chances after 42...♘xh3+ 43 ♔h2! ♘xf2 44 ♕e6+ ♔h8 45 ♘e5!.

43 ♔h2 ♕e4 44 ♕f6 ♕f4+ 45 ♕xf4 gxf4! 46 g4 fxg3+ 47 fxg3 ♘c3 48 ♘d4 h5 49 h4 ♔f7 50 ♔h3 ♔f6 51 g4 hxg4+ 52 ♔xg4 ♔g6 53 h5+ ♔h7

A draw was hidden in the line 53...♔f6! 54 ♔h4 ♔f7 55 ♔g5 ♘e4+ 56 ♔f4 (or 56 ♔h6 ♘d6 57 ♔h7 ♔f6 58 h6 ♔f7 and White cannot win) 56...♘f6 57 h6 b4! 58 axb4 ♘d5+ 59 ♔f5 ♘xb4 60 ♘e6 ♔g8 61 ♔g6 ♘d5 reaching a theoretical draw. The text leads to a lost king and pawn ending.

54 ♔h4! ♔g8 55 h6 ♔h7 56 ♔h5 ♘e4 57 ♘xb5 ♘f6+ 58 ♔g5 ♘e4+ 59 ♔f5 ♘c5 60 ♘e5 ♔xh6 61 ♔d4! ♘a6 62 ♔d5 ♔g6 63 ♘d4 ♔f6 64 ♔d6! ♔f7

64...♘b8 65 ♘c6 ♘a6 66 ♘b4 is also in White's favour.

65 ♘e6 1-0

Game 78
Bologan-Peng Xiaomin
Shanghai 2000

---

1 e4 e5 2 ♘f3 ♘c6 3 ♗b5 a6 4 ♗a4 ♘f6 5 0-0 ♗e7 6 ♖e1 b5 7 ♗b3 0-0 8 h3 ♗b7 9 d3 d6 10 a3 ♘a5 11 ♗a2 c5 12 ♘c3 ♘c6 13 ♘d5

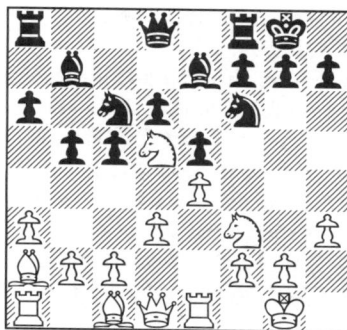

This is a far more logical continuation than the 13 ♘e2?! of Game 76. White immediately seizes control of the vital d5-square and after the imminent exchange on d5 he can start active operations in the centre as well as on the queenside. He can play c2-c3 and later either d3-d4 or b2-b4 according to the circumstances.

13...♘xd5

Or 13...♘d4 14 ♘xe7+ ♕xe7 15 ♘xd4 cxd4 (if 15...exd4, 16 ♗f4 retains the advantage for White) 16 ♗g5 with a small but lasting positional advantage for White due to his retaining the bishop pair.

14 ♗xd5 ♖b8

The alternative is 14...♕d7 and now:

a) 15 ♗e3 ♘d8 16 c4 ♗xd5 17 cxd5 f5 18 b4 ♘f7 19 ♖c1 ♖ac8 20 ♕b3 f4?! (better is 20...fxe4 21 dxe4 c4 with at least an equal game) 21 ♗d2 h5 22 ♕d1 ♗d8 23 ♗c3 ♕e8 24 ♗b2 ♗b6 25 ♖c2 ♕e7 26 bxc5 dxc5 27

♕a1 ♖ce8 28 h4 ♗c7 29 ♕d1 ♘d6 30 g3 ♕f6 31 ♔g2 with some advantage for White in Bologan-Van den Doel, Bastia (rapid) 1999.

b) Practice has shown that Black does not gain full equality after 15 c3!. For example, 15...♔h8 16 b4 ♕c7 17 ♕b3 ♘d8 18 ♗e3 ♖c8 19 bxc6 dxc6 20 c4 ♗c6? (this loses a pawn; correct was 20...♖b8 with only a small positional advantage to White) 21 ♗xc6 ♘xc6 22 cxb5 ♖b8 23 a4 axb5 24 axb5 ♘b4 25 ♕c4 ♗d6 26 ♖ec1 ♕b7 27 ♖a5 ♕b6 28 ♖ca1 f6 29 ♘d2 ♖fc8?? 30 ♕xb4! 1-0 Galkin-Ma.Tseitlin, Biel 2000.

15 c3 ♗f6?!

Maybe Black had to settle for 15...♘a5 but in that case White also retains a very pleasant initiative. The problem for Black is that he cannot generate any counterplay on the other wing while White has the initiative both in the centre and on the queenside.

16 b4 ♘e7 17 ♗xb7 ♖xb7 18 ♗e3 ♕c8 19 ♕b3 ♖c7 20 bxc5 dxc5 21 c4!

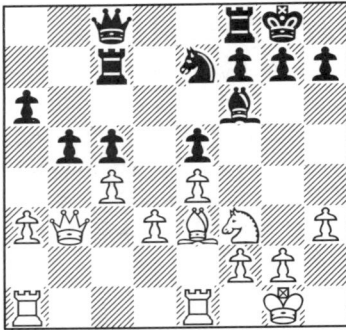

This leads to the opening up of the b-file, along which White will take control with his major pieces. Black's position is very passive and he will have great difficulty in defending his weak a- and c-pawns.

21...bxc4 22 ♕xc4 ♘g6 23 ♖ab1 ♖c6 24 ♖b3 ♖d8 25 ♖eb1 ♘f8 26 ♗d2 ♘e6 27 ♖b7 ♖cd6 28 ♗a5!

Just when Black had hopes of achieving some counterplay along the d-file, White

deflects Black's rook from the d-file because the eighth rank must be kept guarded against the intrusion of the white rook to b8.

28...♖f8 29 ♖1b6 ♖xb6 30 ♖xb6 ♘f4 31 ♗d2 ♕d8 32 ♖b3 ♕d6 33 ♗xf4 exf4 34 ♖b7 ♗d8 35 ♖a7 a5 36 e5 ♕b6 37 ♖d7 g5?

Black's position was very difficult but this is a desperate attempt that weakens his king-side even further and accelerates his defeat.

38 ♕d5 ♔g7 39 e6

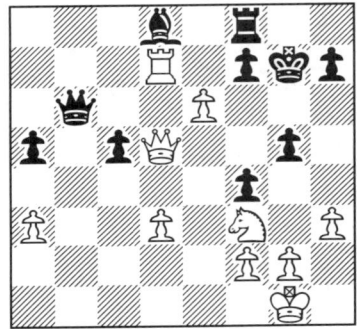

39...♗f6 40 ♘xg5 ♕b1+ 41 ♔h2 1-0

Game 79
Nijboer-De Vreugt
Dutch Championship 2001

1 e4 e5 2 ♘f3 ♘c6 3 ♗b5 a6 4 ♗a4 ♘f6 5 0-0 ♗e7 6 ♖e1 b5 7 ♗b3 0-0 8 h3 ♗b7 9 d3 d6 10 a3 ♕d7

With this move Black connects his rooks and prepares for the manoeuvre ...&a8-e8 followed by ...&c6-d8-e6. As we can see, there are many purposes to this move. Firstly, Black's b5-pawn can be defended by the queen if White starts with the usual plan of a2-a4. Black prefers to keep the pawn on b5 rather than to play ...b5-b4 because this would give White control of the important c4-square. Also, later on, after ...&c6-d8-e6, Black can play ...c7-c5 denying White spatial advantage in the centre.

11 &c3 &ae8 12 &e3

This move has been popularised by the Spanish super-GM Alexei Shirov, who has had some success with it.

12...&d8 13 &e2 d5

Black ended up with a passive position after 13...&e7?! 14 &g3 c5 15 a4 &c7 16 axb5 axb5 17 c4! b4 18 &a4 &c6 19 &g5 &d7 20 &f5 &e6 21 &d2 h6 22 &xc6 &xc6 23 &xd8 &xd8 24 &h2 &f8 25 &g4 &h7 26 &a6 with a strong initiative for White in Shirov-Milos, FIDE World Championship, Las Vegas 1999.

14 &g3 h6

Black was just a pawn down for nothing in the game Shirov-Onischuk, FIDE World Championship, New Delhi 2000 after 14...d4 15 &d2 &h8 16 c4 &g8 17 &c1 g6? 18 cxb5 axb5 19 &c5 f6 20 &xb5. The text takes away the g5-square for White's minor pieces and is therefore a useful preventative move.

15 c3

Also deserving of attention is 15 &f5!? dxe4 16 dxe4 &xd1 17 &axd1 &a5 18 &c5 &xb3 19 cxb3 &xe4 20 &xf8 &xf8 21 &g3 &xf3 22 gxf3 and White is slightly better due to his minimal material advantage.

15...d4 16 cxd4 &xd4 17 &xd4 exd4 18 &d2 c5 19 &f3

After 19 f4 Black has a good reply in 19...c4!, responding to White's kingside play with play of his own in the centre.

19...&h7 20 &ac1 &b6 21 &f5 c4 22 &xg7!?

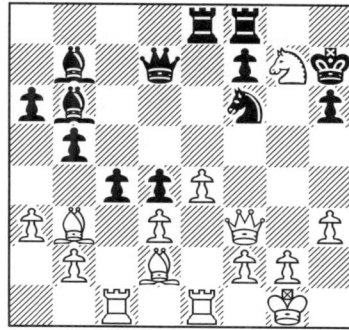

The battle has reached its decisive stage. This sacrifice only leads to perpetual check but White didn't have enough attacking chances on the kingside to look for more.

22...&xg7 23 &xh6+ &xh6 24 &xf6+ &h7 25 &h4+

The point is that 25 &xb6? even leads to a lost position for White after the ingenious 25...&g8!? (of course not 25...cxb3? 26 &c7 and White wins)

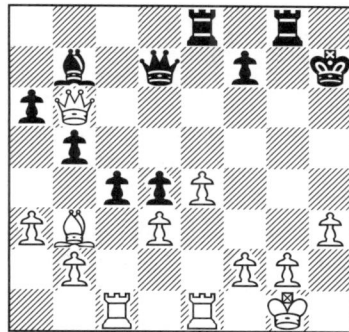

with the following possibilities:

a) 26 g3 &xh3 27 &c7 &c8! and White is unable to defend both the bishop on b3 and the g3-square where Black will sacrifice his rook.

b) 26 &f1 &xg2! 27 &xg2 &g8+ 28 &h2 (forced because if 28 &f1?, 28...&xh3+ 29 &e2 &xd3 is mate) 28...&c8! 29 &e3 dxe3 30 &xe3 cxb3 and Black emerges a piece up with a winning position.

25...♔g6 26 ♕g3+ ♔h7 27 ♕h4+ ♔g6 28 ♕g3+ ♔h7 ½-½

Game 80
Adams-Kosten
British Championship 1997

---

1 e4 e5 2 ♘f3 ♘c6 3 ♗b5 a6 4 ♗a4 ♘f6 5 0-0 ♗e7 6 ♖e1 b5 7 ♗b3 0-0 8 h3 ♗b7 9 d3 d6 10 a3 ♕d7 11 ♘c3 ♖ae8 12 ♘d5

White immediately seizes control of the d5-square, simultaneously freeing a path for his c-pawn. White can thus later on play both in the centre (after c2-c3 followed by d3-d4) or on the queenside (b2-b4 followed by a2-a4).

12...♘a5?

White retains a small advantage after 12...♘xd5 13 ♗xd5 ♘d8, whilst another possibility for Black is 12...♗d8 and now:

a) 13 ♗d2 is given by Adams as slightly better for White after 13...♘d4 14 ♘xf6+ ♗xf6 15 ♘xd4 exd4 16 ♕g4, but also deserving of attention is 13 ♗e3!? and, in the event of Black playing 13...♘a5 14 ♗a2 ♘xd5? 15 exd5 ♗a8 16 b4 ♘b7 17 c4 f5 18 ♖c1, he would end up in a horrible position with the badly placed pieces on b7 and a8.

b) The game Deseatnicov-Khruschiov, Minsk 2000 continued 13 ♗a2 ♔h8 14 ♘e3?! ♘e7 15 ♘h2 d5 16 exd5 ♘fxd5 17 ♘hg4 f6 18 g3? (weakening the a8-h1 diago-

nal is an error) 18...♘b6 19 f3 ♘g6 20 h4 f5 (White must have regretted playing 18 g3?) 21 h5 fxg4 22 hxg6 ♖xf3 23 ♔h2 ♕c6 24 ♘xg4 and White resigned because of the obvious 24...♖f2+! and White is mated.

13 ♘xe7+ ♕xe7

Or 13...♖xe7 14 ♗a2 d5 15 ♗g5! with an unpleasant pin on the h4-d8 diagonal.

14 ♗a2 c5 15 ♘h4!

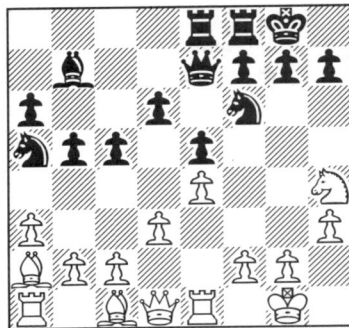

The knight is heading towards f5.

15...♘c6

Little different is 15...♗c8 16 ♗g5 ♗e6 17 ♘f5 ♗xf5 18 exf5 and White's bishop pair grants him an indisputable advantage.

16 c3 ♗c8 17 ♗g5 ♔h8

Black should avoid his kingside pawn structure being damaged by 17...♗e6 18 ♘f5 ♗xf5 19 exf5 ♘b8 followed by ...♘bd7, which was probably a better choice.

18 ♗d5 ♘d8

Or if instead 18...♘b8 then 19 ♖e3! h6 20 ♗xf6 ♕xf6 21 ♕h5! with multiple threats against f7.

19 ♘f5 ♕c7?

Black misses the last chance to free himself with 19...♗xf5 20 exf5 h6 21 ♗h4 g5! 22 fxg6 fxg6 23 ♗b3 ♘e6 with chances for a successful defence, although White would have maintained a positional advantage with his strong bishop pair.

20 ♗xf6 gxf6 21 ♕f3 ♖g8 22 g3 ♘e6 23 ♔h2 ♘g5 24 ♕e3 ♖g6 25 a4!

It is useful to open up the a-file in order to

attack the various pawn weaknesses in Black's camp.

25...bxa4 26 ♖xa4 ♖eg8 27 ♖ea1 ♘e6 28 ♘h4 ♖g5 29 ♕f3 ♕e7 30 ♘f5 ♕f8 31 ♖xa6!

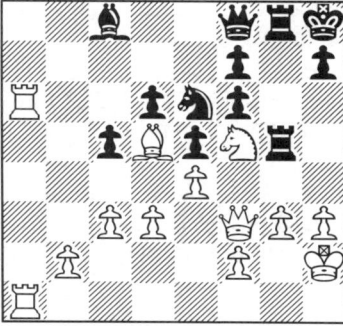

31...♘c7

Black was in time trouble but the game was already lost. Also losing for Black was 31...♗xa6 32 ♖xa6 ♘c7 33 ♘xd6! ♘xd5 34 exd5.

32 ♘xd6!

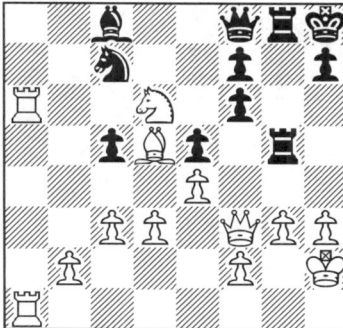

32...♘xd5

Or 32...♘xa6 33 ♕xf6+ ♖5g7 (forced) 34 ♘xf7+ ♕xf7 35 ♗xf7 ♖f8 36 ♕xe5 ♖fxf7 37 ♕e8+ and White wins.

33 ♘xc8 ♕xc8 34 exd5

White is winning both materially and positionally. Little more needs to be said.

34...♖f5 35 ♕e2 ♕d8 36 c4 ♕f8 37 ♖a8 ♕h6 38 d6 1-0

Game 81
Short-I.Sokolov
Wijk aan Zee 1997

1 e4 e5 2 ♘f3 ♘c6 3 ♗b5 a6 4 ♗a4 ♘f6 5 0-0 ♗e7 6 ♖e1 b5 7 ♗b3 0-0 8 h3 ♗b7 9 d3 d6 10 a3 ♕d7 11 ♘c3 ♖ae8 12 ♗a2

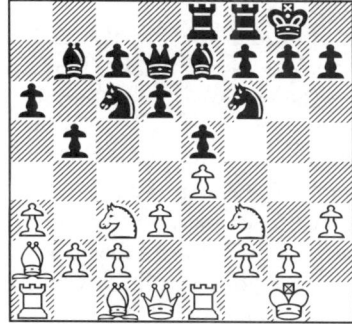

This prophylactic move has the aim of preventing both ...♘c6-a5 and ...♘c6-d8 manoeuvres.

Harmless for Black is 12 ♗g5 ♘d8 (also good here is 12...♘d4) 13 a4 ♘e6 14 ♗xf6 ♗xf6 15 axb5 axb5 16 ♘d5 ♗d8 17 ♘e3 ♔h8 18 c4 ♘f4! 19 ♔h2 (very dangerous for White is 19 cxb5?! f5! 20 ♘xf5 ♖xf5 21 exf5 ♕xf5 22 ♖e3 ♖f8 23 ♖a7 ♕g6 and now 24 ♘e1 loses to 24...♗xg2 25 ♖g3 ♘xh3+ 26 ♔h2 ♕h6! etc.) 19...f5!? 20 ♘xf5 ♖xf5 21 exf5 ♕xf5 22 ♖e3 ♖f8 23 ♖a7 ♗c6 24 ♖a6 (or 24 cxb5 ♗xb5 25 ♗c4 ♗c6 and Black has enough compensation for the sacrificed exchange due to strong pressure on the a8-h1 diagonal) 24...♗b7 25 ♖a7 ♗c6 26 ♖a6 ½-½ Kunte-Van den Doel, London 1999.

White sometimes tries to transfer his knight to the kingside with 12 ♘e2, against which Black equalises by 12...d5 (Black played passively in the game Acs-Heidenfeld, Bundesliga 1999 after 12...♔h8 13 ♘g3 ♗d8 14 c3 ♘g8 15 ♗a2 g6 16 d4 ♗c8 17 a4 f6 18 axb5 axb5 19 ♗b1 ♘ce7 20 ♖a7 ♘c6 21

♖a8 ♗b7 22 ♖a1 ♘b8 23 b3 ♖f7 24 c4 bxc4 25 bxc4 exd4 26 ♘xd4), for example: 13 exd5 ♘xd5 14 ♘g3 ♘d4!? 15 ♘xd4 (after taking the pawn with 15 ♘xe5 ♕d8 16 ♗a2 ♗d6 Black gets excellent attacking chances thanks to his superior development) 15...exd4 16 ♗d2 c5 17 a4 ♗h4 18 axb5 axb5 19 ♕g4 ♕xg4 20 fxg4 ♗xg3 21 fxg3 ♖xe1+ 22 ♖xe1 h6 23 ♖e5 ½-½ Shirov-I.Sokolov, Wijk aan Zee 1996.

12...♗d8!

The strongest reply. Weaker is 12...♘d8 13 d4! exd4 14 ♘xd4 c5 15 ♘f5 ♗xe4 16 ♘h6+ gxh6 17 ♘xe4 with advantage to White.

13 ♗d2

Worthy of attention is 13 ♘d5 ♘xd5 14 ♗xd5 ♕c8 (after 14...♘a5?! very unpleasant for Black is 15 b4!) 15 c3 ♘b8 16 ♗a2 c5 17 a4 and in this position a draw was agreed in Bakre-Heidenfeld, York 2000.

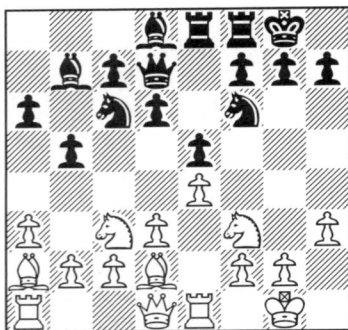

13...♘e7

Also possible is 13...♘d4!? 14 ♘xd4 exd4 15 ♘e2 c5 (I prefer this to 15...d5 16 ♗b4 ♗e7 17 e5! ♗xb4 18 axb4 ♖xe5 19 ♘xd4 with a small advantage to White) 16 f4 ♗b6 with chances for both sides.

14 ♘h4 ♚h8

It is too early for play in the centre with 14...d5?! because of 15 ♗g5! with advantage to White.

15 f4?

White is trying to create a kingside attack

but this will only make weaknesses in his own camp. Better was 15 ♗g5 but even after that Black stands well after the rather odd-looking 15...♘fg8!?

15...exf4 16 ♗xf4 ♘g6 17 ♘xg6+ hxg6 18 ♕d2

Or 18 a4 b4 19 ♘e2 d5! with a promising position for Black.

18...♘h5

Another possibility is 18...d5!? 19 e5 ♘h5 20 ♗h2 ♗h4 21 ♖f1 d4 etc.

19 ♗h2

After 19 ♗e3 play can proceed 19...♗h4 20 ♖f1 f5 etc., which is similar to the text.

19...♗h4 20 ♖f1 f5 21 ♘d5 ♗xd5 22 ♗xd5

Weaker is 22 exd5?! ♕e7! followed by ...♗h4-g3 with advantage to Black due to the poor position of White's light-squared bishop.

22...c6 23 ♗b3 d5 24 exd5 cxd5 25 ♖f3 g5!

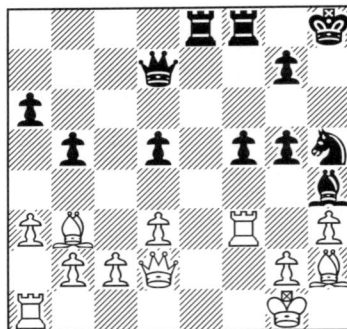

Black has carefully calculated all the consequences and now starts a strong kingside attack. The role of the powerful bishop on h4 will soon be made clear.

26 g3 g4 27 hxg4 fxg4 28 ♖xf8+ ♖xf8 29 ♕g2

Relatively the best move because after 29 gxh4 g3 Black regains the sacrificed piece with a near winning attack.

29...♗f6 30 c3?

Maybe the best chance of surviving was

30 ♕xd5 ♗d4+ 31 ♔h1 ♕xd5+ 32 ♗xd5 ♗xb2, although Black still retains an extra pawn and good winning chances. However, after the text White should lose by force.

30...d4 31 c4 ♗g5 32 cxb5 axb5 33 ♖f1 ♗e3+ 34 ♔h1 ♖xf1+ 35 ♕xf1 ♕c6+ 36 ♕g2 ♕c1+ 37 ♗g1 ♗xg1

Black misses a forced win with 37...♔h7!, which prevents all White's counterplay by improving the position of his king. After 38 ♗f7 g6 White can resign.

38 ♕xg1 ♕xb2

White has counterplay despite being a pawn down after 38...♘xg3+ 39 ♔g2 ♕xg1+ 40 ♔xg1 ♘e2+ 41 ♔f2 ♘f4 42 ♗c2 followed by ♔f2-g3! etc.

39 ♗f7! ♘f6 40 ♕h2+ ♕xh2+ 41 ♔xh2

The ending is a draw despite Black having an extra pawn as his g4-pawn is very weak.

41...g5 42 ♗e6 ♔g7 43 ♗c8 ♘d5 44 ♗xg4 ♔f6 45 ♗d7 b4 46 axb4 ½-½

Game 82
Shirov-Kamsky
Dos Hermanas 1996

---

1 e4 e5 2 ♘f3 ♘c6 3 ♗b5 a6 4 ♗a4 ♘f6 5 0-0 ♗e7 6 ♖e1 b5 7 ♗b3 0-0 8 h3 ♗b7 9 d3 d6 10 a3 ♕d7 11 ♘c3 ♖ae8 12 ♗d2

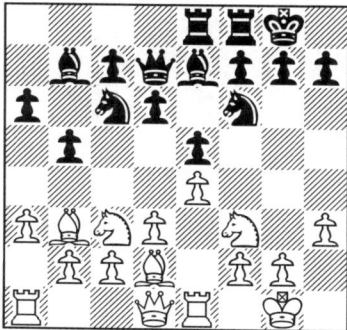

White wants to see what plan Black will employ before deciding on what to do next. He still keeps the option of fighting for the d5-square whilst he also has the possibility of transferring his knight to the kingside by ♘c3-e2-g3. In short, the text can be described as a slow manoeuvring move that should not bring White any opening advantage against best play.

12...♘d8

Much worse is 12...♔h8? 13 a4 b4 14 ♘e2 ♘g8 15 ♘g3 g6 16 c3! bxc3 17 ♗xc3 ♗f6 18 d4 exd4 19 ♘xd4 ♘xd4 20 ♗xd4 ♗xd4 21 ♕xd4+ f6 22 ♖ac1 with a big advantage to White, Lanka-Am.Rodriguez, Albacete 1995.

13 ♘e2 ♘e6 14 ♘g3 c5 15 c3 ♗d8 16 ♗c2 ♗c7

After a series of accurate moves Black has managed to fully equalise. The next move is practically forced because Black was threatening to gain an advantage in space with ...d6-d5. Both sides have weak squares (d5 and d4), leading to a level position.

17 c4 ♗c6 18 b3 g6 19 ♗h6 ♘g7 20 ♕d2 ♔h8!

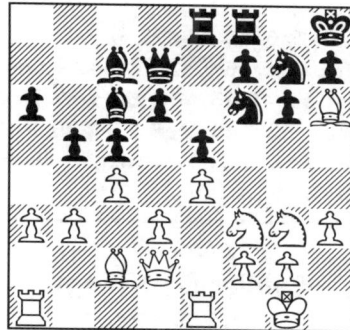

An important move. Black is preparing to dislodge the bishop from h6.

21 b4 ♘g8 22 bxc5 dxc5 23 ♗e3 ♘e6 24 cxb5 axb5 25 ♗b3 ♘d4 26 ♗xd4 cxd4 27 ♖ec1 ♗d6 28 ♕a2 ♔g7 29 a4 ♘f6 30 ♕d2 h6 31 axb5 ♗xb5 32 ♗c4 ♗xc4 33 ♖xc4 ♖a8 34 ♖ac1 ♖fc8 35 ♕c2 ♖xc4 36 ♕xc4 ♖a5

With the obvious threat of ...♖a5-c5! winning material.

37 ♖b1 ♕a7 38 ♕c6 ♖a6 39 ♕c8 ♕a8

40 ♕xa8 ♖xa8 41 ♘d2 ♘d7

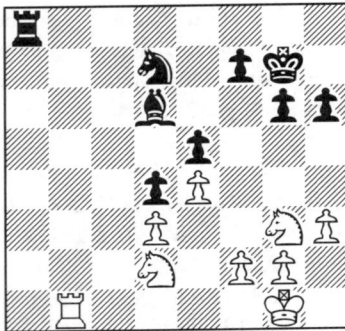

This ending is somewhat drawish due to the symmetrical pawn structure. If anyone is better in this position then it is probably Black but only very slightly due to his control of more squares. However, White will place his knights on good squares and any winning attempt by Black would have an element of risk. The only real weakness in the position is the pawn on d3 but this is not enough to be of a decisive nature.

42 ♘c4 ♖a6 43 ♖b5 ♗c7 44 ♘f1 ♖c6 45 ♘fd2 ♘c5 46 ♘b2 ♘e6 47 ♘dc4 ♘f4 48 ♖b4 f5 49 f3 ♔f6 50 ♔h2 ♖a6 51 ♖b5 ♖a1 52 ♖c5 ♘e6 53 ♖d5 ♖c1 54 ♖d7 ♖c2 55 h4 g5 56 hxg5+ hxg5 57 ♔g1 ½-½

Game 83
Svidler-De Vreugt
Esbjerg 2000

---

1 e4 e5 2 ♘f3 ♘c6 3 ♗b5 a6 4 ♗a4 ♘f6 5 0-0 ♗e7 6 ♖e1 b5 7 ♗b3 0-0 8 h3 ♗b7 9 d3 d6 10 a3 ♕d7 11 ♘c3 ♖ae8 12 a4

One might think about the logic behind this since White is moving this pawn for the second time, but in modern day chess sometimes it is possible to ignore the usual advice of 'never move the same piece or pawn more than once in the opening'. White undermines Black's b5 stronghold, having in mind that

Black's a8-rook has already left the queenside. Statistics confirm that White is doing very well with the text move and to date Black has not been able to demonstrate full equality.

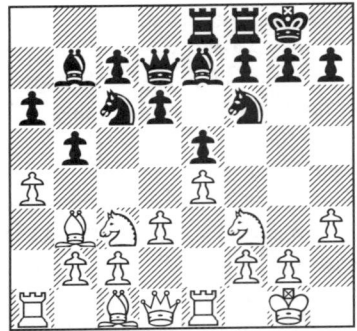

12...b4

After 12...♘a5? White has the devil of a trap with 13 ♗xf7+! (although in Korneev-Kovalev, Minsk 1998 the game went along peacefully after 13 ♗a2? b4 14 ♘e2 c5 15 ♘g3 ♗d8 16 ♗g5 ♔h8 17 ♘h2 ♘g8 18 ♗xd8 ♕xd8 19 c3 ♕b6 20 cxb4 cxb4)

13...♖xf7 14 axb5 and White regains his sacrificed piece with a great positional advantage.

Black can also try 12...♘d4 13 ♘xd4 exd4 14 ♘e2 c5 15 ♗g5 b4 16 ♘f4 a5 17 ♗xf6 ♗xf6 18 ♗d5 with only a tiny advantage for White, who is likely to be able to post a strong knight on d5.

13 ♘d5 ♘xd5 14 ♗xd5 ♘d8

Passive is 14...♗f6?! 15 ♗d2 ♖b8 16 a5!
♘d4 17 ♗c4 ♘xf3+ 18 ♕xf3 c5 19 c3 bxc3
20 bxc3 ♗d8 21 ♕g3 ♔h8 22 f4 ♗f6 23 ♖a3
♕c7 24 ♖f1 ♖be8 25 f5 ♖d8 26 ♕f3 ♕d7 27
♖b1 d5 28 exd5 ♗xd5 29 ♗xd5 ♕xd5 30
♕xd5 ♖xd5 31 c4 ♖d7 32 ♗e3 ♖c8 33 ♖b6
♖a7 34 ♗xc5! ♗d8 35 ♗e3 ♗xb6 36 axb6
♖b7 37 c5 (White's queenside pawns are
unstoppable) 37...♔g8 38 ♔f2 ♔f8 39 ♔f3
♔e7 40 ♔e4 f6 41 ♖xa6 ♖d7 42 c6 1-0
Grünfeld-Bitansky, Israel 1999.

15 ♗xb7 ♘xb7 16 d4 exd4

Or 16...♗f6?! 17 dxe5 ♗xe5 18 ♘xe5
♖xe5 19 b3 ♘c5 20 ♗b2 ♖xe4 21 ♖xe4
♘xe4 22 ♕d4 ♘f6 23 ♕xb4 ♖e8 24 ♕c4
♕c8 25 ♖d1 with a positional advantage to
White because the bishop is stronger than
the knight in an open position such as this,
J.Polgar-Adams, Wijk aan Zee 1998.

17 ♕xd4 a5 18 ♕d5!

The alternative is 18 b3 c6 and here the
game was prematurely agreed drawn in
Galkin-Van der Wiel, Essent 1999. After 19
♗b2 White appears to be better since
19...♗f6 is strongly answered by 20 e5! etc.

18...♕c8

The point behind White's excellent eighteenth move is that after 18...c6?! White has
19 ♘e5!

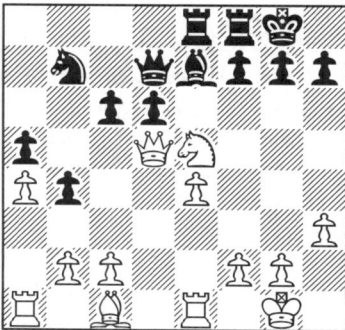

19...♕xh3 (virtually the only move) 20
♘xc6 with a clear advantage for White.

19 ♗f4 c6

Or 19...♗f6 20 e5 dxe5 21 ♗xe5 ♗xe5
(White is also slightly better after 21...c6 22
♕c4 ♗xe5 23 ♖xe5 etc.) 22 ♖xe5 ♖xe5?!
(after this Black's position goes downhill;
better was the alternative 22...c6) 23 ♘xe5
♕f5 24 g4?! ♕g5? (after this Black ends up in
a lost position; the only move was 24...♕e6)
25 ♖d1 ♘d6 26 ♘d7! ♕xd5 27 ♖xd5 ♖a8
28 ♖c5 ♖a7 29 ♘e5 ♔f8 30 ♘c6 ♘b7 31
♖b5 ♖a6 32 ♘xb4! axb4 33 ♖xb7 ♖c6 34
♖xb4 ♖xc2 35 ♔g2 and the rook and pawn
ending is winning for White, Adams-De
Vreugt, Dutch League 1999.

20 ♕c4 ♗f6 21 ♖ad1 ♖e6?!

This was a good moment for Black to free
himself with 21...d5! 22 exd5 cxd5 23 ♕xd5
♗xb2 24 ♖xe8 ♖xe8 25 ♘g5 ♖e7 26 ♕d3
g6 and Black is okay. Considering ...d5 is so
thematic, he should not have missed it.

**22 ♘d4 ♗xd4 23 ♕xd4 ♖d8 24 ♔h2?!
d5 25 exd5 ♖xd5 26 ♕b6 ♖xd1 27 ♖xd1
h6 28 ♕d4 ♖e7 29 ♖d3 ♕f5?**

Black overlooks a strong tactical resource.
Better was 29...c5 30 ♕d5 ♔f8 31 ♖g3 ♕e6
with good chances of survival.

30 ♗xh6!

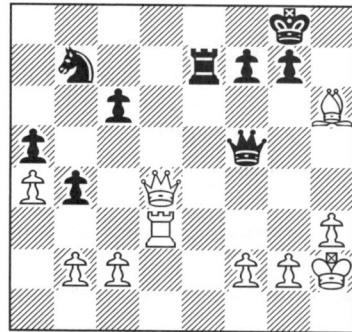

30...f6

Taking the bishop with 30...gxh6? quickly
loses to 31 ♖g3+ and in the case of 30...♕e5+
31 ♕xe5 ♖xe5 32 ♖g3 wins.

**31 ♗e3 ♕e6 32 b3 c5 33 ♕f4 ♔f7 34
h4**

With an extra pawn and a strong bishop

against a weaker knight, White is guaranteed the win.

34...♖e8 35 ♕f3 ♕c8 36 ♗f4 ♘d8 37 ♕h5+ 1-0

Game 84
Anand-Ivanchuk
Monaco (rapid) 2003

---

1 e4 e5 2 ♘f3 ♘c6 3 ♗b5 a6 4 ♗a4 ♘f6 5 0-0 ♗e7 6 ♖e1 b5 7 ♗b3 0-0 8 h3 ♗b7 9 d3 ♖e8

Black delays moving his d-pawn. Perhaps it can move to d5 in one go?

10 a3 d6 11 ♘c3 ♗f8

An alternative, 11...♘d4, was seen in Karjakin-Campora, Dos Hermanas 2003. Play continued 12 ♘xd4 exd4 13 ♘d5 ♘xd5 14 exd5 (Black has not achieved equality as his light-squared bishop is restricted by White's pawn on d5) 14...♗f6 15 ♖xe8+ ♕xe8 16 ♗d2 c6 (Black has to play this to free his position) 17 dxc6 ♕xc6 18 ♕g4 ♖e8 19 ♖e1 ♖xe1+ 20 ♗xe1 ♔f8 21 f3 d5 22 ♕f4 g5?! (an unnecessary weakening of the kingside) 23 ♕b8+ (not 23 ♕f5?! ♕e6 when White has to exchange queens) 23...♔e7 24 ♗b4+ ♔d7 and now with 25 ♔f1?! White began to drift and eventually lost. Instead 25 a4! would have left Black in deep trouble.

12 ♗a2 ♘d4 13 ♘h2!?

White is planning the manoeuvre ♘h2-g4 with the idea of exchanging Black's knight on f6, which might enable him to control the vital d5-square.

13...d5 14 exd5 ♘xd5 15 ♘g4 ♘f4

Also possible was a modest 15...♕d6 with approximate equality.

16 ♘e4

Weaker is 16 ♗xf4?! exf4 because later White must be wary of ...f4-f3 with an initiative against White's monarch.

16...♘g6 17 c3 ♘e6 18 ♕f3 ♖b8 19 g3! h5

Black could have avoided the weakening

of his kingside by playing 19...♖e7!?.

20 ♘h2

The tempting sacrifice 20 ♘gf6+ leads only to a draw after 20...gxf6 21 ♘xf6+ ♔g7 22 ♘xh5+ ♔g8 23 ♘f6+ ♔g7 and now if 24 ♘xe8+ ♕xe8 25 ♗d5 ♗xd5 26 ♕xd5 ♖d8 Black stands well.

20...h4 21 ♕f5 ♗d5 22 ♗xd5 ♕xd5 23 ♘f3 ♖bd8 24 gxh4!?

White sacrifices the d3-pawn in order to achieve a kingside initiative.

24...♕xd3 25 ♕g4 ♘c5?!

Much stronger was 25...♘ef4!, preventing h4-h5, because if 26 h5? f5! and Black wins.

26 ♗g5!

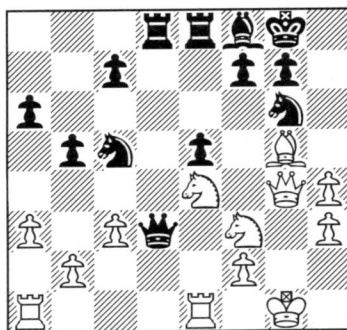

26...♘xe4

The move 26...f6? loses immediately to 27 ♗xf6!.

27 ♖xe4

Less strong is 27 ♗xd8?! ♘f4! (threatening ...♘f4-e2+) and there is no way White can avoid a draw. Also interesting is 27...♘xf2!? 28 ♔xf2 ♗c5+ followed by taking on d8 with promising compensation for the sacrificed exchange.

27...♖d6?

This loses. Black had to play 27...♘e7 28 ♘xe5 ♕d5 with chances for survival.

28 h5 ♘f4 29 ♖e3! f5 30 ♕h4 ♘e2+ 31 ♔f1 ♕d5 32 ♔xe2 f4 33 ♗xf4 exf4 34 ♖xe8 ♕d3+ 35 ♔e1 ♕xf3 36 ♕e7!

Now the game is decided.

36...♖f6 37 h6! ♕g2 38 ♕xg7+ 1-0

Summary

10...♘a7!? leads to a small but lasting advantage to White, with no winning chances whatsoever for Black. 10...♘b8 usually leads to a patient manoeuvring game where White remains slightly better. However, in Game 70 Ivanchuk managed to outplay his fellow countryman and reached a winning position, only to blunder more than once and end up losing.

White maintains a positional grip after 10...♘d4 11 ♘xd4 exd4 12 ♘d2 (Game 73), which is much stronger than Jansa's 12 c3.

Game 74 saw excellent positional play by Murey against Adams, where White's domination on the queenside using the c-file was crowned with success. Black should avoid such uncomfortable positions without any counterplay at all costs – this game demonstrates that 12...h6?! is too slow. The conclusion of Game 75 is that Zaitsev failed to obtain sufficient compensation for the pawn and that 12...b4 is dubious.

Gelfand's 13 ♘e2?! (Game 76) is not great for White – his kingside attack never got off the ground due to Adams' resourceful play over both the queenside and in the centre. Kasparov's 13 ♗g5 (Game 77) also fails to grant White any opening advantage. More to the point is Bologan's 13 ♘d5 (Game 78), which is the main problem for Black if he chooses the system 10...♘a5 11 ♗a2 c5 12 ♘c3 ♘c6. The control of the d5-square grants White a lasting advantage.

After 10...♕d7 11 ♘c3 ♖ae8, Nijboer's 12 ♗e3 (Game 79) allowed Black to obtain a roughly equal position after 12...♗d8! 13 ♘e2 d5 14 ♘g3 h6 15 c3 d4 16 cxd4 ♘xd4 17 ♘xd4 exd4 18 ♗d2 c5. In Game 80, instead of Kosten's 12...♘a5, Black should play as in the previous game with 12...♗d8. Short-Sokolov (Game 81) is quite sophisticated but Black managed to get a playable position, while Shirov's 12 ♗d2 against the now retired Gata Kamsky gave Black no opening problems in Game 82.

The move 12 a4 (Game 83) might look illogical because this is the second time White moves the same flank pawn in the opening, but there is an explanation behind it. After ...♕d8-d7 and ...♖a8-e8 Black concentrates his forces in the centre – Black is ready for White's possible kingside attack. Therefore White switches his intentions and challenges Black on the queenside, namely on his b5 stranglehold, by playing 12 a4!?. It looks like a good idea.

1 e4 e5 2 ♘f3 ♘c6 3 ♗b5 a6 4 ♗a4 ♘f6 5 0-0 ♗e7 6 ♖e1 b5 7 ♗b3 0-0 8 h3 ♗b7 9 d3 d6

9...♖e8 – *Game 84*

10 a3 ♘a5

10...♘a7!? – *Game 69*

10...♘b8 11 ♘bd2 ♘bd7 12 ♘f1 ♖e8

13 ♘g3 – *Game 70*; 13 ♗a2 – *Game 71*

10...♘d4 11 ♘xd4 exd4 12 c3 – *Game 72*

12 ♘d2 – *Game 73*

10...♕d7 11 ♘c3 ♖ae8

12 ♗e3 – *Game 79*; 12 ♘d5 – *Game 80*; 12 ♗a2 – *Game 81*; 12 ♗d2 – *Game 82*;

12 a4 – *Game 83*

11 ♗a2 c5 12 ♘c3 ♘c6

12...b4?! – *Game 75*; 12...h6 – *Game 74*

13 ♘d5 – *Game 78*

13 ♗g5 – *Game 77*; 13 ♘e2 – *Game 76*

CHAPTER EIGHT

Anti-Marshall
with 8 a4

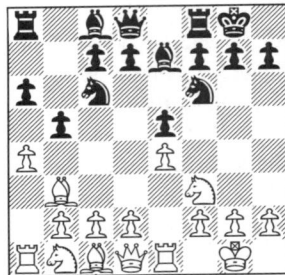

1 e4 e5 2 ♘f3 ♘c6 3 ♗b5 a6 4 ♗a4 ♘f6
5 0-0 ♗e7 6 ♖e1 b5 7 ♗b3 0-0 8 a4

Against the old Main Line Anti-Marshall, 8 a4, I'm recommending that black-sided players should play the system with 8...♗b7 9 d3 ♖e8!?, the main subject of this chapter. I prefer this line to the main move 9...d6 for a couple of reasons. Firstly, by playing 8...♗b7 9 d3 ♖e8, it is no longer necessary to memorise some of the forcing lines that arise after 8...♗b7 9 d3 d6 and 8...b4. For example, after 8...♗b7 9 d3 d6 White can choose between several possibilities including the positional plan with 10 ♗d2, sharper lines after 10 ♘c3 ♘a5 11 ♗a2 b4 12 ♘e2, or Kasparov's favourite 10 ♘bd2 (see Games 90-91). The second reason for choosing 8...♗b7 9 d3 ♖e8 is that it contains an ambitious idea of playing ...d7-d5 in one go. Game 92 is a very instructive example of what can happen after 8...b4. White quickly obtains the excellent c4-square for his knight and Black must be careful as his queenside is rather weak.

In Mainka-Blatny (Game 85) Black succeeds in freeing himself by playing ...d6-d5.

The next 'all Nikolaidis' encounter (Game 86) sees White playing the very straightforward 10 ♘g5, hitting f7. The rare continuation 10 ♘a3 was seen in the super-GM game Ivanchuk-Adams (Game 87). White puts

pressure on the b5-pawn but Adams finds a simple solution to his problems.

Yurtaev-Lau (Game 88) sees 10 ♗d2 followed by ♘b1-a3 in order to challenge Black's b5 stronghold. Yurtaev plays ...♗e7-c5, which leads to a position similar to the Archangel Variation of the Ruy Lopez.

The main continuation against 9...♖e8!? is 10 ♘c3 (Game 89).

Game 85
R.Mainka-P.Blatny
Munich 1992

---

1 e4 e5 2 ♘f3 ♘c6 3 ♗b5 a6 4 ♗a4 ♘f6
5 0-0 ♗e7 6 ♖e1 b5 7 ♗b3 0-0 8 a4
♗b7 9 d3 ♖e8!?

The move 9...罝e8!? has been championed in the past by John Nunn.

10 c3 h6

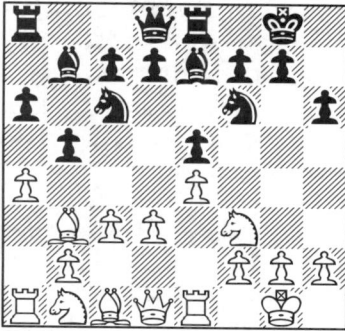

This move is very important because before playing ...罝f8 Black must cover the g5-square. Thus after 10...罝f8 Black must reckon on with 11 罝g5!?, retaining control over the d5-square.

11 罝a2 罝f8 12 b4

Seizing the space on the queenside, but Black will obtain counterplay in the centre.

12...d6 13 罝a3 罝d7 14 罝d2 罝e7

The knight is heading towards the kingside, allowing the move ...c7-c5 and clearing a diagonal for Black's light-squared bishop.

15 罝c2 罝g6

Taking the pawn with 15...bxa4, conceding the c4-square, is inferior.

16 罝e3 d5 17 exd5 罝xd5 18 罝xd5 罝xd5 19 罝e3 罝ad8 20 axb5 axb5 21 罝xd5 罝xd5 22 罝a7?

White should have sensed danger and played 22 d4! e4 23 罝d2 f5 24 f3!, thus forcing further exchanges and heading for the draw. With the text White forgets about the safety of his first rank.

22...e4! 23 罝d4 exd3 24 罝xd3 c5

Or 24...罝xb4!? 25 cxb4 罝xd4 winning a pawn because the queen is taboo.

25 bxc5 罝xc5 26 罝a5 b4! 27 罝b5 罝f4 28 罝c6 bxc3

Black could have won the exchange after 28...罝c8!? 29 罝xd5 罝xd5 30 cxb4 罝xb4 31

罝xd5 罝xe1 but, due to all the pawns being on the same side, a black win would have been doubtful.

29 罝xc5 罝xd4 30 罝c4 罝e5 31 h3 罝d5 32 罝c5 罝e4 33 罝c4 罝d3 34 罝h2 罝e7!? 35 罝e4 罝f5 36 罝xd3 罝xd3 37 罝c1?

The final mistake. After the correct 37 罝f1! 罝xe3 (or 37...罝dxe3 38 fxe3 罝xe3 39 罝e1 罝g4+ 40 hxg4 罝xe1 41 罝xc3 and the endgame is drawn as all the pawns are on the same side) 38 fxe3 the attack on the f7-pawn gives White a vital tempo for defence. For example:

a) 38...罝dxe3 39 罝c1 and White will capture the c3-pawn reaching a drawn rook endgame.

b) 38...罝exe3 is met by 39 罝c8+ 罝h7 40 罝xf7 with excellent drawing chances for White.

c) 38...罝e7 39 e4 and it is very difficult for Black to realise the advantage of the extra pawn.

The text loses a second pawn – the rest needs no further commentary.

37...罝xe3 38 fxe3 罝exe3 39 罝c2 g6 40 罝g1 罝g7 41 罝f2 罝g3 42 罝c6 h5 43 罝c5 罝ge3 44 罝a2 罝f6 45 罝a6+ 罝e6 46 罝a4 罝d2+ 47 罝f3 罝ee2 48 g4 罝h2 49 罝a6+ 罝g7 50 罝g3 罝dg2+ 51 罝f3 h4! 52 罝a7 罝f2+ 53 罝e3 罝f6 54 罝e4 罝xh3 55 g5 罝f5 56 罝xf5 gxf5+ 57 罝xf5 罝g3 58 罝f4 c2 59 罝c7 罝g2 60 罝f5 h3 61 g6 罝f2+ 0-1

> ### Game 86
> ### K.Nikolaidis-I.Nikolaidis
> *Ano Liosia 1996*

1 e4 e5 2 罝f3 罝c6 3 罝b5 a6 4 罝a4 罝f6 5 0-0 罝e7 6 罝e1 b5 7 罝b3 0-0 8 a4 罝b7 9 d3 罝e8!? 10 罝g5

With his last move Black left his f7-pawn defenceless and White immediately tries to take advantage of this. Most monographs assess 10 罝g5 as dubious, which I consider to be a slight exaggeration.

10...d5 11 exd5 ♞d4 12 ♝a2

Bad is the line 12 d6? ♞xb3 13 dxe7 and now the strong 13...♛d5! immediately wins for Black.

Although it has yet to be tried in competitive play, 12 ♜xe5!? ♞xb3 13 cxb3 ♞xd5 14 ♞c3 ♝xg5 15 ♝xg5 ♛d7 16 ♜xe8+ ♜xe8 17 ♞e4 comes seriously into consideration – Black might have just enough compensation for the pawn.

White can only try to retain his extra pawn by the continuation 12 c4. After 12...♞xb3 13 ♛xb3 Black has the choice between the following:

a) 13...♞xd5 14 ♞xf7 ♚xf7 15 cxd5 ♝xd5 16 ♛c2 is roughly even – Black's pair of bishops are compensated by White's better pawn structure.

b) 13...c6!? deserves a closer look – 14 cxb5 cxd5 15 bxa6 (worse is 15 ♞c3?! ♞g4! 16 ♞h3 d4 17 ♞e4 axb5 18 ♛xb5 ♝d5 19 a5 ♜b8 20 ♛a4 f5 21 ♞d2 ♛c7 22 ♞c4 ♝b4 23 ♜d1 ♝xc4 24 dxc4 e4 25 ♝f4 ♝d6 26 g3 ♝xf4 27 ♞xf4 e3 with an initiative for Black, Hitzgerova-Jackova, Jutland 2000) 15...♝xa6 16 ♜xe5 ♝d6 (of course not 16...♞g4? 17 ♞xf7! ♚xf7 18 ♜xd5 with a decisive double check to follow) 17 ♜xe8+ ♛xe8 18 ♛d1 ♝xd3 with an excellent position for Black because the bishop on d3 is taboo (19 ♛xd3?? ♛e1+ 20 ♛f1 ♝xh2+! wins).

12...♝xd5

The main variation is considered to be 12...♞xd5 and now:

a) Risky is 13 ♜xe5? ♝xg5! 14 ♝xg5 ♛d7 15 ♜xe8+ (or 15 ♝xd5 ♝xd5 16 ♜xe8+ ♜xe8 17 ♞c3 ♝f3! with the idea that if 18 gxf3?, then 18...♛h3 19 ♚h1 ♞xf3 20 ♝f4 ♞h4 21 ♛f1 ♛f3+ 22 ♚g1 ♛xf4 wins outright for Black) 15...♜xe8 16 ♞d2 ♞b4 17 ♝b1?? (this loses by force which is no surprise because White has lost control of his first rank; the only move was 17 ♝b3 but after 17...♞xb3 18 cxb3 – forced because after 18 ♞xb3? ♛d5! White loses material –

18...♞xd3 and to play this position as White is no great fun!) 17...♞e2+ 18 ♚f1 ♝xg2+! 19 ♚xg2 ♛g4+ 20 ♚h1 ♞g3+ 0-1 Zapata-Nunn, Dubai Olympiad 1986.

b) 13 ♞f3 ♞b4! 14 ♞xd4 ♞xa2 15 ♞f5 ♞xc1 16 ♞xe7+ ♜xe7 17 ♜xc1 ♜e8 ½-½ Tal-Planinc, Moscow 1975. However, instead of 14...♞xa2, Black can also play 14...exd4 15 ♝b3 ♝d6, which John Nunn assesses as slightly better for Black.

13 ♜xe5?

After this White's rook will be the target of various tactical tricks. Better was 13 ♝xd5 ♞xd5 (stronger than 13...♛xd5?! 14 ♞c3, which just helps White's development) 14 ♜xe5 ♝xg5 15 ♝xg5 ♛d7 16 ♜xe8+ ♜xe8 17 ♞a3 h6 18 ♝d2 ♜e6!, planning ...♜e6-g6 with strong kingside pressure.

13...♝xa2 14 ♜xa2 ♞g4!

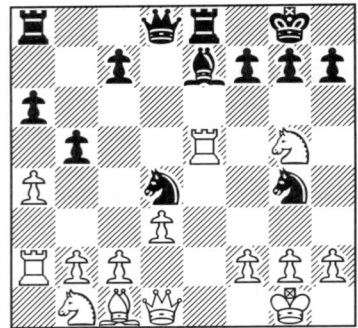

15 ♞xf7!?

The best practical chance because after 15 ♛xg4 ♝xg5 White loses material due to his weak back rank.

15...♛d7!

Perhaps White missed this subtle move? Of course Black is not obliged to play 15...♚xf7? 16 ♛xg4 when White is more than okay.

16 ♜e4 ♝h4! 17 ♞h6+

When playing the move 15...♛d7, Black had to calculate the variation 17 ♛xg4 ♛xf7! (but not 17...♛xg4? falling for the cheapo 18 ♞h6+!

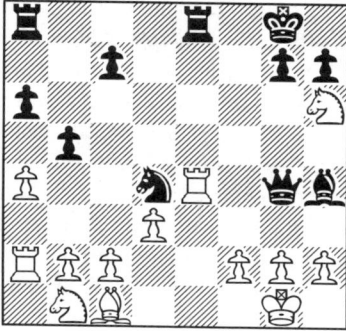

turning the position around) 18 ♕xh4 ♕xa2 19 ♘c3 ♕a1 20 ♕g5 bxa4! followed by ...a4-a3 and Black wins.

17...♘xh6 18 ♗xh6 ♖xe4 19 dxe4 ♖f8

The threat of ...♘d4-f3+ winning White's queen grants Black the decisive tempo for the attack along the f-file.

20 ♘c3 ♖xf2 21 g3

A sad reply but there is no time for 21 ♗e3? due to 21...♘e2+ mating.

21...♖xc2 22 ♗e3 ♕h3 23 ♗f2 ♗xg3! 24 hxg3 ♖c1

Even stronger was 24...♖d2!, which would have forced immediate resignation.

25 ♗xd4 ♕xg3+ 26 ♔f1 ♕d3+ 0-1

Game 87
Ivanchuk-Adams
Linares 2002

---

1 e4 e5 2 ♘f3 ♘c6 3 ♗b5 a6 4 ♗a4 ♘f6 5 0-0 ♗e7 6 ♖e1 b5 7 ♗b3 0-0 8 a4 ♗b7 9 d3 ♖e8 10 ♘a3

This rarely used continuation can be played occasionally as a surprise weapon. White attacks Black's stronghold on b5 and hopes for ...b5-b4, after which White's knight would obtain the dream square c4.

10...♗xa3

Tournament practice has shown that 10...♗c5?!, although it may look attractive at first glance, doesn't promise Black a good position after 11 ♗g5!

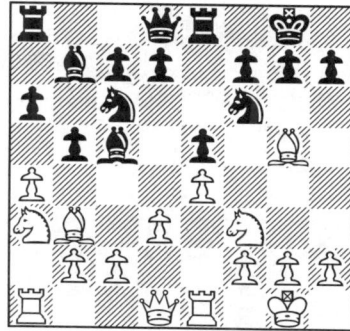

with an unpleasant pin along the h4-d8 diagonal. One example is 11...♘a5 12 ♗a2 b4 13 ♘c4 ♘c6 14 c3 h6 15 ♗h4 g5 16 ♗g3 bxc3?! 17 bxc3 d6 18 ♘e3 ♘e7 (a blunder but Black is already struggling) 19 ♕b3 hitting both f7 and b7, Hechlinger-Olson, Philadelphia 1995. A second example after 11 ♗g5! is 11...♘d4 12 ♘xd4 ♗xd4 13 c3 ♗b6 14 ♕f3! ♗c6 15 ♘c2 bxa4 16 ♗xa4 ♗xa4 17 ♖xa4 ♖e6 18 d4 h6 19 ♗h4 ♕e8 20 d5 ♖d6 21 ♘a3! ♘h7 22 ♘c4 with an obvious positional advantage to White due to the weak pawn on a6, Kupreichik-Dueball, Germany 1993.

11 bxa3!?

Black easily equalises after 11 ♖xa3 b4 12 ♖a1 d5 13 ♗g5 dxe4 14 dxe4 ♘a5 etc.

11...d5 12 exd5

After 12 ♗g5 Black has a good reply in 12...d4, seizing some space in the centre.

12...♘xd5 13 ♗b2?

It will transpire that this is an important loss of time. Better is 13 ♗d2, while Black is fine after 13 ♘g5 f6! 14 axb5 axb5 15 ♘e4 (the overly optimistic 15 c4? runs into 15...fxg5 16 cxd5 ♘d4! 17 d6+ ♔h8 18 dxc7 ♕xc7 19 ♗xg5 ♕c6! 20 f3 ♕g6! and White has trouble along the g-file) 15...♘d4 16 c3 ♘xb3 17 ♕xb3 ♗c6 18 c4 bxc4 19 dxc4 (Black also equalises after 19 ♕xc4 ♕d7 20 ♘c5 ♕f7) 19...♘f4 20 ♗xf4 exf4.

13...♘f4 14 ♗c1

White admits his mistake of the previous

move. The following variation shows that he had to be careful because his kingside is vulnerable: 14 ♕d2 ♕f6 15 ♕e3 ♕f5! 16 ♕e4? (losing) 16...♕g4 17 ♘xe5 ♘xe5 18 ♕xb7 c6 19 g3 ♕h3! 20 ♗xf7+ ♔h8! with the inevitable mate to follow.

14...♘xg2!?

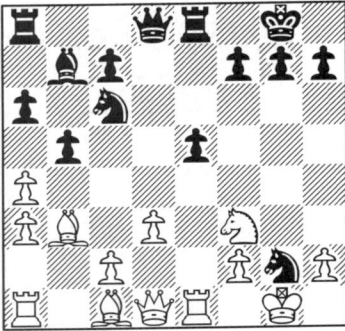

Black doesn't wait for White to exchange the dark-squared bishop for the knight on f4 and immediately sacrifices to destroy White's kingside. Still, even stronger may have been 14...♘d4!?, for example: 15 ♘xd4 ♘xg2! 16 ♕h5 (after 16 ♘e2? ♕h4! 17 ♘g3 ♕h3 White can no longer defend his king) 16...g6! (stronger than 16...♘xe1?! 17 ♗xf7+ ♔f8 – forced because if 17...♔h8? 18 ♗g6 etc. – 18 ♗b3 ♕f6 and now 19 ♗d2! with the idea of ♗d2-b4+ gives White excellent counterplay) and White is in deep trouble, as 17 ♗xf7+ ♔xf7 18 ♕xh7+ ♔f6 19 ♗h6 ♕xd4 20 ♗g7+ ♔f5 21 ♕h3+ ♕g4 demonstrates.

15 ♘g5!

Clearly White needs counterplay because the acceptance of the piece on g2 loses: 15 ♔xg2? ♘d4 16 ♖e3 ♕g5+ 17 ♔f1 ♕h5! and Black regains his piece with a mating attack to follow.

15...♘xe1?!

Great complications arise after 15...♘d4! and now:

a) 16 ♗xf7+ ♔f8 (but not 16...♔h8? 17 ♗xe8 ♕xe8 18 ♖xe5! and if 18...♕xe5?, 19 ♘f7+ wins) 17 ♕h5! ♘f3+ 18 ♘xf3 ♗xf3

transposes to note 'b1'. If White continues 17 ♗a2?! it gives Black a fantastic attack after 17...g6! 18 ♘f7 ♕h4 19 ♗h6+ ♕xh6 20 ♘xh6 ♘xe1 and, despite the fact that White is materially well ahead, Black's cavalry will do White a lot of harm, especially around the f3-square. I am not convinced that White can survive the coming onslaught.

b) 16 ♕h5 ♘f3+ 17 ♘xf3 ♗xf3 18 ♗xf7+ (Black obtains a strong initiative after 18 ♕xf7+ ♔h8 19 ♕xf3 ♘xe1 20 ♕e2 ♕d4 21 ♖b1 bxa4 22 ♗a2 e4! etc.) and now Black has the choice between the following:

b1) 18...♔f8 leads to a roughly equal ending after 19 ♕xf3 ♘xe1 20 ♕f5 ♕f6 21 ♕xf6 gxf6 22 ♗xe8 ♔xe8 23 ♗b2 etc.

b2) Black can play for a win with the more ambitious 18...♔h8!. For instance, if 19 ♖xe5?, then comes the astonishing reply 19...♕f6!!

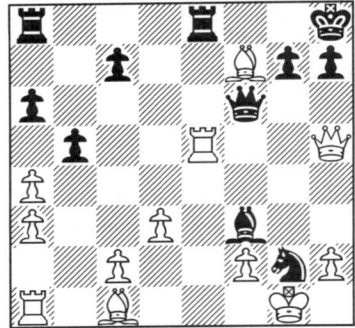

and Black's counterattack is quicker.

16 ♕h5 ♕d7?!

It is very difficult to be critical of this move, which rejects a forced draw. However, it was not easy to calculate the consequences of further complications so maybe it was safer to settle for half a point with 16...h6 17 ♘xf7 (White loses after 17 ♗xf7+? ♔h8 18 ♕g6 ♘f3+! 19 ♕xf3 ♘e7! – White's attack has failed and Black's material advantage decides) 17...♕f6 18 ♘g5+ (White also loses after 18 ♘xh6+? ♔f8 19 ♘g4 ♕f3 20 ♕h8+ ♔e7 21 ♕xg7+ ♔d8 etc., or 19 ♘f5 ♖e6! 20

♗xe6 ♕xe6 21 ♕h8+ ♕g8 and Black has an extra piece) 18...♔h8 19 ♘f7+ ♔h7 20 ♘g5+ etc.

17 ♗xf7+ ♔f8 18 ♗e3!

White can try to hunt down the black king with 18 ♘xh7+?! ♔e7 19 ♗g5+ ♔d6 20 ♖xe1 ♘d4 21 ♖e3, but after 21...♕c6 22 ♕g6+ ♖e6! 23 ♕e4 ♕xe4 24 dxe4 ♖h8! 25 ♗xe6 ♔xe6 Black wins as the knight on h7 is doomed.

18...♘d4 19 ♖xe1

Bad is 19 ♗xd4? ♘f3+! 20 ♘xf3 ♕xf7, while Black emerges in the ending with a strong bishop versus bad knight after 19 ♗xe8 ♕xe8 20 ♕xe8+ ♔xe8 21 ♖xe1 ♘xc2 22 ♖c1 ♘xe3 23 ♖xc7 ♖c8! 24 ♖xc8+ ♗xc8 25 fxe3 bxa4 etc.

19...♘f3+

White has a dangerous attack after 19...g6?! 20 ♕h6+ ♔e7 21 ♕h4! ♕c6 22 ♘e4+!? (also good was the simple 22 f3) 22...♔xf7 23 ♕xh7+ ♔e6 24 ♗xd4 exd4 25 ♔f1! with multiple threats. Note that 25...♕xc2 loses to 26 ♕xg6+ ♔d5 27 ♘f6+ ♔c5 28 ♘xe8 etc.

20 ♔f1! ♘xg5 21 ♗c5+ ♖e7 22 ♖xe5!

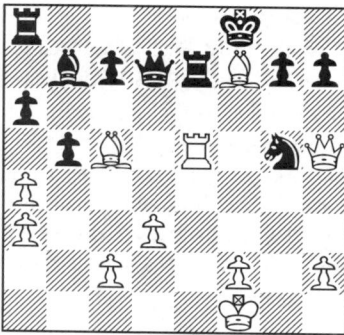

The key position, which White must have calculated before playing 18 ♗e3!. He will regain most of the sacrificed material as well as retaining the initiative.

22...♘xf7 23 ♖xe7 ♕xe7 24 ♗xe7+ ♔xe7 25 ♕c5+

For his lost queen, Black has plenty of material but he needs to play correctly to achieve a draw. So wasn't it better to have played 16...h6 instead of 16...♕d7?

25...♔d7

Also playable is 25...♗e6 26 ♕xc7 ♗d5 27 ♕b6+ ♘d6 28 ♕e3+ ♔d7 29 ♕e5 ♗f7 30 ♕xg7 ♖c8 and Black has managed to coordinate his pieces but at the cost of a couple of pawns.

26 ♕d4+ ♔e7 27 ♕xg7 bxa4?

Black loses a stronghold for his bishop after this move. Correct is 27...♗d5! 28 ♕xh7 ♖h8 29 ♕f5 c6 with chances for a draw.

28 ♕c3! ♔d7 29 ♕d4+ ♘d6 30 ♕xa4+ ♔e6 31 ♕g4+ ♘f5

If 31...♔f6, then 32 ♕d7 etc.

32 ♕c4+ ♗d5

Or 32...♔d7 33 ♕f7+ ♘e7 34 ♕xh7 with a technically winning ending for White.

33 ♕xc7 h5 34 c4! ♗h1

Or 34...♗f3 35 ♕f4! ♗b7 36 d4 ♖f8 37 ♕e5+ ♔d7 38 d5 and White's central pawns are irresistible.

35 f4 ♖f8 36 ♕b6+ ♔f7 37 ♕a7+ ♘e7 38 ♕xa6

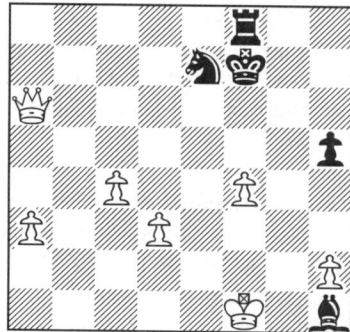

White has both a material and positional advantage. There is nothing Black can do against the march of the white pawns.

38...♖b8 39 d4 ♖b1+ 40 ♔e2 ♖b2+ 41 ♔d3 ♖b3+ 42 ♔d2 ♖h3 43 d5! ♖xh2+ 44 ♔d3 ♘xd5 45 cxd5 ♗xd5 46 f5 ♖a2 47 ♕a7+ ♔f6 48 ♕d4+ ♔g5 49 ♕xd5 ♖xa3+ 50 ♔e4 1-0

1 e4 e5 2 ♘f3 ♘c6 3 ♗b5 a6 4 ♗a4 ♘f6
5 0-0 ♗e7 6 ♖e1 b5 7 ♗b3 0-0 8 a4
♗b7 9 d3 ♖e8!? 10 ♗d2 ♗c5

This rarely seen move looks quite playable for Black. Strangely, in my database I have found only this game with 10...♗c5. With this move Black transposes into the Archangel Variation of the Ruy Lopez with his bishop on c5, albeit a tempo down as his bishop stopped off at e7 en route. However, the extra move for White (♗c1-d2) proves of no great importance, especially as it blocks the d2-square for the knight.

11 ♘a3

White exerts pressure over Black's stronghold of b5 in order to force Black to play ...b5-b4, after which White will obtain the excellent outpost of c4 for his knight.

What about other moves? For example:

a) 11 ♘g5 d5 12 exd5 (worth consideration is 12 ♗xd5 ♘xd5 13 exd5 ♕xd5 14 ♘c3 ♕d7 15 axb5 axb5 16 ♖xa8 ♗xa8 17 ♘xb5 and it still remains to be proved whether Black has enough compensation for the pawn) 12...♘d4 13 c4 and here Black can play either 13...♘g4 or 13...♗c8!?, intending ...♗c8-g4, both with very active positions for Black.

b) 11 ♗g5 ♘a5 12 ♗a2 d6 13 ♘c3 b4 14 ♘d5 ♗xd5 15 ♗xd5 c6 16 ♗a2 h6 17 ♗h4 ♖b8! 18 c3 b3

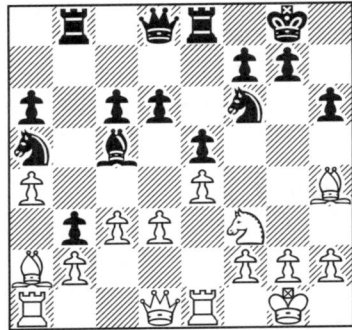

(it is important to remember this motif – the a1-rook and the b1-bishop will temporarily be out of the game) 19 ♗b1 ♗a7 20 d4 c5 and Black can boldly look forward to future events.

c) 11 ♘c3 ♘a5 12 ♗a2 b4 13 ♘e2 d5 or 13 ♘d5 ♗xd5 14 exd5 and now:

c1) 14...♘g4 15 ♖e2 d6 is unclear.

c2) It looks rather risky to open up the game with 14...e4 because then White's pair of bishops spring into life, but it certainly deserves a closer look: 15 ♘g5 exd3 16 ♖xe8+ ♕xe8 17 d6 ♕e2!? 18 ♕xe2 dxe2 19 dxc7 (after 19 ♗xf7+ ♔f8 White has to lose a vital tempo due to the unpleasant threat of ...h7-h6 winning a piece) 19...d5 20 ♖e1 ♖c8 21 ♗f4 ♗b6 22 ♖xe2 ♗xc7 and again we reach a position with roughly equal chances.

11...b4 12 ♘c4 h6 13 c3 d6 14 a5 ♖b8 15 ♗a4 ♘d7 16 ♕c2 ♗a8 17 ♖ab1 ♗a7 18 ♖ec1 ♖e6!

We've had a manoeuvring sequence of moves in which Black was retaining his stronghold on b4 and not exchanging on c3. This would have been wrong because the open b-file would favour White – he would have had various weaknesses in Black's camp to target. Also it is important to note how Black has had to keep an eye open over the d4-square to prevent White from playing d3-

d4.

19 b3?!

White saw that after 19 ♗xc6 Black has the intermediary move 19...bxc3! but the text seriously weakens the key b4-square.

19...bxc3 20 ♗xc3 ♖f6?!

Black was afraid to play the obvious 20...♘b4 21 ♗xb4 ♖xb4 because of 22 ♘xd6? when both 22...cxd6? 23 ♕c8! and 22...♖xd6?! 23 ♕xc7 turn out in White's favour, but he missed the fantastic reply 22...♘c5!!.

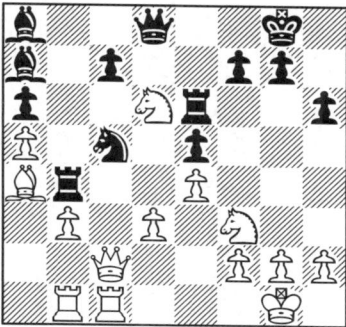

After 23 ♘c4 ♕xd3 Black is dominant and White has a poorly placed bishop on a4.

21 b4 ♘f8 22 ♘e3 ♘e6 23 ♘f5

Again the tactics favour Black after 23 ♗xc6? ♗xc6 24 ♗xe5 dxe5 25 ♕xc6 ♘d4 26 ♘xd4 exd4! 27 ♕xc7 dxe3 28 ♕xa7 exf2+ 29 ♔h1 ♖xb4! – White's position has collapsed.

23...♘e7 24 ♘xe7+?!

Better was 24 ♘e3 ♘f4 25 ♗b3, intending ♗b3-c4, with approximately equal play.

24...♕xe7 25 ♗d2 d5

Once Black plays this move, activating his light-squared bishop, it is obvious that Black has solved all his opening problems. The exchange sacrifice 25...♖xf3 26 gxf3 ♕f6 27 ♕d1 ♕g6+ 28 ♔f1 ♕h5 29 ♔g2 leads only to a draw because the tempting 29...♗xf2? is refuted by the cold-blooded 30 ♗b3!, intending ♗b3xe6 and ♖c1xc7.

26 ♗b3 dxe4

White holds on after 26...♖xf3 27 gxf3 ♘d4 28 ♕d1 etc.

27 dxe4 ♘d4 28 ♘xd4 ♗xd4 29 ♗e1?

This loses a pawn by force. Better was 29 ♖f1!, keeping the game balanced.

29...♖c6

This wins a pawn but also worthy of consideration was 29...♖f4!? 30 ♕xc7 ♕xc7 31 ♖xc7 ♗xe4 with some initiative for Black.

30 ♕e2 ♖xc1 31 ♖xc1 c5

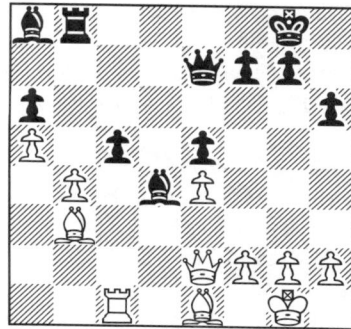

White is in trouble due to the pin along the b-file.

32 ♗d2 cxb4 33 ♕xa6 ♗xe4 34 ♖c8+ ♖xc8 35 ♕xc8+ ♔h7 36 ♕c4 ♗g6?

Black misses a nice win with 36...♕f6! 37 ♗e1 ♕g6 38 g3 ♕f5 39 ♕xf7 ♕xf7 40 ♗xf7 ♗c3 41 f3 (otherwise White has to give up a piece for Black's passed c-pawn) 41...♗xf3 42 ♔f2 ♗d1 43 ♗xc3 bxc3 44 ♔e3 c2 45 ♔d2 e4 and Black is winning the race in the bishop and pawn ending. Now the game fizzles out into a draw.

37 ♗xb4 ♕h4 38 ♗e1 ♕e4 39 ♕c1 ♕b7 40 ♗c2 e4 41 ♗d2 ♕b5 42 ♕e1 f5 43 ♗d1 ♗f7 44 ♗e2 ♕e5 45 ♕c1 ½-½

Game 89
Herrera-N.Mitkov
Cienfuegos 1996

---

1 e4 e5 2 ♘f3 ♘c6 3 ♗b5 a6 4 ♗a4 ♘f6 5 0-0 ♗e7 6 ♖e1 b5 7 ♗b3 0-0 8 a4 ♗b7 9 d3 ♖e8 10 ♘c3 b4 11 ♘d5

11 ♘e2 allows Black very comfortable play after 11...d5! 12 exd5 ♘xd5 13 ♘g3 ♗f8 etc.

11...♘a5 12 ♘xe7+

Sometimes White tries to keep the tension with 12 ♗a2 ♘xd5 and now:

a) 13 exd5 ♗f6 14 c3 c5 15 dxc6 ♘xc6 16 ♕b3 ♕e7 17 ♗d2 bxc3?! 18 bxc3 d5 19 ♖ab1! ♖ab8 20 ♕xd5 (Conquest-P.Blatny, Alma Ata 1989). Black did not manage to prove the correctness of the pawn sacrifice because after 20...♘d4, White has 21 ♕xf7+!. Instead of 17...bxc3?!, correct was 17...a5 with a good position for Black.

b) 13 ♗xd5 ♗xd5 14 exd5 ♗f6 (worse is 14...d6?! because of 15 d4! and White gets control of the centre) 15 ♘d2 d6 16 ♕f3 with a further split:

b1) 16...♗g5? 17 ♘b3! ♗xc1 18 ♖axc1 ♘b7 (a sad retreat, but after 18...♘xb3? 19 cxb3 Black's queenside pawn weaknesses would be difficult, if not impossible, to defend) 19 ♕g4 a5 20 c3 with a clear positional advantage to White, Kotronias-I.Sokolov, European Team Championship, Haifa 1989.

b2) 16...c6! 17 dxc6 d5 or 17 ♘e4 ♗e7 and Black, having managed to free himself from the bind on the d5-square, has now equalised.

12...♕xe7 13 ♗a2 d5!

The strongest continuation, with which Black obtains more space in the centre. Czech Grandmaster Pavel Blatny used to like

the move 13...♖ab8?! with the idea of ...b4-b3, but the following game cast doubts upon that idea: 14 ♗g5 h6 15 ♗h4 c5 16 ♘d2! (White frees the way for his f-pawn) 16...♖bd8 17 f4 d6 18 f5 ♔h7 19 ♕f3 ♖g8 20 ♖f1 ♘c6 21 c3 with a clear advantage to White, who has excellent prospects for a king-side attack (Kholmov-Blatny, Brno 1991).

14 exd5

Or 14 ♗g5 dxe4 15 dxe4 and now:

a) 15...♖ad8 16 ♕e2 h6 17 ♗xf6 (after 17 ♗h4 I recommend 17...♖d6 with equality) 17...♕xf6 18 ♖ad1 ♕e7 19 h3 g6 20 ♕e3 ♔g7 21 ♗d5 ♗xd5 22 exd5 ♘c4 23 ♕b3 ♘a5 24 ♕e3 ♘c4 25 ♕b3 ♘a5 ½-½ Shirov-Adams, Linares 2002.

b) 15...h6 16 ♗h4 ♖ad8 17 ♕e2 and now, instead of 17...b3? 18 ♗xf6 ♕xf6 19 ♗xb3 ♘xb3 20 cxb3 ♕b6 21 ♕c2, when White has both a positional and material advantage (Hübner-Z.Polgar, Biel 1987), the quiet move 17...♖d6 grants Black an equal position.

14...♕d6!

After this move Black regains his sacrificed pawn.

15 ♗d2

15 c4 is known to be harmless for Black. One example is 15 c4 bxc3 16 bxc3 ♗xd5 17 ♗a3 (or 17 ♗g5 ♗xa2 18 ♖xa2 ♘d5 19 ♖c2 c5 20 ♗c1 ♖ad8 with a good position for Black, who has play against the d3-pawn in Short-Nikolic, Naestved 1985) 17...c5 18 ♗xd5 ♕xd5 19 ♕c2 c4 20 ♖ad1 ♘c6 21

dxc4 ♕xc4 22 ♘d2 ♘d4!? 23 ♕xh7+! (Black's tactical idea is revealed after 23 ♕b2 ♘e2+ 24 ♔h1? – better is 24 ♔f1 ♘g3+ with a draw by perpetual check – 24...♘g4!, threatening mate) 23...♔xh7 24 ♘xc4 ♘c2 25 ♖e2 ♖ec8 26 ♖xc2 ♖xc4 27 a5 ♖ac8. Black regains his pawn and the game was eventually drawn, Onischuk-Wahls, Bundesliga 1996.

15...♗xd5 16 ♗xd5 ♘xd5

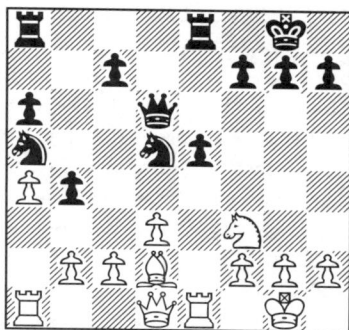

17 ♕e2 ♘c6

Black re-routes his knight towards the centre. The alternative is 17...c5, which doesn't look bad either. For example, Adams-Conquest, British Championship 1986 continued 18 ♘g5 ♕g6 19 ♕f3 ♖ad8 20 h4!? ♘c6 21 h5 ♕f6 22 ♕e4 g6 23 ♕c4 ♘d4! 24 ♘e4 (or 24 ♕xc5 gxh5! with ...♕f6-g6 to follow and Black will have strong play along the g-file) 24...♕f5 25 ♘g3 ♕d7 26 ♗g5 ♖c8 27 ♘e4 ♖c6 with a very complicated position ahead. However, White then blundered with 28 ♘xc5? ♖xc5 29 ♕xc5 ♘e6 30 ♕c4 ♘xg5, but even stronger was 28...♕c8! 29 ♕xd5 ♖xc5 followed by ...♘d4xc2 with an immediate win for Black.

18 ♕e4 ♖ad8 19 b3?!

This creates a weak square in c3. Better was 19 ♘g5, although after 19...♕g6 20 ♕xg6 hxg6 21 ♘f3 f6 the resulting endgame position is somewhat drawish.

19...h6

Controlling g5 and also giving the black king air, which is useful in some variations.

20 ♖ac1

This move indicates that White has no clear plan. The position is probably still balanced but somehow Black has more options.

20...♖e6 21 ♗e3 ♘ce7!

Black's knight heads towards the kingside in order to launch an initiative on that side of the board. The manoeuvring which follows is natural but it is clear than only Black can improve his position. It looks equal but it is not!

22 ♕c4 ♘g6 23 ♖b1 ♕d7 24 ♕g4 ♕c6 25 ♖bc1 ♖f8 26 ♗d2 f5 27 ♕c4 ♕d6 28 ♗e3 ♖fe8 29 a5 ♔h8 30 h4?

This bad move decisively weakens White's kingside.

30...e4! 31 ♘d4?

White had to try 31 dxe4 ♖xe4 32 ♗c5!?, but after 32...♕c6! 33 ♖xe4 ♖xe4 34 ♘d4 ♕b7! White is probably still lost due to his weakened kingside.

31...♘xe3 32 ♖xe3 ♘e5

Trapping the white queen!

33 ♕xe6 ♖xe6 31 ♘xe6 ♕xe6 32 dxe4 f4 0-1

Game 90
Kasparov-Tkachiev
Cannes (rapid) 2001

1 e4 e5 2 ♘f3 ♘c6 3 ♗b5 a6 4 ♗a4 ♘f6 5 0-0 ♗e7 6 ♖e1 b5 7 ♗b3 0-0 8 a4

♗b7 9 d3 d6 10 ♘bd2

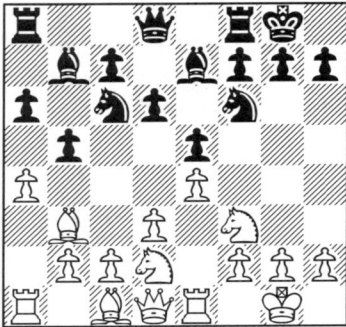

10 ♘bd2 was popularised by Kasparov when he used it with success in his 1993 World Championship match with Nigel Short, and it has now replaced 10 ♘c3 as the main move.

10...♖e8

Black intends to bolster his kingside and e5-pawn with the typical ...h7-h6 and ...♗f8 plan. 10...♘a5 is the subject of Game 91.

11 ♘f1 h6 12 ♗d2!?

Again Kasparov's invention, this move has presented Black with some fresh problems in the 8 a4 Anti-Marshall. White prevents the typical ...♘a5 plan and prepares c2-c4.

Alternatives include the following possibilities:

a) 12 c3 ♗f8 13 ♘e3 ♘a5 14 ♗a2 c5 15 b4 cxb4 16 cxb4 ♘c6 17 ♘d5 ♘xd5 18 ♗xd5 ♕d7 with perhaps a tiny edge for White, Kindermann-Adams, Garmisch 1994.

b) 12 ♘e3 ♗f8 13 ♗d2 ♘e7! (now Black has time to answer c2-c4 with ...c7-c6) 14 c4 c6 15 ♕c2 ♘g6 16 ♘f5 bxc4 17 ♗xc4 d5 with equality, Svidler-Adams, European Team Championship, Pula 1997.

12...♗f8 13 c4!

This advance is not typical for the 8 a4 Anti-Marshall, but here it causes Black headaches because a concession of some sort must be made on the queenside.

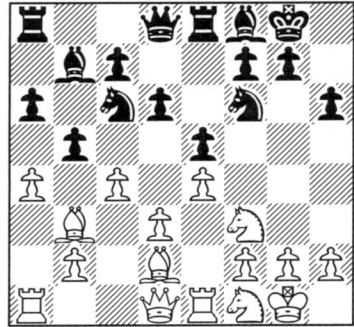

13...bxc4

13...b4 keeps the queenside closed, but after 14 a5! Black's b4-pawn is seriously weakened. One practical example is 14...♘d7 15 ♗a4 ♖b8 16 b3 ♘c5 17 ♕c2 ♘xa4 18 ♖xa4 with an edge to White, Berelovich-Jenni, Bundesliga 2002.

14 ♗xc4 ♖b8

Or 14...♗c8 15 ♗c3 ♗e6 16 ♘e3 ♗xc4 17 dxc4 ♖b8 18 ♘d5 ♘xd5 19 cxd5 ♘b4 20 ♕e2 a5 21 ♖ed1 ♕d7 22 ♘e1! c6 23 ♘c2 ♘xc2 24 ♕xc2 and White's bishop on c3 is far superior to its opposite number on f8, Zatonskih-Reg.Pokorna, Warsaw 2001.

15 ♗c3

Planning the natural d3-d4 advance. White has come out of the opening with a substantial edge.

15...♘e7 16 ♘g3 ♘g6 17 d4 exd4 18 ♕xd4 d5

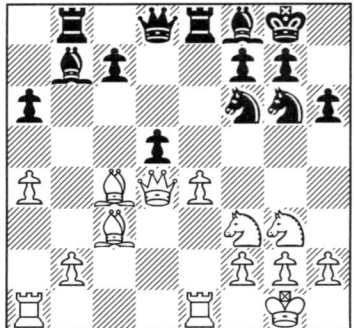

Instead of remaining passive, Black tries to simplify the position.

19 exd5 ♖xe1+ 20 ♖xe1 ♘xd5 21 ♖d1 ♘gf4 22 ♘f5 ♕f6 23 ♕xf6 gxf6

The queens have come off the board but Black is still clearly worse due to his shocking pawn structure.

24 ♗d4 ♗c8 25 ♘e3 ♘xe3 26 fxe3! ♘e6 27 ♗xf6 ♗g7 28 ♗xg7 ♔xg7 29 b3

Black has lost one of his weak pawns, but he still has four left to go! The game doesn't last much longer.

29...♔f6 30 ♖f1 ♖b6 31 ♘d4+ ♔g7 32 ♘f5+ ♔h7 33 ♘e7 1-0

Game 91
Kasparov-Leko
Linares 2001

---

1 e4 e5 2 ♘f3 ♘c6 3 ♗b5 a6 4 ♗a4 ♘f6 5 0-0 ♗e7 6 ♖e1 b5 7 ♗b3 0-0 8 a4 ♗b7 9 d3 d6 10 ♘bd2 ♘a5

Planning typical queenside expansion with ...c7-c5.

11 ♗a2 c5 12 ♘f1 ♖e8!?

Black can block the queenside with 12...b4, after which White probably keeps a slight edge after 13 ♘e3.

13 ♘e3!

Eyeing up the tempting d5- and f5-squares.

13...h6

Or 13...g6 14 ♗d2 b4 15 ♘g5! ♖f8 16 ♘g4 ♘xg4 17 ♕xg4 ♗c8 18 ♕h4 h5 19 ♕g3 with a strong attack, Kasparov-Vladimirov, Batumi 2001. The rest of this game is quite instructive: 19...♗g7 20 ♗d5! ♖b8 21 h4 ♕d7 22 ♕e3! ♗b7 23 ♘h7! ♗xd5 (23...♔xh7 24 ♕h6+ ♔g8 25 ♕xg6+ ♔h8 26 ♕xh5+ ♔g8 27 ♖e3 wins) 24 ♕h6+ ♔g8 25 ♗g5 and now Black played 25...♖xe4? and resigned immediately. After the more tenacious 25...♕d8 White wins with 26 exd5 ♖e8 27 ♖e3! followed by the move ♖f3.

14 ♗d2

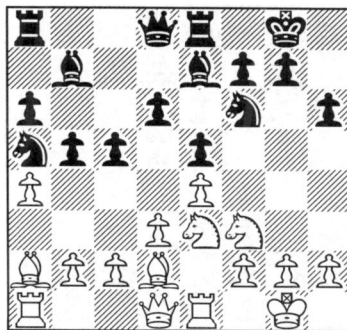

14...c4?!

A committal move. Using a counterattack on the e4-pawn, Black tries to block the long a2-g8 diagonal in order to minimise the influence of the a2-bishop.

14...b4 15 ♘h4! ♘xe4 16 dxe4 ♗xh4 17 ♕h5 (Kasparov) gives White an awesome attack. Relatively best for Black was 14...♘c6 with just a small advantage for White.

15 ♗c3!?

White can probably keep an edge with 15 b4 cxb3 16 cxb3 planning b3-b4.

15...♕b6

After 15...cxd3?! 16 cxd3 Black's plan has failed miserably – the a2-bishop is as active as ever.

16 ♘d2!

Adding further pressure to c4. Leko must have been hoping for 16 dxc4? b4! 17 ♗d2 ♗xe4, when suddenly it is Black who has the advantage.

16...♘c6?!

Now White is able to establish a clear advantage. 16...cxd3?! 17 cxd3 b4 18 ♘dc4 ♘xc4 19 ♘xc4 followed by ♗d2 is also bad for Black, but the best chance is 16...♖ec8 17 ♗xa5 ♕xa5 18 axb5 axb5 19 dxc4 b4 (Kasparov), when Black has some compensation for the pawn, although I still prefer White.

17 ♘d5! ♘xd5 18 exd5 ♘a5 19 ♗xa5?

A slip by the world number one. 19 dxc4! b4 20 c5! ♕xc5 21 ♘e4 ♕b6 22 ♗d2 (Kasparov) would have kept White on top.

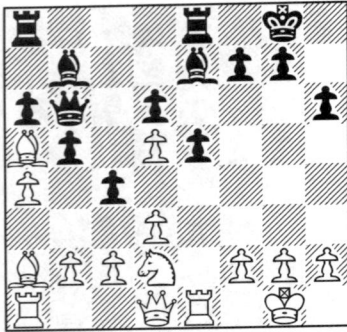

19...♛xa5 20 dxc4 ♛xa4?!

Brave but foolish. 20...b4! would have given Black reasonable compensation for the pawn.

21 c5! ♛b4?

Leko's problems are compounded by another error. 21...♛d4 would have kept Black in the game, although White still stands better after 22 c6 ♝c8 23 c3 ♛b6 24 ♛h5 (Kasparov).

22 ♘e4!

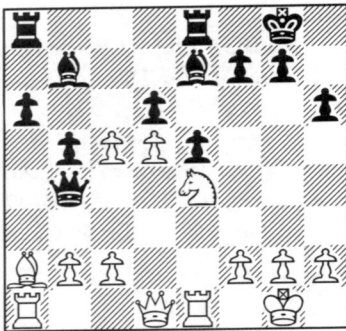

After this move White is already winning and the rest is easy for Kasparov.

22...♛xb2

Or 22...dxc5 23 c3 ♛xb2 24 ♖e2 ♛a3 25 d6 with a double threat of dxe7 and ♝xf7+.

23 cxd6 ♝f8 24 c3

Threatening to trap the queen with 25 ♖e2 ♛a3 26 ♝b3.

24...f5 25 d7 ♖ed8 26 d6+ ♚h8

26...♚h7 27 ♘g5+! ♚g6 28 ♝f7+! ♚f6 29 ♛h5 and Black is quickly mated.

27 ♘c5 ♝c6 28 ♘d3 ♛xc3 29 ♘xe5 ♝e4 30 ♘f7+ ♚h7

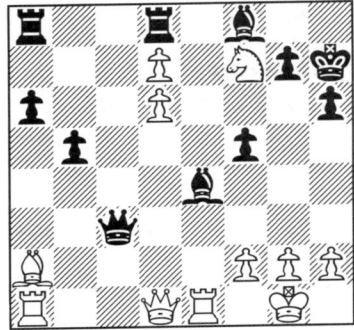

31 ♘g5+ 1-0

31...♚h8 32 ♘xe4 fxe4 33 ♛d5 is not worth playing on for Black.

> ## Game 92
> ## Anand-Ivanchuk
> *Monaco (rapid) 2001*

1 e4 e5 2 ♘f3 ♘c6 3 ♝b5 a6 4 ♝a4 ♘f6 5 0-0 ♝e7 6 ♖e1 b5 7 ♝b3 0-0 8 a4 b4

This advance is much less popular than 8...♝b7. Black can certainly reach playable positions but, as this game shows, it's quite easy to drift into slightly passive ones too.

9 d3 d6 10 a5!

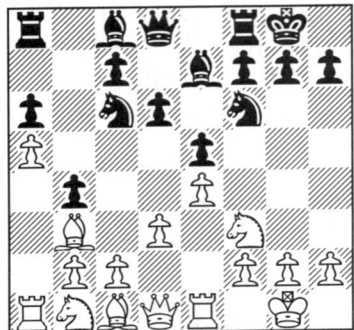

The critical continuation. White prevents

...♘a5 and, more importantly, isolates the a6- and b4-pawns. The only negative feature of this move is that the a5-pawn could become a target itself.

10...♗e6 11 ♘bd2 ♗xb3

An alternative is 11...♖b8 12 ♘c4!? (12 ♗c4 ♕c8 13 ♘f1 is a more common continuation, with White having a slight edge) 12...♗g4 13 ♗e3 ♘d7 14 h3 ♗xf3 15 ♕xf3 ♗g5 16 ♗a4 ♗xe3 17 ♕xe3 and again White has a slight pull, Kasparov-Grischuk, Moscow (rapid) 2002.

12 ♘xb3

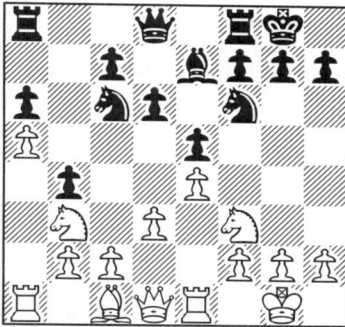

At first glance it looks as though Black shouldn't have any problems here, but he doesn't really have an active plan and the weaknesses on the queenside will eventually become important. Not many black-sided Marshall players have the necessary patience to defend such a position, which probably explains why 8...♗b7 is so much more popular than 8...b4.

12...♖e8

Or 12...d5 13 ♗g5 ♖e8 14 ♕e2 h6 15 ♗xf6 ♗xf6 16 exd5 ♕xd5 17 ♕e4 ♖ad8 18 ♘fd2 g6 19 ♕xd5 ♖xd5 20 ♖e4 ♗g5 21 ♖c4 and White converted his small advantage in this ending, Grischuk-Tkachiev, Prague 2002. Black has weaknesses at b4, a6 and c7.

13 h3

There is no need for White to rush – his

advantage is of a long-lasting nature. That said, 13 d4 ♘xd4 14 ♘fxd4 exd4 15 ♘xd4 ♗f8 16 f3 c5 17 ♘f5 ♖e6 18 ♗g5 h6 19 ♗h4 g6 20 ♘e3 also left Black grovelling in Short-I.Sokolov, Linares 1995.

13...♕d7 14 ♗g5 h6 15 ♗h4 ♘h7 16 ♗xe7 ♖xe7 17 d4 exd4 18 ♘fxd4 ♘f6 19 f3 ♘xd4 20 ♕xd4 ♕b5 21 ♕d3 ♕g5 22 ♕d2 ♕xd2 23 ♘xd2 ♖ae8 24 ♘b3

A few exchanges have been made but if anything these have simply emphasised the pawn weaknesses on the queenside. Note that 24...d5 can simply be met by 25 ♘c5!.

24...c5 25 ♖ed1 ♖e6 26 ♖d2 ♔f8 27 ♖ad1 ♔e7 28 ♘c1 ♖d8 29 ♘d3 ♖d7 30 b3

Objectively White is still only 'slightly better' but defending this type of ending is not really what one plays the Marshall for!

30...g5 31 ♔f2 ♖b7 32 ♘b2 ♖b5 33 ♘c4 ♘e8 34 e5!

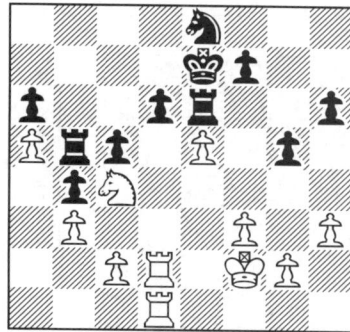

Impressive play from Anand. A temporary pawn sacrifice allows White's rooks to penetrate down the d-file.

34...dxe5 35 ♖d7+ ♔f6 36 ♖a7 ♔g6 37 ♖dd7 f6 38 ♖d8 h5 39 ♖da8

The a6-pawn goes, leaving White with an unstoppable runner on a5.

39...h4 40 ♖xa6 ♘c7 41 ♖xe6 ♘xe6 42 a6 ♘c7 43 ♖a7 1-0

43...♘d5 44 ♖b7 is winning for White.

Summary

Game 86 confirms the widespread opinion that the crude 10 ♘g5 gives Black a promising position. White goes down after he embarks on the greedy pawn-grabbing 13 ♖xe5? at the too great a cost of leaving his pieces uncoordinated. In Game 87 Adams's 10...♗xa3 11 bxa3 d5 etc. looks like it equalises easily. In Game 88, although White forces Black to play ...b5-b4 conceding the c4-square to White's knight, Black keeps the position in the balance as long as White is prevented from playing d3-d4.

In Game 89 the reader should remember the freeing sequence 13...d5! and 14...♕d6!, with which Black achieves an equal position. Later on White plays poorly and apparently without a plan. He then weakens the c3-square after which Black obtains a great spatial advantage culminating in a successful kingside attack. This was a good example of Black's chances in a so-called balanced position.

Finally, Kasparov's powerful opening play in Games 90-91 has certainly put the ball back in Black's court in the line 8...♗b7 9 d3 d6 10 ♘bd2. Black also had an unhappy experience in Game 92 with the committal 8...b4.

1 e4 e5 2 ♘f3 ♘c6 3 ♗b5 a6 4 ♗a4 ♘f6 5 0-0 ♗e7 6 ♖e1 b5 7 ♗b3 0-0 8 a4 ♗b7
   8...b4 – *Game 92*
9 d3 ♖e8 (D)
   9...d6 10 ♘bd2
      10...♘a5 (D) – *Game 91*; 10...♖e8 – *Game 90*
10 ♘c3 (D) – *Game 89*
   10 ♗d2 – *Game 88*; 10 ♘a3 – *Game 87*; 10 ♘g5 – *Game 86*; 10 c3 – *Game 85*

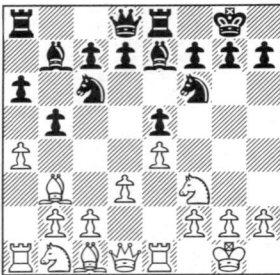
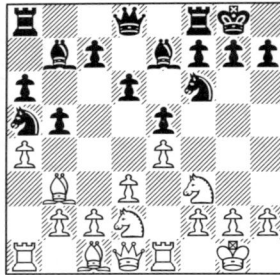
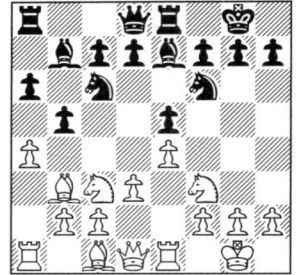

9...♖e8   *10...♘a5*   *10 ♘c3*

CHAPTER NINE

Anti-Marshall with 8 d4!?

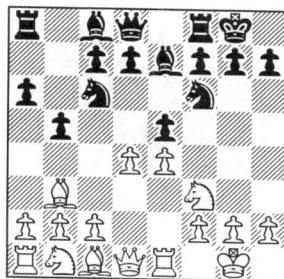

1 e4 e5 2 ♘f3 ♘c6 3 ♗b5 a6 4 ♗a4 ♘f6 5 0-0 ♗e7 6 ♖e1 b5 7 ♗b3 0-0 8 d4!?

By playing 8 d4!? White intends to seize control of the centre and this might lead to positions where it is White and not Black who sacrifices a pawn. In return, White succeeds in pushing away Black's knight from f6 by playing e4-e5 – this grants the first player a lasting initiative. However, with accurate play Black's chances are by no means worse.

Of course after 8 d4!? Black can chicken out by playing 8...d6, after which 9 c3 ♗g4 leads to the Closed Ruy Lopez variation where White doesn't play 9 h3 but plays 9 d4, allowing Black to play ...♗c8-g4. This line is considered quite harmless for Black but in this chapter I will only deal with games where Black accepts the gauntlet by capturing on d4.

In Belotti-Ara.Minasian (Game 93) White embarks on the suspicious pawn-grabbing 8...♘xd4 9 ♗xf7+?!, after which the pair of bishops gives Black a long lasting initiative.

In Games 94-95, after 8 d4!? ♘xd4 9 ♘xd4 exd4 10 e5 ♘e8 it is White who sacrifices a pawn this time with 11 c3!?. In return he obtains strong control over the vital d5-square. Also his light-squared bishop exerts strong pressure on the a2-g8 diagonal. In short, Black must be very careful not to

crumble under White's kingside attack.

Instead of the ambitious 11 c3!?, White can simply recapture on d4 with 11 ♕xd4 (Games 96-97).

Game 93
Belotti-Ara.Minasian
European Championship, Ohrid 2001

---

1 e4 e5 2 ♘f3 ♘c6 3 ♗b5 a6 4 ♗a4 ♘f6 5 0-0 ♗e7 6 ♖e1 b5 7 ♗b3 0-0 8 d4 ♘xd4!

8...d6 9 c3 ♗g4 is by no means a bad choice for Black because theory considers that Black is fine in that line. However, from the psychological point of view I suggest that against 8 d4 Black should be brave enough and take the bull by the horns by playing 8...♘xd4!.

9 ♗xf7+?!

Giving a dubious sign after White's ninth move can only be justified after meticulous analysis and seeing a great number of games. The move by itself is not bad. White wins a pawn but in return Black gets a long-lasting initiative, excellent development and a powerful pair of bishops. In particular, his light-squared bishop will be very strong.

9...♖xf7 10 ♘xe5 ♖f8!

The natural move 10...c5? surprisingly

loses to 11 ♘xf7 ♔xf7 12 e5 ♘e8 13 c3 ♘c6 14 ♕d5+! ♔f8 15 ♖e3! g6 16 ♖f3+ ♔g7 17 ♕f7+ ♔h8 18 ♗h6

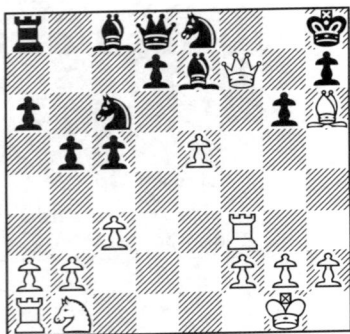

with the inevitable mate to follow. This is an example where two minor pieces are not a match for a rook as the minor pieces have no safe outposts and the side with the rook has the initiative. I am not sure that the late World Champion Mikhail Tal would have enjoyed that variation!

11 ♕xd4 c5

I prefer this to the alternative 11...♗b7. White must decide on which square to place his queen.

12 ♕d3

Black gets excellent compensation for the sacrificed pawn after 12 ♕d2 ♕c7 13 ♘f3 ♗b7 14 ♘c3 ♖ae8 15 e5 b4! etc.

12...c4

I prefer this to 12...♕c7 from the game Vitolins-Ozlins, Riga 1985, which continued 13 ♘f3 ♗b7 14 ♗g5 c4 15 ♕d1 ♗c5 16 ♗xf6 (this knight has to be eliminated as 16 ♘c3? ♘g4!, hitting both the f2- and h2-squares, is clearly bad for White) 16...♖xf6 17 ♘c3 ♖d6 18 ♘d5 ♕a5 19 b3!? (also possible is 19 c3 – I think that with best play Black hasn't enough compensation for the sacrificed pawn) 19...♖e8 (after 19...♗b4 a strong reply is 20 a3! and if 20...♗xe1, then 21 ♘e7+ followed by ♕xd6 etc. is in White's favour) 20 bxc4 bxc4 21 ♖b1 ♗c6 22 ♘g5 g6 23 ♖e2 ♕d8?! (Black had to be brave and

play 23...♕xa2! 24 ♖d2 h6 25 ♘f3 ♔h7 with roughly equal play) 24 h4 h6 25 ♘f3 ♖de6 26 ♕d2 ♔g7?? (a blunder, losing a second pawn; necessary was 26...♔h7) 27 ♕c3+ ♔h7 28 ♕xc4 d6 29 ♕d3 1-0.

13 ♕e2 ♗b7 14 ♘c3 ♕c7 15 ♘g4 b4 16 ♘d5

Stronger than 16 ♘xf6+?! ♗xf6 17 ♘d5 ♗xd5 18 exd5 ♗d4! 19 ♗e3 ♗xb2 and Black has regained the sacrificed pawn with advantage because he now has the better pawn structure.

16...♘xd5 17 exd5 ♖ae8 18 ♗e3 ♗xd5 19 ♗d4 ♕f4 20 ♕e5 ♕xe5 21 ♖xe5 ♗e6

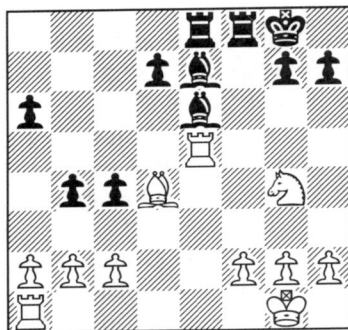

By exchanging queens, White has managed to diminish Black's initiative. However, Black still maintains some advantage in the ending due to his pair of bishops, which can be strong in this type of open position.

22 h3 ♗xg4

I don't think that Black should have parted with his pair of bishops so easily. Worth a try was 22...♗h4!? 23 ♖ae1 h5!, hoping for 24 ♖xh5?? ♗xg4 25 ♖xe8 ♗xh5 and Black emerges a piece up.

23 hxg4 ♗f6 24 ♖xe8 ♖xe8 25 ♗xf6 gxf6 26 ♔f1 ♖e5 27 a3 ♖a5 28 a4 ♔f7 29 ♔e2 ♖e5+ 30 ♔d2

Simpler was 30 ♔f3! and the ending should be drawn.

30...♖g5 31 f3?

White errs again. This time the correct continuation was 31 ♖h1! in order, after

31...♔g6, to respond with 32 f3. Then ...f6-f5 has no effect since White takes on f5 with check.

31...h5!

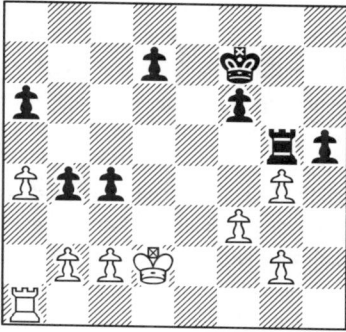

Of course! Black wins a pawn since 32 gxh5? ♖xg2+ is hopeless for White.

32 ♔e3 hxg4 33 ♔d4 gxf3 34 gxf3 d5 35 c3 b3?!

Black reckons that his b3-pawn will be strong (nobody denies it) and that this will decide the game, but what is more important is that with this move Black loses time which could have been better used for bringing his king towards the centre. The following variation shows that Black has excellent winning chances: 35...bxc3 36 bxc3 ♖f5 37 ♖f1 ♔e6 38 a5 ♔d6! (stronger than 38...♔d7 39 ♖b1! ♖xf3 40 ♔xd5 ♖xc3 41 ♖b7+ ♔d8 42 ♖b6 after which White can claim the old saying 'all rook and pawn endgames are drawn') 39 ♖b1 ♖f4+! (less accurate is 39...♖xf3?! 40 ♖b6+ ♔c7 41 ♔xd5 with a draw) 40 ♔e3 ♖h4 41 ♖b6+ ♔e5 42 ♖xa6 f5 and White is in a difficult situation because 43 f4+? ♖xf4 44 ♖e6+ ♔xe6 45 ♔xf4 d4! leads to a lost king and pawn ending by one single tempo.

36 ♖e1!

It is important to cut off the black king from the e-file.

36...♖f5 37 ♖e3 a5 38 ♔c5 ♔g6 39 ♖e2 ♔g5 40 ♔b5 d4?!

This ending is difficult to play from both sides. Maybe a better winning try was the

move 40...♖e5!?. Black seems to be quicker by a split second after 41 ♖h2 ♔f4 42 ♔xa5 ♔xf3 43 ♔b6 f5 44 ♔c5 f4 45 a5 ♔e3 46 a6 f3 47 a7 ♖e8 48 ♔xd5 f2 49 ♖h1 ♖c8!.

41 cxd4 ♔f4 42 ♔c6 ♔xf3 43 ♖e1 ♖h5 44 d5

White's passed d-pawn grants him sufficient counterplay and Black has no more winning chances.

44...♖h2 45 ♖b1 ♖c2 46 d6 c3 47 bxc3 ♖xc3+ 48 ♔b6 ♖d3 47 ♔c7 ♖c3+ 48 ♔b6 ♖d3 49 ♔c7 ♖c3+ 50 ♔d8 ♔e2 51 d7 ♔d2 52 ♔e7 ♖e3+ 53 ♔xf6 ♖d3 54 ♖xb3 ♖xd7 55 ♖b5 ♔c3 56 ♖xa5 ½-½

Game 94
Tseshkovsky-Malaniuk
USSR Championship 1987

---

1 e4 e5 2 ♘f3 ♘c6 3 ♗b5 a6 4 ♗a4 ♘f6 5 0-0 ♗e7 6 ♖e1 b5 7 ♗b3 0-0 8 d4 ♘xd4 9 ♘xd4 exd4 10 e5 ♘e8 11 c3!?

This sharp gambit continuation requires very careful play from Black, especially as White has pressure on the a2-g8 diagonal. This continuation might be psychologically unpleasant for the Marshall player, who expects to attack and not, as in this case, defend.

11...dxc3 12 ♘xc3 d6 13 ♕f3 ♗e6

Too slow is 13...♖b8?!, after which White gets a lasting initiative with 14 ♗f4 and now:

a) 14...dxe5 15 ♗xe5 ♗b7 16 ♕h5 ♗f6 17 ♖ad1 ♕c8 18 ♖d3! (starting a kingside attack when the majority of the black pieces are still on the eighth rank) 18...♗xe5 19 ♖xe5 ♘f6 20 ♕g5 ♕g4 21 ♕xg4 ♘xg4 22 ♖e7 c5 23 ♖dd7 c4 24 ♗xc4 bxc4 25 ♖xb7 with clear advantage for White in the ending due to his total domination of the seventh rank, McShane-D.Pedersen, Abihome (rapid) 2000.

b) 14...♗b7 15 ♗d5 ♗xd5 16 ♘xd5 dxe5 17 ♗xe5 ♗d6 18 ♖ad1 ♖h8 (no better is the alternative 18...♕h4 as White will still retain a strong initiative) 19 ♘e7! ♕d7 (obviously the knight on e7 is taboo) 20 ♕h5 ♖d8? (the last chance to defend was 20...b4!? with the idea of 21 ♖e3 ♖b5! with the unpleasant pin along the fifth rank; 22 ♖h3?? ♘f6 covers the mate on h7 and wins a piece) 21 ♖e3! ♕xe7 22 ♖h3 ♘f6 (the only defence but...) 23 ♗xf6 ♕e4 24 ♗xd8 ♖xd8 25 ♕xf7 and White won material in Vogt-Goldberg, East German Championship 1986.

14 ♘d5 ♖c8

The rook on a8 has been in danger from the white queen on f3.

15 ♗f4 ♗g5 16 ♖ad1

Weaker is 16 ♗g3?! c6 17 ♘b4? c5! 18 ♘xa6 d5!, trapping the knight.

16...♔h8?!

Black removes his king from the a2-g8 diagonal, planning to free himself with ...f7-f5 in some variations.

Bad was 16...♗xf4 17 ♘xf4 ♗xb3 18 ♕xb3 ♔h8 19 e6! and Black is in a mess. Deserving attention, however, is 16...c6!? with the idea after 17 ♗xg5 ♕xg5 18 ♘b6 ♗xb3 19 axb3 ♖c7 20 exd6 to continue with 20...♘xd6! 21 ♖xd6 ♕c5! and Black regains his piece with at least an equal position. In fact, I think that this would be superior to the text, which seems to be a bit too slow.

17 ♗g3

It was later found that the alternative 17 ♗c2! was stronger.

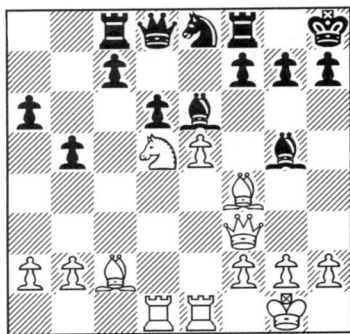

After 17 ♗c2 White retains pressure. For example, 17...f5?! (Black had to play 17...g6

although after 18 ♗g3! it is not easy to play this position for Black – quite simply he is very passive and White has too much pressure) 18 ♕h5! h6? (this is a blunder but it was difficult to find anything better anyway, for instance 18...♗xd5 19 ♗xg5 ♗f7 20 ♕h4! ♕d7 21 g4! ♗e6 22 gxf5 ♗xf5 23 e6 ♕c6 24 e7 ♖f6 25 ♗b3! ♖g6 26 ♗f7 ♗h3 27 ♕g3! and White emerges the exchange up with a technically winning position, or 18...♗xf4 19 ♘xf4 ♗f7 20 ♕xf5 g6 21 ♕h3 and White has regained his sacrificed pawn with a dominant position) 19 ♗xg5 ♗xg5 20 ♕xg5 hxg5 21 ♘e7!, attacking the rook on c8 and threatening a check on g6, I.Gurevich-Nunn, Hastings 1992/93.

17...c6 18 exd6 ♗xd5

Of course 18...cxd5?! is met strongly by 19 ♖xe6! etc.

19 ♗xd5 cxd5 20 ♕xd5

White's strong passed pawn more than compensates for his piece deficit.

20...♖c2 21 d7 ♘c7 22 ♗xc7 ♖xc7 23 ♕d6 ♖a7!

The best defence. The back rank is vulnerable, as can be seen in the following variation: 23...♖c2? 24 h4! (White's first rank is also vulnerable!) 24...♗xh4 25 ♕xf8+! ♕xf8 26 ♖e8 ♔g8 27 d8♕ and White wins.

24 ♕xf8+ ♕xf8 25 ♖e8 ♖a8 ½-½

White has nothing better than 26 d8♕ ♕xe8 27 ♕xg5 h6, which is completely equal.

Game 95
Sznapik-Pytel
Polanica Zdroj 1984

---

1 e4 e5 2 ♘f3 ♘c6 3 ♗b5 a6 4 ♗a4 ♘f6 5 0-0 ♗e7 6 ♖e1 b5 7 ♗b3 0-0 8 d4 ♘xd4 9 ♘xd4 exd4 10 e5 ♘e8 11 c3!? dxc3 12 ♘xc3 ♗b7

This move is playable, although modern day theory considers 12...d6 almost compulsory. With the text Black immediately deploys his bishop on the long diagonal, thus preventing White from playing ♕d1-f3. However, White's queen has other useful squares available, namely g4 and h5, from where he can commence a serious kingside attack. Note that, due to the pawn on e5, White is ideally placed to attack, so Black must be very careful and should initially defend before later making use of his extra pawn.

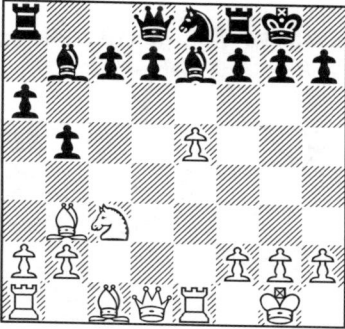

13 ♘d5

A straightforward continuation but other moves here are also possible:

a) 13 ♗f4 d6 (too passive is 13...♔h8?! 14 ♕h5 g6 15 ♕h6 ♘g7 16 ♖ad1 ♗h4!? 17 ♗c2 ♘e6 18 ♖d3? – correct is 18 ♗c1 – 18...♘xf4 19 ♕xf4 ♗g5 20 ♕d4 f6 21 f4 fxe5 22 fxe5 ♖f4 23 ♕xd7 ♕f8 24 ♕xc7 ♖f7 25 ♕b6 ♗e7! and suddenly White was unable to meet the threat of ...♗e7-c5+, Panchapagesan-Stanton, London 1993) 14 ♕h5 dxe5 15 ♖ad1 ♘d6! (stronger than 15...♘d6? 16 ♗xe5 ♕d7 17 ♖e3 ♕c6 18 ♘d5 ♗c5 19 ♗c3 –even better was the immediate 19 ♗d4 – 19...♖d8 20 ♗d4! with multiple threats, Polzin-Montavon, Dresden 1998) 16 ♗xe5 ♗f6 17 ♘d5 ♗xe5 18 ♖xe5 ♗xd5 19 ♗xd5 ♖b8 20 ♖d3 ♕f6 21 ♖h3 ♕g6 22 ♕xg6 hxg6 23 ♖c3 ♖fc8 (inferior is 23...♖fe8?! 24 f4!, which only helps White) 24 ♖e7 c5 25 ♖f3 (weaker is 25 ♖d7?! ♖d8 26 ♖xd8+ ♖xd8 27 ♖xc5? because of 27...♘e4! and White's back rank weakness suddenly decides the game in Black's favour) 25...♖f8

26 ♖d7 ♖b6 (or 26...♖bd8 27 ♗xf7+! ♘xf7 28 ♖fxf7 and, although the rook and pawn endgame is still most probably a draw, it is White who is slightly better) 27 ♔f1 c4 with a possible draw in the ending. White's activity is sufficient compensation for the pawn, but not more.

b) 13 ♕d3!? c5 14 ♗c2 (better than 14 ♗d5?! ♗xd5 15 ♘xd5 ♘c7 16 ♘b6 ♖a7 17 ♗e3 d5 18 exd6 ♘e6! 19 ♖ad1 ♕xb6 20 dxe7 ♖xe7 21 b4 and White was struggling to justify his pawn sacrifice in Romanishin-Tseshkovsky, USSR Team Championship 1978) 14...f5 15 ♕h3 g6 16 ♗h6 ♖f7 17 ♖ad1 d5 18 e6 ♖f6 19 ♗g5 ♖xe6 (naturally forced because after 19...♖f8?! 20 ♗xe7 ♕xe7 21 ♘xd5 ♗xd5 22 ♖xd5 ♘f6 White would be clearly better thanks to the strong e6-pawn, which is a thorn in Black's side) 20 ♖xe6 ♗xg5 21 ♕g3 d4 22 a4!? and although this position is difficult to assess, my gut feeling is that it is probably equal.

c) 13 ♕h5?! yields nothing for White after 13...d5! 14 exd6 ♗xd6 15 ♗g5 ♘f6 16 ♕h4 h6 17 ♗xh6? (overoptimistically played – it was better to settle for 17 ♗xf6 ♕xf6 18 ♕xf6 gxf6 19 ♘d5 and Black is only slightly better) 17...gxh6 18 ♕xh6 ♘h7! 19 ♗c2 f5 20 ♗xf5 ♖xf5 21 ♕g6+ ♔h8 22 ♕xf5 ♕h4 23 g3 ♕g5 with a clear advantage to Black in Rigo-Pinter, Hungarian Championship 1978.

13...♗xd5

Alternatively:

a) 13...d6 14 e6! f5 15 ♗f4 ♘f6 16 ♘xe7+?! (White should have kept up the pressure and played 16 ♖c1! retaining the initiative) 16...♕xe7 17 ♖c1 ♖ae8 18 ♕d4 ♘e4 19 ♕a7 c5 20 ♖xe4? (better was 20 f3 but in any case Black has a clear advantage after 20...c4 21 fxe4 fxe4! attacking both bishops and regaining the sacrificed piece) 20...fxe4 21 ♗xd6 ♕xd6 22 e7+ c4! 23 exf8♕+ ♖xf8 24 ♖d1 (24 ♕xb7 is no better due to 24...e3! 25 fxe3 ♕d2! and if the white rook moves, then ...♕f2+ leads to mate) 24...♕f6 25 ♗c2 ♕xb2 with a winning position due to the extra material, I.Gurevich-Computer Chess System 30, Boston 1993.

b) 13...c6 14 ♘xe7+ ♕xe7 15 ♕h5 ♘f6 16 ♕h4 (also worthy of consideration is 16 ♗g5!? ♘xh5 17 ♗xe7 ♖fe8 18 ♗d6 with a blockade on the dark squares which compensates for the pawn deficit) 16...♘d5 17 ♗g5 ♕e6 18 ♗c2 h6 19 ♗d2 c5 20 ♕g3 f5 with an unclear position in Fedorowicz-Chudinovsky, US Open 1996.

14 ♕xd5

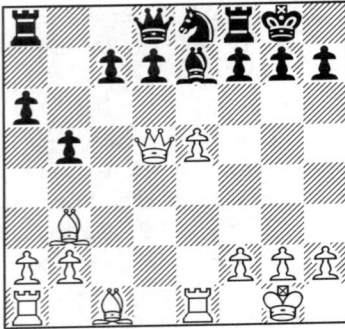

Or 14 ♗xd5!? c6 15 ♗b3 ♔h8 16 ♕h5 g6 17 ♕f3 f6 18 ♗h6 (the alternative is 18 e6 d5 19 ♗h6 ♘g7 20 ♖ac1 ♕e8 21 ♕c3 ♖c8 22 ♕a5 ♗d6 23 ♕xa6 ♗e5 – White has managed to regain his sacrificed pawn but in the meantime Black has succeeded in activating his pieces – 24 a4 bxa4 25 ♗xa4 ♕xe6 26 ♗xc6 ♕d6 27 ♕a3 ♗xh2+ 28 ♔f1 ♕xa3 29 bxa3 ♗d6 30 a4 ♗a3 31 ♖c2 ♖fd8 32 ♖e3 ♘f5 33 ♖xa3 ♘d4! and Black regains a piece and should at least draw) 18...♘g7 19 ♕c3? (correct is 19 e6! dxe6 20 ♗xg7+ ♔xg7 21 ♖xe6 c5 22 ♖d1 – after 22 ♖ae1 Black can defend with 22...♖a7! – 22...♕c7 23 ♗d5 ♖ad8 24 ♖xa6 ♗d6 with equal play) 19...fxe5 20 ♕xe5 ♗f6 21 ♕d6 ♗xb2 22 ♖ad1 ♕h4 23 ♗xg7+ ♗xg7 24 g3 ♕f6 25 ♕xf6+ ♗xf6 26 ♖xd7 c5 and Black has an extra pawn in Nunez-Bandres, Madrid 2000.

14...♔h8

Black intends to free himself by ...f7-f5. Observe how White's e-pawn continues to cramp Black.

15 a4

Deserving of attention is 15 ♗c2!?, which I regard as more logical since White's chances lie on the kingside and not on the opposite wing.

15...c6 16 ♕f3 f5 17 exf6?

This error allows Black to completely free himself. More to the point was 17 ♕d3!, keeping the tension in the centre as well as on the kingside.

17...♗xf6 18 ♗c2 g6 19 ♖a3 ♘g7 20 ♕g4 ♖e8 21 ♖d1 ♖e6!

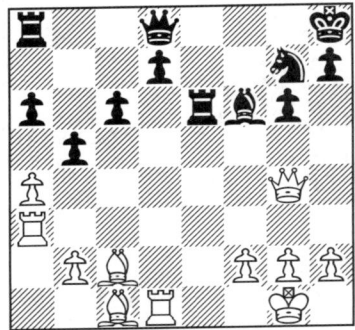

The rook is ideally placed on e6 – it defends the vulnerable kingside as well as giving the option of doubling on the e-file.

22 h4

After 22 ♖h3 ♕e8 23 ♗d2 ♗xb2 24 ♕h4 ♘h5! White's attack reaches a dead end.

22...♕e8 23 ♗h6 ♗xb2 24 ♖a2?

Here White's rook will be misplaced. Correct was 24 ♖e3, although it is doubtful whether this would have changed the result of the game.

24...♖e1+ 25 ♔h2 ♖xd1 26 ♕xd1 d5

White has nothing to show for his material deficit and Black advances his central pawns. Black still has to be careful to prevent a possible kingside attack. However, the position can be assessed as winning for Black.

27 f4

The bishop was taboo – 27 ♖xb2 ♕e5+ and Black wins.

27...♗f6 28 g4 ♘e6 29 h5 g5 30 axb5 ♘xf4 31 bxa6 ♕e3

With the invasion of the black queen, the game is decided.

32 ♕f1 ♗e5 33 ♔h1 ♘e2 34 ♗xg5 ♘g3+ 35 ♔g2 ♘xf1 0-1

Game 96
Marco-Schlechter
Trebic 1915

---

1 e4 e5 2 ♘f3 ♘c6 3 ♗b5 a6 4 ♗a4 ♘f6 5 0-0 ♗e7 6 d4 exd4 7 ♖e1 0-0 8 e5 ♘e8 9 ♘xd4 ♘xd4 10 ♕xd4

Strangely, by transposition of moves, we have reached a position arising from the 6 d4 Ruy Lopez, which is classified under another code in *ECO* – C84.

10...b5 11 ♗b3 c5?!

We shall see the stronger continuation 11...♗b7 in Game 97. The text doesn't solve all the opening problems for Black.

12 ♕e4 ♘c7 13 c4!

Black easily equalises after 13 c3 d5! 14 exd6 ♗xd6 etc.

13...bxc4

ECO stated that 13...♖b8 is an improvement for Black but in fact it doesn't change the position much. For example, 13...♖b8 14 ♘c3 bxc4 (or 14...♗b7 15 ♘d5 d6 16 ♗c2 g6 17 ♘xe7+ ♕xe7 18 exd6 ♕xd6 19 ♕f4 with a clear advantage to White due to his dominant pair of bishops – note how strong

White's dark-squared bishop is compared to Black's knight after the exchange) 15 ♗xc4 ♗b7? (better was 15...d6!?) 16 ♕g4 d5 17 exd6 ♗xd6 18 ♗g5 ♕c8 19 ♕xc8 ♗xc8 (unfortunately for Black 19...♖fxc8 is no better due to 20 ♗e7! ♗f4 21 ♖ad1 with unbearable pressure) 20 ♖ad1 ♖b6 and now in the ancient game Passmore-Leonhardt, London 1904 White missed the chance for 21 ♘e4 ♗e5 22 ♘xc5 ♗xb2 23 ♗e7 ♖e8 24 ♗d8!.

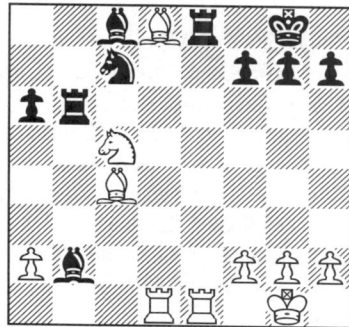

This wins a piece due to the weakness of Black's back rank.

14 ♗c2!

The text is stronger than 13 ♗xc4?! d5! 14 exd6 ♗xd6 15 ♗e3 ♖e8 with a good position for Black.

14...g6 15 ♗h6?!

White maintains a strong initiative after 15 ♘c3! ♖b8 16 ♗a4 ♖b6 (a natural blunder here is 16...d5? 17 exd6 ♗xd6 18 ♗h6, winning the exchange) and now, instead of 17 ♕xc4?! d5! 18 exd6 ♗xd6 with equality, as was seen in Van der Wiel-Ki.Georgiev, Wijk aan Zee 1988, White could have obtained great positional pressure by 17 ♖d1 ♖e6 18 ♗f4 etc.

15...♖e8 16 ♕xc4

Another possibility here is 16 ♘c3 ♖b8 and now:

a) 17 ♖ad1? ♖xb2 18 ♗a4 ♗g5! 19 ♗xg5 ♕xg5 20 ♗xd7 ♗xd7 21 ♖xd7 ♘b5 22 e6 ♖xe6 23 ♕a8+ ♔g7 24 ♖xe6 ♕f5!

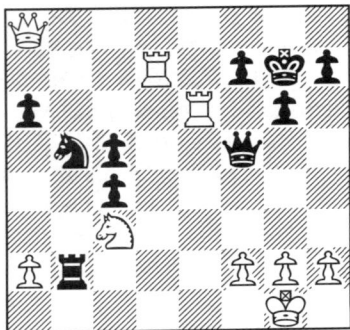

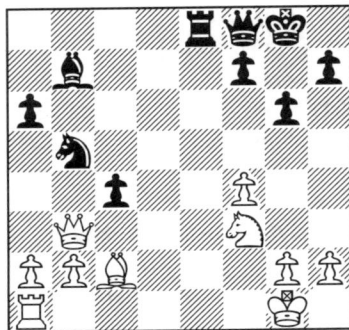

25 h4 ♕xe6 and White must lose material and the game, Blazova-S.Vajda, European Girls Under 18 Championship 1996.

b) 17 ♕xc4 ♖b4! 18 ♕d3 ♖h4! 19 ♗e3 d5 20 exd6 ♗xd6 21 h3? (necessary was 21 g3 although Black still retains good attacking chances) 21...♗xh3! 22 gxh3 ♖xh3 with a strong attack against the white king, Brooks-Kaidanov, New York 1990.

16...♗b7

Also good was the natural 16...d5!? etc.

17 f4?

An ugly move that unnecessarily weakens White's kingside. Better was 17 ♘c3 ♗g5 18 ♗e4! (maybe White did not see this defence?) 18...♗xh6 19 ♗xb7 ♖b8 20 ♗f3 ♗g7 21 ♕xc5 ♖xe5! 22 ♖xe5 d6 23 ♖e8+! (otherwise Black is better) 23...♘xe8 24 ♕a3 ♘c7 with an approximately equal position.

17...d5 18 exd6 ♗xd6 19 ♖xe8+ ♕xe8 20 ♕c3 ♗f8

Possibly even stronger is 20...♘e6 followed by ...♖a8-d8 etc.

21 ♗xf8 ♕xf8 22 ♘d2 ♖e8 23 ♘f3 ♘b5 24 ♕b3?

This loses by force, although White's chances of saving the game are very slim even after 24 ♕d3. For instance, 24...c4 25 ♕f1 ♕c5+ (or 25...♗xf3 26 ♕xf3 ♘d4 27 ♕f2 and for the moment White is holding his own) 26 ♕f2 etc.

24...c4!

25 ♕a4

The only square for the queen because taking on c4 loses to ...♖c8 followed by ...♕c5+ winning the bishop. After the text White's queen is left as a pure spectator, while in the meantime Black rapidly builds up a mating attack.

25...♕d6 26 ♖f1 ♗xf3 27 gxf3

A sad reply but mate was inevitable after 27 ♖xf3 ♕d4+ 28 ♔f1 ♕d2! etc.

27...♖e2 0-1

> *Game 97*
> ### J.Polgar-Nunn
> *Hastings 1992/93*

1 e4 e5 2 ♘f3 ♘c6 3 ♗b5 a6 4 ♗a4 ♘f6 5 0-0 ♗e7 6 ♖e1 b5 7 ♗b3 0-0 8 d4 ♘xd4 9 ♘xd4 exd4 10 e5 ♘e8 11 ♕xd4 ♗b7

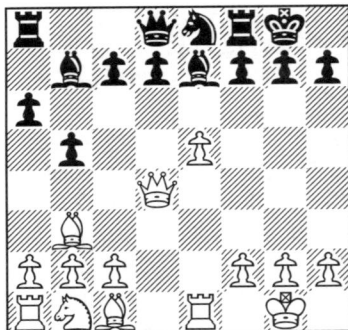

The strongest reply. Black doesn't fall behind in development as after 11...c5?!. Here Black simply develops the bishop on the long diagonal.

12 c4

The alternative is 12 c3 d6 13 ♗f4 dxe5 and now:

a) 14 ♕xe5 ♗d6 15 ♕g5 h6 16 ♕g3 ♕f6 17 ♗xd6 ♘xd6 18 ♘d2 ♖ad8 19 ♖ad1 ♘f5 20 ♕g4 ♘d6 21 ♗c2 ♖fe8 with a roughly equal position, Navarro-Peng Xiaomin, Moscow Olympiad 1994.

b) It is interesting to follow the old game Steiner-Marshall, Bradley Beach 1929 to see how the godfather of the Marshall gambit met 8 d4, That game continued 14 ♗xe5 ♗d6 15 f4 ♕h4 16 ♖e2 ♖d8 17 ♕a7 ♗a8 18 ♘d2 ♕e7 19 ♔f1 ♗c5 20 ♕xa6 ♕h4 21 ♕xb5 ♗e3 22 ♖xe3 ♖xd2 23 ♖e2 ♕xh2 24 ♖xd2 ♕h1+ 25 ♔e2 ♕xa1 26 ♔f2 ♕h1 with unclear play.

After 12 c3, instead of 12...d6 Black also has the possibility of 12...c5 13 ♕g4 d5 14 ♘d2 ♕b6 15 ♗c2 ♗c8 16 ♕e2 (a possible improvement for White is 16 ♕f3!? ♘c7 17 ♘b3 etc.) 16...g6 17 a4 bxa4!? 18 ♖xa4 ♘g7 19 ♘f3 ♘e6 20 h3 ♖d8 21 ♗c2 ♗b7 and here the game was agreed drawn, Xie Jun-Hort, Amsterdam 2001.

12...bxc4

Or 12...c5 13 ♕g4 d6 14 ♗f4! dxe5 15 ♗xe5 ♘f6 (after 15...♗d6 16 ♘c3 ♗xe5 17 ♖xe5 b4 18 ♘a4 Black's c-pawn is very weak) 16 ♕g3 ♕c8 17 ♗c2 ♘h5 18 ♕d3 g6 19 ♘c3 ♖d8 20 ♕e2 ♖e8 21 ♕d2 ♕g4 22 ♘d5 ♗g5 23 ♕d1 ♕xc4 24 ♘b6 ♕e6 25 ♘xa8 ♖xa8 26 ♗f4 ♕f6 27 ♗xg5 ♕xg5 28 ♗e4 with material advantage to White, Pernutz-Kienast, Germany 1994.

13 ♕xc4 d5 14 exd6

White can try to keep his strong e5-pawn alive by playing 14 ♕d3 but Black is absolutely fine after 14...c5 15 ♗c2 f5! 16 exf6 ♘xf6 etc.

14...♘xd6 15 ♕g4 ♗f6 16 ♘c3 ♘b5!

Less to the point was 16...♖b8 17 ♗f4

♗c6 18 ♖ad1 ♖b4 19 ♕g3 ♖d4 20 ♗e5 ♖xd1 21 ♖xd1 ♖e8 22 f4! ♕e7 23 ♘d5 ♗xd5 24 ♖xd5 with a small but lasting advantage to White, Nijboer-I.Sokolov, Dutch Championship 1996.

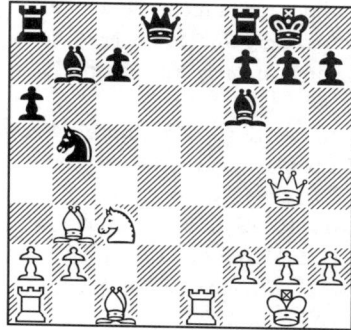

17 ♘xb5

White has to exchange the knights, thus improving Black's pawn structure, otherwise Black will plant his knight on d4 with an excellent position.

17...axb5 18 ♗f4 c5

It's risky to take the hot pawn on b2: 18...♗xb2?! 19 ♖ad1 ♕f6 (or 19...♕c8 20 ♕xc8 ♖axc8 21 ♖d7 etc.) 20 ♖d7 and now 20...♗c8? loses on the spot to 21 ♖xf7!.

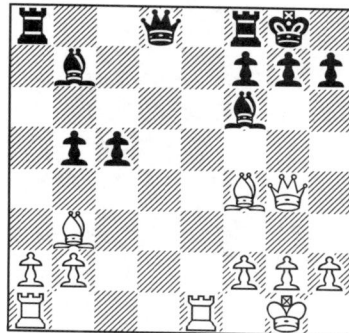

19 ♖ad1 ♕c8 20 ♕xc8 ♖axc8 21 ♗d6 ♖fd8 22 ♗xc5 ♖xd1 23 ♗xd1 ♗xb2 24 ♗b3 g6 25 ♗e3 ♔g7 26 ♖d1 ♗c6 27 f3 ♖c7 28 ♗f4 ♖d7 29 ♗d6 ♗f6 30 ♔f2 h5 31 f4 h4 32 g4 hxg3+ ½-½

Summary

After 8 d4 ♘xd4 9 ♘xd4 exd4 10 e5 ♘e8 11 c3!? I prefer Pytel's 12...♗b7 (Game 95) to the previous game's 12...d6. However, White's main error in Game 95 is 17 exf6?, which frees Black's position on the kingside. White should have instead kept his e5-pawn, which both assists in his attack as well as restricting Black's pieces.

Although Black won the game after 11...c5?! 12 ♕e4 ♘c7 13 c4! bxc4 14 ♗c2! in Game 96, I would not recommend 11...c5?! because White could have played better on various occasions later on in the game. Stronger is the logical developing move 11...♗b7 (Game 97), which gives Black approximately equal chances.

1 e4 e5 2 ♘f3 ♘c6 3 ♗b5 a6 4 ♗a4 ♘f6 5 0-0 ♗e7 6 ♖e1 b5 7 ♗b3 0-0 8 d4 ♘xd4!
(D) **9 ♘xd4**

>   9 ♗xf7+?! – *Game 93*

9...exd4 10 e5 ♘e8 (D) **11 ♕xd4**

>   11 c3!? dxc3 12 ♘xc3 (D)

>   >   12...♗b7 – *Game 95*; 2...d6 – *Game 94*

11...♗b7 – *Game 97*

>   11...c5?! – *Game 96*

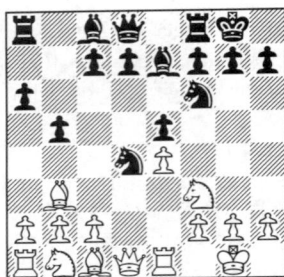

8...♘xd4!

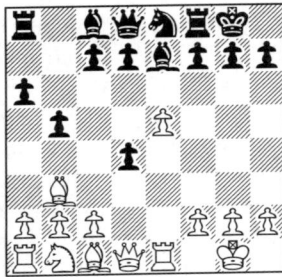

10...♘e8

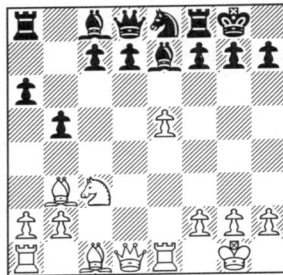

12 ♘xc3

CHAPTER TEN

Other Anti-Marshalls

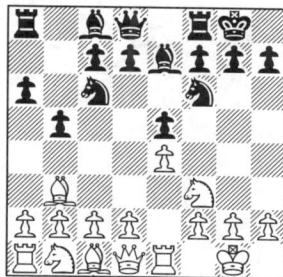

1 e4 e5 2 ♘f3 ♘c6 3 ♗b5 a6 4 ♗a4 ♘f6
5 0-0 ♗e7 6 ♖e1 b5 7 ♗b3 0-0

In this final chapter we shall be dealing with two more Anti-Marshall systems:

1) 8 d3 d6 9 c3
2) 8 c3 d5 9 d4

1) With 8 d3 White adopts a slow set up which is an Anti-Marshall despite being classified under the Closed Ruy Lopez opening code C90 (the same position can be reached after 8 c3 d6 9 d3).

9...♘b8, as in Game 98, leads to a kind of Breyer Variation of the Closed Ruy Lopez, with White keeping a small but lasting advantage.

Games 99-100 see the main line of 9...♘a5 10 ♗c2 c5. Now I recommend for Black the plan of transferring the knight from f6 to the queenside, leading to positions with rich counterplay.

2) Here White does not hesitate to grasp the initiative away from Black and quickly counterattacks in the centre with 9 d4!?. This line first became popular after the famous encounter Botvinnik-Kan (Game 102) and it has now embarked on its second life. From a psychological point of view, 9 d4!? is an unpleasant move for a Marshall devotee to meet as he usually prefers to attack rather than to be put under pressure.

Basically Black now is faced with a difficult choice between three lines: 9...dxe4?!, 9...♘xe4 and 9...exd4.

We begin our study with 9...dxe4?! (Game 101). This cannot be recommended since White enjoys domination of the centre due to his powerful knight on e5.

In Games 102-104 we see the so-called Breslau Variation of the Open Ruy Lopez, arising after 9...♘xe4 10 dxe5 ♗e6 11 ♘d4!. Note that the move order via the Open Lopez would be 1 e4 e5 2 ♘f3 ♘c6 3 ♗b5 a6 4 ♗a4 ♘f6 5 0-0 ♘xe4 6 d4 b5 7 ♗b3 d5 8 dxe5 ♗e6 9 c3 ♗e7 10 ♖e1 0-0 11 ♘d4. This is perfectly playable for Black. However, from the psychological viewpoint I believe it's not suitable for Marshall players because the positions are very different to normal Marshall positions.

In Game 105 Black plays 9...exd4, which I believe is the critical move.

Game 98
Arakhamia Grant-B.Lalić
Port Erin 2001

---

1 e4 e5 2 ♘f3 ♘c6 3 ♗b5 a6 4 ♗a4 ♘f6
5 0-0 ♗e7 6 ♖e1 b5 7 ♗b3 0-0 8 d3 d6

9 c3 ♘b8

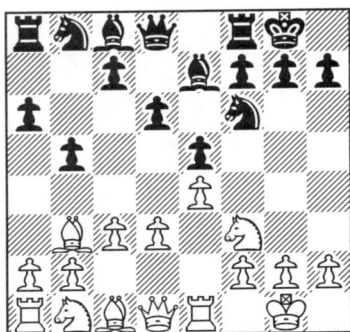

25 f4!

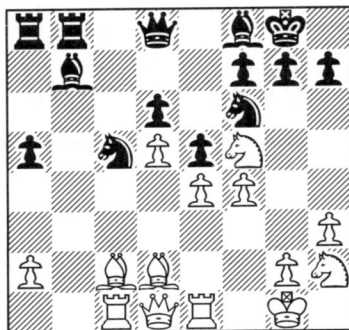

Black tries to transpose play into the Breyer Variation of the Closed Spanish. However this line is somewhat passive and doesn't grant Black full equality.

10 ♘bd2 ♘bd7 11 ♘f1 ♘c5 12 ♗c2 ♖e8 13 d4 ♘cd7 14 ♘g3 ♗b7 15 b3

In the old game Nikitin-Bebchuk, Moscow Championship 1963 the continuation was 15 b4 ♗f8 (also deserving attention is 15...a5!?, looking for counterplay on the queenside) 16 a4 g6 17 ♗d3 c6 18 ♕b3 ♗g7 19 dxe5 dxe5 20 axb5 axb5 21 ♖xa8 ♗xa8 22 c4 ♕b8 23 ♗d2 bxc4? 24 ♗xc4 ♖e7 25 ♘g5 ♕e8 26 ♕a2! ♘b6 and now, instead of 27 ♗b3?!, White missed a direct win with 23 ♗xf7+ ♖xf7 28 ♗e3! ♘fd7 29 ♘xf7 ♕xf7 30 ♕a5! and Black loses material.

15...♗f8 16 d5 c6 17 c4 ♕c7 18 ♗d2 ♖ec8 19 ♖c1 bxc4 20 bxc4 a5 21 ♘f5

Here White is actively placed and if Black ever plays ...g7-g6, then ♘f5-h6+ is rather awkward to meet.

21...cxd5 22 cxd5 ♕d8 23 h3

A traditional Ruy Lopez plan – the knight is heading to h2 and later g4. White's queen will go to f3 with mounting pressure on the kingside.

23...♘c5 24 ♘h2 ♖cb8!

The best move. This enables the manoeuvre ...♗b7-c8 to give Black the option of exchanging on f5, as well as giving Black further counterplay on the b-file.

Thematic! White will need the f-file for her kingside attack, If Black exchanges on f4, White will get possession of the important d4-square.

25...♗c8 26 fxe5 dxe5 27 ♕f3 ♗xf5 28 ♕xf5 ♖b2?

I didn't want to play 28...♘cd7, which allows 29 ♗a4! ♖b2 30 ♗g5 ♖xa2 31 ♗c6, but this was better than the text.

29 ♗c3 ♖xa2 30 ♗b1

This is stronger than 30 ♗xe5 ♘cd7 etc.

30...♖a3 31 ♗xe5 a4 32 ♖f1!

Dark clouds are gathering over Black's kingside.

32...♕d7!?

Offering a pawn in order to diminish the pressure and reach a playable ending, but White prefers to continue with her attack.

33 ♕f4!? ♘h5 34 ♕h4 f6 35 ♗c3

Deserving serious attention was 35 ♕xh5 fxe5 36 ♘g4!, but White was already getting short of time.

35...♘b3?

Playing for tricks. I didn't want to play 35...g6 because of 36 ♘g4! with deadly threats. However, much better instead was 35...♕e8! 36 e5!? ♖xc3 (forced) 37 ♖xc3 ♕xe5 38 ♖cf3 ♗d6 39 ♘g4 ♕xd5 40 ♘h6+!? gxh6 41 ♖f5 ♗e5 42 ♕xh5 a3! and Black's passed a-pawn will save him from defeat.

36 ♖c2!

Avoiding 36 ♕xh5? ♘xc1 37 ♖xc1 ♖c8 38 e5 g6 39 ♕f3 ♗h6 40 ♘g4 ♕a7+! followed by ...♗xc1 and Black wins.

36...♕e8

The intended 36...♘a1!? 37 ♗xa1 ♕a7+ 38 ♖cf2 ♘g3 loses to 39 ♘f3! ♘xf1 40 ♗d4 ♗c5 41 e5! h6 42 ♕e4! ♘g3 43 ♕h7+ ♔f7 44 e6+ etc.

37 ♘g4??

Time trouble. After the game Ketevan said that she didn't know why she played this move – probably she considered this move in many variations earlier on in the game so she played it automatically. The simple 37 ♗b2! would have won easily as it traps the rook on a3.

37...♗c5+

I was aware that the position had changed in my favour but at this point I offered a draw. However, probably from inertia White continues to play for a win although obviously she should have taken the half-point.

38 ♔h1? ♘d4 39 ♗xd4 ♗xd4 40 ♖f3

Or 40 ♖fc1 ♘g3+ 41 ♔h2 h5 42 ♖c7 ♘e2!, avoiding all tricks and winning for Black.

40...♖a1 41 ♖f1 ♕b8 42 ♕xh5 ♖xb1 43 ♖cc1 ♖xc1 44 ♖xc1 a3 45 e5 a2 46 exf6 ♕f4! 0-1

The last trick was hidden in 46...a1♕?? 47 ♘h6+! with a draw by perpetual after 47...♔h8 48 ♘f7+ etc. Note that 47...gxh6??

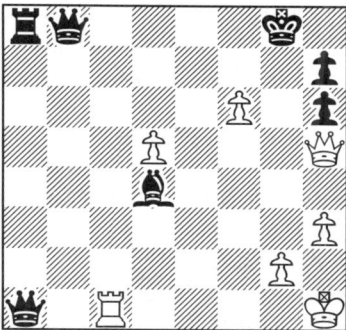

allows mate after 48 ♕g4+.

1 e4 e5 2 ♘f3 ♘c6 3 ♗b5 a6 4 ♗a4 ♘f6 5 0-0 ♗e7 6 ♖e1 b5 7 ♗b3 d6 8 c3 0-0 9 d3 ♘a5

This is most frequently played by Black – he will follow up with the traditional plan of ...c7-c5 The arising position is similar to the Chigorin Variation of the Ruy Lopez. The only difference is that White delays playing d3-d4 until a more convenient moment.

The alternative 9...♗e6 leads to a slow manoeuvring game after 10 ♘bd2 followed by ♘f1 etc., whilst also deserving attention is 10 a4!?, attacking Black's stronghold on b5.

10 ♗c2 c5 11 ♘bd2 ♘d7!

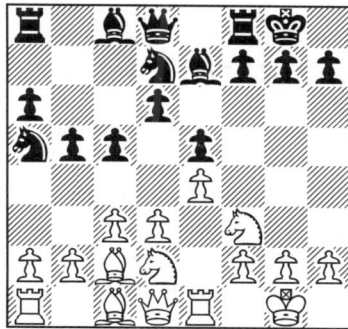

This is the key move, which resembles Keres's ...♘f6-d7 in the Closed Ruy Lopez. As well as freeing the f6-square for his bishop, the knight is heading towards b6 from where it supports queenside play. Should White continue with d3-d4, Black is then ready to play ...cxd4 followed by ...♗f6.

12 ♘f1 ♘b6 13 ♘g3 ♘c6

The knight has done his job on a5 (enabling him to play ...c7-c5) and now returns to the scene of the battle.

14 h3

This is a common manoeuvre in the Ruy Lopez. White prepares ♘f3-h2-g4, which is

163

effective if Black decides to go for ...d6-d5.

14...⌐e6 15 ♘h2 ♖e8 16 ♘g4 ♗g5 17 ♘f5 ♗xc1 18 ♕xc1 ♗xf5

This was not forced. 18...f6 was an alternative, after which White can try 19 ♘xg7!? ♔xg7 20 ♕h6+ ♔h8 21 ♘xf6 ♖e7 22 ♘xh7 ♖xh7 23 ♕xe6 ♗g5 24 ♖e3! (not 24 ♕xd6? ♖g8 25 g3 ♖xh3 with a winning attack for Black) 24...♖h6 25 ♖g3 with approximately equal chances.

19 exf5 f6

Black would like to play 19...d5 but then 20 f6! is very unpleasant for Black. Deserving attention is the recommendation of *Fritz 7*, 19...h5!?, followed by ...d6-d5 – the weakening of the kingside might not be so relevant as it seems at first glance!

20 f4 ♕c7 21 fxe5 ♘xe5 22 ♘f2 ♔h8 23 ♗d1 ♕f7 24 ♕f4 ♘d5 25 ♕h4 g5!

Black needs some breathing space on the kingside otherwise White would play 26 ♗h5! with advantage.

26 fxg6 ♘xg6 27 ♖xe8+ ♖xe8 28 ♗h5

Practically forced due to the threat of ...♖e1+ with an unpleasant pin along the first rank.

28...♖e2 29 ♕g3 ♖e5 30 ♗f3?!

Better was 30 ♗xg6 with an equal position. Now Black takes over the initiative.

30...♘df4 31 d4 cxd4 32 cxd4 ♖g5

Also promising for Black appears to be 30...♖e2!? etc.

33 ♕h2 ♘xg2!

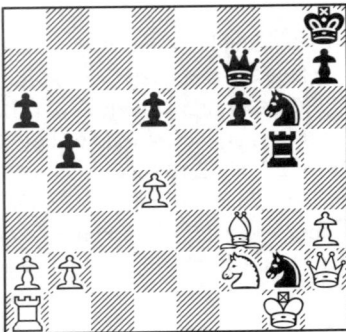

Black had this in mind when playing 32...♖g5.

34 ♘e4

On 34 ♗xg2 ♘h4 Black regains the piece with advantage.

34...♘h4+ 35 ♘xg5 fxg5 36 ♗h1 ♘f4 37 ♖e1 ♕f5 38 ♕g3 ♘xh3+ 39 ♔h2 ♘f4 40 ♖e8+ ♔g7 41 ♗e4?

White misses the draw with 41 ♖e7+ ♔f8 42 ♗e4 ♕f6 43 ♖xh7 ♕xd4 44 ♕xg5 ♕f2+ 45 ♔h1 and Black has nothing more than perpetual check.

41...♕f6 42 ♕g4 ♔h6!

On h6 Black's king feels absolutely safe.

43 ♕d7 ♘fg6 44 ♖e6 ♕f4+

Even stronger was 44...♕f2+ 45 ♔h1 g4!, threatening ...g3, which is an immediate win for Black.

45 ♔g1 ♕c1+ 46 ♔f2 ♕xb2+ 47 ♔e3 ♕a3+ 48 ♔d2 ♕xa2+ 49 ♔c1 ♕c4+ 50 ♔b1 ♕b3+ 51 ♔c1 ♕e3+ 52 ♔b1 ♕xd4 53 ♕xd6 ♕xd6 54 ♖xd6 g4 55 ♖a6 ♔g5 56 ♖b6 ♘f3 57 ♖xb5+ ♔f4 58 ♗b7

This is a very difficult ending, where White's drawing chances are very high. The other possibility was 58 ♗xg6 hxg6 59 ♖b4+ with a likely draw.

58...♘ge5 59 ♖b4+ ♔g3 60 ♖b5 h5!

A nice trap because if 61 ♗xf3?, then 61...gxf3 62 ♖xe5 f2 63 ♖f5 h4 64 ♔c2 h3 65 ♔d2 h2 and Black wins.

61 ♗c8! ♔h2 62 ♗xg4 hxg4 63 ♖b8

With two knights being unable to deliver mate, White 'only' needs to give up his rook for the g-pawn to reach a book draw.

63...♘g5 64 ♖b5 ♘ef3 65 ♖b4 ♘e4! 66 ♔c2

Of course not 66 ♖xe4?? ♘d2+ and Black wins.

66...♘fg5 67 ♖b3 ♔g2 68 ♖a3 ♔f2 69 ♔d3 ♔f3 70 ♔d4+ ♔f4 71 ♔d5 ♘f3 72 ♖a4 ♘d2 73 ♖a3 ♘f1?!

Perhaps a better winning try was with 73...♘b1!? 74 ♖d3 ♘bc3+ etc.

74 ♔d4 ♘fd2 75 ♔d5 ♘f3 76 ♖a4 ♘g5 77 ♖a3 ♘f6+ 78 ♔d6 ♘ge4+ 79 ♔e6

♘e8 80 ♔d5 ♘c7+ 81 ♔c6 ♘e6 82 ♔d5 ♘6g5 83 ♖b3?

White is getting tired and puts a rook on a square from where it will be difficult to control Black's g-pawn. Correct was 83 ♖a1! ♘f3 84 ♖a4 ♘fd2 83 ♖a3 etc.

83...♘f3 84 ♖b2 ♘fd2!

Of course not 84...g3? 85 ♔g2! with an immediate draw.

85 ♖c2 g3 86 ♖c1 ♘f3 87 ♖c2 0-1

Or 87 ♖c4 g2! 88 ♖xe4+ ♔f5 and Black wins.

White resigned without waiting for the obvious reply 87...♘ed2 88 ♖c1 g2 and the g-pawn promotes. An example is 89 ♖a1 ♘f1 90 ♖a4+ ♔f5.

Game 100
Korchnoi-Petrosian
Curacao 1962

---

1 e4 e5 2 ♘f3 ♘c6 3 ♗b5 a6 4 ♗a4 ♘f6 5 0-0 ♗e7 6 ♖e1 b5 7 ♗b3 0-0 8 c3 d6 9 d3 ♘d7 10 ♘bd2 ♘b6 11 ♘f1 ♘a5 12 ♗c2 c5 13 ♘e3

From e3 the knight controls not only the f5-square but also the vital d5-square, which means that Black's ...d6-d5 break has virtually been prevented once and for all.

13...♘c6 14 h3?!

This seems a bit slow. White should have played 14 d4! at once, leading to interesting play after 14...cxd4 15 cxd4 ♗f6 16 d5 ♘b4

(better than 16...♘d4? 17 ♘xd4 exd4 18 ♘f1!, after which Black's pawn on d4 is really weak, Bologan-Savon, Nikolaev 1993) 17 ♗b1 a5 18 ♕e2 ♗d7 19 ♗d2 ♘a4 20 a3 ♘a6 21 b4 axb4 22 axb4 ♕b6 23 ♖c1 ♖fc8 24 ♗d3 ♘b2!, Koc-Shamkovich, Leningrad 1957.

14...♗e6 15 d4 cxd4 16 cxd4 ♘xd4 17 ♘xd4 exd4 18 ♕xd4 ♖c8 19 ♕d3 g6 20 ♗b3 ♘c4 21 ♘d5 ♗xd5 22 ♕xd5 ♗f6 23 ♖b1 ♖e8

Black has obtained the more promising position due to his active rooks and minor pieces. In particular, his knight on c4 is strong.

24 ♖d1 ♕e7 25 ♗xc4 ♖xc4 26 ♕xd6 ♕xe4 27 ♗e3 ♖e6

Despite the symmetrical pawn structure, Black's advantage is indisputable due to his excellently placed centralised pieces.

28 ♕b8+ ♔g7 29 b3 ♖c2 30 ♖bc1 ♖ec6

Black keeps things under control, not allowing White any counterplay like in the case of 30...♖xa2?? 31 ♖c8! with a mating attack to follow.

31 ♖xc2 ♖xc2 32 a3 ♖c3 33 ♕d6 ♗e5! 34 ♕d2

There is no time for pawn grabbing with 34 ♕xa6? ♖xe3! 35 fxe3 ♕xe3+ 36 ♔h1 (forced as 36 ♔f1? ♗g3 is an immediate win for Black) 36...♕xb3 37 ♖f1 ♕g3 38 ♔g1 ♕h2+ and Black should be winning.

34...h5! 35 ♖e1 ♕f5 36 ♕d1 ♖d3 37

♕b1

The only move because 37 ♕c2?? ♖xe3! is curtains.

37...♕d7 38 ♕c1 ♗c3 39 ♖f1 ♕d5 40 b4 ♕b3 41 ♗c5 ♗f6 42 ♕f4 ♕e6! 43 ♕c1 ♖c3

Black's initiative has finally borne some fruit – he is winning a pawn.

44 ♕d2 ♖xa3 45 ♖e1 ♕xe1+

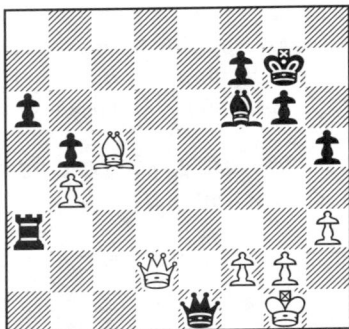

This was the simplest way – converting to a winning bishop ending with an extra pawn.

46 ♕xe1 ♖a1 47 ♔f1 ♖xe1+ 48 ♔xe1 a5 49 bxa5 ♗c3+ 50 ♔d1 ♗xa5 51 ♗d4+ ♔f8 52 ♔c2 ♔e7 53 f3 ♔d6 54 ♗e3 ♔d5 55 ♔b3 ♔c6 56 ♗d4 ♗b6 57 ♗f6 ♗c5 58 ♗b2 ♔d5 59 ♗c3 ♔e6 60 g4 ♔d5 61 ♗f6 ♗d6 62 ♗b2 f5 63 gxf5 gxf5 64 ♗c3 f4! 65 ♗b2 b4

White is in zugzwang – there is no way of him preventing the intrusion of Black's king to the kingside.

66 ♗f6 ♗e5 67 ♗g5 ♔d4 68 ♔xb4 ♔e3 69 ♔c4 ♔xf3 0-1

Game 101
Khalifman-Adams
Wijk aan Zee 2002

---

1 e4 e5 2 ♘f3 ♘c6 3 ♗b5 a6 4 ♗a4 ♘f6 5 0-0 ♗e7 6 ♖e1 b5 7 ♗b3 0-0 8 c3 d5 9 d4!?

This old continuation has just become popular again. White refuses to be the de-

fending party and declines to accept the pawn sacrifice. He accelerates the development of his own queenside and commences the struggle for the centre.

I would like to add that this continuation was at its peak in the middle of the last century due to the efforts of the late World Champion Mikhail Botvinnik (an example of a Botvinnik game follows this one).

White can avoid the Marshall Gambit by playing the quiet move 9 d3 which theory, with very good reason, gives as harmless for Black. One such example is 9...dxe4 10 dxe4 ♕xd1 11 ♗xd1 ♗b7 12 ♘bd2 ♘d7! 13 ♗c2 (or 13 ♘b3 a5 14 ♗e3 a4 15 ♘bd2 ♖fb8 16 a3 ♗c8 17 ♗c2 ♘c5 18 ♖ad1 f6 19 ♘f1 ♗e6 20 ♘h4 ♘a5 21 ♘f5 ♗f8 22 ♗xc5?! ♗xc5 23 ♘5e3 c6 24 h3 ♔f7 25 ♖d2 g6 26 ♖ed1 h5 27 ♔h2 ♔e7 with advantage for Black, who has the bishop pair, Damljanovic-Franzen, Trnava 1982) 13...♖fd8 14 ♘f1 ♘c5 15 ♘e3 ♘d3 16 ♖d1 ♘xc1 17 ♖axc1 ♔f8 18 a4 f6 19 ♘h4 ♖xd1+ 20 ♖xd1 ♘d8 21 ♘hf5 g6 22 ♘xe7 ♔xe7 23 f3 c5 24 ♔f2 ♗c6 25 ♖a1 ♘e6 26 axb5 ½-½ Yudasin-Tseshkovsky, Simferopol 1989.

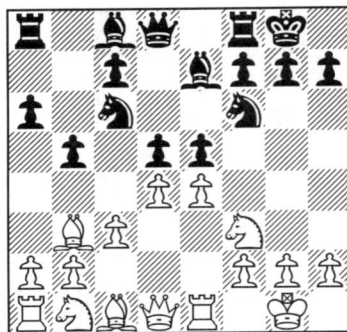

9...dxe4?! 10 ♘xe5 ♗b7

Black couldn't manage to solve his opening problems after 10...♘xe5?! 11 dxe5 ♘g4 12 ♖xe4 ♕xd1+ 13 ♗xd1 ♖d8 14 ♘d2 ♗g5 15 ♗xg4 ♗xg4 16 ♖xg4 ♗xd2 17 ♖d4 and White had an extra pawn in the rook ending, Del Rio-Illescas, Dos Hermanas 2002.

11 ♘d2 ♗d6 12 f4!

The computer engine *Nimzo 8* suggests 12 ♘xf7 as much better for White but I prefer the text – why play the position with rook and two pawns versus two minor pieces if White can reach a simple position with an extra pawn? Note that after the text White's e5-knight has been reinforced and Black has no choice but to play what he does.

12...exf3 13 ♘dxf3 ♘xe5 14 ♘xe5 ♗xe5 15 dxe5

White is also better after 15 ♖xe5, but the line played is more forcing.

15...♕xd1 16 ♖xd1 ♘e4 17 ♗e3?

Much stronger is 17 ♖d7! ♘c5 18 ♖xc7 ♘xb3 19 axb3 and, despite opposite-coloured bishops, White has excellent winning chances with his extra pawn. With the text White lets Black off the hook.

17...♖ae8 18 ♖d7 ♖xe5 19 ♖xc7 ♗d5 20 ♗d4 ♖f5 21 ♖e1 ♗xb3 22 axb3 ♘d2 23 ♗c5 ♖d8 24 b4 ½-½

┌─────────────────────────────┐
│ *Game 102*   │
│ **Botvinnik-Kan**   │
│ *Training Game, USSR 1952* │
└─────────────────────────────┘

1 e4 e5 2 ♘f3 ♘c6 3 ♗b5 a6 4 ♗a4 ♘f6 5 0-0 ♗e7 6 ♖e1 b5 7 ♗b3 0-0 8 c3 d5 9 d4!? ♘xe4

This move leads to the Breslau Variation of the Open Spanish, where White has played c2-c3 and Black, ...♗f8-e7. Maybe

such positions do not suit the player on the black side of the Marshall but I still think the reader should play through these next three games because it leads to sharp tactical play where both sides have their trumps.

10 dxe5 ♗e6 11 ♘d4

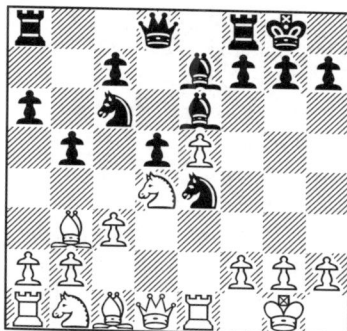

The most straightforward continuation. White prepares to play f2-f3 to drive away the enemy knight from e4.

11...♘xe5?

This sharp continuation is the start of a planned piece sacrifice by Black in which he hopes to gain a dangerous attack. However, we shall see that 11...♘xd4 is more accurate.

However, 11...♘a5?! cannot be recommended. Play continues 12 ♗c2 and now:

a) 12...c5 13 ♘xe6 fxe6 14 ♕g4! ♘xf2 15 ♕xe6+ ♔h8 16 ♗e3 ♘e4 17 ♘d2 with a big positional advantage to White, Botvinnik-Ragozin, USSR 1951, because after 17...♘g5 18 ♗xg5! ♗xg5 19 ♖ad1 Black has to worry about defending his vulnerable d-pawn.

b) Even worse is the move 12...♕d7?, which simply loses a pawn after 13 f3 ♘g5 14 h4 c5 15 hxg5 cxd4 16 cxd4 ♖ac8 17 ♘c3, as in the very old game Mackenzie-Taubenhaus, Frankfurt 1887(!).

Black also failed to equalise after 11...♕e8 12 ♗c2 ♖d8 13 a4 ♕d7 14 axb5 axb5 15 f3 ♘c5 16 b4 ♘xd4 17 cxd4 ♘a4 18 ♗xa4 ♖a8 19 ♘c3 bxa4 20 ♗a3 ♕c6 21 ♕d3 ♕b7 22 b5 ♗xa3 23 ♖xa3 ♖fb8 24 ♖b1 g6 25 ♖b4 because of the weakness of his dark squares,

Sulskis-Svidler, FIDE World Championship, Moscow 2001.

Finally, 11...♕d7?? is a blunder: 12 ♘xe6 fxe6 13 ♖xe4! wins a piece, Tarrasch-Zukertort, Frankfurt 1888.

12 f3 ♗d6

Due to the pin along the e-file, Black had no means of saving his piece. Probably untested but possibly much better for White is 12...♗h4 13 g3 c5 14 ♘xe6 fxe6 15 fxe4 ♘f3+ 16 ♔g2 ♘xe1+ 17 ♕xe1 etc.

13 fxe4 ♗g4

13...♕h4 is discussed in the next game.

14 ♕d2

From d2 the white queen defends the rook on e1, which is important in some lines. Weaker is 14 ♕c2 c5! 15 ♗xd5 cxd4 16 ♗xa8 ♕h4! 17 ♖f1 d3 with complications that favour Black.

14...♕h4 15 h3

Or 15 g3 ♕h5 and now White has a choice between the following:

a) 16 ♗xd5? c5! 17 ♗xa8 cxd4 18 ♖f1 d3 19 ♗d5 ♗c5+ 0-1 B.Parker-Melody, correspondence 1996.

b) 16 exd5 ♖ae8 17 ♖f1 ♗c5 18 ♕g5 ♕h3 19 ♘d2 ♘f3+ 20 ♘xf3 ♗xf3 21 ♕d2 ♖e2 with advantage to Black because, in order to avoid being mated, White had to sacrifice his queen with 20 ♕xe2 in Szabo-Balogh, Budapest 1937.

c) 16 ♕g5 might be White's best choice and now, according to Dutch IM Leon Pliester, Black should continue 16...♕h3! 17 ♕h4 ♕xh4 18 gxh4 c5 19 ♘f5 ♗xf5 20 exf5 ♘f3+ 21 ♔f2 ♘xe1 22 ♔xe1 c4 23 ♗c2 ♗xh2 with an unclear position.

15...c5

This is Black's only move because all others are virtually losing:

a) 15...♗d7? 16 ♗xd5 c6 17 ♗b3 c5 18 ♘f5 ♗xf5 19 exf5 ♘d3 20 ♖e3 c4 21 ♗c2 ♗c5 22 ♗xd3 cxd3 23 ♕f2, Wolf-Tarrasch, Teplitz-Schoenau 1922.

b) 15...♖ae8? and now:

b1) 16 ♗xd5 c6! (but not 16...c5? 17 hxg4

cxd4 18 ♕f2 ♕xg4 19 ♖f1 dxc3 20 ♘xc3 and Black had nothing to show for the material deficit, although he managed to draw after errors by his opponent in Loman-Euwe, Dutch Cup 1925) 17 ♘xc6 ♘xc6 18 ♗xc6 ♗c5+ 19 ♔h2 ♗e6! with a strong attack, Teichmann-John, Breslau 1913.

b2) The alternative 16 ♖e3! is far stronger. Now 16...♖e6!? is an original manoeuvre by which Black quickly redevelops the rook. White should not capture on e6 as it opens the f-file and assists the Black attack. The refutation of Black's play is hidden in the strong 17 ♕e1! after which Black's attack reaches a dead end.

16 ♖f1!

Although this was a training game, Botvinnik finds an important improvement that refutes the brave but risky 11...♘xe5?.

Other continuations are clearly weaker:

a) 16 ♘e2?? loses very quickly after 16...♘f3+! 17 gxf3 ♗h2+!

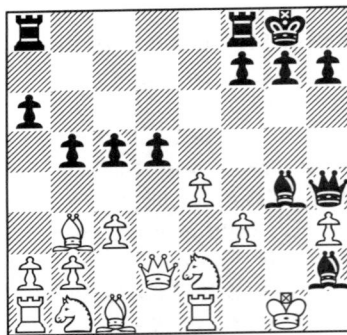

as was played in Hessmer-Negulescu, correspondence 1997.

b) Against 16 ♕f2 the simplest continuation for Black is 16...♕xf2+ 17 ♔xf2 ♗d7! 18 ♗xd5 ♘d3+ 19 ♔f1 ♘xe1 20 ♔xe1 cxd4 21 ♗xa8 ♖xa8 22 cxd4 ♖e8 23 ♘d2 ♗c6 24 ♔f2 (even worse is 24 e5?! f6, when Black regains the sacrificed pawn and emerges with a strong pair of raking bishops – these are very useful in endings where there are pawns on both sides of the board) 24...♗xe4 25

♘xe4 ♖xe4 26 ♗e3 f5 with the better ending for Black.

c) 16 hxg4 was successfully met by 16...cxd4 17 ♕f2 ♕xg4 18 ♗d1 ♕g6 19 ♕xd4 ♗c7! 20 ♗e3 dxe4 21 ♘d2 f5 22 ♕c5 ♖ac8 23 ♖f1 ♘d3 24 ♕d5+ ♔h8 25 ♖f2 ♘xf2 26 ♗xf2 ♖fd8, when Black's pieces clearly dominate, Wolf-Tarrasch, Carlsbad 1923. This variation was very popular in the early part of the last century, with Tarrasch being one of its strongest followers.

16...cxd4

Other continuations are no better:

a) 16...dxe4 17 ♘f5! is very difficult to meet.

b) 16...♕g3 17 ♕f4! ♘f3+ 18 ♖xf3 ♗xf4 19 ♖xg3 ♗xc1 20 ♘c2! ♗h5 21 ♗xd5 ♖ad8 22 a4 ♗f4 23 ♖e3 and White is winning.

17 cxd4 dxe4?!

Slightly better was 17...♘f3+!? 18 gxf3 ♗xh3 19 ♕g5! ♕xg5+ 20 ♗xg5 ♗xf1 21 ♔xf1 and, with two minor pieces against rook and pawn, White is still clearly better.

18 ♕g5

Also deserving of attention is 18 dxe5 ♗xe5 19 ♕e1!? with excellent winning chances for White due to his material superiority.

18...♘f3+ 19 ♖xf3 ♕xg5 20 ♗xg5 exf3 21 hxg4

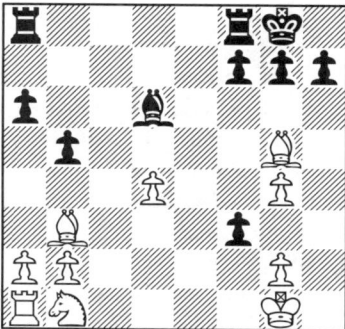

Although Black is not doing too badly from the material point of view, White's position is clearly better because of the activity of his minor pieces, while Black's bishop on d6 is not a very active piece. Botvinnik later used these advantages to claim the full point.

21...♖ae8 2 ♘c3 b4 23 ♘d5 fxg2 24 ♔xg2 ♖e2+ 25 ♔f3 ♖xb2 26 ♘e7+ ♔h8 27 ♘f5 ♗b8 28 ♗e7! ♖c8 29 ♗xb4 h6 30 ♗c5 ♔h7 31 ♖e1 g6 32 ♘e7 ♖c7 33 ♗xf7 ♔g7 34 ♗b3 ♗a7 35 ♗d6 ♖c3+ 36 ♔e4 ♖g2 37 ♗e5+ ♔f8 38 ♘xg6+ ♔e8 39 ♗e6 1-0

Game 103
Jaracz-Krasenkow
Glogow 2001

---

1 e4 e5 2 ♘f3 ♘c6 3 ♗b5 a6 4 ♗a4 ♘f6 5 0-0 ♘xe4 6 d4 b5 7 ♗b3 d5 8 dxe5 ♗e6 9 c3 ♗e7 10 ♖e1 0-0 11 ♘d4 ♘xe5? 12 f3 ♗d6 13 fxe4 ♕h4 14 ♖f1?

The old analysis of Dr Tarrasch shows that Black gets excellent compensation for the sacrificed material after 14 ♕d2 c5 15 ♘f5 ♗xf5 16 exf5 ♖ae8 17 ♖e2 ♘c4 18 ♗xc4 ♗xh2+ 19 ♔f1 ♗g3 20 ♖e3 dxc4, but Black can play even more strongly after 14 ♕d2 with 14...♘c4 15 ♘f3 ♗xh2+! 16 ♔h1 (or 16 ♘xh2 ♘xd2 17 ♗xd2 dxe4 with a near winning position for Black) 16...♘xd2 17 ♘xh4 ♘xb3 18 axb3 ♗g3 19 exd5 ♗xe1 (not so clear is 19...♗xd5?! 20 ♖d1 ♗xb3 21 ♖d4 c5 22 ♖g4 or 19...♗xh4?! 20 ♖e4!) 20 ♘f3 ♗xd5 21 ♘xe1 ♗xb3. White has survived the worst but Black is better in the forthcoming ending.

The correct way of defending the vulnerable h2-square is by playing 14 g3! ♕h3 15 exd5 ♗g4 16 ♕d2 ♖ae8 17 ♗d1!. Although Black, as before, has pressure, my gut feeling is that the first wave of attack has been repelled. White is close to consolidating and he can look forward to the future with his material advantage.

14...♘g4 15 h3 ♕g3! 16 hxg4 dxe4!

Black stops his opponent from running his monarch out via f3. Although White is well ahead in material, Black's attack is so strong that there is no adequate defence.

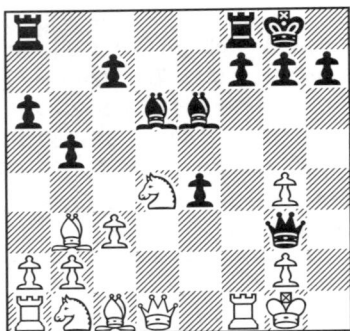

17 ♘f3

Or 17 ♘f5 ♕h2+ 18 ♔f2 ♗xf5 19 gxf5 ♗c5+ 20 ♗e3 ♕f4+ and Black picks up a piece as well as maintaining a deadly attack.
17...exf3 18 ♖xf3 ♕h2+ 19 ♔f1 ♗xb3 20 axb3 ♕h1+ 21 ♔e2 ♕xg2+ 22 ♔d3 ♖ad8 23 ♘d2 ♗f4+ 24 ♔c2 ♗xd2 25 ♗xd2 ♖xd2+ 26 ♕xd2 ♕xf3

White's king has managed to run away to safety. However, the cost is too great. Black has regained all his sacrificed material with interest. The fight has been decided.
27 ♖xa6 ♕xg4 28 ♕d5 h5 29 ♔b1 h4 0-1

Game 104
Hübner-Piket
Dortmund 1992

---

1 e4 e5 2 ♘f3 ♘c6 3 ♗b5 a6 4 ♗a4 ♘f6 5 0-0 ♘xe4 6 d4 ♗e7 7 ♖e1 b5 8 ♗b3 d5 9 dxe5 ♗e6 10 c3 0-0 11 ♘d4 ♘xd4 12 cxd4

Of course out of the question is 12 ♕xd4?? ♗c5 etc.

After the exchange of knights White gets a small but lasting advantage due to the following reasons:

1) Black's backward c-pawn needs constant attention, which means that Black's queenside pawn majority is not as effective as White's kingside pawn majority. Having said

that, note that Black will opt for playing ...c7-c5 to free his position.

2) White is going for a kingside attack and, at the same time, expel Black's knight from the centre by playing f2-f3-f4. In order to prevent White from starting a kingside attack Black will, sooner or later, play ...f7-f5, which will leave White with a strong protected passed e-pawn.

Although 11...♘xd4 is better than the 11...♘xe5? from the previous games, it gives White the better long-term position with practically no winning chances for Black.

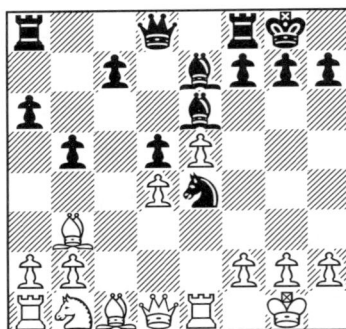

12...h6

In view of the imminent 13 f3, Black vacates the h7-square for his knight. White kept the advantage after 12...♗b4 13 ♖e2 ♕h4 14 a3 ♗a5 15 ♗c2 ♗b6 16 f3 ♘g5 17 ♗e3 f6 18 ♕d2 ♖ae8 19 exf6 gxf6 20 ♘c3 in Engels-Bogoljubow, Stuttgart 1939. The move 12...f5? is clearly a mistake, as was demonstrated in Abbasov-Saidov, Bratislava 1993 which continued 13 exf6 ♖xf6 14 f3 ♘d6 15 ♖xe6! ♖xe6 16 ♗xd5 and the weakness on the long diagonal led to decisive material losses for Black.

13 f3 ♘g5 14 ♘c3

Even stronger was 14 ♗e3! preventing Black from playing ...c7-c5. The old game Chalupetzky-Exner, Gyor 1922 continued 14...f5 15 ♕d2 ♖f7 16 ♖c1 ♕d7 17 ♘c3 ♘h7 18 a4!, when White enjoyed a queenside initiative.

14...c5 15 f4

Stronger than 15 dxc5?! ♗xc5+ 16 ♔h1 d4, when Black obtains counterplay.

15...cxd4 16 ♘e2!

White avoids 16 ♕xd4?! ♖c8! with the idea of ...♗c5 etc.

16...d3

Black tries to make the game messy because the natural continuation 16...♘e4 17 ♘xd4 ♗c5 18 ♗e3 leads to a huge advantage for White – he has a strong grip over the d4-square whilst Black's isolated d-pawn is a big weakness.

17 ♕xd3 ♗c5+ 18 ♘d4 ♗f5 19 ♕xf5 ♘e6!? 20 ♗e3 ♘xd4 21 ♕d3

White had a very interesting alternative, as mentioned by Robert Hübner. He can paradoxically enter an opposite-coloured bishop position a pawn down but with a promising attack, against which it would be very difficult to defend. The critical continuation was 21 ♗xd4! ♗xd4+ 22 ♔h1 ♗xb2 23 ♖ad1 d4 24 ♖d3 etc.

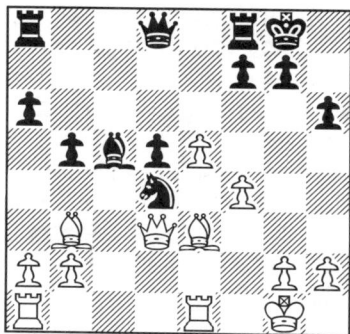

21...♘xb3 22 axb3 d4 23 ♗f2 ♕d5 24 h3 ♖fe8 25 ♔h2?!

White loses all his advantage with this superficial move. Better was 25 ♖ec1!? followed by the doubling of the rooks along the c-file with some advantage.

25...a5 26 ♖ec1 ♗b6 27 ♖c2 ♖ec8 28 ♖ac1 ♖xc2 29 ♖xc2 a4 30 bxa4 bxa4 31 ♗e1 ♕b3! 32 ♕xb3 axb3 33 ♖c6 ♗a5

After this move we reach a drawn rook

and pawn ending.

34 ♗xa5 ♖xa5 35 ♖b6 d3 36 ♖d6

Of course not 36 ♖xb3?? ♖d5 when Black's passed d-pawn is unstoppable.

36...♖a2 37 ♖xd3 ♖xb2 38 ♔g3 g5 39 f5 ♖e2 40 ♖xb3 ½-½

Game 105
Kruppa-Vladimirov
Frunze 1988

---

1 e4 e5 2 ♘f3 ♘c6 3 ♗b5 a6 4 ♗a4 ♘f6 5 0-0 ♗e7 6 ♖e1 b5 7 ♗b3 0-0 8 c3 d5 9 d4 exd4 10 e5

Of course this is more logical than 10 exd5?! because White gains space both in the centre and on the kingside.

10...♘e4 11 ♘xd4

An alternative is 11 cxd4 ♗g4 12 ♘c3. Now the simplest way for Black to get a good position is 12...♗xf3 13 gxf3 ♘xc3 (I don't trust 13...♘xf2? 14 ♔xf2 ♗h4+ etc.) 14 bxc3 ♘a5 15 ♗c2 ♘c4 16 ♗h6!? ♖e8 (bad is 16...gxh6? 17 ♕d3 f5 18 exf6 ♗f7 19 fxe7 ♖xe7 etc. when Black's kingside has been seriously damaged) 17 ♕d3 g6 18 e6 ♗g5! 19 exf7+ ♔xf7 20 ♖xe8 ♔xe8

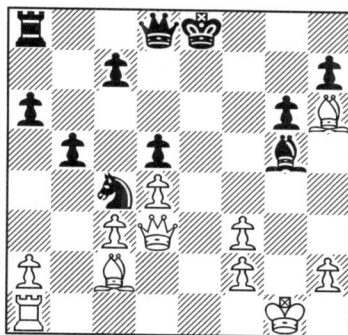

and, with a strong knight on c4, Black can boldly look to the future.

11...♘xe5 12 f3?!

More critical is 12 ♗f4 c5 13 ♗xe5 cxd4 14 ♗xd4 ♗b7 15 ♘d2 ♗f6 16 ♘f1 and White has a small but lasting advantage because of the isolated pawn on d5. Instead of 12...c5, I prefer 12...♗f6!? which transposes to our game after 13 f3 c5 etc. White can also try, after 12...♗f6!?, 13 ♗xe5 ♗xe5 14 ♘f3 ♗g4 and now:

a) 15 ♕xd5 ♗xf3 16 gxf3 (or 16 ♕xe5 ♕h4! with an irresistible attack) 16...♗xh2+! 17 ♔g2 ♕g5+ 18 ♔xg5 ♘xg5 with material advantage to Black. Note that the bishop is taboo on h2 because of ...♘g5xf3+ winning the rook on e1.

b) 15 ♗xd5 ♗xf3 16 gxf3 ♗xh2+! 17 ♔f1 ♘xf2 18 ♕d4 (the only move because if 18 ♔xf2?, 18...♕h4+ with a mating attack) 18...♗g3 19 ♗xa8 ♕xa8 20 ♔g2 ♖d8! and White's queen has no great square to retreat. The position can be assessed as almost winning for Black.

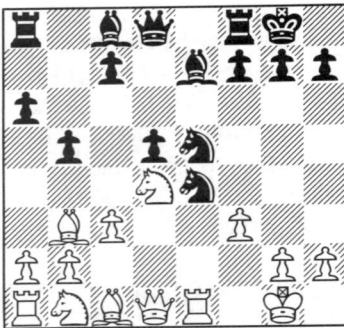

12...c5 13 ♗f4

Or 13 fxe4 cxd4 14 ♗xd5 (after 14 ♕xd4 ♕c7! has the unpleasant threat of ...♗e7-c5 winning the queen) 14...dxc3 15 ♗xa8? (safer is 15 ♘xc3) 15...♗c5+ 16 ♔h1 ♘d3 17 ♕e2 ♗g4 18 ♕f1 ♕h4 19 ♘xc3 ♘f2+ 20 ♔g1 ♗e2! and, regardless of how White takes the

bishop, ...♘f2-g4+ and mate follows.

13...♗f6 14 ♗xe5

Or 14 fxe4 cxd4 15 ♗xe5 ♗xe5 16 cxd4 ♕b6! with a clear advantage to Black.

14...♗xe5 15 ♘c6 ♗xh2+!

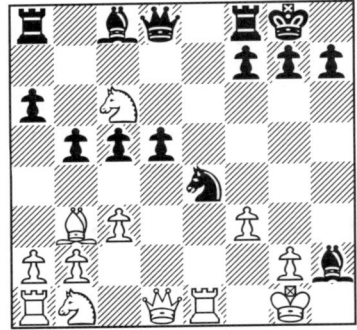

16 ♔xh2 ♕h4+ 17 ♔g1 ♕f2+ 18 ♔h2 ♕g3+ 19 ♔g1 ♘g5!

The attack continues. This strong move shows that Black is not interested in a draw.

20 ♔h1

No better is 20 ♕e2 ♘xf3+ 21 ♕xf3 ♕xe1+ and Black wins, or 20 ♔f1 ♗h3! 21 gxh3 ♘xh3 22 ♔e2 ♕f2+ 23 ♔d3 c4+ 24 ♗xc4 bxc4 mate.

20...♕h4+ 21 ♔g1 ♘h3+! 22 gxh3 ♗xh3 23 ♘e7+

White must close the e-file for the time being because if 23 ♖e2, 23...♖ae8 wins.

23...♔h8 24 ♖e2 ♖ae8 25 ♕e1 ♕g5+ 26 ♔h2 ♖xe7 27 ♔xh3 ♖e6!

Opening the f-file has devastating effects. Black's attack is decisive as White's queenside pieces are out of play.

28 ♖xe6 fxe6 29 ♕g3 ♕c1! 30 ♕h2 ♕f1+ 31 ♔h4 ♕xf3 32 ♘a3 g5+ 0-1

Summary

Games 102-104 confirm that White retains the better chances due to his strong e5-pawn. White gains a spacious advantage on the kingside in Game 104, while if Black sacrifices a piece with 11...♘xe5?, the compensation obtained is insufficient against accurate defence, as demonstrated in both Game 102 and 103.

So after 9 d4!? Black should play 9...exd4 10 e5 ♘e4 (Game 105), yielding sufficient counterplay. That game saw complications with minor pieces being mutually attacked in the centre by pawns. At the end of the day, Black's attack managed to break through despite initially looking like there was nothing more than a draw by perpetual check.

1 e4 e5 2 ♘f3 ♘c6 3 ♗b5 a6 4 ♗a4 ♘f6 5 0-0 ♗e7 6 ♖e1 b5 7 ♗b3 0-0 8 c3
    8 d3 d6 9 d3
        9...♘b8 – *Game 98*
        9...♘a5 c5 11 ♘bd2 ♘d7 12 ♘f1 ♘b6 (D)
            13 ♘g3 – *Game 99*; 13 ♘e3 – *Game 100*
8...d5 9 d4!? (D) ♘xe4
    9...dxe4 – *Game 101*; ...exd4 – *Game 105*
10 dxe5 ♗e6 11 ♘d4 ♘xe5?
    11...♘xd4 – *Game 104*
12 f3 ♗d6 13 fxe4 (D) ♗g4 – *Game 102*
    13...♕h4 – *Game 103*

12...♘b6	*9 d4!?*	*13 fxe4*

INDEX OF COMPLETE GAMES